THE KEEPERS' TATTOO

GILL ARBUTHNOTT

Chicken House
SCHOLASTIC INC.
NEW YORK

Text © 2010 Gill Arbuthnott

First published in the United Kingdom in 2009 as *The Keepers' Daughter*
by Chicken House, 2 Palmer Street, Frome, Somerset BA11 1DS.
www.doublecluck.com

Library of Congress Cataloging-in-Publication Data

Arbuthnott, Gill.

The Keepers' Tattoo / Gill Arbuthnott. — 1st American ed.

p. cm.

Summary: Months before her fifteenth birthday, Nyssa learns that she is
a special member of a legendary clan, the Keepers of Knowledge, as she
and her uncle try to escape from Alaric, the White Wolf, who wants to
use lines tattooed on her to destroy the rest of her people.

ISBN 978-0-545-17166-3

[1. Identity—Fiction. 2. Tattooing—Fiction. 3. Dreams—Fiction.
4. Uncles—Fiction. 5. Fantasy.] I. Title.

PZ7.A6722Kee 2010
[Fic]—dc22

2009026327

10 9 8 7 6 5 4 3 2 1   10 11 12 13 14

Printed in the U.S.A.   23
First American edition, May 2010

The text type was set in ITC Legacy Serif.
The display type was set in Profundis Sans One.
Book design by Lillie Howard

TO EVERYONE WHO TRAVELS
BY BUS IN EDINBURGH
— THANK YOU!

TABLE OF CONTENTS

1

THE DROWNED BOY

The baby cried. Not a normal infant cry of hunger or fear, but a long hopeless keen of pain that went on and on as the priest bent over his meticulous work.

The baby's mother rocked back and forth in distress as she watched from the other side of the room, tears trailing down her face. In a crib at her side her other child slept, exhausted. Her husband stood by the priest as was the custom, holding a small bowl of ink, his face clamped shut on whatever emotions he was feeling.

The rest of the villagers had shut themselves away in their own houses so that they would not have to listen to what was happening.

Afterward would come the ritual celebration, even though no one really understood anymore what it was they were celebrating.

-‡-　-‡-　-‡-

Nyssa slid her fingers through the handles of six empty tankards and lifted them out of a puddle of ale on the table. She put them down on the bar with a thud and picked up a cloth to wipe the table dry. One of the drinkers had left a handful of small coins as a tip, and she scooped them up and slid them into her apron pocket. They weren't worth much, but money was money.

It was a hot night and strands of her brown hair stuck to her sweaty forehead. The rest was pulled back into a thick braid that came halfway down her back.

The inn had been busy earlier but customers were thinning out now. She shoved the stools under the table and went back behind the long wooden bar to start washing out tankards. The water in the big black iron kettle was still reasonably hot as she poured it into the washtub.

She rinsed the tankards one by one, gave them a cursory dry, and returned them to the shelves above the big-bellied ale kegs and the smaller casks of brandy. William was tapping a new keg; the hot weather was making people drink more than usual.

"Can I go out for a few minutes?" she asked him. "Just to cool down a bit."

He smiled at her, his red face shiny with sweat. "Go on then. We can spare you for ten minutes. That's all, though."

Grateful for even that short break, Nyssa pushed through the drinkers to the front door of the inn and went out. It wasn't much cooler outside. Not a breath of wind stirred the hair from her brow as she wiped her face with a corner of her apron.

The sun had long since set, leaving the town lit by lamps and torches and moonlight. She walked slowly along the narrow street away from the center of town, saying hello to the few people who wandered past. The air smelled of fish and salt, hot brick and herbs. The street led downhill toward the harbor, but the last thing she wanted was the long climb up again so, instead of following it down, she leaned against a waist-high wall and simply looked. Setting her hands on the warm stones she leaned over, trying to catch any trace of moving air, but even here there was nothing.

Lights shone from houses on the hillside and the moon made a track of silver across the calm surface of the sea. A few lights moved on the water some way from the shore: squid boats, luring the curious animals with lamps set just above the water. She always felt sorry for the poor things, hooked and clubbed just for being interested. Not so sorry that she didn't eat them, mind you. They were one of her favorites.

Her time must be nearly up: better not be late.

She made her way back to the noise and light and heat of the Drowned Boy Inn. William had told her once that it was named for his grandfather, who'd washed up on the shore one day, aged about six, apparently dead, and been licked back to life by a fisherman's dog.

He had no memory, so William said, of who he was or where he came from. A childless couple in the town took him in and raised him as their son, and when they took over the inn, they renamed it for the strange and momentous event.

The sun-blistered paint on the sign was faded now, and if she hadn't known it showed a dog licking a boy's hand, Nyssa would have had difficulty making it out.

"Bit of a family tradition, taking in foundlings," William would say from time to time as he told the story to a new customer, with a sideways glance at her, and she would smile back, well aware of how lucky that was for her.

William and Oonagh, his wife, had found her playing in the dust outside the inn one day, a tiny child of three or four years old. No one knew who she was or where she came from. At first they told themselves and others that they were just looking after her until her parents were found, but they never were. She might have dropped out of the sky for all that anyone could find out about her. All she had were the clothes she wore and, clutched in one small fist, a broken bamboo flute. Even now she often took it out of the box in her little room and looked at it as though it could tell her who she truly was.

So she had stayed at the inn and been looked after well, not quite as though she were their daughter, but well enough. Oonagh had died three years ago, and Nyssa had thought that perhaps William would send her away to find work elsewhere then, but instead he had come to rely on her more.

She was about to push the door open when she heard her name called softly from the shadow of the building opposite. She peered into the gloom and thought she recognized the face of the girl standing there.

"Cidryn?"

"I heard you'd made rabbit pies," she said.

Nyssa laughed. "Yes. Give me five minutes and come to the kitchen door."

The girl nodded and walked away.

Back inside, Nyssa was met by a loud chorus of raucous singing. One of the men was to wed the next day, and his friends were intent on making sure he did it with a hangover.

She recognized most of them, but a few were strangers, part of the bride's family presumably, from another town. One of them reached an arm out as she passed and caught her around the waist. He pulled her toward him and tried to kiss her.

She twisted quick as an eel and slid from his grasp, at the same time bringing her foot down so that the edge of her wooden heel scraped right down his shin. He yelped and let go and she moved quickly out of reach.

"Sorry, Nyssa," the groom yelled over the laughter of the others. "He's not from around here. He'll not make the same mistake twice."

She slipped back behind the bar. William raised an eyebrow. "All right?"

"Of course. You know I can look after myself."

"Oh, I know," he laughed.

She'd become adept over the years at turning away unwanted attention. When she was a little girl, it had just been people telling her how pretty she was and feeling sorry for her because she was a foundling, but recently she'd had a different sort of unwanted attention to deal with as she left her childhood behind. There always seemed to be some lad stammering at her about meeting him later, or some drunk trying to steal a kiss.

Mostly it was easy to deal with, but William and the regulars kept an eye out for her as well.

One of them was here now: Marius. He caught her eye and gave her a solemn wink and she smiled back. She liked him. He had been a regular for as long as she could remember and had always tipped generously, but it wasn't just because of that that she liked him.

Marius got to his feet and tossed a coin onto the table, picked up his jacket, and raked a hand through his untidy black hair. As he walked past the revelers, the man who had grabbed her somehow lost his balance and landed in the rushes with his ale all over him.

Nyssa covered her mouth with her hand to hide a smile. How had he done that? She was sure that Marius was behind it.

Later, when the bridegroom and his friends had finally gone and they were closing up, William said, "You've grown again, you know. You need some new clothes. Look at that dress: The sleeves are barely down to your elbows."

She stuck her arms out and considered. "I haven't grown *that* much; the dress shrunk in the wash. But you're right, I do need some new things. Sorry."

"That's all right, lass. You earn your keep."

—¦— —¦— —¦—

She looked at the dress properly a little later, upstairs in her own room under the eaves. The sleeves were certainly far too short—they barely covered the little bird tattoo just above her left elbow. She had often wondered what the tattoo meant. Almost everyone on the island had some sort of tattoo of course—or several—and no one really paid any attention to them. They were symbols of birth signs or birth years, clan signs, good-luck charms, or just family traditions, but she'd never seen another one like hers. It was a long-legged bird of some sort:

a heron maybe, black against the pale skin where her tan stopped. Probably it had been something to do with the family she had never known.

She had grown long legged herself lately; her shins seemed to poke a long way below the hem of her skirt, even though she'd let it down as far as she could.

She undressed and put on her nightgown, brushed and rebraided her hair to stop it tangling as she slept, and splashed her face and hands with cold water.

Remembering the coins she had pocketed earlier, she retrieved them from her apron and added them to the tiny nest egg in the little wooden box on top of her bureau.

The broken flute lived in there, too. The mouthpiece was there, and a couple of finger holes, but it had obviously been snapped in two long ago, though she had no memory of how. She took it out, as she did most nights, and turned it between her fingers, but whatever secrets it held, it kept them to itself, as it always did.

-+-   -+-   -+-

Some nights, when she dreamed, it was as though she lived someone else's life, or at least glimpsed it. These dreams came once every couple of weeks or so. They always had, so far as she knew. She had never tried to explain them to anyone else for fear it would make so little sense that they'd think her crazed.

She had come to realize over the years that the dreams always took place in the same town; not the one where she lived, either. It was by a shore — no — it *was* the shore. The land and the sea seemed to merge into each other, and the town petered out in a fringe of half-drowned and rotting buildings, with pitched, red-tiled roofs sticking out of the water.

There was never any sound: not the sea, nor voices, nor animals, even though some of the scenes she glimpsed showed markets or crowded rooms.

Sometimes there was a man in the dream who seemed to have had all the color leached out of him. His skin was a milky pale; his eyes were a blue so light it was hardly a color at all; his hair was white. His clothing, on the other hand, was always black.

Often he was looking straight at her, sometimes with an expression that woke her in fear. Sometimes he laughed at her. Sometimes he spoke, but she could never hear what he said.

They were not comfortable dreams.

That night she stood on a slipway made of huge blocks of dressed stone, waves pushing at her ankles. She looked out to sea for something—but for what? Eventually she turned and trudged out of the waves and back up the slipway. As she looked over the edge into the water she found the blank, weed-fringed eyes of a sunken statue staring back at her.

She continued up a narrow street to the market, where she had often been before. Although it was busy, no one spoke to her or glanced at her. She might as well have been invisible.

She went into a glassblower's workshop, and the man there wrapped a goblet of blue glass and handed it to her with a smile. She made her way back through the crowded streets holding it carefully to her chest.

And then disaster struck: A man holding a struggling chicken barged into her and the package slipped from her grasp and shattered at her feet.

She woke in a sweat of fear, knowing that she would be beaten, or worse, for this, and it was a few minutes before she was able to properly disentangle herself from the dream. There was no goblet; there would be no punishment.

She sat up in bed, shuddering, gradually seeing her familiar room settle into place around her. After a few minutes she lay down and closed her eyes, but she did not sleep again until she heard the cocks begin to crow.

-:-   -:-   -:-

The child crouched among the flowers, sure she was hidden. A little way off, her mother made a great play of looking for her, as though she couldn't see her daughter's blue dress among all the greens of foliage.

"Where are you?" she called. "Come out. I give up."

The little girl put a hand over her mouth to stifle a giggle as her mother straightened, squinting toward the village, shading her eyes so that she could see better.

She crept out of the bank of flowers and tiptoed up behind her mother.

"Boo!"

She shouted as loud as she could, but her mother didn't react, still looking to where a trail of smoke rose from the village.

"Mamma! Here I am. Mamma?" She tugged at her mother's skirt. "Can I hide again, Mamma? Play a song for me!" She pulled at the bamboo flute, held forgotten in her mother's hand.

Her mother turned to her with a strange smile. "No songs just now, my love. You're going to hide again." She grabbed her daughter's hand and began to walk as quickly as she could away from the village. "You curl up small . . ."

"Like the baby?" The girl patted her mother's rounded stomach.

"Like the baby. Stay quiet and curl up still and small and keep hidden. How long do you think you could stay still?" All the time she was pulling the little girl along.

"A long, long time."

"Until it gets dark?"

"Maybe." She sounded less sure now.

"Let's see if you can. Look, here's a good place."

It wasn't much of a hiding place, really; just a little hollow under some rocks, screened by long grass. The child tucked herself obediently into it.

"Like this, Mamma?"

"Just like that. Remember now, stay in there until it gets dark."

"Why are you crying?"

"I'm not. I've got something in my eye. Bye-bye, Nyssa darling."

"Bye-bye, Mamma."

Nyssa walked along the narrow beach, her shoes in one hand. She was supposed to be at the harbor, buying fish for the inn, but the catch wasn't all unloaded yet and she wanted to be sure of the best choice.

The tide was out and on the turn. She walked on sharp white sand and watched terns dipping in and out of the surf, stitching the waves with their beaks as they fished for sand eels.

It was cooler than it had been for days, and a breeze had sprung up at last. She could see the harbor from where she was. It looked as though the boats had finished loading at last. She set off to buy enough fish to keep the Drowned Boy's customers happy for the evening.

Despite the breeze, it was a hot walk up the path to the main part of town carrying the two canvas bags of slithery fish. Some had still been gasping when she bought them, but they had stopped now. She put the bags down for a minute and looked back toward the harbor, absently scratching at an insect bite on one heel.

There was a boat she didn't recognize making its way under oar through the narrow harbor entrance. It was much too sleek and narrow for a fishing boat, and not big enough for one of the regular ferries. At this distance she could make out nothing of the crew, but she could see that around the harbor activity had come to a halt as everyone watched the boat berth. She was tempted to wait and see who came ashore, but the smell of the fish was a reminder of what she ought to be doing. Oh well, if it was anything interesting, news would soon reach the Drowned Boy. It always did.

She walked on, buying a few more ingredients for the cooking. At the dressmaker's she stopped to look at bolts of fabric.

"Nyssa!" said a girl who was waiting for something to be wrapped.

"Cidryn, hello. I didn't get a chance to ask you last night. Have you heard from Aria recently?"

"A letter arrived at the house a couple of weeks ago. She's settled in. It's a good place, she says. They treat her well. Lots of customers. If that's a good thing." She gave a little grimace. "She'll be saving hard, anyway."

A woman appeared from the back of the shop with a wrapped package, her mouth a thin line. She put it down on the counter rather than handing it straight to the girl.

Cidryn picked it up without comment and raised her eyebrows at Nyssa as she turned to leave. The woman's attention was focused on Nyssa even before Cidryn was out the door.

It took her some time to make her choices, torn between practicality, frivolity, the knowledge that she shouldn't spend too much of William's money, and her awareness of the bags of fish sitting outside in the sun. Eventually, however, it was done, and she set off back to the inn, turning down the narrow street where most of the town's livery stables were.

She was halfway along, her mind still at the dressmaker's, when it happened.

A hand clamped over her mouth and another around her waist. Before she could do anything she was dragged in through a narrow doorway and the door was kicked shut behind her.

Instinctively she dropped the fish bags and drove an elbow backward as hard as she could, but it didn't connect well enough to have any effect. The man who had hold of her was speaking into her ear, but she wasn't listening. She kicked back at where she thought his knee would be, then bit down hard on the hand clamped over her mouth, still kicking.

Suddenly she was free.

She heard muffled swearing from her assailant, but didn't even bother to look back as she ran for the door. She almost made it before he tripped her and she went down hard next to him among the dusty straw.

This time she heard the words he hissed in her ear.

"Nyssa, be quiet! It's me, Marius. There are men outside who want to kill us. Just stay still and quiet for a minute."

He pushed himself away from her as if to show he wasn't a threat. Now was her chance to scream for help.

She flailed up into a sitting position, gulping air. Clouds of dust rose around her. She glared at him and opened her mouth to yell. From outside came the noise of booted feet moving along the street. There was something about the sound. . . .

They both froze.

It sounded like three or four men. Marius put a finger to his lips, apparently unaware that blood was dripping from it where she had bitten him. He rolled to his feet, cat-quiet, and she saw for the first time that he was wearing a sword. He was no longer the mild, friendly man from the inn; instead a stranger stood between her and the door, tense as a spring, his hand on the sword hilt.

Together they listened to the footfalls grow louder, then diminish to silence. Nyssa remembered to breathe.

"What on earth . . . ?"

"Wait!" He put up a hand to silence her and opened the door a crack to check the street. Satisfied, he closed it and turned to her, loosening his grip on the sword.

"I'm sorry I did that," he said. He looked ruefully at his bleeding hand. "For a number of reasons."

Nyssa got to her feet, picked up the fish bags in one hand, ready to run, and began to edge toward the door.

"Wait! You're still not safe. Let me explain."

She threw the handful of dust she'd had ready in his face, wrenched the door open, and took to her heels.

-¦-   -¦-   -¦-

Her heart was still pounding when she crashed in through the back door of the Drowned Boy. She dropped the fish bags and shouted to William. There was an answering shout from the big public room and he came into the kitchen, wiping his hands.

"What on earth's the matter, Nyssa?"

"It's Marius. He hauled me into one of the stables — told me there were men trying to kill us. He had a *sword*. I thought I knew him; I don't understand what he was doing." The words tumbled out. She folded her arms to stop her hands trembling. There hadn't been time to be frightened before, but now . . . "I thought I was safe with him at least, but he grabbed me and . . ."

For the first time she took in William's white-faced expression.

"Are you hurt? Where's Marius? Did anyone see you come back here?"

"No, I'm all right. I ran away from Marius in the stable — I threw dust in his eyes. What do you mean, did anyone see me? Who?"

He was silent.

"William?"

"I have to go out," he said abruptly. "I'll close up. Stay inside, out of sight. Don't let anyone in but me."

"William, what's wrong? What's happening?" She was yelling at him now.

"*Sshh!* I'll explain when I come back. *Please* trust me and do as I say for now." He took her hands and looked her straight in the eye. "Let me keep you safe, girl."

-|-   -|-   -|-

He was away for almost three hours.

She had assumed that he'd gone to find and confront Marius, though there had been something in the way that he'd spoken that made her doubt this.

She sat in her room for a while, but the inactivity became unbearable, so she went down to the kitchen and set about making the fish stew for the evening. She gutted the fish, hands working automatically, mind elsewhere, then wiped her hands before she took Oonagh's recipe book down from the shelf where it lived.

In truth, she didn't really need to look at it, but it was comforting, as though something of Oonagh herself still lived in the pages. It was one of the first things she remembered about her life here, standing on a chair in the kitchen, watching Oonagh cook. She had learned to read from this handwritten book. It had been Oonagh's mother's and grandmother's before her, each generation adding recipes and comments so that it was as much about family history as food.

She'd assumed at first that it was the only book in the world, until she was big enough to be allowed into the yeasty-smelling brew room, and found that William had a book of recipes, too, but that his were for making stout.

Those, and the inn ledgers where she'd learned to enter the takings and expenses, were her only reading material as a child. Still, what more did she need?

She began to chop herbs.

At last there was a knock at the door and she heard William's voice. Relieved, she rushed to unbar the door and let him in.

Marius stood behind him.

"What's *he* doing here?" She spat the words out.

William looked from Nyssa to Marius and back, then took a deep breath. "You have to leave. Tonight. Marius will look after you."

2

FAMILY

"Leave? What do you mean? I'm not going anywhere — especially with *him*."

Marius crossed the threshold after William and pushed the inn door shut behind him. She saw that his hand was bandaged.

"You're in danger, Nyssa," William went on. "You have to get away from here. Go and pack a bag. You should leave as soon as it's dark. Marius will look after you."

"How can I be in danger? What do you mean?" None of this was making sense. *It must be a dream,* she decided. Nothing else could explain this bizarre scene.

William looked around helplessly at Marius, who waited at the edge of the room, his back against the door.

"What do I tell her?"

"Enough to make her come. There will be time for the rest later. I hope."

"Don't talk about me as though I'm not here!" shouted Nyssa.

William passed a hand over his face as he tried to order his thoughts.

"The bird on your arm — you always used to ask what it was. It's a Crane: just like mine."

"But yours isn't . . ."

William rolled up his sleeve and she looked at the familiar geometric design on his arm.

"Look more closely." He traced lines with a finger and she suddenly saw the bird concealed by a network of other lines. "I had it changed years ago, so you wouldn't ask about it. It's a clan tattoo. The badge of the Keepers of Knowledge."

"But they're just a legend. They're not . . ."

"We both belong to that clan — Marius, too. Show her, Marius."

Still silent, Marius moved toward her a little and pushed back his sleeve until she saw another long-legged bird.

"The Keepers exist all right, Nyssa," William went on, "although they were almost wiped out hundreds of years ago. Those who survived were scattered all over the Archipelago. You know the Legend."

"Everyone on the Archipelago knows the Legend, but that's all it is, even though people on some of the islands say they wish it were true these days."

William shook his head. "No. We're Keepers. The Legend is true. After the flood, the clan was shunned for the destruction they had brought on the Archipelago. Until then, all the other clans had looked to the Keepers as their teachers, their leaders, really. The Keepers were the ones who spread knowledge to everyone else. They knew about all sorts of things, and they shared what they knew freely. Thira must have been a place of wonder back then. . . ."

"Even if it was," said Marius impatiently, "it's done us no good."

William ignored him and went on. "The clan was shunned. No one would help them. Those who survived scattered and lived secretly, trying to guard what was left of their knowledge. Over the centuries, people more or less forgot about them. Most people thought they didn't exist anymore. Some thought they never had. Secrecy became a habit for the Keepers, a habit that resulted in their knowledge fading. Secrecy and tradition. That's why we all still have the clan tattoo."

"Tradition — some help that's been," said Marius.

William pulled out a chair and sat.

"Twenty years ago — you know this already — the Shadowmen came in boats from far to the north and east. One island fell to them, and then another. At first no one really tried to stop them, because they came every few years and raided and went home again. It never seemed worth the extra bloodshed. But this time they stayed. They had a new leader — Alaric. Seems he was after more than plunder and decided to stay and build himself an empire.

"They spread fear wherever they went. Took what they wanted. Occupied islands, stripped them, moved on. It was as if they had stepped out of the old legends: That's why folk started calling them Shadowmen.

"And now these Shadowmen are seeking out the remnants

of the Keepers to destroy them, and so, more than ever, we must live out our days in hiding, always watching."

"Why are they looking for Keepers? And why destroy them? How do they even know about them if they're such a secret?" Nyssa's voice was insistent.

William was silent for a few seconds. "Their leader thinks that we still have power. We don't, of course, or we wouldn't spend our lives hiding what we are, but it's become an obsession. He knows the Legend and believes it. He wants the power he thinks we have for himself, or he wants to destroy us so we can never threaten him."

"But they're nowhere near here, anyway. They don't have anything to do with us. They've never even set foot on this island," she said.

"They have now. Shadow scouts came in on a ship this morning."

She remembered the strange boat, wolf-sleek, and shivered.

"The Shadowmen are coming for *you*, Nyssa."

There was silence for a few heartbeats.

"For *us*, you mean," she said.

"What?"

"You said they're coming for *me*. You mean for *us*." She saw William and Marius exchange a look she didn't understand.

"Of course," said William, not meeting her eyes.

"Why did you never tell me this before?"

"I wanted to protect you. I thought maybe they would never track you—us—down and you could live here in peace. I didn't want you to be frightened for no reason."

"So what now? We abandon the Drowned Boy and run — where?"

There was a silence so thick you could have sliced it.

"What? What else?"

"I'm not going, Nyssa," said William. "They don't know about me. If they find you or Marius, they'll know you by the tattoos, but mine is disguised. Marius will look after you, and I can send them the wrong way if I stay here."

"I'm not going with him. He's practically a stranger."

"He's your uncle."

At last Nyssa was shocked into silence. She sat down on a table and put her head in her hands. *I'll never complain about the other dreams again,* she thought, *if I can just wake up from this one now.*

William tried again, struggling to keep his voice calm, so that she wouldn't realize how frightened he was for her.

"Nyssa, you know how dear you are to me. You're in terrible danger; I'm not. If they find you, they'll surely kill you. Marius can take you to safety; I can't. You *must* go with him. Please go and pack. I'll get some food together for the pair of you." He turned and went into the kitchen, coming back a moment later with the canvas bags.

Numbly she took them from him, went up to her room, and began to pull things out of her dresser, and stuff them in the bags. She didn't know what else to do.

When she'd finished she tucked the little wooden box that contained her few personal belongings and the tiny cache of money in among the clothes. A few tears dropped onto the bags then. Her mind was a blank, but somewhere she knew that if she was taking the box, she was admitting that this was real and not a dream at all.

She went back downstairs and into the kitchen. William and Marius stopped talking as she came into the room. There was an uncomfortable silence.

"What now?" she asked into it.

William cleared his throat. "I'll open up as usual. You stay out of sight here. As soon as it's dark, the two of you will leave; but you must be ready as soon as we open, in case one of the scouts comes in."

✢   ✢   ✢

Time passed with painful slowness. Nyssa and Marius sat silent in the kitchen, Nyssa's bags stowed in a cupboard with her jacket. Marius's hand rarely strayed far from his sword hilt as he listened tensely to the sounds from the front of the inn.

Business was quiet this evening, after the bachelor roistering of the night before, and the fish stew bubbled on the stove, mostly uneaten.

Nyssa fell into a half doze, tired out by this strange day. But she was jerked back by William's voice from the bar, unnaturally loud and hearty.

"Good evening, sir. Always good to see a new face in town. You off that ship that docked this morning?"

Nyssa froze, but Marius was on his feet lifting the trapdoor in the kitchen floor that led to the tavern cellar. They went silently down into the malty darkness, and Marius closed the trap carefully after him.

After a few seconds their eyes adjusted to the dimness. Narrow shafts of light came down where there were knotholes and gaps in the floorboards above them.

The cellar ran the whole length of the Drowned Boy, as familiar to Nyssa as the rooms upstairs. Heart pounding, she began to edge forward between the rows of kegs, drawn by the indistinct mutter of voices above her. She ignored Marius's furious whisper to keep still, and worked her way forward until she was right under the big wooden bar, where William was continuing his unnatural conversation with the stranger.

"Are there many of you come ashore? Restocking your supplies, I imagine." There was the noise of a full tankard being put down. "Your drink."

"Thank you." Coins sounded on the wood. "We wanted to have a look around your island," a harsh voice said, in an unfamiliar accent, ignoring the rest of the question. "We're looking for something special to take back to Lord Alaric."

"Ah," was all William said.

Nyssa realized that Marius had crept up beside her and was listening as intently as she was.

"This must be a busy place," the strange voice went on. "Surely you must have help to run it?"

"Oh yes, when it's busy. It's quiet tonight, so there's no one else in, but I've extra help if and when I need it."

Nyssa wished she knew who else was in the room above her. Her heart was in her mouth waiting for some helpful busybody to say "Nyssa's here somewhere, surely, William?" but no one did. In fact, no one else seemed to be saying anything. They must all be listening to the man from the ship, too.

The conversation from above had lapsed into silence. Nyssa and Marius stayed where they were, afraid that they might betray their presence to the stranger if they moved.

The minutes dragged out, but at last they heard the unfamiliar voice say, "Good night, then. That was a good brew. I might bring some of the others next time I come."

"Good. Yes. 'Night then."

Footsteps moved away from them and they heard the door open, then shut. Nyssa moved to go back up to the kitchen, anxious to see William, but Marius put a restraining hand on her shoulder.

"Wait. It could be a trick," he said quietly.

Only when they heard William's footsteps overhead moving toward the kitchen did they thread their way back through the kegs.

The trapdoor swung open above them to reveal William's strained face. He gave them a hand up.

"You're sure he's gone?" asked Marius.

William nodded. "I watched him from the window until he was out of sight."

"What do you think?"

William shook his head. "Hard to say, but I think he was just having a look around. If I was a betting man, I'd lay odds they'll have a man in every inn in town tonight asking questions, but I don't think he had a particular reason for being here. One thing's certain, though: You need to get out of town."

Darkness had come while they hid in the cellar. They retrieved Nyssa's bags and jacket from the cupboard. William helped her put it on. Their hands were shaking.

"Good-bye, girl. Don't worry: Marius'll take good care of you." He tried to force a smile and failed. "I'll miss you, you know. Don't know who else can do the cooking for the Boy like you."

She desperately wanted to slow time down, to stop what was happening to her, but for once she couldn't think of anything to do or say that would help.

"Don't fret, William." She found her voice from somewhere. "I'll be back soon."

William was silent.

"Won't I?"

"When it's safe. But I don't know when that'll be, Nyssa." He threw his arms around her and gave her a hug that nearly crushed the breath out of her. His eyes when he stepped back were suspiciously bright.

She realized she was crying.

Marius put a hand on her arm. "We must go now."

William opened the door and checked that the road was empty.

As she went out she put her arms around him once more and reached up to kiss him.

"I love you. I'll come back."

He gave her what might have been a nod.

Marius led her in silence through the backstreets to a stable and tied her bags and the satchels of food William had given them on to a bay horse already laden with his own gear.

"Up you go." He laced his hands together to help her mount.

"I can't ride." Her mouth was dry.

"You'll learn," he said shortly, and boosted her up onto the horse's back.

+ + +

They rode until it began to grow light. Nyssa dozed, clinging to Marius as she grew used to the steady motion of the horse. Marius didn't talk and she was glad of this: She had enough to think about, trying to make sense of the last few hours without attempting a conversation as well.

Several times during the night he drew the horse in under the shadow of the trees, thinking he heard sounds of pursuit. Once it was a deer trotting along a path; the other times probably just his overstrained imagination.

As the sky grew light, Marius turned off the road and went deep into the pine wood. They rode on until the sun was up, moving slowly along narrow hunting trails. Finally, when it was fully light, Marius stopped and helped her down, tired and stiff, from the horse's broad back.

"Now what?" she asked.

"We rest, then when it's dark we move on again."

"Where are we going?"

He heaved the saddle off and the horse shook itself. "I don't know yet. It depends on whether we're followed or not." He tossed her the satchels of food. "Best have something to eat, then get some sleep."

She sat down and began to unpack what William had sent with them.

"I don't want to sleep. I want you to explain exactly what's going on."

He left the horse to graze and sat down near her, his back against a tree trunk. She passed him a hunk of bread and a cold pork chop. He smiled, and briefly he was the good-looking half stranger from the Drowned Boy again. He pushed his hair out of his brown eyes and bit into the chop.

"Are you really my uncle?"

He nodded, chewing a mouthful of pork. "Your mother was my sister."

Mother, sister, uncle. She tried the unfamiliar words in her head. *Her mother's brother.* She thought of the bamboo flute in her bag, until now her only evidence that she had ever had a family. She wanted to know everything, but there were so many questions jostling for space in her head that she didn't know where to start.

"What age am I?"

The question that escaped first was as unexpected to Nyssa as to Marius. "What?"

"How old am I? I've never known."

"You'll be fifteen in a couple of months."

"Tell me about my family. Tell me what happened to them." She twisted a piece of grass nervously around her fingers.

"All right, but you must eat something. We'll be on the move later—you need to eat now."

She cut herself a piece of white sheep's cheese and pulled an apple from the bag. Marius swallowed the last of the pork and threw the bone into a tangle of brambles.

"We all lived in the same village until ten years ago. It was a village of the Keepers, almost a hundred of us. There weren't many Keeper villages then; now there are none. It was where I grew up."

He remembered so clearly, even now . . .

He had resented what it meant to be a Keeper's child for as long as he could remember: the meaningless rituals that had to be learned, the chanting of verses that no one understood. The Legend, over and over; the Legend, until he knew every word, was sick of every word.

Sitting in a hut stinking of smoke, day in, day out, while one or another of the priests droned on at them and hit them around the ears until their heads rang if their attention strayed, as it so often did.

Ten years old, twelve years old, fourteen years old—still it went on. He and two of his friends talked about what they would do. They would leave the village and forget everything they had been so unwillingly taught, become normal people, live like everyone else. Instead of living frozen in the past, they would live in a present where the Legend didn't affect them, where no one knew how to recognize the house of another Keeper.

They would escape.

He wouldn't tell her about all that, of course.

"There had been rumors for some time that the Shadowmen were interested in information about the Keepers.

"We thought that was all they were—rumors—and no one really believed them. No one knew anyone who had been touched by them. And then . . ."

And then . . .

They'd gone away for a couple of days, Marius and his friends, all just turned fifteen, ostensibly to hunt; but really they were laying plans for their escape. That was too dramatic a word for it of course; they were hardly prisoners. But they did mean to leave for good. It needed a plan, for the rest of the villagers wouldn't want them to go. So they'd hunted, successfully, but they'd also rehearsed all the arguments their families would make to try and keep them from going. Nothing would take them by surprise.

Except what they found.

". . . we went hunting. Late in the afternoon we came out of the woods and saw a column of smoke rising from the village . . ."

Black, oily smoke that stank of death. They spurred their horses on as fast as they could, but it made no difference. It was already over. Everyone was dead, every building burned to smoking timbers. Most of the bodies had been dragged inside to burn as well, jumbled together.

Numbly, they'd gone from ruin to ruin, hoping to find someone still alive, until they could stand it no longer. All their families were dead. Except . . .

"I couldn't find your mother anywhere. We rode out of the village calling to her, hoping she had managed to hide with you somewhere. Your brother had been in the village that morning. He'd had a cough and your grandmother — my mother — had been looking after him. They stood no chance. The children's bodies were so badly burned that I was never able to tell who they were."

They'd ridden calling — screaming, really — desperate for there to be someone left . . .

"I knew your mother liked to walk beside the dunes and the salt marsh, so we went that way, hoping for a miracle, I suppose. She was dead, too, and the baby she was expecting, of course, but you were sitting beside her, trying to get her to wake up. I don't know how long you'd been there. You were only four; you couldn't explain what had happened. You just said Mamma had told you to hide."

He paused to take a drink from the water bottle.

-‡-   -‡-   -‡-

Mother, father, brother, grandmother, baby . . . In a few sentences she had gained and then lost a whole family. She had no memory of any of them, nothing before William and Oonagh and the Drowned Boy.

She suddenly felt exhausted. It must have shown on her face. Marius reached across and very carefully took hold of her hand.

"I'm sorry. We wanted to spare you all this. That's why we never told you."

She pulled her hand away. "I'm all right," she said stubbornly.

Give her time, Marius told himself. *It's going to take time.* He rummaged in his pack and passed her a blanket. "See if you can sleep. I'll keep watch."

She lay down and tucked the blanket around her. Every stone and clump of grass dug into her. "I'll never sleep lying on the ground," she said, and was asleep in moments.

Her dreams were a jumble of smoke and blank faces and the howling of wolves. She woke, unrefreshed and aching from the ride and the stones. The sun was high in the sky, its hot light filtered by the canopy of needles. Marius had dozed off where he sat. For a while she lay still, thinking, trying to fit the revelations of the past twelve hours into her picture of the world.

It didn't work. There was a lot more she needed to know before any of this would make sense, and it was clear that William and Marius had told her as little as possible to make her leave.

She stared at the sleeping figure of the man she was now suddenly supposed to think of as her uncle. There was no resemblance between the two of them that she was aware of. She wondered if he looked like his sister. Her mother. The strangeness of it hit her anew.

It struck her just how little she knew about him. She had no idea how he made a living, although she did know that he lived in rooms rented from the father of her friend Nicos, near the harbor. He'd always been friendly in a distant kind of way, and she'd liked him vaguely, but now she felt angry that he had kept all this from her.

She let Marius sleep until the sun told her it was mid afternoon, then kicked his ankle to get his attention. He woke with a start, disoriented, his hand going reflexively to his sword hilt, to find Nyssa standing in front of him, arms folded, face stern.

"I thought *you* were supposed to be taking care of *me*," she said, forcing him to meet her eyes.

He was appalled. All sorts of excuses leaped to his tongue, but he forced them down. He wasn't going to let her fluster him.

"It's a good thing I was awake to keep watch."

"I'm sorry. It won't happen again."

"How do you know that?" she said sharply. "We need to take turns, not just assume you'll be able to stay awake all the time." She sat down. "I want to know where we're going."

He fought to remember that he was meant to be the one in charge.

"You do know where we're going, don't you? There *is* a plan of some sort?"

"Not . . . exactly. In case you hadn't noticed, we left in a bit of a hurry." He didn't trouble to keep the annoyance from his voice.

"But I thought that you and William had been on the lookout for Shadowmen for years? You're not going to tell me you'd never thought through what to do if they actually turned up?"

"We had to keep things flexible," he yelled. "We didn't know how things would happen!"

They had both risen to their feet now, and were staring at each other truculently.

"Huh! Unbelievable!" Nyssa turned on her heel and stalked off to the other side of the clearing.

Fuming, he stared at her stiff back. This was not what he had seen in his mind's eye when he imagined fleeing from the Shadowmen again. He'd imagined rescuing a cooperative child, a bit tearful perhaps, but mostly frightened — and grateful, definitely grateful.

And instead here he was in the middle of a wood shouting at a stroppy teenager who was mostly . . . furious.

It had been much easier the first time he had rescued her.

"*Mamma won't wake up*," she had said, squinting up at him through her disheveled hair.

He knelt down beside her to close his sister's eyes.

"*They broke the flute.*" *She showed him the remains of the bamboo flute clutched in one chubby fist.* "*It won't work.*"

He picked her up and carried her away from her mother's body.

"*Why won't Mamma wake up?*"

"*Sshh, Nyssa. We'll let her sleep just now.*"

As they rode away, thoughts settled like stones in his brain. She's all that's left. Do they know they missed her? I have to keep her safe. Somehow I have to keep her safe.

At first, there were the three of them, to look after the little girl, to keep watch, to discuss what they should do as they made their way across the island; but one night, a couple of weeks after the village had been destroyed, the others must have slipped away while he slept. He didn't blame them; Nyssa was his responsibility, his danger, not theirs, and hadn't they become such close friends because of their determination to leave behind the Keepers' way of life?

So the two of them had made their way across the Archipelago, helped by the hidden network of Keepers, whose houses he was able to find because of the lessons he had so despised. He hadn't told anyone what she was of course, just that she'd been orphaned in a Shadow attack. He'd told no one until she was settled at the Drowned Boy and he'd decided to take William and Oonagh into his confidence. They'd have found out soon enough, anyway.

They'd looked at the little girl playing in the straw as though seeing her for the first time.

"*Should we tell her when she's older?*"

Marius shrugged. "It would only be a burden to her. What good would it do, anyway, when it's her alone? Perhaps if both . . ." He shook his head. "Even then it would be pointless. We don't even understand it."

"Of course there's a plan," he said, keeping his voice level with an effort. "We head for the south of the island, then cross to the Mainland."

"Won't they be watching the ferries?"

"We won't be going by ferry. We'll be going on a squid boat." He hoped fervently she wouldn't detect in his voice the fact that the plan was so freshly minted he hadn't known it himself until the words emerged.

They set off again just before sunset. At first they took the road, Marius noticeably less tense than the night before, until after just half an hour the sound of hoofbeats drove them back under the trees again.

This time his fears were justified. As they crouched behind a pine, his hand over the horse's muzzle to keep it quiet, two figures came into view, riding fast. They were cloaked, but the moon glinted off chain mail under the cloth. There were no men-at-arms on the island. These could only be Shadow scouts from the ship.

Nyssa watched with horrible fascination as they drew nearer. She saw swords, powerful arms controlling the horses. Their faces seemed dark and intent to her. Surely they would see her? Suddenly the trees in front of them seemed pitiful camouflage.

Any second now one of the men would glance around and then . . . and then they were past, oblivious.

They waited in breath-held silence as the sound of hooves faded to nothing. Even then, it was a long time before they moved again.

"We stay off the road," said Marius as he helped Nyssa mount. Her legs shook so much she could hardly do it. There was no need for a reply.

THE LEGEND

This is the Legend, as it has been passed down through the generations from the days before the earth and the sea rose up and destroyed so much.

Long ago, long, long ago, the Archipelago was peaceful home to many clans. Some fished and some farmed, some wove and some carved.

The Keepers worked with knowledge. They watched the stars wheel and predicted the times when the sun or moon would be swallowed by darkness, so that it was no longer a thing of terror to the people. They studied the human body in health and sickness, and learned how to cure many ills. They learned to melt metal out of stone, to move water uphill so that even the highest villages had enough. It seemed there was no question that they could not answer, and they shared their knowledge freely with the other clans. For this they were revered, and if there could be said to be any leaders among the people of the Archipelago, then they were the Keepers of Knowledge.

Thira was the island that was theirs: a place of learning and light, science and music, and joy. The towns of Thira were of great beauty, built of white marble and mosaics, tiled and carved.

All was as it should be in the Archipelago.

And then the Shadow rose.

The Shadow clan came in harsh black boats from the north with their twin priests and their strange gods of death and destruction. The people of the Archipelago welcomed them at first, for they were strangers. But the Shadowmen broke the sacred bond of hospitality and turned on those who would have made them welcome, killing and enslaving.

They spread as the plague spreads, from island to island, more and more of them, and the people of the Archipelago suffered and despaired. And in their despair, they turned to the Keepers to save them.

Then the most learned men and women of the Keepers searched among all their stores of knowledge for something that would stop the spread of the Shadow. For one hundred days and one hundred nights they searched and planned and worked.

And when the hundred days and nights were over, they looked at the few lines of writing their search had yielded and they were afraid.

They looked out to sea and saw the swift, cruel boats of the Shadowmen heading for Thira, and this is what they did.

The wisest man and woman among the Keepers went down into the belly of the Earth Goddess and spoke aloud the lines that were written: the only time those lines have been uttered.

And the Earth Goddess heard, and shook her husband, the God of the Sea, from a deep sleep, and together they rose up and cleansed the Archipelago of the Shadow.

Many of the islands were riven by the shaking of the Earth and half drowned by the fierce anger of the Sea. Thira, beautiful Thira, was cleft in two. The land tilted and the waves swallowed the temples and libraries and places of learning. The Keepers were scattered and Thira was abandoned to become a haunt of spiders and snakes and scorpions.

In this way the Keepers were punished for their presumption in awakening the gods.

3

THE WHITE WOLF

After that, they kept to hunting trails. Nyssa had no idea how Marius could find his way, for one trail looked just like another to her in the scant light, but he seemed to have no doubts about which one to take.

"How do you know where you're going? They all look the same."

He gave a short laugh. "I'm often out here hunting. It's what I do to live—well, one of the things. I can mend your roof, or break a horse for you, or dig a well and fix up the pipes to bring water to your house."

In spite of herself she smiled as she bumped along behind him. "I'll be sure to remember that." She fell silent for a moment, then said to his back, "I still don't understand why the Shadowmen are hunting us."

"Because of what we are. We told you. Their leader thinks we still have the power the Keepers used to have in the old times.

"As if we'd be skulking around like this if we did," he added as an afterthought.

"But it doesn't make sense," she persisted. "If they've captured Keepers in the past, they must know that we don't have any special power. So why carry on hunting us?"

She felt him shrug. "I don't know. They're foreigners. Maybe they're just stupid."

"Oh, come on! No one that stupid could have overrun half the Archipelago. It makes no sense."

But she got nothing further from him.

As they traveled, the ground rose slowly, and deep in the night they emerged from the far side of the wood, high up on the spine of the island. The moonlight picked out the pale rocks that pushed everywhere through the thin soil like pieces of broken bone.

There was little cover here and they rode silently, alert for any sign of pursuit. The ground leveled under the horse's hooves, then began to fall away as they made their way slowly down toward the fertile floodplains that fed most of the island. As dawn crept closer, Marius was looking for somewhere to lie low for the day, but the orchards and olive groves through which they now rode offered nothing in the way of a hiding place.

"No luck," he said. "I'd hoped there would be somewhere here, but we can't risk it." He pulled the horse's head around and they started back up the slope, heading northeast.

The light was growing now, and he urged the horse on as fast as he dared over the rough ground. After half an hour, they came to the place he'd been heading for: an ancient village, hundreds of years old, deserted lifetimes ago; each house made of great stone slabs fitted together and half-buried in the hillside.

He tethered the horse in one house and went to cut some fodder while Nyssa unpacked their small store in another.

When he came back, he helped himself to some food, stretched until his joints cracked, and sat down with his back against a wall and his legs stretched out in front of him.

"You sleep first; I'll watch," said Nyssa, her mouth full of bread and cold pork.

"I'm not tired."

"You look it." She stared at him.

How was it that she could make him feel uncomfortable so easily? He seemed to have lost the ability to lie to her.

"All right. Just a couple of hours, then it's your turn." He reached for bread.

"You'll sell the horse?"

He nodded. "Tomorrow, once we reach the coast. We'll buy another one once we get to the Mainland."

"We'll need two. Can we afford that?"

Again she had surprised him. "You can't ride."

"You said I'd learn. You were right. And I'm not bumping along behind you like baggage any longer than I have to. Just choose me something that isn't too high or too fast."

He nodded and decided to go to sleep before she said anything else unexpected.

While he slept she rummaged in the bags she had brought. All her clothes reeked of fish. Her hand closed around what she was looking for, and she wriggled the box out of a tangle of cloth, the coins in it clinking slightly as she did so.

Apart from the money, it held a few strings of beads and a little mirror that Oonagh had given her, a small pearl she'd found once as she shucked an oyster, a few dried flowers, and the broken flute. It wasn't much to show for fifteen years.

She turned the flute between her fingers, wondering who else in her dead family had held it. She would ask Marius about it when she woke him.

In the end, she let him sleep for four hours.

"Why didn't you wake me sooner?"

She shrugged. "I didn't want you dozing off again when you were supposed to be keeping watch."

He closed his mouth hard on what he was about to say in reply. He was not going to let her provoke him.

She held up the flute. "Tell me about this. Tell me about my family."

"Your father was called Julius, and your mother — my sister — was called Kira. The flute was hers. Julius made it for her the winter you were born. You used to love her playing it." He smiled. "You made her take it everywhere. She used to play it every night when she put you and your brother to bed."

"What was his name?"

"Kit."

"What age was he? Would he be? Compared to me, I mean."

He was silent for what seemed an inordinately long time before he spoke again.

"You were twins."

For some reason that rocked her afresh.

He looked at her stricken face. "I'm sorry, Nyssa. It would have been so much easier if you had never had to find all this out."

She sat silent for a long time. Marius sneaked a look to see if she was crying, but her face was dry.

"You're wrong," she said at last, gathering herself. "It might have been easier for you, but not for me. For as long as I can remember, I've wondered who I really was. Now, whatever happens, at least I know that."

-:-   -:-   -:-

They set off again just after sunset, both equally anxious now to get off the island and away from their pursuers.

After three or four hours, Nyssa heard the sea lapping against rocks somewhere off to her left and saw a few lights moving gently against the night sky. She realized with a jolt that once more she was watching squid boats.

"We're here," said Marius quietly.

"Where's here?"

"Gavos."

She hadn't realized they had come so far.

"There's a house where we can hide until tomorrow night. I'll be able to buy us passage on a boat by then."

Ten minutes later they came into a little town. Marius soon turned off down a side street. About fifty feet along he stopped, dismounted, and helped Nyssa down.

The door of the nearest house was peeling and splintered. Boards covered a couple of splits in the wood. Marius looked around, then put a shoulder to it. It gave unwillingly with what seemed to be a horribly loud screech, the damp wood catching against the floor.

He pushed her inside. "Wait here. I'll see to the horse." The door shut behind him with another screech.

Left alone in the silent and, she assumed, deserted house, Nyssa forced herself to stand still and wait for her eyes to accustom themselves to the lack of light. After a few moments she saw a gleaming line where the shutters didn't quite meet. A table and a couple of chairs emerged from the gloom. A chest stood in one corner, a little stove in another. She wished she could light a lamp, but until Marius returned she wouldn't have tinder, even if she could find one.

There was another door on the far side of the room. She thought briefly about opening it, but decided to wait until Marius came back. Instead she made her way over to the table, pulled out a chair, and sat waiting tensely, alert to every creak and breath of air.

It seemed a long time before the door screeched open again and Marius appeared, an indistinct silhouette. He dumped their things on the floor and pushed it shut again.

"Let's get some light in here," he said.

"I didn't know if it was safe. I didn't have a lamp or a tinderbox, anyway."

"There should be one. . . ." He edged over to the stove. "Here it is." There was a scrape of tinder and a small light bloomed on the other side of the room.

"What is this place? How did you know about it?"

"It belongs to my landlord—you know, Nicos's father. I'm meant to be putting a new roof on it in the next few weeks." He grimaced. "Won't be doing that now. Still, I never enjoy mending roofs, anyway."

Nyssa picked up the lamp and moved around the room, looking at what it contained. "I wonder who lived here?" she mused.

"I don't know. It's been empty for a few years, I think. The bedroom's through there."

Nyssa pushed open the door. The word *bedroom* had suggested that there might be beds in it, but as she looked around she saw that rats had long ago eaten the mattresses. She shut the door again. "I think we'll be better off in the main room," she said.

Marius had found and lit another lamp, pushing the shutters properly closed before he did so.

"Now what?" asked Nyssa.

"We get some sleep just now. On the floor I suppose. Once it's light I'll go out and buy some food and find a fisherman who'll take us across to the Mainland tonight. Hopefully I'll manage to sell the horse as well, but we'll have to see about that."

-:-   -:-   -:-

It was late afternoon. A screech announced Marius's return. Nyssa looked up expectantly.

"Everything's arranged. We'll be away as soon as it gets dark. The weather's set fair and no one's talking about having seen any strangers who might be Shadowmen. I even managed to sell the horse. We'll be on the Mainland by morning."

"And safe?"

He shrugged noncommittally. "I wish I could say I was sure. *Safer*, anyway. We can lay up in the port and wait for word from William, and we'll have a few hours' notice if the Shadow ship appears. Who knows? Maybe them turning up on the island like this will turn out to be a coincidence and you'll be back in the Drowned Boy in a week."

He threw a bundle toward her. "Put these on. It's just as well that no one remembers a girl leaving secretly. Can you act like a boy?"

She rolled her eyes. "Now that really is a stupid question. There's nothing to it, you just have to behave like an idiot. You've seen me dealing with them often enough in the inn. Acting like one is no challenge."

✦   ✦   ✦

"Time to go."

At last. Nyssa had thought it would never get dark as she sat waiting, dressed in a frayed pair of trousers now, her hair pushed up under a cap, looking to a casual observer like any other fisherlad. She smelled the part, too, she thought, after days with the reeking bags. She picked them up and followed Marius out of the house.

They made their way without obvious haste down the narrow streets to the quayside. Some of the boats were already out, yellow lights moving slowly across the water. They picked their way among fish boxes and crab shells and piles of rope.

"This one."

The boat was tied up beside a weed-slippery wooden ladder, the lamp in the stern already lit. A tall man got up from his place beside it as they arrived, and nodded to them. Marius tossed down a small bag that chinked as the man caught it, and then they were handing down their packs and climbing into the boat to settle themselves where they wouldn't be in the way, all in silence.

The fisherman untied the boat and pushed away from the quayside, then pulled up the sail. The wind filled it suddenly, snapping the canvas, and they left the island behind them.

-:-   -:-   -:-

With a favorable wind, they made fast time. Once they were far enough from the coast for the action not to be noticeable, the boatman snuffed the squid lamp, and they sailed on under the stars in almost total silence. They reached the Mainland hours before dawn and put in at a little bay just down the coast from the nearest port in order to avoid arousing interest by arriving at night when the place was quiet.

Nyssa managed to find enough room to lie down on a pile of netting, her head pillowed rather lumpily on her fishy-smelling bag, and fell asleep, rocked by the boat's gentle motion.

She was on her knees staring at an ornately tiled floor. Her hands were spread in front of her, and blood dripped slowly from her nose onto the tiles. She would not cry. She took a long, painful breath. Her ribs hurt. She raised her head and looked up into the face of the bleached man; she knew at once that it was he who had hurt her.

Sitting back on her heels, she wiped blood and snot from her face with one hand, watching his face. He looked back at her with satisfaction, raised one slippered foot, and kicked her in the ribs.

She woke choking, gasping for breath as Marius scrabbled across the bottom of the boat toward her.

"Nyssa, what's wrong? You were dreaming."

She sat up, feeling the cool wood of the gunwale under her fingers. There was enough light now to see Marius's face, close and anxious. From the stern of the boat came the undisturbed snores of their ferryman.

"He was hurting me, kicking me. It *hurt*, even in the dream." She spoke wildly, feeling for blood on her face, running her hands cautiously over her ribs.

Marius touched her shoulder gently. "It's all right. You're safe. Who did you dream about?"

"I have these dreams every two weeks or so — I always have. It's as though I'm someone else, in another town. And *he's* there. It seems so real." She realized she was gabbling and forced herself to slow down. "He seems so real, but I've never seen anyone like him."

"What do you mean?"

"He's so pale: It's as though someone bleached all the color out of him. White hair, white skin, cold, pale eyes. Always black clothes."

It was growing lighter by the minute. Light enough for Nyssa to see the expression of shock on Marius's face that he didn't even try to hide.

"What?" she whispered.

"The White Wolf," he said, half to himself. "How can you dream of him? You've never seen him."

"What are you talking about?" she said, more loudly this time.

"The man you describe is Alaric. The White Wolf."

"He's real?" she breathed, an edge of panic in her voice.

He nodded. "He is the leader of the Shadowmen. He ordered the killing of our family, and he controls the men who hunt you now."

"How can I be dreaming about someone I've never met? I'm not a seer. I must have seen him when my mother was killed."

He shook his head. "He didn't take part in the raid himself. He never does."

The horizon was pink and gold now as the sun rose.

"You have these dreams regularly?"

"Yes, but he isn't always part of them. It's as though I'm really there."

"Do you know *where* you are?"

She shook her head. "But things don't move around like they do in normal dreams. If I'm in the marketplace, I know where the streets that lead from it will take me, and they do always go there. It's as though the town's being eaten away by the sea. Some of the buildings are half under water, some are covered."

Marius drew his breath in with a hiss.

"Thira. You are dreaming of the White Wolf and of Thira. It used to be the foremost city on the island of the Keepers, so the stories say: full of learning and light and music. But the cataclysm that the Keepers drew down to stop the ancient Shadowmen destroyed Thira as well.

"And now the White Wolf sits among the ruins with his own Shadowmen, building the Archipelago into an empire of fear. He wants to crush us all."

She was more frightened by the idea that these dreams were somehow real than by any of the other revelations of the last couple of days, but this was a chance she wouldn't miss, however terrifying the answers might be.

"Why . . . ," she said slowly, grasping the moment, but dreading what Marius might tell her, ". . . is he so interested in *me*? It's not just because of the clan I belong to, is it? I'm bound to this man in my dreams. Tell me the truth: Why does he want me dead?"

Marius was silent, chewing a knuckle as he wrestled with himself. There was another thunderous snore from the back of the boat. He cast a glance at the sleeping fisherman and moved to sit beside her. "You have information that he both wants and fears," he said in a low voice.

"Information? I don't know about anything except cleaning and cooking."

"No. Just listen." He rubbed a hand across his eyes as he tried to work out how to explain.

"When you were a baby, a few months old, you were given your clan tattoo." She nodded. "But you were given another tattoo at the same time: three lines of text in a language that no one understands anymore."

She frowned. "But I don't have another tattoo."

"You do." He touched the back of her head. "It's here, under your hair."

She stared at him, baffled, and slid her fingers into her hair, probing her scalp as though it might suddenly feel different.

"But why does this matter to this man—the White Wolf?"

"The Keepers saved the Archipelago from the Shadowmen hundreds of years ago. These lines, whatever they are, are what allowed them to do it. They brought down the cataclysm that destroyed the first Shadowmen and half the Archipelago and scattered the Keepers. The White Wolf probably wants to obliterate them utterly, by killing you, so that they can't ever be used against him and people will know that no one can save them this time."

"Probably?"

"There is another possibility. He may believe he is powerful enough to twist the text and use it against the other clans so that the threat of destruction will enslave them. He's wrong about that, though."

"How do you know?"

"The text is six lines long. It has always been divided between twins, generation after generation. The other three lines belonged to your brother and died with him."

She took a moment to absorb the implications of this. "But surely then we could persuade him to stop? If I've only got half the lines, then they're useless, whatever they mean."

"He may not know about the text being divided. Even if we could stay alive to tell him, why would he believe us? And if he already knows, then it hasn't stopped him, anyway."

After a long silence, Nyssa spoke, trying to get her voice steady. "If what you say is true, and I'm not sitting in a boat with a madman, then the White Wolf will never stop hunting me."

"No," said Marius bleakly.

Nyssa made a sound that was half laugh, half sob. "All this time, carrying this with me and not knowing. And there's no way to get rid of it. Is there even any point in running?"

"Of course!" Marius gripped her shoulders and turned her to face him. "Your mother died protecting you. I will, too, if I have to."

"I don't want you to."

"But I'll do it, anyway; because it *is* worth running and it *is* worth fighting. It's worked for ten years already. You won't give up. I know you, remember. I've known you all your life. You can't think clearly just now. All this is too much of a shock. Let it sink in for a few days while we wait to hear from William."

+ + +

Nyssa stood motionless, a honey cake suspended halfway to her mouth, watching a great scarlet and blue bird. It was telling fortunes by dipping its scaly foot into a bag and pulling out twists of paper, three for each customer. As far as she could tell the people of this little town must be extraordinarily lucky, judging by the varied and optimistic prophecies they received.

"Your fortune, miss?" The bird's owner was looking at her, shrewd brown eyes in a wrinkled, nut-brown face. She forced a smile, shook her head and moved off, eating the cake.

It was market day and the square was crowded with stalls. Some were stoutly built of wood, with awnings of striped canvas and careful displays of goods, others were no more than a piece of cloth spread on the ground. Creels of salted fish jostled with scryers' booths, cloth merchants, and spice sellers. She was half deafened by a cacophony of crated ducks and hens and exhortations to buy. Under one stall laden with glassware a piglet slept, tethered by a cord to one of the supports. A small boy ran here and there in pursuit of two escaped geese, and a moment later fled yelling, his quarry turned pursuers.

It was the third day since they had arrived and, to her relief, Nyssa no longer smelled of fish. Her clothes had all been cleaned and the fish bags replaced by something more suitable as luggage.

The initial shock of what Marius had told her was beginning to wear off, and with it some of the despair she had felt at first, though she still wasn't about to ask the bird to tell her fortune. They had taken rooms at an inn—Nyssa back to being a girl now—and for the first day she had stayed there, alternately trying to think and sleep and having little success at either. Good meals and a comfortable bed seemed to have had a powerful restorative effect, however, and this morning she had woken determined to act as though she still had a normal life, whatever Marius thought.

"I'm going out to the market," she had said.

"Oh no, you're not," he replied. "You're not wandering around on your own."

"Then you come, too."

"I'm going down to the docks to see if there's any word from William. Come with me if you want to get out."

"I can't buy a new dress at the docks, can I? I'm going to the market. I'm not going to spend my life hiding in inn rooms. I want a normal life back!"

"Nyssa, you are *not* going. I forbid you!"

She had stared at him in total disbelief for a couple of seconds, stormed off to her room in fury, and immediately climbed straight out the window and went to the market, anyway.

She stopped at a dressmaker's booth and bought two dresses, already made, that looked as though they would be a reasonable fit, then headed back to the inn, carrying her parcel of clothes and the sticky bag containing the rest of the honey cakes.

She hadn't stayed out for all that long in the end. She didn't really want to worry Marius after all, but she had needed to find a way to be in charge of herself again, even if it was only for a couple of hours.

She knocked on his door, ready to proffer the rest of the cakes as a peace offering, but there was no answer and the door was locked. She guessed that he would still be down at the quayside on the lookout for a message. He was sure to be back soon, though, to escape the midday heat behind closed shutters like everyone else.

She tried on the dresses while she waited. The sleeves came all the way to her wrists and the skirts almost to her ankles. At least there would be no danger of her tattoo being visible now.

There was a knock and Marius came in, hot and sweaty. They stared at each other for a moment and Nyssa wondered if he was about to try to give her a row for disappearing, but he had other things on his mind.

"There's word from William," he said, shutting the door behind him. "Another Shadow ship has arrived. It's not a random visit: The scouts are searching for a girl of your description."

Nyssa sat down heavily on the bed. "Is William all right?"

"As far as I know. I can't imagine any of the Drowned Boy regulars giving useful information to strangers, can you? Though they must have put two and two together since you disappeared."

Nyssa was forced to smile, imagining the delight her regulars would take in giving nothing away, just to be disagreeably difficult; but her smile was short-lived.

"They've got men in every town. Sooner or later they'll find someone who'll tell them something about you. We were lucky to get away when we did. We can't go back, and we can't stay here any longer, either. Get packed up."

ALARIC

THIRTEEN YEARS EARLIER

Alaric's aim was to bring the whole of the Archipelago under his yoke. He would be acknowledged as ruler by all of them.

King? Emperor? The title wasn't important to him. What mattered was the power.

He understood better than any of his men the importance of titles, of symbols. Everyone wanted to think of themselves as someone of significance—as a hero, not just a thief and a murderer. He watched their faces when they listened to the poets and singers at the end of a night's drinking. He saw their eyes go blank as they imagined themselves into the tales, imagined a poem being written about *them* one day. These islands were a superstitious place, he thought, full of strange beliefs and stories and legends. He wanted to become a figure in their stories so they would truly believe in him, and in what he could do to them.

So he chose a new name for himself, although of course he let some of his lieutenants believe it had been their idea. Now he was the White Wolf. The name made it easier for people to fear him.

As far as he could see, there was no single island that dominated the others. They just formed a loose confederation of alliances and rivalries. Look at any of the stories from their past, however, and there was one place that stood out: Thira.

Thira had been at the center of everything once. Now it was just a broken-down island of ruins swooning into the sea, where the streets ended in clots of weeds, and crabs stared out of temple windows, but it was still a potent name in the Archipelago. He decided to make it his base.

He moved most of the men and boats there, and took one of the beautiful decaying buildings farthest from the sea to be his palace.

For the next couple of years he concentrated on building up a network of spies, letting it be known that he had agents on every island, creating a climate of fear.

The number of men under his command grew, swollen both by more of his own people, who came from the northeast to seek the ease and good living that the south seemed to promise, and also by local men, who wanted to make sure they were on the winning side, or who saw a chance to settle old scores.

The islanders called his followers Shadowmen, although it could scarcely have been less appropriate. There was nothing shadowy about them as they swaggered across the islands they had already taken, but the name linked them with the ancient legends of this place.

Here he heard more about the early Shadowmen, his ancestors maybe, and about Thira's role in their defeat; and that was when he first became properly aware of the Keepers and of the ancient rumor that they had somewhere preserved the words of power that had allowed them to wreak that destruction.

What if these words still existed and could be used against him?

Then again, if he had those words, the people of the Archipelago would obey him or die. He had to have them.

And so he began to search. . . .

4

TROUBLE ON THE ROAD

Nyssa looked anxiously out the window at the narrow strip of water separating the Mainland from the island. She dreaded seeing the sleek black silhouette of a Shadow ship, but there was nothing to alarm her. Marius was right, though: They had to leave quickly. It was only a matter of time before the Shadow scouts realized she had eluded them and crossed to the Mainland to continue the hunt.

It had been too late for them to get away the day before: They had horses and tack to buy, and to have shown that much urgency would only have made them stick in people's minds. It was important that they left without looking as though they were fleeing.

She was a silent spectator as Marius haggled over prices with the horse merchant; she wasn't even sure which horses he was trying to buy. Half an hour later, though, the trader spat on his palm and shook hands, and they took possession of a tall bay gelding for Marius and a little dun-colored mare for her. At least Marius said the mare was little. Sitting tense and alone in the saddle, it looked a long way to the ground as far as Nyssa was concerned, and she didn't object at all when Marius took hold of her reins in the busier streets on their way back to the inn.

"So," she said conversationally, as they were pushed close together by a passing cart. "Where do we go now?"

"We leave here this afternoon, when there's plenty of other traffic on the road, so we'll be as inconspicuous as possible."

"And go where exactly?"

"Some nice big town where we can be anonymous. I'll find work—maybe you as well. We'll keep our heads down, live quietly."

"Quietly, *pointlessly*—until the next scare comes and we have to move on again." There was an edge to Nyssa's voice that made Marius uneasy. "Looking over our shoulders, never trusting a stranger. What sort of life is that?"

"The sort of life I've lived all the time you were at the Drowned Boy," he said shortly, turning the horses into the stable yard of the inn.

After a moment she said, "I'm sorry, of course you have. That was stupid of me," apparently chastened as they clattered across the cobblestones.

Marius got down and held the mare's head while Nyssa dismounted carefully. For a moment he thought, thankfully, that she had let the subject drop.

They led the horses inside and found stalls for them. Nyssa watched Marius, then copied him, unfastening the girth and heaving the saddle down. She stumbled, caught off guard by the unexpected weight.

"I think we should go to Rushiadh."

His back was to her as he set the saddle down on the partition. She watched it stiffen. He turned around slowly.

"Why?" he said, in a voice that suggested he didn't want to know the answer.

She lugged her saddle across and plonked it beside his with a bright smile. "It's big, it's anonymous — just like you said. And most important, it's not under Alaric's control."

"It's in the middle of a desert, it's ruled by some religious cult, and it's hundreds of miles away," Marius countered. "There are other places that would serve almost as well, much closer.

"And they wouldn't be full of foreigners," he added as an afterthought.

She began unbuckling the mare's bridle straps. "Won't we be safer if we're farther away?"

He scratched the gelding's ear. "Not necessarily. They won't just have one set of scouts looking for you, you know. And just because Alaric doesn't have authority in Rushiadh doesn't mean he couldn't have you kidnapped if he found out you were there." He turned his attention to the bridle. "Anyway, I thought you'd want to stay a bit closer to home."

She pulled the bridle off the mare's head, and a strap fell to the ground where she'd unfastened the wrong buckle. She bent to pick it up, and when she straightened said, "What's the point? You're right. We can't go back there. I need to stop thinking of it as home now." He dropped his gaze, not wanting to meet the bleak look in her eyes. "In which case, if we have to make a new start, why not start somewhere *totally* different?"

He tried to think of an obvious argument against the idea, but couldn't seem to find one.

"I'll think about it," he said, and went to get water for the horses.

Alone in the stall, Nyssa allowed herself a small smile of triumph.

✠   ✠   ✠

They set off in the middle of the afternoon, joining the steady procession of travelers on the dusty road that would lead them to their new lives. The road led south at first, toward the ports for Rushiadh.

"It goes to a lot of other places, too," said Marius. "Just because we're on this road doesn't mean that's where we're going."

"No, of course not," agreed Nyssa, the expression on her face so innocent that it made him immediately suspicious.

The road climbed gently from the sweltering coastal plain into the cooler air of forests and hills. The air smelled of earth and growing things when Nyssa rose next morning from her hard bed in the travelers' hostel where they had spent the night.

They ate bowls of porridge, then saddled the horses. Nyssa's legs ached already. She thought of the hours ahead and sighed. The night before she had been so stiff she could hardly get down at all.

"Come on, Pollux," Marius had said as he led the gelding out of the stable.

"Is that what you've called your horse?"

"It's what I call *all* my horses. What about yours?"

For some reason it hadn't occurred to Nyssa to name her, but she only had to think for a few seconds.

"Mouse."

He raised his eyebrows. "That's an outright silly name for a horse. She'll get confused."

Nyssa giggled and stroked the mare's soft nose. "You're quite happy to be called Mouse, aren't you?"

The mare tossed her head and let Nyssa lead her out of the stable.

They mounted and nosed the horses out into the broken column of travelers already on the road. For half an hour or so they rode in sleepy silence, until they came to a place where the road ran close to the edge of a bluff, high above the sea.

Looking back, they could see the town they had left yesterday, like an abandoned toy.

A line on the horizon showed the coast of the island. Nyssa looked at it with a pang, then caught her breath. Two tiny, unmistakable silhouettes moved on the water.

"Marius, look." She pointed.

He squinted at the distant sea. "What?"

"Shadow ships—can't you see them?"

He screwed up his eyes, shook his head. "No. Your eyes must be a lot better than mine. You're sure?"

She looked again. "Yes. Definitely. They're heading across from the island just like we did."

"Then it's as well we left when we did. Let's go."

They turned the horses back onto the road, Nyssa resisting the urge to kick the mare into a faster pace. Beside her, Marius was muttering.

"They'll dock in the early afternoon. Then they have to find someone who remembers us, buy horses — or do they have their own on the ships? — split up to cover all the likely routes. They won't be on the road before tomorrow morning, so that puts us a day and a half, maybe two days, in front of them."

"But they'll be riding faster."

He nodded. "I know. I think it's time you learned to trot."

⁃⁝⁃   ⁃⁝⁃   ⁃⁝⁃

She dreamed of Thira again that night, but not of the White Wolf. Instead she wandered through a succession of dusty rooms that seemed to contain nothing except occasional bits of broken furniture and scattered fragments of torn parchment. It was no place that she'd seen before. She woke from this dream more puzzled than frightened. She thought she'd been looking for something, but had no idea what it was.

It was too early to get up and she knew she wouldn't sleep again. Marius breathed regularly in the other bed. At least he didn't seem to snore.

Assuming they could stay one step ahead of the Shadowmen, how could she win him around to the next part of her plan? He wouldn't be keen. Already he was suspicious of her sudden interest in Rushiadh. Once she realized that she intended to consult the Great Library of the Moon Priestesses to try to find out what the tattoo meant, she was sure he wouldn't help her; instead he'd want to stop her in case it drew attention to her.

She tried, and failed, to imagine a whole building full of books. How many books could there be altogether everywhere? Enough for a room; yes, she could imagine that. But a whole building? Well, if things worked the way she intended, she wouldn't have to imagine. She'd actually see it.

She wouldn't let him stop her going, of course; she'd run away from him if she had to. Once she was better at riding.

⁘   ⁘   ⁘

Three days passed without incident. They pressed on as fast as they could without arousing suspicion. Mostly the road wound through trees, but sometimes it dipped down from them so that for a while they rode with views of terraces of red earth covered in vines or olive trees or wheat, red-roofed villages, and the sea glittering and tranquil as a mirage beyond them.

Nyssa's dreams were coming more frequently, every two or three nights. Maybe it was because she knew what they were about now, or maybe just because all the rhythms she used to live her life by had ceased to exist.

On the third night they stopped in a proper town: not large enough or far enough away to do as a hiding place, but a town nevertheless, grown up around the junction between two trade routes. Marius decided they could risk a rest day.

They rose late the next morning, and to her surprise he didn't object when she said she wanted to go out alone. "You might be safer like that," he said. "If they really are on our trail, they must know by now you're traveling with a man. We might be less noticeable apart."

Today she had no desire to idle her way around a market. She had some very specific purchases to make, and then she was going to have a soak in the inn's bathhouse.

Marius had equally definite aims for the day. The first was to send a carefully worded letter to William via a carrier, to try to find out how much the Shadowmen actually knew.

The second was to find the best alehouse in town and wash the dust of several days' travel out of his throat.

-‡-   -‡-   -‡-

Nyssa put her small collection of packages on the bed. Sitting down, she unwrapped a pen, paper, ink, and a small pair of scissors. She fetched her wooden box of possessions and took out her little mirror, studied her face for a minute, then went to close the shutters.

-‡-   -‡-   -‡-

Marius got back to the inn later than he had intended, and with more ale inside him than he'd planned. He wasn't drunk—far from it—but he couldn't honestly have claimed to be completely sober, either.

He'd thought Nyssa might be in the common room having something to eat, but there was no sign of her there, so he went up to her room and rapped on the door. There was a muffled response that he took to mean *come in*, so he pushed the door open.

Nyssa stood in front of the mirror on the wall, obviously caught off guard. She was wrapped in a robe, having come straight from the bath by the looks of it. Some of her hair was piled in a haphazard knot on top of her head. A small mirror was in her left hand and a pair of scissors in her right.

They stared at each other in wide-eyed silence. Marius felt the pleasant effects of the ale drain away through his boot soles.

"What are you doing?" It didn't sound like his voice at all.

"Trimming my hair?"

"What are you doing?" he asked again. Although, as was so often the case when he asked her a question, he found that he didn't really want the answer.

She stared at him defiantly, and he caught himself wishing once more that she'd somehow stayed a child. Then she put down the mirror and scissors and moved to sit on the bed.

"Come in and shut the door," she said. "You know what I'm doing, but I can't do it properly on my own."

He pushed the door closed behind him, heard the latch click, and moved slowly across the room toward her.

"Why can't you leave it?"

"How can you ask that? Don't pretend you don't understand. If this is why my family was killed, I want to see what it looks like. I want to understand it."

"That's why you want to go to Rushiadh." It was a statement, not a question.

She nodded. "Please." She picked up the scissors and held them out to him. "If you help, it shouldn't be obvious when my hair's braided, and it'll grow out, anyway." She looked him in the eye and said, with an odd sort of dignity, "I have a right to know why I'm being hunted, don't you think?"

That was the moment he finally accepted that she was no longer a child.

He sat down beside her and took the scissors from her hand. "Hold still," he said, and began to cut her hair. He thought as he snipped that he would have to shave away some of the hair to see the tattoo properly but, as he cut close to her scalp, he could see the lines of lettering shining through.

He could remember standing in the hut as the priest did this: Nyssa bawling; Kira crying silently; her husband, Julius, tight-lipped; and Kit, exhausted by his own ordeal, already asleep in his crib.

So long ago, so far away — another life, almost another world.

The tattoo still looked almost as sharp as the day it had been done, when she was only a few months old, though the ink had faded a little: clear tight lines that covered a surprisingly small area of her skin.

He moved to fetch the pen and ink and paper. Nyssa sat so still she might have been made of wood. He began to copy, slowly and patiently, wishing for the first time in his life that he had paid more attention to this part of his tedious education, trying to recreate perfectly every curve of the lettering since he had no idea how small a mistake could fatally alter the meaning of whatever it was that gradually appeared on the paper in front of him.

When he had finished he handed it wordlessly to her.

She took it and stared at it intently, as though she could force the meaning to make itself clear. Absently she reached one hand up to unpin her hair and shook her head. When her hair settled it looked almost as it had before.

"And no one knows what this means or how to say it?" she asked.

"No one. That knowledge must have died out generations ago."

"Did no one ever try to rediscover it?"

"If they did, nothing was ever passed on about it; we all spoke the Common Tongue. Perhaps there never seemed to be a need; the Shadow had been gone for such a long time. It was nothing more than a legend. Don't forget — just a couple of weeks ago you thought the Keepers didn't even exist. That's what most of the Archipelago thinks."

"And what would they do if they found out that the Keepers are still here?"

He shook his head. "I've often wondered. I think most people wouldn't care," he said bitterly. "Though now the Shadowmen are here again maybe there are some who wish there were Keepers with power and spells to help them again. They don't realize that we don't mean anything anymore. We're not what we were in the stories. Some people would laugh at us for the way we've clung to traditions we don't even understand. But for all those who might welcome us, there would be some who would be afraid of us, in case we're what the legends say. They're the dangerous ones."

"Why?"

Marius gave her a look of surprise. "Think, Nyssa. If people are afraid of something, they destroy it. It nearly happened to us all those years ago. There are still plenty of people who would finish the job."

Nyssa thought about that in silence for a minute. It was hardly a cheering thought. She turned her attention back to the paper in her hand.

"I thought it would be longer. If it's supposed to be so powerful. Of course, it could be meaningless, couldn't it? People could have made so many mistakes copying it over the centuries that it doesn't mean anything anymore." She turned to him. "Imagine if I'm being hunted for nothing." She gave a rather desperate laugh.

Marius shrugged. "Maybe if we could prove it was something useless, we could persuade him to leave you alone."

"Does that mean we're going to Rushiadh?"

"Oh, I suppose so. Tell me," he said, trying to lighten the gloomy mood, "did you always get your own way with William?"

Her mouth curved upwards and she gave a genuine chuckle. "Oh yes. Even when he didn't realize I had."

-∤-   -∤-   -∤-

Aware that they had no reason to assume they had lost their pursuers, they left the next morning before the heat built up.

Nyssa felt that she and Mouse were getting used to each other, although she was still a long way from Marius's careless ease with Pollux.

They continued along the same road for one more day, then struck off southwest, toward the coast. The plan now was to take a ferry from the port of Korce to Trabzyn, from where it was only a three- or four-days' ride to the city of Rushiadh on the southern Mainland. There were other ports from which they could have left, but Marius wanted to go this way because there was supposed to be a Keepers' house along the road, and he hoped he could send another message from there to William, telling him their change of plan.

"Have you been here before?" asked Nyssa.

"No. We had to learn where there were Keepers' houses." She looked at him, puzzled. "In the village, when I was growing up." He gave a sigh at her look of incomprehension, and started to explain to her a little of the hated lessons that had nearly driven him away from the Keepers altogether.

"We were made to learn so much that had no point or made no sense. The Legend, obviously. The Legend. We had to repeat it, word perfect, every day from when we were six, or maybe it was seven."

"Why?" Nyssa interrupted.

"Exactly! But if you asked, the priests just hit you around the ears and made you repeat it again."

"What else?"

"Lists. Lists of dates, of names. Some of them were the names of stars — maybe all of them were, for all I know. But I've no idea what the dates meant. Some were in the past, some in the future. If I asked, all I ever got was 'This is how the knowledge has been passed on for generations.' That was after they'd hit me, of course.

"Sometimes there were things mixed in that almost made sense. There would be a list of crops and advice about how to plant them. And there were bits — scattered — about digging to find water and bringing it to a house or field. It took me about three years to put it all together in my mind, though. It was all mixed up with more cursed lists.

"It was almost as though someone had once torn up a lot of books and mixed all the scraps together in a sack and then read them in whatever order they came out.

"Actually, though," he added, looking thoughtful, "to be fair, I *have* used the stuff about the water. I've dug wells for a few people, or piped water to their houses. It pays well.

"What you really can't imagine, though, is the hours and hours of rubbish — no, years and years of it — that the few useful morsels were buried in.

"As far as the priests were concerned, we were taught these things because that was what had been done for hundreds of years. It was as though they were afraid that if they didn't do it, we'd all fade away, like smoke, and there would be nothing left. Gods — they must always have chosen the most stupid people in the village to be priests!"

He shook his head.

"Don't get caught up in any fanciful notions of what it is to be a Keeper. If anything about the Legend was ever true, it was all lost hundreds of years ago. There's nothing left for us to be heirs to except trouble."

Nyssa opened her mouth to say something, saw the expression on Marius's face, and decided that, for once, silence might be the best option.

-+-   -+-   -+-

The road they were traveling now was much quieter than the one they had left behind. They were taking a very indirect route to Rushiadh. *No bad thing*, Marius mused.

The forests of which Nyssa had grown so weary were far behind now. She was glad of the open views that had replaced them, even though she regretted the loss of shade. There were times she was sure she could actually feel her brain drying up.

On either side of the road, slopes of white stone and thorny scrub stretched away, singing with grasshoppers. Whenever the horses brushed against plants the scent of thyme rose around them. Flocks of ragged goats moved over the rough ground, cropping the sharp leaves, their bells speaking to the goatherds and their big rangy dogs.

On the sixth day they found themselves alone on the road for almost the whole morning, apart from the occasional sound of hooves in the distance behind them. The road dipped down now, and they began to see areas of woodland again.

They had stopped in the middle of the day to eat and doze in the shade of the trees, and were preparing to set off again, still sleepy and talking of inconsequential things. Nyssa was tightening Mouse's girth, telling her what a good girl she was, when there was a noise she didn't recognize, and Marius gave a grunt and fell to the ground beside Pollux.

It took her a few seconds to realize that the thing sticking out of the front of his left shoulder was an arrow, and when she did so, she couldn't suppress a scream.

She dropped to the ground and scrambled over to him, retaining just enough presence of mind to keep hold of Mouse's reins.

He managed to sit up and haul himself behind a tree.

"Get over here!" he hissed. "Keep down."

She grabbed Pollux's reins, too, and crawled over beside him. His hand was clamped over the arrow and his breathing was harsh.

They peered around the tree trunk, looking for any signs of the archer. Nyssa's jaw was clenched so hard to prevent a whimper escaping that it hurt.

Five minutes passed; ten. Nothing.

"We have to move," Marius said. "If we stay here, whoever shot will just wait until dark, then finish things off." He fumbled awkwardly for his knife as he spoke.

"Is it *them*?" Nyssa couldn't stop shaking.

"I don't know. If we're lucky, it's just a bandit out to rob and kill us."

"That's all right, then," she said weakly, pulling crumbs of courage from his bravado. "I thought for a minute we were in trouble."

He handed her the knife. "Here. Cut through the shaft of the arrow."

"Shouldn't I try to take it out?"

He shook his head, loosening the hand that held the arrow

and squinting down. "No. It isn't bleeding all that much. If you take the arrow out it'll be worse, and I need to be able to ride."

She began to cut at the shaft while he tried not to watch. At first she was too tentative, afraid that she would hurt him, but after a minute or so he said, "Get on with it, Nyssa, just do it fast," so she did. He grunted as she snapped the shaft, but collected himself enough after a few seconds to smile at her and say, "Well done."

"Now what?"

"We have to get away from here."

Their gear was already strapped onto the horses. Nyssa helped Marius to his feet, and they stood behind the horses, looking intently back down the road and into the trees, watching for any sign of movement, a flash of metal, perhaps.

"Do you think they've gone?" asked Nyssa hopefully.

"I doubt it."

They moved a little farther into the trees so that they would have some shelter as they mounted. Marius pushed his left hand inside his jacket and caught Pollux's reins in his right hand.

"Now what?"

"Now you find out if you can gallop."

He jammed a foot into Mouse's flank and she leaped away with a squeal, Pollux hard on her heels. By the time they reached the road, the ride was already faster than anything Nyssa had done before. Mouse was completely out of her control, hooves pounding along the packed earth, ears flat. Nyssa crouched as low in the saddle as she could, knotted her hands in Mouse's mane, and tried not to shut her eyes in terror.

After what seemed an age, but could only have been a few minutes, she heard Marius shouting from behind her.

"Slow down now! Sit up. You don't want to run her ragged."

Nyssa straightened and hauled on the reins as hard as she could. For a moment it had no effect, but she kept pulling and gradually she felt Mouse's pace slacken a little. The horse slowed to a canter, Marius and Pollux keeping pace beside her here where the road was wider.

Realizing that Mouse wasn't going to crash into a tree, Nyssa twisted to look back down the road. So far as she could tell, there was no pursuit. Perhaps everything was going to be all right.

"I can't see anyone behind us."

"Good."

"Do you think they've gone?"

He gave a mirthless laugh. "Not for a minute."

"But we can outrun them?"

Marius shook his head. "Afraid not. I'll not be able to ride like this for long. I'm just trying to get far enough ahead to give me a chance to ambush *them*." He did his best to sound calm. It wouldn't help if she realized just how much trouble they were in and how frightened he was himself. The horses had slowed to a trot now as he scanned the woods for a good spot. "I want you to ride on, Nyssa, as fast as you can. I'll catch up if everything goes well."

"I'm not leaving you!" She was appalled.

"Please. There isn't time for an argument." He closed his eyes wearily for a moment.

"I know that. So please believe that I mean it. I won't go. Don't waste time trying to make me."

"Then for once in your life, shut up and do what I say." She nodded. "In here." He had spotted whatever it was he'd been looking for. They checked back down the road again. There was still no one to be seen, but it was possible to imagine, very faintly, the sound of hooves.

Marius slid awkwardly down from Pollux, leaning against the gelding's flank for a few seconds as he spoke. "Get the horses out of sight of the road. Tie them up, then find yourself somewhere to hide, and don't come out until I tell you it's safe."

"And if you don't?" The words were out before she could stop them.

He looked hard at her. "Then do what seems best," he said, and handed her the knife she'd used to cut the arrow.

She nodded, forcing down panic, trying not to think about what he meant.

He handed her Pollux's reins, then bent, and pulled another knife from his boot.

"Now go."

ALARIC

TEN YEARS EARLIER

All the spies knew that the White Wolf paid well for scraps of information about the Keepers, though none of them was quite sure why. Surely the Keepers were just the ragtag remnants of a clan who legend said had once been powerful enough to destroy a Shadow fleet, along with half the Archipelago, by their temerity in awakening the old gods. But they were no threat now. Most people in the islands thought they only existed in the old stories, never dreaming that they still lived inconspicuously among them.

Then a man came with new information. He made his report to Alaric in the great hall he liked to use for such things, with its cracked floor of patterned marble. Alaric appeared to listen with only half his attention as he continued with the meal he had been eating when the man arrived.

Afterward, though . . . afterward, he sat alone, turning a cup of wine in his fingers, considering the potential of what he had just heard.

They placed such stock in their tales and legends down here. In that respect they were little better than children. What a blow this might strike in his quest to take the whole Archipelago. He would prove he was stronger than the Shadowmen of old, and no Keepers' spell could stop him this time.

He didn't rush into anything, of course. He spent time and effort on having the man's story thoroughly checked without raising any suspicions.

He considered briefly whether he should involve himself directly, but that was not his style. Better to simply stretch out a hand and have his Shadowmen do it.

When he gave the commander who would be in charge of the expedition his instructions, the man had a single question for him.

"We are to leave no one at all alive in the village?"

"No one."

The man nodded and left to carry out the White Wolf's orders.

5

THE FACE IN THE MIRROR

As she pulled the horses deeper into the trees she could definitely hear hooves. *Only one horse*, she thought. She pulled their own two horses behind a thicket of new growth that would screen them from the road and tethered them, then looked around for somewhere to hide. There was nothing that really offered enough cover. Instead she quickly climbed up a small knoll and lay on her stomach peering around a tree at the top. At least from here she would be able to see what was happening and try to escape if things went wrong.

The hoofbeats were louder now, but not hurried; no more than a trot. She could see Marius pressed against a tree, his white face set, the knife blade held between his fingers. Along the road a horse and rider appeared.

Just one. Nyssa's hand tightened on the hilt of the knife she held. Their attacker was a wiry, sallow man on a piebald horse. He looked about, alert but unhurried, obviously thinking they would be easy prey now. He didn't look like what she imagined a Shadowman to be. *That doesn't mean he can't kill you, though. After all, if he's a bandit, this is how he makes a living.*

There was a short bow and a quiver of arrows at his back, a sword and a knife at his belt. He scanned the road for hoof-prints, but Marius had chosen the spot well and the dry earth gave few signs. It shouldn't be immediately obvious where they had turned off.

If only they'd had a bow as well . . . but no, that wouldn't have helped. She couldn't shoot and, at the moment, neither could Marius.

She realized she was holding her breath and let it out carefully as the man drew level with Marius. She tensed, waiting for him to make his move.

Marius waited until the bandit had gone about fifteen feet, then stepped into the road and threw the knife as hard as he could. It spun silently through the air and hit the rider squarely in the back, knocking him from his horse.

He pulled himself to his knees, roaring curses, and reaching for his sword as Marius rushed at him, hauling out his own sword, knowing that he might have little chance if it came to a proper fight. He had no idea how badly he had already wounded the other man.

There was no more time to think. He was on him, hacking and thrusting as best he could, not letting the robber get to his feet.

Nyssa was up and running to help without even thinking what she was doing, but by the time she reached the road it was already over. Marius stood white-faced and panting, his sword patched with red. Sprawled in the dust at his feet, the man was clearly dead. He'd broken his bow when he fell, and blood oozed and soaked into the parched earth around him. Nyssa stared in sickened fascination. It could so easily have been Marius lying there like that, and then what would have become of her?

Marius's voice, sharp with pain, broke into her thoughts. "Get the horses, Nyssa," he said. "Don't look anymore." He sat down suddenly on a boulder at the roadside.

For once she made no argument. Fighting down nausea, she hurried back to where the horses were tied and brought them back.

"Are you all right?" A stupid question, but she asked it nevertheless.

He tried to smile. "I'll do, for a bit longer, anyway." She could see that the dark stain on the shoulder of his jacket had spread since she last looked at it.

"Are we just going to . . . leave him?"

Marius nodded. "There's nothing else we can do. It'll take me all my strength to stay on Pollux, and it'll be dark soon. You're in charge now, Nyssa. Get us away from here. The Keepers' house shouldn't be far. Look for an eye carved into the gatepost. That's how to recognize this one."

Marius putting himself in her care frightened her more than the attack had done.

⊹   ⊹   ⊹

Nyssa bit her lip, scanning the landscape ahead for an inn, a house . . . even a ruin would do. The sun was beginning to sink; soon it would fall below the horizon. She had to find somewhere before dark and, despite Marius's assurance that the Keepers' house was nearby, so far she hadn't seen any house at all, let alone a gatepost. He rode at her side, silent and grim-faced, the reins of the bandit's horse tied to his saddle. He hadn't spoken for a long time now.

The road descended gradually. Soon they would reach cultivated land. There had to be safety *somewhere*.

Something caught her eye to the left of the road. Across a shallow valley, lamps were blooming. Through the thickening light she could just make out a fortified house, almost lost in the swift twilight. Without the lamps she would never have noticed it.

"There's a house! There's a house across the valley. Not far now."

"Good," was all he said.

She turned Mouse off the road and onto a smaller trail that seemed to lead in the right direction. Ten minutes later, the house came into view again. It was protected by a high stone wall.

She'd given up on the thought that this might be the house they'd been looking for. She didn't care, just so long as the people inside let them in. They'd ask questions. . . . She'd just have to think of something.

They had arrived at the gate. Torches burned on either side of it so that anyone outside would be clearly visible and dazzled coming in out of the dark. Nyssa squinted into the light, looking for any sign of a carved eye, but unable to see one.

"Hello!" she shouted. Nothing but the cicadas answered her.

"Hello! Please let us in."

There was a creak, and a small hatch opened in the gate, bright light flooding through.

"What do you want?" a deep voice asked.

"We were attacked on the road earlier. My uncle's hurt. Please let us in."

There was a sound of muttered conversation from behind the gate, then the voice said, "I'm opening the gate. Don't move until you're told to."

Nyssa nodded. Instead of the relief she had thought she would feel, she was more worried than ever. Once they were shut behind that gate, they would be completely in the power of whoever was inside.

Get a grip, she told herself. *It's far too late to be thinking like that. Just stay alert.*

The gate opened with a screech to reveal a torch-lit court-yard, and five men with drawn bows.

"You can come in now," said the same voice, which belonged to a burly, dark-bearded man.

They rode slowly forward, hearing the gate shut behind them as soon as they were through. Once it had done so, the bowmen relaxed.

The man who had already spoken came forward and took Mouse's reins from her. "Get down. You'll be safe here." He gave her a searching look, then his eyes moved to Marius and he nodded to another of the guards to help him down.

"Is that your horse, too? What happened to the rider?" The man who held her reins nodded to the robber's mount.

She couldn't think of anything to do except tell the truth. "It belonged to the man who attacked us. My uncle killed him."

For an endless second there was silence. The archers looked at each other.

"Good," said the burly man, his face splitting in a grin. "That's one less of the bastards to prey on decent folk."

Any reservations there might have been about offering Marius and Nyssa help had apparently evaporated on the spot. The horses were led away to be stabled, their bags were carried indoors, and Marius was helped inside. Nyssa started to follow when he was taken off down a corridor, but her host put out a hand to block her way.

"Best leave him to us for a bit, girl. I'll come and get you when we're done. Let's get you something to eat." Without warning, he roared, "Luccia!" and after a few seconds a hugely fat old woman, her hair hidden in a coif, appeared around a corner.

"We have guests for the night. Find some food and drink."

He turned back to her. "What's your name, anyway?"

"Nyssa — and my uncle is called Marius."

"Get Nyssa something to eat now," he instructed the old woman. "We've to take an arrow out of her uncle."

"Trouble on the road?"

"Aye — but they killed the thieving —"

"Well done, dear." Luccia's face split in a melon grin. "Come with me now."

"I'd rather —"

"I'll come and get you," the man said firmly.

Luccia led her off around the corner with such swift small

steps that it looked as though she was rolling along on tiny wheels. Feeling helpless and unable to do anything else, Nyssa followed and found herself in an enormous kitchen, with an open window looking onto a central courtyard.

Already it was completely dark outside, but several of the windows showed lights. Luccia bustled around fetching food and drink and talking continuously, half to herself and half to Nyssa, about the lawless state of the roads.

Nyssa sat down at a huge scrubbed table and, to be polite, picked at food that she was much too tense to eat. She jumped when she heard Marius yell.

"That'll be the arrow coming out." Luccia pressed a glass into her hand. "Try not to worry, my dear; Bruno knows what he's doing."

Nyssa had drunk half the glass before she realized it was wine so strong it made her head swim.

Another ten minutes passed, then Bruno's voice rang out from a window on the other side of the courtyard.

"Luccia! You can bring the girl around now."

Nyssa shot to her feet so quickly that she knocked over her half-drunk wine. Luccia waved away her apologies as she trundled along the corridors in front of her.

They met Bruno coming out of a room.

"Is he all right?"

"Yes. No need to worry. Rest, and food and drink, and he should be fine. See for yourself."

Nyssa pushed open the door not quite knowing what to expect, but there was Marius looking fairly normal, if you discounted the fact that he was more or less the same color as the bed linen, propped up on a number of pillows. He gave her a wry smile as he pushed the hair out of his eyes with his good hand. He was wearing someone else's clean shirt, and she could see the edge of a bandage where it was open at the throat. She realized that Luccia and Bruno had shut the door and left them alone.

What she really wanted to do was hug him, but instead she sat carefully in the chair beside the bed and smoothed her skirts.

"Are you all right?"

"Much better. A few hours' sleep and I'll be fine. You did well to get us here, Nyssa."

"But I don't know if it's the right place. It was too dark to see any carving on the gatepost."

"Well, they've been friendly enough so far. There was nothing else you could have done. I couldn't have gone on much longer."

A silence developed.

"Well, what is it?" he said with a sigh after a minute or so.

"What?"

"I'm getting to know how your mind works. You want to say something. Get on with it."

She gave a sheepish smile. "I was just wondering. . . . You threw that knife at his *back*."

Yet again, she had confounded him. "What—you think I should have given him a fair chance? He'd already tried to kill us."

"No . . . no, that's not what I meant. It's just that . . . wouldn't it have been better to throw sooner, because if you'd missed, wouldn't he have been too far away for you to have a second chance?"

Marius burst out laughing. "And there I was thinking you had some moral scruples!" He shook his head. "Obviously I don't know you as well as I thought."

She was frowning at him. "You're not taking me seriously. I want to understand. If you'd missed . . . I want to be able to defend myself. All I've ever used a knife for is cutting up food. I want you to teach me to use one properly."

He sobered immediately. "Of course I will. I should have thought of it before."

"That's all right. There hasn't exactly been much time to think about things like that so far. Hopefully I'll never need to do it, anyway."

At that moment the door opened and Bruno came in with a cup in his hand.

"This'll make sure you get a good night's sleep. Stop the wound from keeping you awake." He handed it to Marius, who sniffed the contents and then drained it, grimacing at the taste. "It should only take a few minutes to work." He made no move to take the cup back and turned as though to leave, but instead of doing so he suddenly grabbed Nyssa's wrist and pushed her sleeve back to expose her clan tattoo.

Nyssa pulled her arm away with a gasp, as Marius tried and failed to get out of bed.

Bruno smiled. "I thought so. We saw yours, of course," he

nodded to Marius, who had fallen back groggily against the pillows, "when we were tending to your shoulder; but you weren't in a state to realize it at the time."

Nyssa thought wildly. What could she do? Oh God, what could she do?

"Two Keepers on the road. Unusual these days. I know it's said that long ago a Keeper could travel the length of the Archipelago and rely on the Crane tattoo for bed and board and passage. Everyone thought it was an honor to help a Keeper then. But nowadays . . . nowadays they tend to stay still, where they think they're safe. Of course, nowhere's really safe for us, is it?"

In the short silence that followed, Nyssa wondered if she'd misunderstood, until Bruno pushed up his own sleeve, grinning.

As she looked at the familiar tattoo, she suddenly knew what people meant when they used the phrase *weak with relief.*

"So I *did* find the right house. I couldn't see the carving."

"The eye? We took that away years ago. Doesn't do to advertise what we are now. How did you know about it?"

"Marius told me — didn't you?"

But the sleeping draft had overtaken him.

"Best thing for him, girl. You look as though you could do with a good sleep yourself. You know you're among friends now, so there's nothing to stop you having one, either. Come on, I'll show you your room."

"Can I sleep in here? In case he needs anything."

"Of course you can, though he'll not wake before morning. I'll get bedding brought in."

·⊹·   ·⊹·   ·⊹·

They slept late next morning, exhausted by the events of the day before. Nyssa was relieved to see that Marius, though his arm was in a sling, seemed almost his usual self.

Bruno looked at his shoulder and rebandaged it. "Could have been much worse," he said drily.

Late that afternoon a couple of men brought in the body of the bandit and tumbled it unceremoniously off a horse into the dust outside the gates.

"What do you want done with him?"

Bruno stared at the corpse, considering. It smelled terrible, the features already discolored and bloated. Nyssa felt her throat constrict, and edged away with her hand over her mouth, trying not to be sick.

Bruno was frowning. "I thought I'd recognize him. Odd. Well, I won't have anyone waste energy burying him. Throw him in the ravine. The wolves can have at him."

He beckoned Marius and Nyssa to follow him into the stables.

"Did you look through his baggage?"

Marius shook his head. "Never had the opportunity."

The robber's belongings lay in a small forlorn heap just inside the door. Bruno crouched down and began to rummage in the saddlebags.

"Here," he said with a grin, and handed Marius a leather pouch.

Nyssa watched as he opened it awkwardly, one-handed. It was full of gold pieces.

Marius whistled. "It looks as though he was quite successful in his chosen line of work."

"I'll count it," said Nyssa, taking it from him.

Bruno continued to search the bags, tossing things to the ground as he finished with them. Engrossed in her counting, Nyssa didn't see him take out a length of thin cord, but his exclamation of surprise made her look up in time to see Marius frantically pantomiming to him to be quiet.

"What?" she said, eyes narrowed.

"Nothing."

She gave Marius a hard look. "Don't treat me like an idiot." She turned to Bruno. "What is it?"

He looked at Marius and shrugged helplessly. He held up the cord. "He wasn't just a bandit. This means he is—was— a Shadowman. They—"

"They all carry a cord like that," Marius broke in quickly. "It's a sort of badge, like our tattoos."

The coins Nyssa had been counting slid through her fingers. She had convinced herself during the frightening ride to find safety that the man Marius had killed had simply been a thief, that they had been random targets. Fear formed into something that felt like a stone and sank into the pit of her stomach.

Bruno looked from one to the other of them, eyes full of questions. "Was he after you? How did he know you were Keepers?"

Marius, almost as pale as he had been the day before, licked his lips, collecting himself.

"I don't know. We thought he was just a robber. No one on

the road knew we were Keepers. He couldn't know . . ." He shook his head. "I don't know."

Bruno looked at him for a few seconds, seemed about to ask him something else, then changed his mind and closed his mouth. Nyssa bent to pick up the coins she had dropped, not wanting to say anything in front of Bruno.

"I'll send some of my people out to check the roads, see what they can find out. You'd best stay here until they come back and we know a bit more about what's going on."

Marius nodded absently. "Thank you. But we shouldn't stay; it will bring danger on your household."

Bruno snorted. "We're all Keepers. You're not any more dangerous to my household than I am."

Nyssa handed the pouch of coins to him. "I'm sorry. I didn't finish counting it."

He made to pass it to Marius.

"It's yours. Take it."

"It's not mine."

"You killed him; you've earned it."

Marius shook his head. "You took us in, gave us help. We didn't even know the money was there."

It was a stupid thing to have a stalemate about, Nyssa decided.

"Why not keep half each?"

Bruno nodded slowly. "That sounds like sense."

Nyssa held her hand out for the pouch. "I'll start counting again."

-¦-   -¦-   -¦-

They stayed another two nights, waiting for Bruno's men to return. None of them brought any news when they did so. If other Shadowmen were abroad in the area, they were well hidden.

For Nyssa, it was a struggle to leave. Here she felt reasonably safe, and was sure she was among friends. Back on the road anything could happen. But they couldn't hide here forever. They needed the anonymity of a big town to give them a measure of security.

At least when they left, they were not only reprovisioned and rested, but with much heavier pockets. Marius's arm was out of the sling, though his shoulder still pained him.

"You've kept saying money isn't a problem, anyway," said Nyssa as they rode through the vineyards that now covered the terraced hills. "How much do we have?"

"One hundred and sixty-four gold pieces."

"Altogether?"

"Altogether."

"Of which we were just given a hundred and four." She skewered him with a glance. "So, in fact, you were lying to me, and I should have been worrying about money."

"No." He had the grace to look embarrassed. "No, I lied to you so you *wouldn't* worry about money."

"I thought we were being honest with each other. How do I know when to believe you?"

"I'm sorry. I just—well, I just thought you probably had enough to worry about already."

They rode on in silence for a hundred yards.

"You were probably right," she said.

Now that they were alone, they could at last discuss the attack properly. They seemed never to have been alone together in the past three days.

"How did he know who we were?" asked Nyssa. "I swear I hadn't seen him before — had you?"

Marius shook his head and kicked Pollux into a trot so they could stay within sight of the cart rumbling along in front of them.

"I certainly don't remember him," he said over his shoulder as Nyssa urged Mouse to keep up. "Maybe he didn't know who we were: We just fit the description of who he was looking for, so he decided to shoot us so he could make sure."

"They wouldn't just . . . would they? What if we were just two ordinary people and he'd killed us?"

"Nyssa, they wouldn't care. They think about the people of the Archipelago the way they think about insects. They wouldn't care *how* many of the wrong people they killed."

"That's *terrible*." She gulped. "That means other people are in danger because of us — of *me*. What can we do?"

He caught hold of her arm. "Nothing. There's nothing we can do about that. Nyssa, this isn't your fault. It's him — Alaric — doing this. It's not your fault."

She nodded, but he could tell she didn't believe what he'd said. They rode on in silence.

✢ ✢ ✢

The road stayed quiet around them during the two days it took to reach Korce, but they were careful never to be as isolated from other travelers as they had been on the stretch where they were attacked.

A couple of times each day, Marius turned off the road so that he could begin to teach Nyssa how to use a knife properly. To his surprise, she quickly picked up how to throw accurately.

"You've a good eye," he said, levering the knife out of a tree trunk. "Not everyone can do this."

"Did you learn how to fight in the village?" she asked.

He shook his head. "We only used weapons to hunt. That's one reason the Shadowmen were able to do what they did to the village.

"No. Once I knew you were safe at the Drowned Boy, for a while at least, I went off and enrolled with a sword master for a few months."

"Wasn't it too late by then?"

He frowned at her. "Not for you. I wanted to be able to protect you."

She flushed. Day by day she was coming to understand the enormity of what he had done, and was still doing, for her.

"Come on," he said. "We should get back on the road."

✢ ✢ ✢

They rode into Korce late the next day, found lodgings at the second inn they tried, and both went to bed early: Marius still feeling the effects of the arrow, and Nyssa for want of anything else to do.

It proved to be a long night. Her sleep was broken, plagued with fragmentary dreams of the drowned city, though tonight at least, she didn't have to look into the White Wolf's eyes. It was a relief when dawn came, and she was up and dressed early.

After they had breakfasted they made their way to the docks to book places on the next ferry to Trabzyn. They looked about constantly, alert for anyone who could be a Shadowman, but saw nothing to arouse their suspicions.

They could see masts as they picked their way down to the harbor with its wharves and jetties. A smell of tar rose to meet them as a vessel had its seams caulked. There were skiffs and small boats tied to the wooden piles, and a few fishing vessels, but the only ships of any size were three big-bellied cargo vessels.

The jetties were littered with the usual ordered jumble of drying nets, creels, and coils of tarry rope. Men hung on cradles over the edge of one of the barges, daubing her seams with tar, and there was all the normal bustle of a working port.

They found the ferry office and booked places on the next sailing, in four days' time.

"Four days . . . I didn't think we'd have to wait that long at this time of year."

"You'll just have to find somewhere to carry on teaching me how to use a knife. And you can help me choose one of my own," she added as an afterthought. "There must be a shop here somewhere that sells knives."

In fact whole streets in Korce seemed to consist of nothing *but* shops, some hardly more than booths, and most buildings that weren't shops were inns. On either side of the narrow lanes they rose three or four stories high, leaning toward each other like drunks. The majority of shops seemed to specialize in just one thing: honey or boots or ropes for rigging, dusty herbs or candles or cheese — or knives.

In the end, she bought two on Marius's advice: one long-bladed and sheathed in calfskin, to wear obviously at her belt if it seemed advisable, and another, much smaller but wickedly sharp, that could be easily concealed.

"May as well do it properly," Marius commented, handing over coins.

-+-   -+-   -+-

In all the time that she had afterward, she would always think of that night, rather than the one in which she fled her former life at the Drowned Boy, as the night everything changed.

Once again she headed for bed early, leaving Marius nursing his tankard in the common room of the inn. She undressed, braided her hair, and hoped as she lay down that tonight would bring her only ordinary dreams.

She trailed her fingers through a film of dust on the surface of a marble balustrade as she climbed a magnificent staircase, some of the treads shattered or crazed with a spiderweb of cracks.

At the top of the stairs she set off along a corridor. Most of the windows were shuttered, but here and there a little moonlight seeped in where they were broken. It didn't do much to lighten the gloom of the corridor, though, and she was glad of the small oil lamp she carried.

At the end of the corridor was another staircase, narrow, plain, and wooden, in contrast to the first, twisting up out of sight. She began to climb it, avoiding the fragile skeletons and bird droppings that lay thick in the corners, where pigeons and sparrows found their way in from time to time through the broken shutters and fluttered in distress until they died, unable to find a way back out.

The only light coming into the dark, dusty passage at the top of this flight was from the star-sprinkled sky showing through the missing tiles, for here she was directly under the roof.

She pushed open a door and saw before her a tiny room with a pathetic sprinkle of someone's belongings: a burst mattress on the floor with a couple of torn blankets, some bits and pieces of clothing neatly folded on a chair that had lost its back.

Her dream-self crossed the room and unhooked a scrap of ancient tapestry that seemed to serve as a curtain across a tiny window.

The building she was in must be set high in the town, for she could make out a jumble of roofs fanning out below, and lights burning at other windows.

Her mind empty, she stared out the window for several minutes, then turned back into the room.

There were candle stumps on a small table pushed against the wall, stuck into the wax left by their forerunners. She lit them carefully and blew out the oil lamp.

The candle flames steadied and she looked at the wall behind them; no, not the wall—a mirror, doubling the flames. She leaned forward and saw her dream-face.

She wasn't looking at her own reflection. Gazing back at her was a pale, bruised face surrounded by matted hair the color of oat straw — the face of a boy. Her hand moved and he probed gently at a black eye with a thin, filthy finger.

She wasn't looking at her own reflection. She was looking at her own eyes, in this strange, battered boy's face.

And suddenly she understood.

"Marius! Marius, let me in!"

It was the hammering on the door that roused him, then a surge of fear as he heard the terror in her voice.

"I'm coming," he yelled, pulling on clothes as he lunged for the door. She was through it the second he unlocked it, in her nightgown, hair awry, eyes wide, on the verge of complete hysteria.

"What is it? What's wrong?" he asked, trying to envisage what scene could have reduced her to this state.

"It's Kit. It's him. I've seen him. He's not dead."

6

THE HOUSE OF WHITE LILIES

He gaped at her blankly. *Oh no,* he thought. *She seemed to be coping so well with all of this. . . . She's having some sort of breakdown. What do I do?*

He shut the door, checking automatically as he did so that there was no one to eavesdrop.

"Come, sit down," he said. He put an arm around her shoulders and led her to the bed. He could feel her trembling as he smoothed the covers to make a place for her. She sat, obedient as a little child for once, and he thought for a moment it was going to be all right.

Crouching in front of her he looked into her dilated eyes and took her hands.

"You've been dreaming, Nyssa. It's hardly . . ."

"I know I've been dreaming," she interrupted him sharply. "That's the whole point. I've had these dreams for as long as I can remember, as if I was living someone else's life as I slept. It never made sense, but now it does. I looked in a mirror tonight in my dream and I saw him. I saw Kit. I've been dreaming bits of his life. He's alive, Marius!"

After a few seconds, he managed to catch his breath.

"Nyssa, this can't be real. You've been caught up in your dreaming and you're still half-asleep. It's only natural that you long for someone else in your family to be alive. This is how it's coming out."

She snatched her hands away angrily. "No, it isn't. This is *not* my imagination. As soon as I saw him I knew who he was. We're twins. People always say twins have a special bond. Perhaps he's been dreaming my life as well."

"Nyssa, Kit is dead," he said patiently. "The Shadowmen killed him with the rest of your family."

"You don't know that. You just assumed they did. You told me the children's bodies were too badly burned to know who was who."

He didn't have a ready answer for that. She pushed herself to her feet and began to pace the room.

"You were quick enough to believe I was dreaming about the White Wolf. Why won't you believe this?"

"You described him. It couldn't be anyone else."

"Well then: Kit has pale, pale hair, and eyes just like mine and he's thin and . . ."

"That means nothing. I haven't seen him since he was four. What's wrong?"

Nyssa stood rooted to the spot, hands over her mouth.

"He has him, Marius. The White Wolf has Kit; he's had him

all this time. He keeps him as a sort of slave. He beats him. . . .
I've seen it. I've lived bits of his life with him."

Marius pulled himself up to sit on the bed. Against all logic
he almost found himself believing her.

He forced himself to recall what he'd spent so long trying
to forget; what he'd seen in the village that day. The jumble of
bodies, the stench of burned flesh. He'd recognized what was
left of his mother from the ring she always wore, and knowing
that she'd been looking after Kit that morning, he'd assumed
that one of the small bodies nearby must be him.

Could he have been wrong?

If what Nyssa said was true . . . ? He felt sick at the thought.
All the time she had been safe at the Drowned Boy, Kit would
have led a life of fear and misery that he could hardly imagine. He pushed away the thought that it would have been better
for the boy to have died. And despite the horror, he felt a faint
glimmer of hope. Could Kit really be still alive? Surely it was
impossible.

"What did he look like?"

He pulled his thoughts back from the abyss to answer her.
"He was pale and quiet, with hair the color of straw and eyes
just like yours."

"Just like he was—is—in my dream."

He was silent, casting about for a reason why this wild idea
couldn't be true, but try as he did, he could not think of one. In
fact, it could make sense of the otherwise inexplicable fact that
she had dreams of the White Wolf.

Kit alive, and in the White Wolf's hands . . .

"Just suppose you were right. What would we do?"

"We have to go and get him," she whispered.

"No." He found to his surprise that he had already made the decision. She opened her mouth to shout at him, but for once he managed to silence her with a look. "Not you. I'll go. I'll send a message to Bruno and Luccia. They'll look after you, and I'll go to Thira."

"No! I'm coming with you."

His face was implacable. "You are not going to walk into the White Wolf's lair. If you are right, he already has Kit's half of the message. Would you hand him the rest? It must be what he's dreamed of for years. That's why he wants you. I won't let you put yourself—and everyone in the Archipelago—in that danger."

"Oh, come on, Marius! Think straight! I'll be safer there than anywhere." She leaned back against the washstand, her hands behind her. "It's the last place he would expect me to be—right under his nose. I'd have to be mad to go there. And he has no idea that I know Kit is alive, much less that he's there."

"No." He didn't raise his voice, and he didn't say another word. They glared at each other for a few seconds, then Nyssa turned on her heel and ran from the room. Marius went after her just in time to see her door slam behind her and hear the key turning in the lock.

He went back to his own room, his mind seething. What would Nyssa do next? How could he rescue Kit from the White Wolf's clutches—if he was even there at all? Without Nyssa standing in front of him, he couldn't quite understand why he'd been so quick to believe her; but even as he thought that, he found himself infected by her urgency. If Kit was there, then every day of delay was an additional day of fear and torture for him. He'd send word to Bruno tomorrow to come and fetch Nyssa. She'd be safe there until he came back. If he came back.

-:-   -:-   -:-

Locked in her room, Nyssa sat on her bed thinking furiously, her fingers still curled around the handful of gold coins she had taken from the washstand in Marius's room a few minutes earlier. She had known there was no point trying to argue or persuade him at that moment; in fact she doubted that there was any point at all. She was more or less certain that about this they would both be equally intransigent.

But not equally cunning.

As soon as they'd headed for Korce, she'd thought of Aria, and wondered idly if they might see each other, but now Aria's presence here seemed like a gift. Surely she would hide her for a couple of days while Nyssa decided how to elude Marius and get to Thira? They'd been friendly enough back home.

It was one of the few things she and William ever fought about. He was almost as much of a soft touch as she was when beggars turned up at the kitchen door, and seldom turned anyone away without food except the drunk and angry ones, but he wouldn't even sell kitchen scraps to the cabaret dancers, much less let them through the door of the Drowned Boy, although the girls were never short of money. Even if they came to the back door after dark, he would have nothing to do with them, closing the door in their faces without a word.

"Oonagh wouldn't like it," was all he would ever say on the matter.

When she was a child, of course, she'd just accepted it, but as she got older it seemed to her more and more unfair. Everyone had to make money to live somehow, and the girls didn't rob or hurt anyone. Why should they be shunned on the street—half the time by the same men who were so eager for their company behind the gauzy curtains of the cabaret windows?

So she had managed to let it be known that she was happy to sell them a jug of ale or a flask of spirits or a bowl of stew if they came to the Drowned Boy when she was working in the kitchen and William was out. It soon became a regular occurrence, and that was how she came to know Cidryn and Aria, who weren't much older than she was herself.

She didn't want to appear nosy, but she had to admit she was inquisitive about their lives, and gradually they came to trust her enough to tell her a little. With Aria in particular she found she had much in common—not in the way they lived, obviously—but in how their minds worked. They often talked of what they would do when they were older.

"I'm saving money as fast as I can," said Aria. "Once I have enough, I'll quit dancing and buy a little house just for me."

"And how will you make a living?"

"I'll be a weaver. I'm good at weaving—quick, too. I'll manage to make enough." She flashed Nyssa a dazzling smile. "And then maybe I'll be able to come in through the front door of the Drowned Boy."

Nyssa gave a rueful smile. "And I'll still be there behind the bar, like as not."

"With a husband and children around you," said Aria, a little wistfully.

Nyssa shrugged. "I don't know about that. What about you?"

Aria flushed. "No honest man will want me after what I've been. It doesn't matter, anyway. I won't want a man around. I can take care of myself."

A few weeks after that, Aria came to say good-bye.

"They're looking for girls for a new hall in Korce. I'm going at the end of the week. It'll be a bigger place, more money. I'll be able to get out sooner, with any luck."

And now here Nyssa was in Korce, too, in need of a hiding place that Marius would never think of. She went through the plan in her head once more, then got into bed and waited for morning.

┼   ┼   ┼

She'd been hoping that Marius would wake early, and sure enough he knocked at her door before she had heard anyone else come out of their rooms.

Still in her nightgown, she let him in.

"I'm sorry," he said. "I thought you'd have slept as badly as me and be up and dressed."

"I haven't slept at all. I'm exhausted. I'm going to try to sleep now."

"Oh." He paused, at a loss.

"I understand why you don't want me to go to Thira. I suppose it makes sense."

His face brightened. "Then you'll stay with Bruno?"

"I might." She yawned hugely. "Can we talk later?"

"Yes, of course. I'll see you . . ."

"Lunchtime, maybe."

He left and she closed and locked the door, then leaned against it listening to the sound of his receding footsteps. As soon as she heard him go down the stairs, she dressed quickly, packed up her things, and climbed out the window onto the flat roof of the storeroom below.

She dropped her bag and let herself down, landing neatly.

She was fairly sure that Marius would eat breakfast, then go down to the docks to book his passage to Thira. She headed off in the other direction, to search for Aria.

Although she knew that many of the clubs and dance halls would be near the docks, she didn't want to risk wandering around there in case she ran into Marius, so she tried another tack and headed for the street she had noticed the day before, which seemed to be full of shops selling cosmetics. If there was one thing dancing girls bought frequently, it was makeup.

She found herself — who had always gone about decently bare-faced — hesitating on the threshold of the first one. Chiding herself mentally, she walked in. There were no other customers, just a tiny wizened man sitting in a high chair behind the counter, grinding pigments in a mortar. The air in front of him was hazed with blue powder.

"What can I get you, my lamb?" he asked with a mild smile.

She gave him her best smile in return. "Nothing, thank you. I'm trying to find someone—a girl called Aria. I'm not sure where she works."

"Aria . . . Aria . . ." He stopped grinding and licked his lips as he thought. "No, my lamb, she's certainly not a regular. You her little sister, are you?"

"No. Just a friend."

"I could make some inquiries. Give you some . . . introductions, if you like. Lots of opportunities in Korce for a pretty girl like you."

"No. Thank you. That's all right." She felt her smile turn queasy as she hurried from the shop.

She wasn't propositioned in the next two places, but neither of them knew anything about Aria, either.

The fourth shop contained two customers being served by a thin woman who was an arresting advertisement for her own products. Nyssa was fairly sure she would have looked unremarkable without them, but she had used them to transform herself into a haughty, queenlike creature, who gazed down from magnificent kohl-rimmed eyes at her tiny kingdom of scent and pigment.

Nyssa hung back until the other two women had left, then asked her question.

"Who wants to know about Aria?"

"I do," said Nyssa, surprised and excited. "Do you know her?"

"Depends." She scratched her head with a long nail. "You say you're a friend. You don't look like her kind—if you know what I mean."

Nyssa explained.

"Ah." The woman smiled. "She's mentioned you — from back home, aren't you? I know her. You'll find her at the House of White Lilies, down by the docks."

A few minutes later, Nyssa left the shop with directions to the House of White Lilies. All the way there she was on edge in case Marius appeared around a corner and her plan collapsed.

Despite the fact that she had so few belongings with her, her bag seemed to be getting heavier by the minute, so she was doubly glad when she saw the carved and painted sign that hung outside the House of White Lilies.

She knocked, waited, knocked again, waited again. She was just considering trying to find a back door when she heard the sound of a bolt being drawn and she found herself looking at a sleepy-eyed servant girl.

The girl stared dumbly at Nyssa.

"I've come to see Aria. I was told she worked here."

The girl raised her eyebrows and drew the door a little wider, then turned and walked off. Nyssa gathered she was to go in.

She followed the girl into a shuttered room at the rear of the building, and stood as she opened one shutter just enough to let in some light.

"Wait here," she said, and went out.

As her eyes grew accustomed to the dim light, Nyssa wandered around the room, which was furnished with couches and small tables. It smelled faintly of tobacco smoke and frangipani. She pushed the shutter open a bit more and saw in front of her a small paved courtyard, bright with pots of flowers and singing finches in little cages. Her thoughts ran here and there like mice. *What if Aria wasn't here? Or wouldn't help her? What would she do then?*

"Don't be stupid," she said to herself under her breath. "You'll think of something. You have to."

At that moment she heard the door open and turned to see Aria wrapped in a robe, her hair braided for sleep, and the remains of her kohl smudged around her eyes. When she saw Nyssa, her puzzled expression changed to one of delight.

"Nyssa! What on earth are you doing here? I couldn't imagine who could be waiting to see me. I never would have thought of you. Sit down. I'll get Yana to bring us something to eat and drink."

She called to the servant girl to bring refreshments, then came and sat down by Nyssa.

While they waited, Nyssa asked Aria about life in the House of White Lilies.

"There are more girls than where I used to work — and more cabarets and dance halls here, of course; but then, Korce is a big place, lots of people passing through. I'm earning good money, saving hard." She gave a rueful smile. "It'll still be a few more years before I can leave, though, unless some rich man takes a real fancy to me and buys out my contract."

Yana came back with a jug of fruit juice and some bread and dates, then left again without a word. Helping herself thirstily, Nyssa said, "I thought you didn't want to be stuck with a man?"

Aria shrugged. "Might not be so bad, with the right one. We'll see. You have to be realistic in this job. But tell me what you're doing in Korce."

Nyssa gave her a very truncated version of events that left out tattoos and Shadowmen and Keepers and massacres. She did tell her that Marius was her uncle and that she had discovered she had a brother, but that Marius thought she should wait here while he went to find him.

"I'm here asking for your help," she went on. "I've run away from my uncle. I'm not going to be left here like a piece of luggage. I want to go to find my brother."

"Of course you do," Aria breathed, her eyes wide with delight at the story. "How can I help you?"

"I want you to hide me here and help me get on the ferry for Thira."

"I'm sure you'll be able to stay here, but won't your uncle be on the ferry?"

"Yes, but as long as he doesn't find me before it sets sail . . . Once we're at sea there's nothing he can do."

Aria's smile widened. "And he certainly won't think to look for you *here* in the meantime, will he?"

It was Nyssa's turn to smile. "Somehow, I doubt it."

-:-   -:-   -:-

Marius returned to the inn well pleased with his morning's work. He had canceled their tickets for Trabzyn and bought passage for himself to Thira instead. He decided to talk to Nyssa right away, while he was in a good mood. The ferry for Thira left the day after tomorrow: She would be pleased at how little delay there would be.

He tried to avoid confronting the fact that he had no idea how he was going to find Kit, let alone rescue him.

He knocked on Nyssa's door and, when he got no answer and found it locked, knocked again.

She hadn't mentioned going out.

She'd been so reasonable this morning; surely she wouldn't have done anything stupid, would she? A worm of doubt began to gnaw in his head.

He persuaded the innkeeper to open the door for him, and found it empty of any sign that Nyssa had ever been there.

Mouse was still in the stable, so for the rest of the day he tramped the streets in a fruitless search, swearing fluently under his breath almost every step of the way.

At the ferry office he waited behind a sleepy-eyed servant girl buying tickets for her mistress to ask if anyone who might have been Nyssa had been in, but the man selling the tickets shook his head.

Eventually, at a loss to know what to do next, he went back to the inn.

╬   ╬   ╬

Nyssa spent the rest of the day at her ease in the little courtyard with its songbirds. She and Aria talked away the morning, then Aria excused herself, yawning, and went off to sleep before it was time to prepare for work.

She'd had to ask permission for Nyssa to stay, of course, and the owner of the house, curious, had come to have a look at the fugitive before agreeing. Nyssa found herself being observed with a measuring eye by a woman who looked to be in her fifties, with pale skin and implausibly red hair. She wasn't fat, exactly; there was just a lot of her, Nyssa decided, trying not to stare in fascination as various outposts of flesh settled themselves as she sat down to talk.

She patted Nyssa's knee with a beautifully manicured hand. "We can find you a room for a couple of nights. It won't be longer than that, will it?"

"No, no, I'm sure it won't be. I'll pay, of course."

She waved a hand in a magnanimous gesture of dismissal. "No. The room's empty just now, anyway. Aria tells me you're a good cook?"

"Well, I'm used to cooking for the inn . . ."

"You can do some cooking in payment, then. It's always good to have a change."

"Certainly, I'll be glad to."

The room was on the second floor, away from the street. Aria showed her the way. "It's a servant's room, I'm afraid — there's not much space."

"It's fine, thank you. All I need is enough space to lie down."

A little later Yana had come back, looking as semicomatose as ever, clutching the tickets to Thira that Aria had dispatched her to buy. She handed them over to Nyssa with a great show of not being interested.

Maybe she really wasn't, thought Nyssa. After all, presumably all sorts of things went on in the House of White Lilies. This probably didn't pique her interest even slightly.

At the start of the evening, Aria came in briefly, dressed in a gauzy saffron dress, her hair curled and her face painted.

"You'd better stay in your room for the rest of the evening. Just shout for Yana if you need anything."

Nyssa stared in fascination at her pomegranate-red lips, her eyes lengthened by kohl, the lids stained with malachite powder. She'd never seen her like this before. Aria had always been unobtrusively dressed and bare of cosmetics during her visits to the Drowned Boy.

There was a slightly awkward pause, then Nyssa said, "Thank you again. I'll see you tomorrow."

From time to time during the evening, sounds of music and laughter drifted up from the open windows of the ground floor she'd been in that morning, but that was all.

She hardly noticed, anyway. There was only one thought in her head now; none of the rest mattered — Keepers, legends, tattoos, Shadowmen — none of it.

Only Kit.

ALARIC

THE FIRST TWIN

Alaric stared at what they had brought him. It was only half of what he had told them to bring and, as such, useless.

The commander of the raiding party was sweating.

"We searched every building," he said. "Checked everybody. The other one wasn't there. We rode out from the village, too, found a few stragglers — killed them, as you ordered — but there was no sign of the other one."

He waited, throat dry, for his fate.

Alaric was angry of course, but it didn't show in his pale skin, in his bleached eyes. He never let others see how he felt. If you kept your emotions hidden, it gave you an advantage. People didn't know how to react, deprived of the cues they didn't even realize they relied on.

He stared coldly at the sweating man in front of him. Pathetic, what fear could reduce a grown man to. He considered what to do with this failure. . . . He rather thought that the most effective thing in this case would be . . . nothing. Just leave him wondering what might happen to him, and when, and if there was any tiny chance that he might escape it.

"Leave it here," Alaric said, "and get out."

The man turned on his heel and began to walk away, resisting an urge to run.

Alaric looked at the filthy thing on the floor in front of him, curled up like a wood louse, silent. It didn't move, but he knew it wasn't dead. He could see it breathing. Tomorrow he would have its head shaved and copy whatever was inked onto its skin. After that, of course, the creature would have absolutely no value.

Should he have it killed?

Perhaps he would keep it. There were times when he was bored. It would be good to have a diversion.

And, just maybe, the other one was out there somewhere still.

7

THIRA

The discovery that Nyssa had robbed him (or so he chose to think of it, although arguably the money belonged to them equally) had done little to improve Marius's frame of mind.

He supposed she must have gone to another inn, and was almost sure that she would try to board the ferry for Thira, with or without a ticket.

The only alternative he could think of was that she would head back to the Drowned Boy, but despite the succession of nasty surprises she'd given him, he really didn't think for a moment that she was stupid enough to do that. In fact, she wasn't stupid at all.

Which left unanswered the question of what he should do now.

It was tempting to use Nyssa's disappearance as a reason — an excuse — not to go to Thira. He wasn't a hero, wasn't even a warrior: The idea, if he was honest, frightened him.

Even if he could get to Kit and persuade him to trust him, how would he ever get him off the White Wolf's island?

A treacherous small part of his brain said, *Nyssa would have an idea. She always has ideas*, but he ignored it. She was just a girl, however shrewd. This was a man's job.

And what would happen to her if, as seemed all too possible, he was captured or killed on this mad but unavoidable errand? He hadn't had the chance to tell Nyssa enough about the Keepers' network for her to be able to make contact with anyone else. He had no idea how much Bruno knew, or indeed, how much he would be willing to help.

She'll manage somehow, said the same small bit of his brain. *It's yourself you should be worrying about.*

❖ ❖ ❖

Marius dumped his bags on the dockside, pushed his tousled hair out of his eyes, and massaged his aching shoulder. He'd been walking around the town since he settled the inn bill, hoping against hope that he'd spot her, but he hadn't, of course. Just like the two days before, which he'd spent uselessly combing the streets and asking questions at inn doors.

Not that he was convinced that he'd even got truthful answers from the ones who didn't just shut the door in his face. She might have told some sympathetic innkeeper that he'd been bothering her, or worse.

After some thought, he'd sold the horses and tack. Serve her right to be left without a horse.

He was disgusted with himself: After watching over her for all these years to lose her like this. . . . He felt, as he waited to get on the ferry, that he was abandoning her.

He was first to board. He took his luggage quickly down to the tiny cabin and shoved it in, then returned to the deck to scrutinize everyone else arriving in dribs and drabs over the next three hours as the tide rose.

Most of the passengers were men, alone or in small groups, probably going to Thira to look for work. There were a few women, but no families. He recognized the servant girl he'd seen in the ferry office, accompanying two women who were clearly dance hall girls, veiled except for their tinted and kohl-edged eyes, who went past him, giggling. The servant stayed only long enough to see to the luggage, then disembarked.

The bell was rung to signal that the ferry would leave in ten minutes, and activity on board increased as ropes were coiled, the last chests and baskets of cargo were loaded, and the few people who weren't sailing went down the gangway.

Five minutes to go. The gangway was hauled up, the rowers unshipped their oars.

Still no sign of Nyssa.

The mooring lines were cast off, and the vessel edged away from its berth into open water.

Marius scanned the dockside, hoping to see her there, come to watch him leave. The waving figures dwindled as the sails were run up and caught the wind.

Well, he'd done it. For good or ill he'd left her behind, and at least she would be safer than if she had come to Thira.

He heaved a sigh that was half relief, half regret.

-|-   -|-   -|-

With a favorable wind filling the sails, they were soon scudding along in the afternoon sunlight. Marius stayed up on deck, trying to enjoy the peace and air and light. On two occasions a pod of dolphins raced beside them for several minutes as they headed southeast, the Mainland present for a while as a smudge of gray-green on the horizon; and they were accompanied constantly by seabirds wheeling and diving for the fish that schooled in the warm waters.

It was a three-day journey to Thira, if the weather stayed fair. Of course if the wind dropped or veered to an unfavorable direction, they would be dependent on the rowers and it would take far longer.

Three days should be long enough to come up with a plan.

"Hello," said a familiar voice beside him. He jerked around as though he'd been stung and stared in horror at Nyssa, leaning on the rail three feet or so from him, traces of kohl and pigment still smudged around her eyes. Her hair was twisted and braided up at the back of her head, and she wore unfamiliar clothes.

He stared stupidly at her.

"Please try not to be too angry with me. I *have* to go to Thira. You couldn't possibly have stopped me. Now that I know it's Kit in the dreams, I can't not go to him as soon as possible. Surely you see that? I'm sorry I lied to you and I'm sorry I took the money."

"The money doesn't matter," he said automatically. The thing was, he wasn't angry. Horrified, relieved, devastated, happy, and God knew what else, but just at the moment, anger wasn't part of what he was feeling.

He buried his head in his hands on the rail and breathed in the smell of tarry wood as he tried to make sense of his thoughts.

"Where have you been? In Korce, I mean. I searched for you."

She hesitated. "Staying with a friend."

"A friend?"

"Someone I knew from the Drowned Boy. I remembered she lived here now."

"Do I know her?"

Nyssa looked confused—no—flustered. "I don't know."

"And she helped you sneak aboard with that tawdry girl, in disguise?"

She took a deep breath, but all she said was "Yes."

She'd expected him to be furious, to rant at her, and she'd had all her barbed replies at the ready. It was disconcerting to find she didn't need them.

"You *do* understand, don't you?" she asked.

"Yes, I suppose I do. But do you understand how *I* feel, after all these years of keeping you hidden, keeping you safe? It feels as if it's all being thrown away."

"I know. I'm sorry."

He gave her a faint smile. "Perhaps we are all fated to do what we do.

"Anyway," he said, more briskly, "you're here, the ferry doesn't stop anywhere except Thira, so I suppose I have to accept that you're coming with me. I don't suppose there would be any point asking you to find a nice quiet place to stay on Thira while I try to get to Kit?"

"None whatsoever."

"No, I thought not." They watched the birds for a moment. "Are you sharing a cabin with that . . . girl you came on board with?"

"Yes."

He raised a disapproving eyebrow.

"This is a holiday for her," Nyssa said quickly.

"Hmmmf!"

"Actually . . . *she* is the friend from the Drowned Boy."

"What? William never let those girls come into the inn."

"That's why they used to come around to the kitchen door and talk to me instead. I got to know quite a few of them. Aria's been a good friend to me over the last few days: She took me in, got my ticket, disguised me, and got me aboard."

"How much did you tell her?"

"Not too much, don't worry. But she knows I'm going to Thira to find my brother. She's over there, by the way. Come and talk to her."

Aria was hanging over the ship's stern rail, watching something. She was wearing an unremarkable and entirely modest dress. Nyssa called her name as they approached and she turned around, smiling, her face unveiled and scrubbed clean of cosmetics.

"This is Marius," said Nyssa. "And he isn't nearly as angry as I'd expected."

She glanced at Marius and saw that he had flushed scarlet to the roots of his hair.

Aria seemed quite oblivious. "Hello. It's good to meet you. I'm sorry if I've spoiled your plans, but I had to help Nyssa when she came to me."

Marius seemed temporarily to have been robbed of speech. After an excruciating few seconds, he muttered something incomprehensible under his breath, turned on his heel, and went below deck.

Nyssa turned to Aria, who gave her an innocent smile. "He's probably just uncomfortable to be asked to talk to someone like me in broad daylight. It happens all the time." She turned back to her inspection of the boat's wake.

-:-   -:-   -:-

Three days had seemed long enough to come up with a plan when the boat left Korce, but by the time Thira came into sight over the horizon they still didn't have one, though at least there was a chance Nyssa would be able to find her way around, based on what she had seen in her dreams. They continued to torment her every night, but she did not speak of them anymore. It was too painful now that she understood what they meant.

Marius, of course, had never set foot on Thira before. In fact, he couldn't think of a Keeper who had — voluntarily, anyway — for many years. He had overcome his embarrassment enough to speak to Aria, albeit in a somewhat strained way. Nyssa scrupulously pretended to notice nothing odd about the careful way Marius acted toward her.

"Have you decided yet if you'll go straight back to Korce?" Nyssa asked her.

Aria wrinkled her nose. "I think I might stay on for a few days. They said I could take a couple of weeks and they'd keep my place open. I can't see much reason to rush; it's not as if I've got something wonderful to hurry back for."

This was the answer Nyssa had been hoping for, and she took it at once to Marius in his minute cabin.

She found him sharpening his sword, his pack already trussed on the bed beside him.

"It's hours yet until we dock, you know," she said.

He shrugged. "I know. Nerves." He flashed her a sheepish smile.

"I've got an idea."

He cringed away theatrically. "God help us all."

She ignored that and plowed on. "The Shadowmen are looking for me — and maybe for you as well. A man and girl together. Aria's going to stay on Thira for a few days. If we all stay together, we're not what they're looking for: one girl alone, or one girl with a man."

There seemed nothing immediately lunatic about the suggestion.

"What does Aria have to say about that?"

"I haven't asked her yet. I thought I'd talk to you first."

"That makes a change. It might well be a good idea, but we'd have to be very careful what we said in front of her, for her sake as well as ours."

She nodded gravely. "I know. I'll go and ask."

Aria was delighted. She had found the whole quest-for-long-lost-brother story irresistibly romantic from the moment that Nyssa had told her, and now she had the chance to prolong her involvement.

"Maybe I'll be there when you find him, Nyssa. Goodness . . ." She put her head on her hand and stared dreamily at the growing bulk of Thira ahead of them. "He could be over there now, watching the ship come in, never dreaming . . . It's just like one of these tales the ballad singers bring around the inns, or something in a play."

She clapped her hands. "I'm going to enjoy this."

Nyssa tried to mirror her carefree smile, despite the growing knot of anxiety in her stomach. "Come on, then. We should pack."

‡   ‡   ‡

Once she had finished packing—which didn't take long—Nyssa came back up on deck, wanting to take her first proper look at Thira as soon as possible.

The ship would not put in at the city of Thira itself: The drowned buildings were too much of a hazard, the original harbor now lying far below the water, wrecked hulls crusted with barnacles still visible when the sea was calm if you floated over them in a small boat. Instead they would dock a few miles down the coast at Mili, which now served as Thira's port.

The island was all fairly low-lying, so as they drew closer their view of it contracted down to a strip of coast, and then to a medium-sized harbor, the striking thing about which was the lack of any town behind it. Instead there was a series of sheds, housing donkeys, horses, and carts for hire, to carry the passengers to Thira town itself, and a few stalls selling water, fruit, and grilled fish.

All the passengers were up on deck now, waiting as ropes were flung ashore and the gangway was secured.

Nyssa, Marius, and Aria shuffled down onto the quayside with the others, and Marius left the girls with the bags while he went to hire a donkey to carry the baggage, though they themselves would walk. A dusty breeze blew smells of sage and thyme from the scrubby bushes beyond the stalls to join the smell of fish.

Aria drifted off to one of the stalls and came back with three wedges of watermelon. The girls ate theirs as they waited, crunching the black seeds as the stones seemed to sway beneath their sea-accustomed feet.

Compared to Korce, it was eerily quiet. There was none of the bustle you normally found in a port: no shouting or singing, not even a dog running loose. It made Nyssa uncomfortable; suddenly she felt very conspicuous, although Aria seemed blithely unaware of anything strange.

Marius returned with a small, resigned-looking donkey and took his slice of melon gratefully from Aria.

"Are you sure that's a donkey?" she teased him. "It's awfully small. I've seen bigger dogs."

"We don't exactly have much luggage," he said, tying on the bags. "It would have been a waste to pay for a bigger one."

Nyssa stroked the little beast's muzzle and fed it the rind from her melon.

"Let's go," said Marius, and they set off for Thira.

Those who had hired carts were already far ahead, and the twenty or so people on foot were soon strung out over a long section of road. Nyssa, Marius, and Aria were near the front of the group, being young and fit and keen to find somewhere to lodge in the city before darkness drew in.

The road climbed gently and goat-nibbled pines replaced the thorny scrub on either side, so that sometimes they lost sight of the sea on their left.

They had been walking for just over an hour when the road took them across the shoulder of a rocky outcrop to give them their first close look at the town of Thira.

It was smaller than Nyssa had expected, but then half of it was in the sea. It seemed to melt into the water. The tide was out, exposing weed-swagged columns and fragments of walls, roofs of faded terra-cotta with gaping holes like open mouths, the remains of houses, shops, temples — all sorts of buildings.

A broad slipway of dressed stone, fraying now at the edges, led down into the blue water. As she looked at it, Nyssa realized it must have once been a processional way, leading down to a great temple whose column caps and shattered roof she could just glimpse breaking the waves, the farthest out of any of the visible drowned buildings.

Everywhere there were remnants of the great city that Thira had once been, but now it was a shadow and a memory: a ghost of its past.

There were still some buildings left above water from the time of the Keepers. You could see how beautiful they must once have been, but most of them were half-ruined now. Roof tiles were missing; weeds pushed up the stones in courtyards; empty spaces gaped where once there had been windows.

Around these remnants had grown up a new Thira of narrow streets and anonymous rows of buildings. It was a gray place, dusty and dispirited. Seen from its outskirts, the whole city had an air of neglect.

They had decided not to stay at an inn if that was possible, preferring to rent a couple of rooms or a house where they could keep themselves to themselves and have more privacy. Aria was happy with this suggestion, too. She had no option but to be sociable in the House of White Lilies; quiet and semisolitude were just what she craved.

The donkey took them straight to the livery stable, making the list of directions Marius had been given in Mili superfluous. They asked the stable boy who took her about somewhere to stay. He thought for a moment, looking as though he was wrestling with himself.

"There's my aunt Niobe," he said doubtfully. "She rents out the top floor of her house. It's empty just now; the last people . . ." He stopped, seeming to think better of finishing the sentence. "I'll take you to see her, if you want."

Marius glanced at the others, who nodded in agreement, and they picked up their bags and followed him out of the stable. The boy led them through streets that were busy but still, Nyssa thought, oddly quiet. None of the people she passed met her eyes. That in itself was unsettling. At home everyone would have stared openly at a newcomer. The boy took them to the inland side of the town and stopped in front of a sun-faded blue door in a street lined with shops and carpenters' workshops. The whole street smelled of wood shavings.

"You'd better let me talk to her first," he said, and left them at the door with their bags.

After a few minutes he reappeared. "You can come up."

Nyssa bent down to pick up her bags. As she did so the ground shifted under her feet without warning and she heard a low rumble. Caught off balance, she fell to her knees. She thought for a moment it was another aftereffect of being at sea, but when she looked up she saw that Aria had a hand against the wall of the house and was looking around wildly.

"What was that?" said Marius, helping Nyssa up.

"Earth tremor," said the boy, with a total lack of concern. "They come every few days. Nothing to worry about. My granny says it's one of the gods turning over in his sleep."

And indeed, when Nyssa looked around, no one was acting as though anything out of the ordinary had happened.

"Come on, then," their guide repeated impatiently.

They followed him into the house, dim after the sun outside.

"This is my aunt Niobe," he said. "She'll see you right. I've got to get back to the stable now."

Niobe was a tall, thin woman, her brown hair piled haphazardly on top of her head. She was having a good look at them, mouth pursed, obviously weighing whether they were the sort of people she wanted to share her house with.

After a few seconds she shook her head and sighed as though reaching a decision against her better judgement. "I'll show you the rooms," she said. "See what you think."

She led them up a narrow wooden staircase. There were two rooms at the top.

"I can put another bed in the big room for you," she said. "I suppose you girls will be sharing?"

"Yes," agreed Nyssa.

There was a ladder leading up to a flat roof that they could use, with a charcoal stove for cooking.

Niobe left them alone for a minute to talk.

"What do you think?" said Marius. "This is good," he went on without waiting for an answer as he looked from the roof into the street below. "We can see anyone outside without being seen ourselves."

"Goodness," said Aria, "you make it sound as though we're looking for a hideout, not just somewhere to stay."

"It's fine," said Nyssa quickly, trying to cover Marius's slip. "Let's see how much she wants for it."

⊹   ⊹   ⊹

Every few minutes since they'd arrived in Thira, Nyssa had caught glimpses of places she half thought she recognized from the dreams. She had tried not to think about it too much until they found themselves a place to stay, but now that they had, she was anxious to look around and try to find her bearings.

She hadn't told Aria about the dreams, of course, which meant she would have to be circumspect about what she said.

They all went out together, ostensibly to buy some food, though there wouldn't be much left this late in the day. They followed their noses down the street and around a corner to the nearest bakery and bought some rough salty bread, the dough mixed by local custom, the baker said, with seawater.

"Arrived on the ferry this morning?" he asked, with the air of a man who makes it his business to know everything about everyone. "Found lodgings?"

Marius counted out coins. "Yes. We're staying with a woman called Niobe, just around the corner." *It wouldn't do to look as though they were trying to keep it secret.*

The baker looked at them with sharpened interest.

"Are you now? I hope you're less trouble to her than the last lot. Poor Niobe." He shook his head. "Did she tell you about them?"

"No."

"Two men from the south coast. Builders, supposedly. Shadowmen came for them after a week. Not builders at all. *Conspirators.*" He gave a dismissive sniff. "Idiots, if you ask me. Stirring people up. Pointless. *He* knows about everything that goes on. Knew about them before they even arrived, if you ask me."

They didn't need to ask who *he* was.

"Anything else, folks?"

Marius shook his head and they left, rather silently.

They wandered at random for a while, taking in the air of watchfulness that seemed as much a part of the city as the stone from which it was built. A gust of wind blew a sheet of paper against Aria's skirt. She picked it off and looked at it curiously.

The ink had been smudged by the moisture in the air, but it was still more or less legible.

The three of them read it, their hearts beating faster as they did so.

CITIZENS OF THIRA!
Be ready.
Do not despair.
The Tyrant will not prevail.
We must be ready to fight back.

There was something odd about the way it was written, but Nyssa couldn't think what it was.

Wordlessly, Marius took it from Aria's hand, crumpled it into a ball, and, making sure no one was watching, tossed it over a nearby wall.

"Well, that's interesting. Definitely not the sort of thing we want to be carrying around, though."

They walked on until they came out by chance onto the street above the slipway. Nyssa was drawn to the ramp immediately: Here was something she recognized clearly from the dreams.

Marius stood awkwardly with Aria in front of the row of narrow shops at the top, while Nyssa walked down to the edge of the ebbing tide. It was a feeling so strange that she had no words to describe it, to stand here where she had stood in her dream, where Kit must have stood, now not only looking at the sea, but hearing and smelling it as well.

When she turned back to rejoin the others, she glanced down automatically to where she knew the blank eyes of the sunken statue watched her from under the water. They looked back at her, unseeing.

On the way back to Niobe's house she was unusually quiet, more shaken than she had expected by this transformation of her dreams into reality. She could feel Marius watching her, waiting for a chance to speak to her privately, and as soon as they were inside she left Aria in the room they were to share, where a second bed had indeed appeared, and went to Marius's room.

"You recognized that place, didn't you?" he asked as soon as she came in.

She nodded.

"How close was it to what you saw in your dream?"

"It was exactly the same."

It was this that had shaken her the most. She had assumed that the dreams were . . . well . . . *dreams*: an approximation of reality, but no more. If everything she'd seen in her dreams was precisely true . . . Suddenly the enormity of what they had embarked on settled like a piece of ice in her stomach. She thought of the smile of the White Wolf and was afraid. *He knows everything that goes on.* She thought of the three of them, alone in the very center of his web of power. What on earth had made her think they could steal Kit away from under his nose?

The Shadowmen were coming for her.

ALARIC

TWO YEARS EARLIER

Eight years passed. The White Wolf and his Shadowmen spread out from Thira, quickly at first, until they held half the Archipelago. But then their spread faltered and slowed. Alaric sat in his crumbling palace and tried not to let his frustration show.

There were too many islands. It was that simple. Even with twice as many men, he couldn't have kept them all as subdued as he wanted. Armed resistance seemed beyond them, and they cooperated as much as was necessary to stay alive. But unless he kept an island well garrisoned, it would neglect to pay its dues or fail to send the slaves he demanded to Thira, and he would have to send more men. And where was the other twin? He wanted both children and the secret they possessed. He wanted them in chains, so that people would know who was in charge and he, Alaric, would be acknowledged as absolute ruler of the entire Archipelago.

So he mused in his crumbling palace until the twins became an obsession.

The answer came quite unexpectedly one afternoon.

A man had arrived at the palace, ragged and haunted looking, claiming to have information that the White Wolf would pay to hear. Lunatics of this sort turned up of course, from time to time. Usually they had nothing that was of any interest to him, let alone any value. Sometimes he let them leave again. It depended on his mood, and on how amusing they were.

This one showed the captain of the guard a tattoo, though, which made him of interest immediately and ensured that at least he got as far as Alaric's great hall.

Alaric kept him waiting on the chilly marble for an hour or so, then went in with half a dozen guards, in case the man had any misguided thoughts of hopeless heroics.

He certainly didn't look like a hero. Scrawny and scruffy, in clothes that were hardly better than rags, he stood scratching nervously at a sore on one cheek.

Alaric settled himself comfortably in the great chair he liked to use for such occasions.

"Well?" he said, and waited.

"I hear you pay for information about the Keepers."

Alaric waited in silence.

"The Shadowmen massacred everyone in the village where I grew up. But they missed someone. A little girl — she'd be eleven or twelve now — with a tattoo on her head."

"Go on."

"She survived the massacre. Her uncle took her. As far as I know she's still alive. Being hidden by the Keepers."

"How do you know all this?"

The man pushed his sleeve back again to show the Crane tattoo of his clan. "The uncle — Marius, he's called — was my friend. I was with him when he found her, next to her mother's body."

"And where are they now?"

The man looked shifty. "I don't know. I split up from them after a few weeks. He planned to find shelter for the girl with other Keepers."

"These were your friends, even relatives perhaps. . . . Why betray them? And why now?"

"Isn't it obvious? I can't sink any lower. I'm half-dead with hunger. I need money to survive, and I have nothing else to trade but this information. Being a Keeper never brought me anything but trouble, anyway. I owe them no loyalty."

"How sad, to feel no loyalty toward your own people." Alaric smiled gently, then gestured to one of his men. "Find him some clothes and a decent horse and a purse of, let's say . . . twenty gold pieces, I think. This information is of some interest after all."

The man began to make some sort of stuttering thanks, but Alaric silenced him with a wave and dismissed him and the guards.

After about fifteen minutes, one of his men came back in.

"Any further orders, sir?"

"You've given him what I said?"

"Of course."

"Let him take ship to wherever he wants, but make sure he doesn't get off again. You know how I feel about disloyalty."

"Sir."

Alone again, Alaric sat deep in thought. Suddenly his stalled plan from almost a decade ago was back in action. This time there would be no mistake. He would make sure he found the girl, however long it took. Once he had both parts of the riddle, the Archipelago would be his and there would be no one left out there to stop him.

And if the Legend were true. . . . He thought of the power, of the terror. . . . It almost made him dizzy.

He wondered briefly whether to send for the boy, to tell him the happy news of his sister's survival, but thought better of it. No, let it come as a surprise when they were reunited here, in his palace.

He smiled as he pictured the scene.

8

KIT

That night there seemed to be no respite from the dreams, but they were no more than fragments, and in the periods that she spent awake, she could find nothing in them that might be useful. There had been no sign of Kit or Alaric, just glimpses of rooms and a darkened courtyard with a donkey tethered to a waterwheel.

Beside her, Aria slept curled and quiet beneath a sheet, apparently undisturbed by dreams or by the mosquito whining somewhere in the room. One of her feet was poking out and on her ankle Nyssa could see a tattoo, a swirl of dots. It was only a few weeks ago that Nyssa had thought tattoos didn't really matter, but now she wondered about all of them. Did this one mean something to Aria? Aria must have seen Nyssa's Crane tattoo by now; clearly it carried no significance for her. For a moment Nyssa wondered what it would be like to swap lives with her. Different, obviously, but by no means better, when she thought about it properly. She wondered how Aria had come to live the way she did. She had never asked; it had always seemed too much of an intrusion.

When morning came, the air sticky with humidity, and she rose unrefreshed, she saw Aria looking at her shadowed eyes.

"I don't mind being woken if you want to talk, you know."

Nyssa smiled. "Thank you. I just had some bad dreams. They kept me awake for a while."

Aria smiled sympathetically and went back to brushing her hair.

They finished yesterday's bread for breakfast, then set out to explore Thira properly.

From Niobe's house the streets sloped down rather haphazardly to the sea, as though the long-ago earthquake had crumpled the ground like cloth.

Down near the slipway was a market square that Nyssa recognized. It didn't give her as much of a jolt, though, to find that this, too, was exactly as it had been in her dreams. She even recognized two or three of the people, and was surprised for a few heartbeats that they looked at her blankly, until she realized it was Kit's face they knew, not hers.

She scanned the square constantly for the sight of a white-blond head, of her eyes in someone else's face.

The market was well ordered and well stocked, but again the people seemed oddly subdued. That sense of watchfulness was everywhere in the city of Thira, as though the inhabitants were braced and ready for something.

The three of them were paying for some fruit and vegetables when the bustle and sound around them seemed to drain away. Business carried on, more or less, but people's eyes slipped sideways as they talked, and Nyssa saw the woman next to her pull her child tight to her side.

They turned to find out the cause of the sudden change. Half a dozen men had come into the market square and were walking slowly through it. They were all tall and well muscled, and walked with the swaggering assurance of those who know that they are feared. They were dressed alike in dark trousers, boots, and sleeveless tunics. Long knives hung at their hips, beside lengths of thin cord.

Nyssa stared as though spellbound. By her side Aria had watched the men for a few heartbeats, then turned back to the market stall. She felt Marius's fingers pressing her arm. "Look away, Nyssa," he said quietly in her ear. "Don't let them see you staring. We don't want to draw their interest. Look away."

But she couldn't. She stared in sickened fascination at these men. Was it one of them who had killed her family? If they knew who she was . . .

Aria spoke to her, and with immense difficulty she turned her gaze away and made some sort of answer.

The Shadowmen walked unhurriedly through the market, their dispassionate gaze sweeping across the faces of the ordinary people, looking for someone. But whoever they were seeking evidently wasn't here, and they disappeared off down a side street. As soon as they went, there was a palpable sense of released tension, and the hubbub of the market returned to what passed for normal here.

Aria eyed Nyssa inquiringly.

"I've heard about them of course, but I've never seen any

before, although I know they've passed through Korce. I'm glad it's not me they're looking for. They don't look as if they'd listen to much in the way of explanations before they decided whether to throttle you or not."

"Throttle you?" said Nyssa through dry lips.

"I don't think . . . ," Marius began.

Aria ignored him. "They usually throttle the people they execute. They're famous for it. That's what those cords they carry are for. It's probably what happened to those men the baker was talking about."

Nyssa's mind went back to Bruno holding up the cord in the stable. Throttled. Is that what would have happened to her if Marius hadn't killed the man on the road?

There were black spots in front of her eyes. She shook her head, but they wouldn't go away. Sounds were suddenly muffled by a buzzing in her head. There were hands on her arms and someone — Marius? Aria? a Shadowman? — said in her ear, "Come on over here where you can sit down."

Somehow she found herself sitting on the dusty ground against a wall. The buzzing and the spots receded, and she was looking at Marius, crouched in front of her, frowning.

"Sorry," she said. "It was just—"

"It's all right." He cut her off as Aria appeared from somewhere with a cup of water and handed it to her.

Nyssa sipped it gratefully, put her fingers in it, and dabbed it on her brow and the back of her neck. Looking around properly again, she was relieved to find that no one was paying them any attention.

Aria, however, was looking at her curiously.

Nyssa forced a smile. "Pathetic, I know. Heat and lack of sleep I suppose."

Aria smiled back, saying nothing.

"Come on," said Marius, reaching down an arm to help Nyssa up. "We need to go back to the house with all this food, anyway. You can have a bit of a rest."

If Aria noticed that Marius, too, was rather pale beneath his tanned skin, she chose to ignore it, and they made their way back to Niobe's house.

They stayed there for the rest of the morning. Nyssa lay on her bed with closed eyes, but the last thing she wanted to do was sleep. She was afraid that the Shadowmen would now be part of her dreams, too, and she wasn't ready to face them, even there.

Aria sat near the window, apparently unconcerned, humming to herself as she embroidered a bodice. She finished the bird she was working on, bit through the thread, and put the cloth down.

"I'm not trying to find out any more than you want to tell me, but if it would help to talk, I'm here," she said.

"I'm asleep," said Nyssa.

"No you're not. You're pretending."

"How did you know?"

"Experience. I can always tell now when someone's really asleep and when they're not."

Nyssa opened her eyes and sat up, since there was obviously no point in continuing with the pretense any longer. She was sure she could trust Aria, but how much should she tell her?

Ignorance might be the only protection that Aria had. And what about Marius? He'd be furious if he found out she'd confided in her friend.

Never mind Marius, she thought. *Trust your instincts.*

She spoke slowly, trying to give herself a chance to check every word before she said it.

"Kit *is* here. I only found out recently. I thought he was dead. I think he's a slave in the White Wolf's household. Marius and I will have to try to smuggle him out. And I suppose if we manage to do that, the Shadowmen will be looking for us."

Aria drew a breath and nodded. "Well, that explains what happened in the market." She fell silent, thinking. "How long is it since you've seen your brother?"

"Not since we were four, and I don't even remember that."

"Then how are you going to recognize him?"

"I dream about his life here. I've been having these dreams for years, but I had no idea what they were about until . . . until a few weeks ago." She suddenly remembered how careful she had to be talking to Aria.

"How sure are you that you've got this right?"

"Totally. I can't explain it. I just know."

Aria looked at her curiously, but only said, "Well, I suppose that explains the bad dreams, too. So you'll recognize him. Will he recognize you?"

Nyssa shook her head. "I don't think so. Not unless he's been dreaming about me the way I've been dreaming about him."

"And how are you going to get him away from here when you *do* find him?"

"We'll hire a small boat — or steal one. Both Marius and I know how to sail. We'll head for Drakona, then island-hop to the Mainland and find somewhere to lie low."

"Well, I don't suppose Alaric's going to set the Shadowmen on you forever. Not just to get a slave back." Nyssa decided not to disillusion her on this point. "But he is going to be angry. Which means I should be off this island before you do anything, unless I want to be part of what you do."

"You must go. We won't do anything until you're on a ship. It makes no sense for you to put yourself in danger."

Aria smiled. "If there's one thing I do have, it's a good sense of self-preservation. Don't worry about me. I'll be gone the moment I think I'm in any danger. But for now, surely the more eyes and hands you have available, the better?"

"Well . . . yes."

"Do you know where to look for him, or do we just have to wander around hoping to bump into him?"

"Wander around, more or less. I see bits and pieces of places when I dream of him: the market, the slipway yesterday, shops, the insides of buildings. I know he sleeps in a little room at the top of a great, crumbling building, but I don't know what the outside looks like."

She stopped talking.

"What?" said Aria.

"I looked out the window of Kit's bedroom in the dream. It was night, and I was looking down on the roofs of all the other buildings I could see."

"So we just need to find the highest building in the city; it doesn't matter about knowing what the outside looks like."

"That sounds too easy."

"Nothing is ever too easy."

The room had been growing darker as they spoke. A great bank of bruise-gray clouds had come up out of the northwest, piled high and ominous, tinged with sulfur yellow. Now there was a growl of thunder.

Aria pushed the windows wide. "Just what we need to clear the air a bit."

The clouds swept in on a rush of wind now, and suddenly the storm was upon them, rain thrumming down in huge drops that made dark circles the size of gold coins where they hit the dusty street, until they overlapped and then blotted each other out.

People ran here and there in the street seeking shelter, though a few stood with their faces turned up to the dark sky, letting the welcome rain wash over their hot skin.

Shopkeepers hurried to pull their wares under cover before the rain spoiled them, bundling things haphazardly back into their shops.

Nyssa and Aria watched this street theater below as the thunder cracked and growled, much closer now, and lightning printed itself across their eyes.

There was hardly anyone out on the street now; just a boy hurrying toward the middle of town, his corn-silk hair flattened by the rain, his tunic clinging to him in sodden folds.

Nyssa watched him and felt her heart stutter. She stared at his retreating back, at the pale blond, rain-darkened hair, for an endless second.

"That's him!" she gasped, and ran for the door.

"Wait, Nyssa! Wait!"

Nyssa hurtled down the stair and out of the street door into a torrent of rain and noise and lightning. She was soaked in seconds, her hair dripping into her eyes, her dress plastered to her legs as she ran.

The street now was quite empty; no sign of Kit, or of anyone at all. She was tempted to call his name, but knew that that would be madness, so she ran on instead, though she didn't know which way to go, turning down one street then another, always heading away from the sea, always heading uphill.

-⁝-   -⁝-   -⁝-

Marius heard the sound of running feet on the stairs, and seconds later Aria burst into his room.

"Quick! Nyssa thought she saw Kit—she's gone after him. She's . . . Just come!"

He was on his feet, grabbing his jacket before she'd finished speaking, and they raced down the stairs together and out into the storm.

"Which way did she go?" yelled Marius.

"I don't know. Maybe she went to the slipway." Marius looked at her hard. "No—wait; we were talking about the building she saw in her dreams. Maybe she went there; we decided it must be the highest place in the town."

Marius stopped dead, grabbed Aria's arm, and pulled her around to face him.

"What has she been telling you?"

Aria pulled her arm free angrily. "Don't worry—I know you think I can't be trusted, but you're wrong." She spat the words out. "Nyssa told me that Kit's a slave. I know you're going to have to smuggle him away."

They stared at each other for a few seconds.

"This is ridiculous. We're wasting time," said Marius.

"I know," said Aria. "Shall we go now and argue later?"

They hurried on in charged silence.

-:-   -:-   -:-

Aria was right. They found Nyssa in front of the highest habitable building. From a distance it was still impressive: all domed turrets and dormers and marble facing. Closer, though, you could see the cracks in the façade, the ivy forcing its way in around window frames, the green water stains marking the white marble. Nyssa stared up at it as the thunder clashed almost directly above them and a sheet of lightning backlit the whole scene.

"Nyssa, come away," a voice in her ear said gently, and she turned to see Marius, and beside him Aria, both as wet as she was.

"He's here. I know he's here."

"*Sshh*, my dear, I know he is. But we can't just knock at the door and ask to see him, can we?" said Aria. "We must go away and plan."

"Aria's right. Now we know where he is, we can plan properly how to get him away."

"Come along, Nyssa. Let's go home."

They each put an arm around her and led her away from Kit.

They got back to Niobe's house, soaked and shivering, and stayed there for the rest of the day. Once Aria had persuaded her to change into dry clothes, Nyssa lay down and slept dreamlessly for five hours, and woke that evening refreshed and able to focus properly on the task ahead for the first time since they had reached Thira.

With the rain gone, the three of them sat around the little charcoal stove on the roof, cooking a rabbit for supper, and began to plan.

Marius and Aria were being icily polite to each other. He knew now just how much Nyssa had told her and, more important, what she hadn't. It wasn't that he didn't trust her—he found to his surprise that he did—but he didn't want her any more involved than she already was. He had extracted a promise from Nyssa not to tell her any more, knowing even as he did so that she would have no qualms about breaking it if she thought it would help Kit.

Together she and Marius tried to persuade Aria to leave the island before they did anything that might endanger her, but she refused flatly.

"We need a boat," said Marius. "Stealing one is too risky. What if we can't find one when we need it? No, we'll buy one now, take it out a couple of times, then moor it up somewhere far enough away from the city that we won't be seen going. We'll have to hide until it's dark . . . and watch the weather of course before we make a move. . . ."

They ate the rabbit, cooling their burnt fingers in their water glasses as they talked.

"So, a boat first—we do have enough money, don't we?" said Nyssa.

Marius nodded and swallowed a mouthful of rabbit. "Yes. I got a good price for the horses and tack back in Korce. I think that'll almost cover the cost of a boat. After all, we just want something small that's seaworthy. The older and tattier it is, the better in some ways: It'll draw less attention."

"And then all we have to do is find Kit again, somewhere we can talk to him, explain why we've come, and get him to the boat."

"Before Alaric realizes he's missing," Aria reminded her.

She nodded with a rueful smile. "I'm not forgetting."

"Have you thought about what he looks like?"

Nyssa frowned. "What do you mean?"

"That hair," said Aria who had also seen the figure from the window. "It stands out too much. It'll attract attention everywhere we go. We need to dye it. A nice, safe, dull brown. I'll see to that, shall I? I'm guessing I know more about dyeing hair than you two."

"I imagine you do," said Marius drily. "So, tomorrow a boat."

✙   ✙   ✙

The storm's passing had left fresher weather behind it, and they walked back to Mili the next morning along a road that was no longer a dust bath.

The harbor was quiet when they arrived: just local fishermen tinkering with their boats or mending nets. It didn't look as if a ferry was expected that day. The sheds were largely empty of their donkeys, horses, and carts.

Marius spoke to one of the net menders, and was directed to a fat balding man with a magnificent moustache whose name ("The man or the moustache?" muttered Nyssa mischievously) was Anto.

Anto sucked his teeth and shook his head reflectively a few times when he heard what they were looking for, as though it was unheard of that someone should want to buy a small boat on an island.

He thought, theatrically, for several moments, then wagged a large finger at them and said, "I may have just the thing. This way."

He led them past the sheds and on for a few hundred feet, to where a small boat lay forlornly in front of a scrubby thicket of thornbushes.

Marius raised his eyebrows. "We want one that floats."

Anto looked cut to the quick. "What do you take me for? Of course the boat is sound. I'd go out in her myself."

"I want to see her in the water."

"Very well, very well. Wait here and I'll get someone to take her down to the water for you."

While he was gone, they took a closer look at the little boat. Marius had to admit that under the peeling paint the timbers looked quite solid. There was a faded blue eye painted on each side of the prow. The mast was true, and Anto was going to bring the sails back with him, as well as manpower.

"She'll do, won't she?" asked Nyssa.

Marius nodded. "If she floats."

-:-   -:-   -:-

An hour later, after a short demonstration of her seaworthiness and a lot of haggling, the boat was theirs.

They sailed her along the coast for a couple of hours to get a feel for how she handled, then brought her back and moored her in a cove with two or three others about a mile outside Mili.

"So now we're ready?" asked Nyssa.

"So now we're ready," said Marius.

-:-   -:-   -:-

From that moment, the search for Kit began in earnest. They reasoned that they would need to talk to him and convince him of who they were and, if that worked, arrange to meet him somewhere to spirit him away from Thira.

Nyssa was torn between having them search separately and cover three times as many places, and her complete conviction that even if the others recognized him, it would have to be her who spoke to him first.

In the end they compromised: She and Aria would stay together, and Marius would search separately, hoping that his tattoo would provide enough reassurance if he were to encounter Kit first.

For two frustrating days they didn't have so much as a glimpse of the boy with corn-colored hair, though they quartered the town and spent as long as they dared watching the comings and goings from the great, crumbling building where they thought he slept.

If Niobe wondered what her new tenants spent their time doing, she kept her own counsel. Although she lived in the rooms on the ground floor they saw little of her, but they heard visitors come and go with some regularity.

It was the third day when everything changed.

There was a sea fog that morning: an autumn chill that hung in the streets. They pulled on jackets before Marius went one way and the girls another to buy the slivers and fragments of food that justified their daily visits to the markets and quayside.

Wrapped in mist, sound muffled, the drowned city seemed even stranger than usual. With the smell of rotting weed in her nostrils, Nyssa had a mad fancy that the whole place, themselves included, was submerged, that if they came out of the mist they would choke in the air like landed fish. It was impossible to tell simply by looking where the boundary was between sea and land. In this uncertain half world, Nyssa found her steps drawn to the great slipway and the blind, submerged statue.

The mist lapped at it even as the tide did, turning driftwood over against the blocks of stone. The girls stopped at the top, their hair beaded with droplets of fog. There was hardly anyone out on the streets yet, but at the bottom of the slipway Nyssa thought she saw a figure sitting on the stones, rags of mist sliding over and around it.

Her heart missed a beat.

She clutched Aria's arm. "That's him. I'm sure of it." Why she was so sure, she couldn't have said.

Aria squinted at the figure. "It could be anyone. I can't even tell what color his hair is."

"It's him. I know it. Wait here."

Nyssa let go of Aria's arm and walked down the slope toward the figure, the sound of her steps deadened by the fog.

As she drew closer she saw a white-blond head, hunched shoulders, arms encircling drawn-up knees.

She licked her lips, her mouth suddenly gone dry. She didn't know what to say.

"Kit?" The word came out as no more than a cracked whisper, to which the figure gave no response. She edged a few steps closer and tried again. "Kit? Hello? Kit?"

The figure turned slowly and she stared at the face from her dreams, at her own eyes, at her brother's face.

His lip had been split recently, and an old bruise, faded to green, shadowed one eye. He stared at her, wide-eyed and frightened.

She quashed an impulse to take the few steps toward him and throw her arms around him, and dug her nails into her palms instead.

"Don't be afraid, Kit. I'm here to help you. Do you know who I am?"

Still he stared, unmoving, unspeaking. His concentrated gaze was unnerving.

She tried again.

"Do you recognize me? My name is Nyssa. I've come to help you. I'm your sister — your twin. Talk to me, Kit."

He shook his head, stood up, and began to edge away from her back toward the top of the slipway.

"Wait, Kit, please. Don't run away. I know you've been hurt for a long time. We've come to take you away, so you'll be safe from the White Wolf."

She had thought that he looked frightened before, but his expression at the mention of Alaric was close to terror. She couldn't let him go like this.

She moved toward him, stretched out a hand, and took hold of his shoulder.

He twisted and slid out of her grasp and ran off up the slipway, easily eluding Aria as she tried to block his way at the top.

"Kit!" Nyssa yelled. "Wait!"

But he was gone, lost in the fog.

9

SHADOWMEN

"It stands to reason," said Marius for the third time, "that he'd be frightened. He probably had no idea that he *has* a sister. He may not even know his real name after all these years. Think what a shock you must have given him."

"I know," said Nyssa wearily. The three of them sat, rather despondent, in the girls' room in the fading evening light. "I had this picture in my head—I knew it was stupid even before this, mind you—that he'd see me and smile and we'd hug and we'd all sail away and be safe. I suppose I thought that somehow he'd know who I was."

"But he didn't say *anything*?" asked Marius, although she'd already told him.

"Not a word. Just stared and stared and then ran. Maybe if I hadn't mentioned Alaric . . ."

"You said he was already moving before you did that," interjected Aria.

"Yes, he was. I wish I knew what I did wrong."

"I don't think you did anything wrong. It was just the surprise. Think how shockingly unexpected you were to him, given the life he must have led." Once again it was Aria, the voice of reason.

"I'll go back to the slipway tomorrow morning. I've often dreamed of it—I'm sure it's somewhere he goes whenever he can—and I can't think of anywhere I'm more likely to be able to talk to him privately."

"And if he doesn't come back there?" Aria looked doubtful.

"We carry on searching elsewhere," said Marius grimly. "Even if that means going into the palace of the White Wolf." Though he knew without doubt now that Kit was alive, the reality of what it meant for them had suddenly hit home.

-∤- -∤- -∤-

That night, she did not dream. At least, she did not dream Kit's life. She was too close to it now in her waking hours. But she did dream of her mother, something that had never to her knowledge happened before.

She and her mother were in a firelit room, in what she somehow knew was the house where she'd been born. Kit was there, too, but hiding in a shadowy corner.

Her mother was playing a lullaby on the bamboo flute, and Nyssa closed her eyes, dozing in the firelight, knowing she was safe.

The music stopped. She opened her eyes and saw her mother holding the flute out to her.

"It's your turn," she said and Nyssa woke and lay in the gray dawn and tried to hold on to the dream. It was no good. Sleep

wouldn't come back. On the other side of the room she could hear Aria's steady breathing.

After a while she got up and opened the shutters just enough to let her see her way around. She went to the little wooden box, took out the broken flute, and turned it between her fingers, considering.

Was it possible that Kit might remember it? That it might unlock for him, although it didn't for her, a time when they were all together?

That, and the bird on her arm, were all the evidence she had that once they had shared a life. She had no idea whether it would be enough.

She dressed as quietly and as fast as possible, trying not to wake Aria. She scrawled a note so that the others wouldn't worry, crept down the stairs, opened the front door, and found herself face-to-face with Marius.

"Where are you going?"

"Where have you been?"

They spoke simultaneously.

Marius gestured that they should go outside so they didn't disturb the rest of the household.

"Where are you going?" he asked again.

"To the slipway. I dreamed about my mother last night, play-ing the flute." She showed him what was closed in her hand. "I thought he might remember it. I know it's a bit of a long shot . . ."

"No. It's a good idea. But you shouldn't go out alone." She opened her mouth to protest. "I know. You think someone else will frighten him even more. I'll stay well back, I promise. But remember, I haven't even seen him yet. Come on. We can talk as we walk."

She fell into step beside him. "So, where have you been?"

"I couldn't sleep, so I decided to have a look at the White Wolf's palace at night, just in case we have to try to get in."

"And?"

He shook his head. "I just hope we don't have to try: far too many guards. God, Nyssa, this place at night — you know during the day it's as if everyone's watching their back, watching their neighbor?"

She nodded.

"It's much worse at night — gave me the shivers — and the place is crawling with Shadowmen, coming and going, pulling people out of their homes, out of inns; taking them up to the palace, bringing them back. I was probably lucky they didn't pick me up just for being out on the street with no good reason. It's as if the town has a whole different life at night. I can't imagine *anyone* sleeps well in Thira."

"Except Aria."

He smiled. "It doesn't surprise me somehow. She's an interesting girl, Nyssa. I'm glad she's with us. I'm sorry if I seemed . . . shocked . . . at first. It was just . . ." He didn't finish the sentence.

The unspoken words hung in the air between them and kept them silent until they reached the little street that led to the slipway. The empty slipway.

"I'll wait here," said Marius, sliding into the shadows in a doorway.

Nyssa nodded and walked away from him. The tide was in, water lapping far up the stony slope. In the early morning quiet, the suck and scour of the waves was the loudest sound. Wet stone showed where the water had receded.

She went as far as possible without getting wet, sat down, and took out the flute.

It still made a noise, though you couldn't call it music. Its spirit was broken, but it could still find three cracked notes. She put it to her lips and played them, her fingers moving gently over the remaining holes.

Over and over she played the notes, over and over, until she fell into a sort of reverie.

She had heard no sound of approach, but suddenly she knew he was there, behind her, well out of arm's reach, listening.

She carried on playing for a little longer, then let the sound die away.

"Do you remember?" she said without turning. "Our mother used to play, and sometimes she would sing. Do you remember? This was her flute." She turned slowly then to look behind her.

Kit stood poised for flight, torn between longing for the music and fear of her. He was smaller than her, she realized, and looked much younger. Her heart lurched with pity and guilt as she thought of her comfortable life at the Drowned Boy compared with the nightmare childhood he must have endured.

She put the flute down carefully where he could see it, and spoke again, pushing up her sleeve as she did so.

"You have a picture of a bird on your arm, don't you? One that won't come off. I've got one the same. Look." She held her arm out so he could see, realizing as she did so that she was talking to him as if he was a child, not someone her same age.

Shaking visibly, he pushed his own sleeve back to compare their tattoos. Nyssa had to bite back a cry as she saw his arms, crisscrossed with scars, narrow white lines against the tan. *What had been done to him?* With an effort she kept her smile in place and held her arm still so he could look his fill at the two birds.

At length he let his sleeve fall and shuffled a pace or two closer. She covered her own tattoo again with relief and picked up the flute.

"You do remember this, don't you? And you remember our mother?"

He gave a very small nod.

She held out the flute on her open palm, as you would hold out food to a nervous horse.

"Here. You can take it. It's your turn to have it."

His eyes flicked to her face, wide with surprise, then he began to edge forward.

Hardly daring to breathe, she kept quite still as he came just close enough to grab it from her hand, then scuttled back a few paces. He put the flute to his lips and produced a wavering note.

He gave her a sudden quick smile and turned to leave.

"Wait!"

He paused and looked back, frightened again.

"I'll be here tomorrow morning, Kit. I'll bring you some food."

He looked at her but didn't reply.

"Kit? You can . . . talk, can't you?"

He stared at her for a few seconds, then ran off.

She got stiffly to her feet and walked up the slipway to meet Marius emerging from the shadows. He was paler than on that awful day on the road when he had the arrow in his shoulder.

"I didn't know," he muttered. "I didn't know." He put his hands on her arms and stared at her as though he was seeing her for the first time. "I never imagined he would be like this. My God, Nyssa, it's bad enough that you should have dreamed the life that has done that to him, but that he should have lived it all that time . . ."

He released her arms.

"It's my fault," he said bleakly. "If I'd checked properly in the village when I found the children . . ."

"Don't be ridiculous," Nyssa said sharply. "What could you have done? One man with a four-year-old girl against a party of Shadowmen—you'd have ended up dead, and Alaric would have got me as well as Kit. You did the only thing you could. You saved me so that we could both save Kit."

"Maybe."

"Marius, I'm worried."

"You think I'm not?"

"That's not what I meant. I haven't heard Kit say anything: not a word. I'm worried that he can't speak."

Marius considered this. "He can certainly hear. Not *any* sound?"

She shook her head. "Not so far."

"He was never a talkative child. Couldn't get a word in edgeways with you as a sister, I suppose." His mouth curved a little. "Let's hope it's just that you're new to him and he's frightened." His expression turned grim. "He's probably learned in that place that it's safer to keep your mouth shut."

"We'll have to get his trust before we try to get him off the island. We can't do it unless he comes with us willingly."

"*Mmnn* . . . I wonder how long that will take? Let's hope he comes back tomorrow. . . . We'd better be getting back before Aria gets worried."

✛   ✛   ✛

When they got back to their lodging, they found the door to the street open. As Nyssa stepped through, something turned under her foot. She bent to pick it up and looked at it curiously. It was a tiny square of metal, with a raised letter *E* on it. She was about to show it to Marius when they heard voices from the room Nyssa and Aria shared, and she slid it into her pocket instead.

As they climbed the stairs, Marius signaled to Nyssa to be quiet, his hand going automatically to the sword that wasn't there, for he hadn't worn it since they arrived on Thira for fear of attracting unwanted attention. Instead, he had to content himself with loosening his knife in its sheath.

At the top of the steps they paused to listen more closely, and heard Aria's voice and then her laugh.

Puzzled, for they didn't think she knew anyone here, Marius knocked, then opened the door without waiting for a reply.

The scene before them was so utterly unexpected that Marius and Nyssa stopped dead in the doorway.

Two Shadowmen were in the room: one stood, arms folded, by the window, and the other lounged at his ease in the cushioned chair. Aria sat curled on her bed, neat as a cat, in a pleated dress of fine terra-cotta-colored linen that they had never seen before. Her face was carefully painted as if for a performance, her hair artlessly coming down from its knot, a cloud of perfume hanging around her. She was smiling.

Marius and Nyssa stared wordlessly.

"Ah, here they are, Captain. Marius, Nyssa, what are you thinking of, going out without asking my permission? The captain thinks I have very poorly trained servants.

"Not a word" — she held up her hand as though to stop them from speaking, a gesture quite unnecessary as the circumstances had struck them temporarily dumb — "and I'm not interested in your excuses, or in where you've been.

"Captain Jaxom, Lieutenant Merrick, my maid, Nyssa, and my bodyguard, Marius."

Though her wits seemed slow as honey, Nyssa had the sense to drop a curtsy. Beside her, Marius moved his head in what a charitable person might have taken for a bow.

The man in the chair stared at them as though they were beasts in a field. He was heavyset, with short dark hair that was going gray at the temples and a nose that had been broken at least once.

Merrick was younger, blond haired and clean shaven, with shrewd blue eyes.

"You do your mistress little credit by your behavior," Jaxom said in a cool voice.

Nyssa hung her head. That way, she didn't have to look at him, could avoid seeing the cord that hung at his waist.

What dangerous game was Aria playing? And what roles did they play in it?

"Oh, get out," said Aria irritably. It took Nyssa a second to realize she was speaking to them. "I won't have the pair of you sulking there. Wait in the other room. I'll deal with you later."

There was no choice but to play along with whatever Aria was doing. They shuffled out and into the other room and shut the door.

"What on earth is going on in there?" hissed Marius, face down on the floor, reaching for the sword concealed under his bed.

Nyssa had her ear pressed against the timber of the door. Marius moved to stand beside her, the sword in his hand, and passed her his knife.

"I don't suppose you're carrying your own. I just hope you remember how to use it," he whispered.

Swallowing, she nodded.

For ten minutes they stood, straining in vain to hear anything from the next room, tense as springs. Disaster was a hairsbreadth away.

After what seemed an interminable wait, they heard the other door open and Aria's voice again.

"My thanks to you once more, Captain. You've been most understanding. I'll certainly pay heed to your advice — and I'll look forward to seeing you again."

A man's voice said something too quietly for Nyssa to make out the words. Aria gave a coquettish giggle, footsteps descended the stairs, and the other door shut.

They moved to the window and watched the Shadowmen walk out of sight around a corner, then hurried to Aria's room.

As they opened the door, she was pouring a glass of water, her fingers shaking. She drained it in one draft and sat down rather abruptly.

"Well," she said, "what did you think of the performance?"

"What in the world was all that about? Why were they here? When did they come?" Marius fired questions at her without giving her a chance to answer.

"They came about an hour ago. I was still asleep — Niobe woke me and told me they were downstairs and wanted to see all of us. A routine check, they said: They call to see everyone who stays more than a couple of days to verify what their intentions are."

"What did you tell them?"

She gestured impatiently at her appearance, rolling her eyes.

"What does it look as if I told them?" she said, pulling pins out of her hair and letting it fall. "I said I was looking into the possibility of the House of White Lilies opening a place here. I'd been dressing plainly in public to avoid notice and taking you — my servants — around with me."

She shivered and got up to fetch a shawl.

"They weren't impressed by the fact that I didn't know where my own servants were."

"You must have been convincing. The captain seemed to have taken a bit of a fancy to you," said Marius grumpily.

"Of course I was convincing," Aria snapped. "I am a performer, after all! Or had you forgotten?"

"Of course not! I mean . . ." Marius opened and closed his mouth like a newly landed fish.

"Oh, go away and let me get this muck off my face," said Aria in exasperation.

Nyssa stood in silence, feeling the currents swirl around the room as Marius left without another word. Aria stared at the door for a few seconds, then got up and began to rub cream on her face to take off the paint.

"We were at the slipway," said Nyssa, rummaging in her pack for the smaller of her two knives. "I took Kit a flute that used to be our mother's. I thought he might remember it and be convinced he could trust me." She found the knife and stuck it down her boot, resolving now to have it within reach as long as they were on Thira.

"Did it work?" asked Aria, wiping off cream and color.

"Well, he took it, and he smiled at me. But, Aria, I'm not sure he can speak."

Aria paused in her cleaning. "He's said nothing?"

Nyssa shook her head. "And Marius was so shocked when he saw him — more than I was. I hadn't realized it would be so bad for him."

"I shouldn't have bit his head off like that," said Aria remorsefully, changing into a more sober dress so that now only the scent of her other persona remained.

"How could you be so brave with these Shadowmen in the room?"

"It's just acting—all of it." She gestured at the dress and the smeared cloth. "You put on the clothes and makeup and become someone else. *This* is me."

"Do you think they'll come back?"

"Not for a few days at least, although as far as I can make out the whole town's on edge just now—this conspiracy against the White Wolf that the baker was talking about. I've told them I'm looking at buildings where the House of White Lilies might open up, so that'll explain us wandering around town. Merrick even suggested one, so I suppose we'd better make a show of looking at it. But I think if we're still here in a week, they'll be back to find out why. Captain Jaxom wants to see me again, anyway." She gave a shudder.

"Aria, you must leave on the next ferry, whatever happens."

"We'll see. With any luck we'll all have sailed away in that little boat by then. How are you going to see Kit again, anyway?"

"I told him I'd be at the slipway tomorrow with some food for him."

"Well then, we'd better get out and buy some."

There was a knock at the door just then and Marius came in. He didn't even glance at Nyssa before he spoke to Aria.

"I apologize if I offended you. You dealt with those Shadowmen magnificently, and kept us safe for a little longer."

Aria had colored faintly as she listened.

"I'm sorry I snapped at you," she replied. "Nyssa told me it was quite a shock for you, seeing Kit."

Marius looked down. "Yes. I don't know what I'd expected, but not what I saw. We have to get him away as soon as possible."

"Well, now that you two are talking to each other again, maybe we could go and buy some food for me to give him tomorrow," Nyssa said, a little more acerbically than she'd intended.

-¦-   -¦-   -¦-

She was at the slipway early the next morning, with a rabbit leg and some bread and cheese wrapped in a cloth. Marius was concealed as he had been the day before; though he longed to speak to Kit himself, he was unwilling to risk frightening him away.

They waited until the sun was well up and the streets were busy with people going about their business. Small children fished for crabs off the upper end of the slipway, but Kit did not come.

Eventually Marius unfolded himself from his doorway and went down to where Nyssa sat staring disconsolately at the weedy roofs appearing below her as the tide went out.

"We should go," he said gently, "or people will begin to notice how long we've been here. We don't want that. We'll come back tomorrow."

Nyssa took the hand he offered and got stiffly to her feet. "But why hasn't he come? He could be hurt, you know."

"I know, but don't you think it's more likely he can't get away from his tasks? After all he's a slave, remember."

She nodded, then took a deep breath and squared her shoulders. "Right. Let's go home, get Aria, and go looking around now that she's invented a plausible excuse for us."

They decided to make a pretense of looking at the building that Merrick had suggested as a possible site for Aria's imaginary cabaret, following his directions toward the center of town.

Here, the ruined buildings from the Keepers' time were more in evidence than around Niobe's house. The sense of emptiness in these streets was palpable, as though people avoided them.

"Merrick's not much of a businessman if he thinks this would be a good place," said Aria grumpily. She looked at the directions on the slip of paper she held. "It should be the next street on the right."

A minute or two later they stood in front of the place, which was as empty as Merrick had said it would be. It looked as though it had been the house of a rich man. The doorway was an arch of white marble carved with vines, a little cracked in some places, but still sound, though the wooden door itself was in a sorry state and gave as soon as Marius put a shoulder to it.

Beyond lay a courtyard with a broken fountain and an empty lily pool. Trees grew among the shattered paving.

Aria looked around in disgust.

"What on earth made him think I'd be interested in a derelict building?" She seemed to have forgotten temporarily that the whole thing was a ruse, anyway.

Marius gazed around the place, taking in the graceful proportions of the buildings around the courtyard, the ornamentation crumbling above the empty windows.

"Do you think this is from the Keepers' time?" Nyssa asked him quietly, as Aria picked her way across the tangled courtyard.

"I think it must be. No one builds like this now. Look at all the work, all the time that's been put into simply making it beautiful. Imagine what it must have been like . . ."

Nyssa tried to see it.

The sound of water, cooling a hot summer afternoon. Fish flashing in the pool. The air drenched in the scent of jasmine. A woman reading at a table under a vine pergola. The house gleaming around her, alive. Children's voices. Laughter. The smell of herbs from the kitchen. Music.

She tried to picture the people who had once lived here, but all she could see was the Crane tattoo that bound them all, made them the focus of this vivid but disappeared world. For the first time, she felt a faint sense of the Keepers as real people, connected to her. People whose loss had somehow diminished the whole Archipelago.

"What a waste of time!" Aria's voice broke into her reverie. "Still, I suppose we had to come and look to keep the story up. Come on, let's go."

Nyssa and Marius exchanged a glance and followed her back toward the street.

⊹   ⊹   ⊹

Their steps led them, seemingly without intent, to the square below the White Wolf's great crumbling palace. They sat on the edge of a long-dry fountain and passed a bottle of water back and forth as they looked at it.

Nyssa had hardly taken in its appearance the last time she had been here. Then she had been consumed by the likelihood that Kit was somewhere inside. Now she looked at it with a more measured eye, trying to remember exactly what she had seen of it in the dreams, trying to calculate which of the high, cobwebby windows could be his.

Marius was counting guards, trying to work out their routines, in a futile attempt to find a moment when, if they had to, it might be possible to slip inside to search for Kit.

Aria had turned aside to watch something happening on the other side of the square.

"Nyssa! Marius! Over there—look!"

Coming into the square on foot were a number of Shadowmen. In their center, a man rode a tall bay stallion. He was dressed in black from throat to heel, and his skin and hair were so pale that he looked like a figure carved from snow.

Behind the horse trotted a smaller figure, with corn-colored hair and a bruised face.

10

A GLASS OF MINT TEA

Marius was quick to realize the danger. "Don't let Kit see you, Nyssa — we don't know what he might do. If he runs over here, we're all finished."

Nyssa ducked down a little behind Aria's shoulder, but continued to stare at the little procession. There were a dozen Shadowmen, but it was the rider at their center that drew her eyes. It was her first sight of Alaric, the White Wolf, outside her dreams, and she shuddered to see him made flesh here in front of her.

This was the man who had ordered her family killed. This was the man who kept her brother as a slave, who had mistreated and beaten and done who knew what else to him. She fantasized for a second or two about pulling the concealed knife from her boot and trying to kill him, here, now. A ridiculous impulse, of course — she'd be cut down before she got near him.

Alaric himself seemed oblivious to the people watching him, paying them no more attention than he might give a beetle that wandered into his path.

Kit wasn't looking around, either. His eyes were fixed on Alaric's back and his expression was fearful. The Shadowmen were alert for trouble, their gaze constantly flickering around the square for any sign of a threat to their leader.

The group reached the gateway and guards drew aside to let them pass, the horses' iron shoes clattering on the paving.

Alaric dismounted and, as he turned, looked Nyssa full in the face. She felt paralyzed, her fingers numb, the breath frozen on her lips, impaled by his pale, cold gaze. But he looked away in a couple of seconds, undisturbed by any shred of recognition.

She felt Aria's hand tighten around hers as her body came back to life.

Alaric threw his reins to Kit and they watched as, with difficulty, he led the big bay out of sight. The White Wolf strode up the crumbling marble steps in front of his palace and disappeared into the inner gloom.

Marius let out a long, careful breath. "That's the man you dreamed of?"

"That's him."

"God help us all."

-‡-   -‡-   -‡-

In their lodgings that night there was a renewed sense of urgency. Seeing Kit with Alaric made her twin's vulnerability appallingly clear.

"We have to get him to come with us the next time we see him," said Marius. "We can't afford to wait—for his sake and our own. It gets more dangerous for us here every day. Sooner or later someone will spot you with him, Nyssa. We need to get him away soon or we'll lose the chance altogether."

"I think the slipway early in the morning is still the best place. I'm sure he often goes there."

"Right. We go there first thing tomorrow. If he's not there, we keep a watch on it and on the palace."

"He'll only go with Nyssa, though — if he'll even do that," said Aria. "As far as he's concerned, we're strangers. And if Nyssa's right about him being mute, we can't even start a conversation with him."

"I know that. We have to get him to Nyssa, or get Nyssa to him."

-+-　　-+-　　-+-

Gray dawn came, and Nyssa, Marius, and Aria walked to the slipway. Marius and Aria folded themselves into a doorway, and once again Nyssa walked across the sloping blocks of stone.

The tide hadn't yet ebbed as far as the day before. She stood, waiting for the weed-thatched roofs to break the surface.

The sun came up through low clouds, like a disc of beaten copper.

And he was there.

He must have made no sound as he approached; he was suddenly there beside her. Once more she crushed the urge to grab his hand and run. Instead she smiled at him and held out a honey cake.

He looked at her and smiled hesitantly in return, then reached out and took the cake with his right hand. She saw the broken flute clutched tightly in his left fist.

He crammed the honey cake into his mouth, chewed, and swallowed.

"Can you play it?" she asked, pointing to the flute.

He swallowed the last crumb and nodded. Raising the flute to his mouth, he blew gently and moved his fingers over the holes to produce the same three mournful notes she had so often played.

"That's very good," she said, smiling again. Her mouth was dry now and her heart was beating fast. "Would you like some more honey cake?"

He nodded.

"Will you come with me to get some? It's in my house, just up there." She pointed vaguely. "I have cheese, too, and bread, and cold rabbit if you want some."

His smile faded.

Careful, she thought. *Everything depends on this moment.*

"There are lots of honey cakes," she said. "It's not far. It won't take long."

She held out her hand to him and stood quite still. She imagined he could see her heart beating against her ribs. It felt as though it was about to burst out of her chest altogether.

Kit turned his head and looked carefully back up the slipway. Nyssa prayed that Marius and Aria were well concealed.

When he had satisfied himself that there was no one to see, he turned, gave her an almost-smile, and slipped his hand into hers. It was dry and calloused and very cold. Ragged nails pressed into her flesh. She closed her fingers around it carefully, and they walked slowly up the slipway together, away from the falling tide.

When they reached the top, Kit quickened his pace, glancing around constantly, nervously. Nyssa didn't dare look toward where she knew the others were hidden.

The plan was that they would follow at a distance so as not to frighten him, and if she managed to get him back to Niobe's house, she would explain them to him then.

Nerves made her want to jabber, to talk to him about inconsequential things, but she could feel that he needed quiet, needed to be able to concentrate on his watching, so she contented herself with saying every couple of minutes, "Not far now. We'll be there soon."

The farther they went, the more nervous he got and the tighter he clutched at her hand. She was increasingly afraid that he would simply bolt. She slowed and stopped and turned him to face her.

"I'm your sister, Kit. Your sister. I'll look after you, don't worry. I won't let anything happen to you."

He stared at her with his mirror-image eyes, and he didn't smile but he didn't bolt, either, and they began to walk again.

When they reached the house, the outer door was locked: Niobe was out. *Just as well*, thought Nyssa, unlocking it. She was almost weak with relief when Kit went with her, after only a little hesitation, up the stairs and into her room.

She motioned for him to sit and went quickly to get the rest of the honey cakes and a glass of water.

She found that he had sat down on the floor, so she did

the same, carefully situating herself between him and the door, leaning back against the bed and wrapping her arms around her bent knees.

He ate quickly, licking his fingers, picking up and swallowing the crumbs that fell to the floor.

"You're safe here, you know. You're safe with me. I'll look after you."

He didn't answer.

"Do you believe me?"

He stopped eating for a moment and cocked his head to one side, thinking about it, then gave a hesitant "don't know" shrug.

She got up and brought him plates with bread and cheese and rabbit and sat down again.

"Do you believe that I'm your sister? Do you remember me?"

This time he nodded with complete certainty, smiling as he did so.

So he did remember her! Surely he would come with her in that case?

"I want to look after you now that I've found you. I want to take you to a safe place to live with me. Would you like that? Safe and warm and plenty to eat."

He frowned and looked away from her and went back to his meal. Her mouth was dry again. She was so afraid that if she said the wrong thing he would run from her.

The others would be here any minute. She would have to explain about them before they arrived.

"We'd be a family again," she went on carefully. "You and me and Marius. He's our uncle, our mother's brother. He helped me to find you."

He stared at her, his expression unfathomable.

"He'll be back soon. He went out with my friend Aria. The three of us came to Thira to find you and take you home with us and keep you safe."

He looked alarmed at the prospect of dealing with other people. Nyssa tried to think of something to distract him, make him relax a bit more.

"You go to the slipway a lot, don't you? Do you like the sea?"

It seemed she had chosen the right thing. He smiled widely, eyes shining.

"Do you like sailing?"

A shrug.

"Do you ever go anywhere in a boat?"

Head shake.

"We have a boat. Would you like to go out in it?"

Emphatic nod.

"We'll go out in it later today."

He began trying to convey something with his hands, but she couldn't make it out, and at that moment she heard the sound of footsteps coming up the stairs and Aria's voice.

At once Kit looked up, terrified.

"It's all right," Nyssa tried to reassure him, going to the door. There was a soft knock, and she opened it. Aria and Marius came in and Nyssa shut the door behind them.

"Kit, this is Marius, our uncle, and this is my friend Aria."

Kit had backed himself up against the wall, wide-eyed. Aria sat down on the bed, gave Kit a brief smile, took her shoes off, and rubbed her feet.

Marius hadn't moved from the door. Nyssa could see his throat working as he took in the pitiable spectacle that was his nephew, who for so many years he had believed dead.

"Marius, you're frightening him," Nyssa whispered.

Marius took a difficult breath. "Hello, Kit," he said very gently.

"Marius, come over here and play cards with me," said Aria brightly. The two of them moved to the table by the window and pretended to ignore Kit and Nyssa.

Kit relaxed a little, watching Aria's quick fingers deal the cards. After a few seconds he went back to the last of his food, finishing it quickly. Aria got up from the table and did something at the cupboard where they kept the food. Kit watched her move, but didn't seem so frightened.

He got up, though, to Nyssa's consternation, pointing out the window to the street and then to himself, pantomiming *I'm going now.*

Aria caught Marius with a look as he was on the verge of rising to block off the door. He subsided again.

She gestured toward the glasses stacked on the cupboard shelf. "Have some mint tea before you go. You must be thirsty."

She handed a glass to Nyssa and one to a suddenly confused Kit, took one herself, and drank. So did Nyssa, following her lead.

Kit looked uncertainly from one to the other, then raised his own glass and drank. Aria gave him an encouraging smile. "It's good, isn't it?"

He nodded and drank again, and the glass slipped from his fingers and fell to the floor, the remains of the tea splashing out. Somehow Marius got to him in time and caught him as he fell.

"What in heaven's name have you given him?" he asked angrily, lifting Kit with appalling ease and carrying him to the bed.

It took Nyssa a moment to comprehend what had happened.

"Something to make him sleep for three or four hours, that's all," said Aria.

"You've *drugged* him?" Nyssa was taken aback.

"You wanted him to stay here, didn't you? This gives us a bit of time to think without worrying about him making a run for it. Anyway," she said, glancing over to where Kit lay peacefully asleep on her bed, "he looks as if he needs a rest."

Marius had sat down by the boy's side and was looking at him closely, taking in how small and frail he was compared to Nyssa, looking at the dirt and the bruises and the scars, at the little tattoo on his arm that marked him as a Keepers' child.

"You're probably right about that," he said with a sigh.

"How do you know how to drug someone?" asked Nyssa.

Aria's face was closed. "It's useful to know sometimes," she said, then was silent.

Nyssa spoke into the weighted quiet. "Could we get him to the boat like this?"

"If we could get hold of a cart," said Marius. "We could hide him under our gear . . . maybe we could have him in the boat before he wakes. How long did you say we've got?"

"Only three or four hours, but we could give him more when he wakes."

"How will he ever trust us again if we drug him?" said Nyssa miserably.

"He probably won't even realize," retorted Aria. "You can tell him he just fell asleep."

"Not if he wakes up and finds he's on a boat."

"Maybe we'd be better to wait for dark," Aria suggested.

Marius shook his head. "No. Alaric will have his men searching for him soon. We'll never get out of the city if we leave it until then." He rose from the bed. "I'll go and see if I can hire a cart from Niobe's nephew. There isn't a ferry today, so they shouldn't be too busy. I'll just go and get some money from my room and get my stuff together. You two start packing up here."

Absorbed in their task, Nyssa and Aria didn't hear the footsteps until they were nearly at the top of the stairs, and by then it was too late to do anything about it.

They stood with their arms full of clothes and listened to doom approach. There wasn't even time to lock the door.

There was a sharp knock. Aria and Nyssa looked at each other desperately. Another knock, and this time a voice as well.

"Don't be coy now. I know you're in. I heard you from downstairs." It was Captain Jaxom's voice.

Aria's face was a white mask of horror.

"You should have sent me word you were coming," she called, and Nyssa was amazed to hear barely a tremor in her voice, "so that I could have made sure to be ready for you. As it is, Captain, I'm afraid it's not convenient just now. Perhaps this evening?"

There was a snort from outside the door. "Don't worry, dearie. I'll make it worth your while for it to be convenient right now."

The door swung open.

The captain was a big man, and he filled most of the doorway. He looked around the room as though he owned it, and took in the two horrified girls, and then his eyes came to rest on the towheaded figure on the bed.

He frowned. "What's this?"

"I brought him in." Nyssa found her tongue somehow. "I found him on the street. He seemed to be ill. My mistress has a soft heart and I thought she might give him some money for food."

The man looked from one to the other, made suspicious by the fear in their faces.

"This is one of my master's slaves. He would be displeased to find the boy sleeping when he should be at work."

Before they could reply he crossed to the bed in a couple of strides and cuffed Kit around the head.

"Get up, boy!"

When he got no response, he bent closer, sniffing. He straightened and turned, a very different expression on his face now.

"He's been drugged. What's going on here?"

"That must be why . . . ," Nyssa began.

"Shut up, girl. It's your mistress I'm speaking to." He crossed to where Aria stood in two strides. "Well?"

Aria's tongue failed her at last, and she stood, mute and terrified, as he closed one hand around her throat.

"What's going on? Why is this slave here? There's something going on and you'd better tell me what it is while you still have the breath."

Nyssa tried to pull him off Aria, but he swatted her aside with his other arm so that she sprawled, dazed, on the floor. Aria fought to pull his throttling hand away from her throat, but he was much too strong.

At that second the door crashed open. Half choked and stunned, to Aria and Nyssa the next couple of minutes had the quality of a nightmare.

Marius burst in, knife in hand. He took in the scene in a heartbeat, hardly pausing before he ran straight at Jaxom. The captain shoved Aria aside and reached for his own knife. Marius was on him before he could free it from its sheath, but Jaxom caught his wrist so that he couldn't strike. For a few seconds they grappled, watched in frozen horror by the girls, then Nyssa remembered the knife in her own boot and dragged herself to her feet. She hesitated briefly, looking at the broad back in front of her, then jabbed him with the blade as hard as she could.

The knife jarred horribly as it hit a rib and skidded off, but it didn't matter that the blow was a glancing one, or that Nyssa had dropped the weapon. The surprise and pain distracted Jaxom for a fatal second, enough for Marius to pull his knife hand free and plunge the blade into his chest, into his heart.

Jaxom toppled to his knees, then forward onto his face, gave a sort of groan, and was still.

At first no one moved, then Aria sat up with a struggle, rubbing her throat.

"Are you both all right?" Marius asked, never taking his eyes from the figure on the floor.

"Yes," said Nyssa shakily, picking up her dropped knife and staring fixedly at the blood on the blade.

"I think so. Is he dead?" Aria couldn't suppress a shudder.

Marius knelt and felt for a pulse. After a pause he said, "Yes, he's dead."

On the bed, Kit slept a drugged, untroubled sleep. Nyssa helped Aria up to sit beside him, then hurriedly found a rag to wipe her knife clean and stuck it back in her boot with a shudder. They all stared dumbly at the dead man for what seemed like several minutes.

Marius was the first to pull himself together, getting up and crossing to look out the window.

"He must have come on foot. That's good: No horse to hide." He was thinking out loud as he looked for a way to get the situation under control. "He's not in uniform—he must be here on his own time, so maybe it'll be a while before anyone notices he's missing." He came to a decision and swung around from the window.

"Get a grip on yourselves and finish packing," he said sharply. "We have to get out of here as soon as possible." There was no place for sympathy or kind words here. Someone had to take control or they would completely go to pieces.

They stared at him, then Nyssa got to her feet and began to pick up the armful of clothes she had dropped.

Marius went to his room and hauled the cover off the bed. When he came back in, Aria still hadn't moved, staring at the dead man on the floor. He knelt again, ignoring her, and pulled his knife loose. He heard it scrape against a rib as it came free. There was surprisingly little blood. Another stroke of luck.

He arranged the bedcover on the floor and, rolling the body onto it, wrapped the corpse as best he could.

With Jaxom's face hidden from sight, the spell that seemed to have held Aria immobile was broken. She got to her feet and without a word went back to her packing.

Nyssa gave her a sidelong glance and saw how her hands shook as she folded a dress, but she carried on.

Marius took a deep breath. "I'm going to get a cart." They stared at him. "Lock the door behind me," he went on before they could protest, "and don't answer to anyone but me. Nyssa, keep your knife within reach."

She swallowed hard and nodded.

"I'll be as quick as I can." He tried a reassuring smile, but it didn't work. "We'll be away from here soon."

And before he or they could change his mind, he turned and left.

11

WAVES

The cart creaked as it rolled along the road. Marius, Aria, and Nyssa sat on the board, Marius driving. No one spoke.

Nyssa wanted nothing more than to sleep, exhausted by stress and fear. She supposed the others must feel the same.

It seemed like days since they'd stood staring at the dead body in front of them, but it was barely two hours. As soon as Marius had left, Nyssa had locked the door and dragged the table against it as an extra precaution.

She and Aria had bundled up the rest of their belongings and packed up all their food and water. In silence.

Aria had seemed lost, dazed, moving mechanically through their room. Nyssa had mopped up the surprisingly small blot of blood on the floor and scrubbed the stain away as best she could, trying not to touch the wrapped bundle of the body as she did so. With the rug pulled over the damp patch on the boards, the room looked almost normal. Apart from the body, of course.

In a mercifully short time Marius had returned.

"I've got us a cart," he said as Nyssa opened the door. "Are you ready?"

She nodded.

"Right. Let's get him downstairs." He jerked his head toward the bundled body.

"What?" Nyssa thought she must have misunderstood.

"We can't leave him here, or as soon as they find him, they'll be searching for us. We put him on the back of the cart under the luggage and get rid of him somewhere quiet along the road."

Nyssa looked at him as though he was crazy. Aria didn't look at him at all.

"Our best chance is now. The streets are quiet because it's the middle of the day. Come on, help me get him downstairs."

Reluctantly, they moved to help him. With difficulty, they got the dead body down the stairs. Now Nyssa understood what people meant when they talked about deadweight.

Marius sent Aria outside to watch for a moment when the road was empty. She gave him an unfathomable look and went out without a word. "Is she all right?" he said to Nyssa. "She seems upset."

Nyssa quashed a desire to punch him. He had, after all, just saved them. Possibly.

"Upset for someone who's been half strangled, then seen a man knifed to death in front of her?"

"Well, yes, actually. Much more upset than you were when I . . . when the robber died."

Nyssa thought back to that day in the woods — it seemed so long ago — and he was right. Aria *was* much more distressed by what had happened than they might have expected. She opened her mouth to say something just as Aria's head appeared around the door.

"Now. The street's clear."

Somehow they heaved and hauled the body into the back of the cart, where Marius flung the canvas cover over it. Nyssa ran upstairs to get their gear while Marius kept an eye on the cart, and on Aria, who was silently organizing the cargo. Once their baggage was stowed and the cart looked a bit more normal, they all went back upstairs for the last time.

Nyssa stuffed the rest of Marius's belongings into his bag while he counted out the money they owed for the rooms.

"I may be a murderer, but I'm not a thief," he said with grim humor.

Nyssa took the bags and Marius bundled up the still-sleeping Kit in his cloak and carried him down the stairs. Aria watched for another quiet moment on the street and they put the rest of the bags, and Kit under the cloak, on the back of the cart.

"So far, so good," said Marius as they drove away.

-|-   -|-   -|-

They'd left the city with no problems and were now making their way at an apparently unhurried pace along the coast road, waiting for a chance to dump the body.

"This looks as if it might do," said Marius, pointing to a track that led away from the road and into trees.

Luck was on their side again and no one saw them turn off. They went along the path for a few minutes, until they were well out of sight of the road, then stopped the cart.

Of course, to get to the body, they had to take everything else off, including Kit. As Marius lifted him out and put him down gently on the ground, he stirred and gave a sigh.

"How much longer do we have before he wakes up? Aria?"

"I don't know." She shrugged.

"Come on, think! You seemed to know what you were doing when you gave the drug to him. What was it you said then?"

She made an obvious effort to think as she pulled bags off the cart. "Three hours. Maybe a bit longer, he's so small. So, another hour at most."

Marius nodded. "Have you got any more of whatever it was you gave him?"

"Yes."

"Find it in case we need it. We can't have him waking up now, before we're on the boat."

While Aria searched for the drug, Marius and Nyssa shoved the body off the cart and dragged it into the trees a short distance. Marius straightened, panting for a few seconds, then bent again to pull it free of the bedcover.

"Why are you doing that?"

"It links us to him. If we're lucky, when he's found, they'll think he was killed here." He tied the cover in a tight bundle around a fist-sized rock. "We'll drop this off the boat."

Back at the cart, Aria was loading their belongings again. They settled Kit, making sure he was hidden from view, turned the cart with some difficulty, and rejoined the road.

In the twenty minutes it took to reach the nearest point to the boat, they met two carts and four people on foot, none of whom showed the slightest interest in them.

"This is it," said Marius a little later. "Take the reins while I check things."

He handed Nyssa the reins, jumped down, and disappeared among the scrubby bushes that lined the seaward side of the road.

In a few moments he was back.

"It looks all right. There's one old man down there cleaning out fish traps, but we can't help that. We'll get everything out of sight of the road, then I'll get rid of the cart." He climbed up and lifted Kit again. The girls each took as much as they could carry, and they picked their way down the almost invisible path between thorny branches.

When they were well out of sight of the road, Marius found a place to put Kit down and went back for the last of their things. They could see the sea a little way below them, shining like a handful of aquamarines, but the boat was still hidden.

Marius returned with the final bags. "I won't be long," he said, and started back to the road.

Nyssa and Aria settled themselves as comfortably as they could. Nyssa pulled open the cloak swathed around Kit. His face was hot and sweaty. As she stroked his hair back from his forehead, he stirred and flinched away from her hand, and she heard the rhythm of his breathing change.

"He's waking up."

"Already? That's sooner than I expected." Aria scrabbled through a bag and brought out a little twist of paper. She poured half a cup of water, tipped the contents of the paper into it, and stirred it with a finger.

Beside them Kit moved, rubbing his neck with one hand.

"He'll be drowsy when he wakes. Get him to drink some of this. Just a couple of mouthfuls should be enough. We don't need much more time."

Aria moved out of Kit's line of sight as he opened his eyes, and Nyssa sat down where he would see her, hating herself for what she was about to do to him. It felt like a betrayal.

Kit blinked sleepily and yawned, then smiled a little as he saw Nyssa. Before he could realize where he was, she said, "You fell asleep. You must be thirsty." She held the water out to him and helped him sit and drink, then watched him lie down again, close his eyes, and drift away from her.

She poured out the rest of the water and handed the cup back to Aria and they sat in silence, waiting for the sounds of Marius's return. Aria stared out to sea and Nyssa watched her.

"Are you all right?"

Aria came back from wherever she had been with a jolt. "What?"

"Are you all right? I know what happened back in Thira was terrible, but you seem . . . I don't know . . . lost."

Aria gave a laugh that held no humor. "I suppose I am. It's over for me, you see. Until that man was killed, this was all a delicious, dangerous game and I could walk away from it whenever I chose.

"But not now. They'll find him dead, and he'll have told someone where he was going, then they'll find we've disappeared, and there's a bloodstain on the floor. . . . They'll know I was involved in his death and they'll come after me.

"I can't go back to the House of White Lilies. I can't go back to Korce. All that part of my life has ended, just like that. I can't walk away. So, yes, I'm upset.

"I know that most people have nothing but contempt for the life I led, but I had friends, and a place to stay, and I was saving some money; and most of the time I felt safe.

"Now I've got nothing."

Nyssa was appalled, for it was all true. Aria, who had so lightheartedly agreed to help her, was ruined because of it.

"I'm so sorry. This is all my fault."

"No, it isn't. I chose to get involved—you didn't try to persuade me. I thought I was clever enough to spot danger coming and get out of the way. I know better now."

Nyssa couldn't think of anything to say that might comfort her and not be a lie, so Marius found them sharing a morose silence when he returned a few minutes later.

"Right. Let's get off this island."

They loaded themselves with as much as they could carry and made their way down the steep slope that led to the water's edge, where the boat rocked at its mooring, a comforting sight. The old man was still there a little way off, tending to his fish traps, but he hardly spared them a glance.

It took them fifteen minutes to get everything down to the boat and stowed to Marius's satisfaction. As they were loading the last bags of food, Aria gasped and said, "Look at the water," pointing to the sea's edge.

The water was falling away from the shore, as fast as water running out of a bath. It only lasted a few seconds, and then it turned and began to run back in, but as it did so there was a grinding rumble, and the earth shook as it had on their first day in Thira. A large wave rushed in from nowhere and rocked the boat violently against its mooring lines, then died away just as abruptly. Everything was suddenly still.

They looked at each other.

"Let's get out of here," said Marius.

There was a brisk breeze blowing from the west, and the sail snapped to and fro as Marius hauled it up. Nyssa untied the mooring lines and pushed off with an oar, and the wind caught the sail and shook them free of Thira.

Once they were well offshore, Nyssa leaned over the side and dropped the weighted cover that had served as a shroud. She watched it spiral down through the blue water, trailing a faint plume of red as it sank.

They waited for Kit to wake.

-+-   -+-   -+-

This time it took longer than they had expected, for he seemed to have gone from drugged sleep straight to normal sleep. No one wanted to wake him, though; they were all anxious about how he was likely to react when he found himself inexplicably on a boat.

Nyssa found herself staring at the back of his head, wondering about his half of the tattoo. Eventually she would try to explain it all to him, with Marius's help, but for now it didn't matter. All that mattered was keeping him safe.

It was a couple of hours before he stirred, and by that time the others had begun to relax slightly, seeing no sign of pursuit so far. Thira shrank behind them as the afternoon wore on and they took turns steering. Nyssa felt almost safe, though she knew that was premature. Alaric would search relentlessly for Kit once he realized that he had escaped, and if one of the Shadowmen's fast boats left Thira now, it would overtake them before nightfall. Out here they couldn't be more exposed. Safety was very far away.

When she saw Kit begin to wake, she handed the tiller to Aria and went to sit beside him in the front of the boat so that he'd see her first.

This time he woke quickly, and was instantly alert, sitting up suddenly. For a moment Nyssa was afraid he would simply jump overboard as he stared around him, wide-eyed and incredulous. But after he had stared his fill at the blue water, he looked at Nyssa and smiled.

She gave a sigh of relief.

"I told you we'd go out on a boat later. You fell asleep before we got here. Thira's back there." She pointed over the stern and he turned to look. But instead of Thira, he saw Aria and Marius and squirmed back against Nyssa.

"It's all right. They're friends. Remember? My friend Aria and our uncle, Marius."

Marius held out a hand to Kit. "Come on over here, Kit, and you can steer."

He shook his head and pressed harder against Nyssa, his ragged nails digging into her arm. Marius let his hand drop, his expression unreadable.

"Give it time," said Aria softly. "He can't be used to kindness from men."

Marius nodded and made a show of attending to one of the ropes. Nyssa tried again.

"Thira's back there. See how far away it is?" Kit nodded. "You don't ever have to go back. You're safe now. We'll look after you. No one will hurt you anymore."

Kit looked at her and shook his head sadly.

"You'll see," said Nyssa, trying to convince herself as much as him.

-:-   -:-   -:-

It was close to dark when they reached the tiny island that was the closest refuge to Thira, and there was still no sign of any pursuit. They beached the boat and built a fire against the autumn chill, then ate a frugal meal and lay down to sleep as well as they could on the bare ground, exhausted by the day's events.

Kit dropped into sleep as quickly as an animal, and in the firelight Nyssa could see that he was still clutching the flute like a talisman. She turned over and saw Marius watching him, too.

"He'll get used to you. Aria's right: It'll take him a while to trust you, but he will. He'll grow to understand what you've done for him and for me."

"I hope so."

‡   ‡   ‡

Nyssa opened her eyes to find it was daylight and Kit was gone, his blankets an empty, twisted nest. She sat up in a panic, looking around for him. Marius and Aria were still asleep nearby. She got to her feet and was on the verge of waking them when she saw him at the sea's edge, toes in the surf, staring out over the ocean. It was clear that the sea held a deep fascination for him. She wished she could ask him to explain why.

For the moment, though, there were more immediate concerns. The horizon was still clear of any suggestion of pursuing vessels; just a normal sprinkling of fishing boats much like their own. They needed to replenish their supplies before they started on the next leg of their journey, for circumstances had meant they'd not been prepared when they fled Thira.

The others were awake now, and after they had broken their fast, they decided that Marius and Aria should go to buy food from the few herders and farmers who lived here. It seemed wise not to advertise Kit's presence, so he and Nyssa would replenish the water stores and pack up the boat again for what would probably be a three-day journey northeast to Drakona.

Kit's relief at seeing Marius depart was palpable. Nyssa wished she could find a way to convince him that Marius was very different from the men he had known on Thira, for she could see how his distrust wounded Marius like a knife. She knew, however, that only time could really help.

She talked to him about nothing in particular as they filled the water bottles at a spring, packed up, and stowed their belongings. This time at least, there was a chance to rope them properly in place, in case the weather turned rough.

Where would they go after Drakona? She and Marius hadn't had a chance to think beyond that yet, but they couldn't stay there: Although it was not the most obvious destination for them to seek, it was still much too close to Thira and much too small to provide any real measure of safety.

She put the thought aside for the time being. *One step at a time, Nyssa. It's got you this far.*

The others came back about an hour later with fresh bread and apples and a piece of smoked mutton. Kit retreated along the beach as soon as they appeared, and Nyssa's heart went out to Marius, for she could see the hunger in his eyes to touch, to embrace, to reassure this damaged boy.

Marius contented himself with saying, "You two have been busy. Well done."

Within half an hour they were at sea again, Kit hanging over the prow watching fish flick past beneath him and once, to his delight, a pod of dolphins that raced along beside them for several minutes.

They left the little island in their wake and began to sail by compass bearing now, for soon they would lose sight of any glimpse of land for two days.

Marius and Nyssa were both competent sailors; Aria could steer, but was less good with the sails. It was clear that Kit knew nothing, nor did he seem in the slightest bit interested in understanding how they controlled the boat, although Nyssa tried to explain it to him. He never tired of staring at the white-flecked water that now stretched away unbroken on all sides.

They took turns steering and snatching uncomfortable sleep on the damp boards. It was noticeable that Kit stayed as far as possible from Marius, but no one made any comment.

The first two days passed without incident, and a numbing sense of boredom crept up on Nyssa, Marius, and Aria, though not on Kit, who still hadn't tired of fish and water.

The wind began to rise during the afternoon of the second day. At first they were pleased, for it came from the right direction, and they would reach Drakona more quickly, but by nightfall it was strong enough to make them reef the sail hard. Fortunately, the sky stayed clear, and they sailed on under the stars.

The wind dropped a little around dawn, and for a couple of hours they thought the gale had passed, but with full daylight it came back like a fury, and they were soon bailing out the boat.

Now only Marius was strong enough to keep any control over the tiller, even when they fought the sail down altogether and ran on under a bare mast.

Kit lay curled in terror near the prow, clawing at his arms with his broken nails until they bled. He showed no sign of responding to anything Nyssa said to him until, half-frantic with fear, she grabbed him by the arms and yelled, "Stop it! Stop it!" in his face.

He did stop, an expression of shock on his face, and from that moment lay curled, mute and unmoving in the water that was gathering in the boat's belly.

Nyssa and Aria scooped water out as fast as they could, but each time a wave broke over the boat, the water seemed to grow a little deeper.

Marius hung grimly on to the tiller, checking the compass when he could, scanning the horizon for a glimpse of land. Surely Drakona should be in sight by now, at the speed they must be traveling? He couldn't fight this wind for much longer, nor could the boat. Was this how they would all end, after everything? And no one would ever know what had become of them.

As Aria bailed frantically, a small, detached part of her mind considered how odd it was that she should come to this. Of all the ways she had considered that she might die, drowning had never figured into her speculations. She thought of all the things that she would never see now, or do, and the sadness she felt left no room for fear.

Nyssa was furious. They deserved better than this from the gods, after what they had managed to do. She paused a moment from bailing to look at Marius. His face was gray with fatigue. How much longer could he keep the boat from being swamped completely? Had they saved Kit from a life of misery in order to deliver him to the peace of death? She bailed harder.

Marius thought his vision was beginning to cloud. He couldn't focus properly on the horizon anymore. It was overlaid by a violet smudge.

He blinked and shook his head, but it stayed obstinately there, and he realized he was looking at Drakona.

"Look!" he yelled to the others, not daring to take a hand off the tiller to point. He saw the girls glance around, heard Nyssa whoop with something like triumph.

Two more hours. If they could just keep the boat afloat for two more hours.

The world shrunk down to the simple and desperately difficult task of keeping the boat aimed at the island growing on the horizon. Nothing but determination kept him on his feet now, a determination that they would live long enough for Kit to learn to trust him.

They almost did it.

They were two hundred yards offshore when there was a terrible sound of splintering, and suddenly there was a great gash in the side of the boat and there were rocks all around them, wickedly sharp, breaking through the wild water.

"We're holed!" yelled Nyssa. "We're going to sink."

Somehow the boat was still moving forward, even as it foundered. Nyssa abandoned the hopeless bailing and hauled Kit to his feet.

"Kit! The boat's sinking. We have to swim. See the island?" She spun him around and pointed. "Swim for the island." An appalling thought surfaced. "You can swim, can't you?"

He shrugged, frowning.

Behind them, Marius had abandoned the tiller at last, and he and Aria were trying to pry loose anything that might float, so that they could hold on to it. And suddenly there was no more time as the boat broke its back on another rock in a collision so violent they were hurled into the roiling water.

Nyssa came up coughing, saw Kit nearby, and tried to swim toward him. She could hear Marius yell "Try to stay together!" There were broken planks in the water around them. She grabbed hold of one of them, saw Kit do the same, and looked around. Eventually she spotted Marius, but there was no sign of Aria, though against the pitching waves it was difficult to make anything out clearly.

She was being swept away from Kit and Marius, caught by the trailing edge of some current. She tried to fight against it, but it was all she could do to keep her head above water enough to breathe.

The sea embraced her and she closed her eyes.

12

WRECKAGE

"Nyssa."

A voice from another world, from a time before the sea took her. Something rough against her cheek. Gritty sand. Ears full of the sound of the sea, eyes full of salt. Cold. Clothes full of water, tangled around her like a shroud.

"Nyssa."

She forced her eyes open to find what sea spirit was talking to her. A strange voice, cracked and dry as a husk. A ghost's voice. Nothing to see but her own salt-tangled hair.

She pushed it out of her eyes and sat up. Pain. All of her right side beaten and battered. She held on to her ribs so that she could breathe.

"Nyssa."

In front of her an empty shore, pathetic flotsam from the boat: a shoe, half an oar, pieces of unrecognizable clothing. Who had called her name? She turned around slowly. Kit was kneeling on the sand behind her. She forgot about the voice.

"We're alive, Kit! We're alive." Her own voice cracked with salt, with the pain of drawing breath. "Are you hurt?" He shook his head. "The others. Where are the others?" She began to struggle to her feet.

He helped her up.

"Have you seen them?"

He shook his head sadly and pointed at the sea.

He couldn't mean — surely he couldn't mean . . .

"But who spoke to me?" She looked around wildly.

"Me."

She stared at him, everything else forgotten for an instant. "You? You can speak?"

He nodded.

"Oh, Kit." She went to put an arm around him and he retreated slightly. "Why didn't you tell me?"

He shrugged.

"I'll keep you safe, Kit, I will. Even if . . . even if we don't find Marius and Aria. Maybe they came ashore somewhere else. They might be all right. We should look for them." She held out a hand and, cautiously, he took it. "We have to look for them; we have to find shelter, and water, and decide what to do . . ."

Hand in hand, they set off along the beach.

-:-   -:-   -:-

They'd been walking for half an hour or so, Nyssa now with her arms wrapped around herself so it didn't hurt so much to breathe. From time to time she glanced at Kit's bedraggled figure beside her, silent as though he'd never spoken to her. She'd tried to get him to speak again, but he wouldn't. She was beginning to wonder if she'd imagined it all as she woke, washed up and battered, on the shore of Drakona.

She scanned the beach constantly for any clue to what had become of Marius and Aria, but there was nothing. Where she and Kit had come ashore there had been some bits and pieces of wreckage, but here there was nothing at all.

They would have to get off the beach before darkness fell and find some sort of shelter, but she was unwilling to leave the shore yet, still clinging to the hope that the others would be around the next outcrop of rock. There was no way off the beach just now, anyway: Black rock faces reared up to her right, forty to fifty feet high. Even if fit, she would have thought twice about trying to climb them, and in her present state it was impossible.

Maybe they'd be around the next corner.

They weren't, nor around any corner that they came to. They trudged on. The cliffs gradually became lower, until they were no more than fifteen feet high. She'd have to get up there somehow. They had to get off the beach.

Every time they had come to any group of rocks that could have concealed Marius or Aria her heart had lurched with a mixture of hope and dread, followed by plummeting disappointment when once again there was no trace of them.

Kit suddenly grabbed her arm, pointing to the top of the rock face. There were two men in a cart looking down at them.

For a few seconds, Nyssa was at a loss. Friends or enemies?

What should she do? She realized that there was nothing to decide. The men had obviously seen them—already they were climbing down from the cart—and there was no way they could escape even if they wanted to.

They needed help. Nyssa hoped fervently that they had just found it.

One of the men waved and called something that she couldn't make out; he started down the rock face while the other, older one stayed with the cart.

Kit edged nervously toward Nyssa.

"It's all right, Kit," she said through the pain in her chest. "I think they've come to help us."

The younger man jumped down the last few feet from the rocks.

"We saw the boat go down from the village," he said in an accent Nyssa had never heard before. "How many people were on board?"

"Four of us," said Nyssa. "Have you found the others?"

He shook his head. "I'm sorry, we haven't. There are others out searching, too," he added. "Maybe they've found them." But he didn't meet her eyes as he said it.

"Let's get you back to the village," he went on. "There might be some news there. Are you hurt? Can you get up here?"

Nyssa looked doubtfully at the steep rocks. She would just have to do it. She nodded.

Kit went first, scrambling up with an agility that surprised her. Somehow, with help from her rescuer, and with Kit and the older man reaching down to pull from above, she got up, in spite of the pain in her side. They lifted her into the cart and put blankets over her, and she let herself drift away for a little as the cart creaked gently along a track.

Dusk was falling, lights from the village shining out as they drew near. Nyssa had kept her eyes shut for most of the journey, not wanting to answer questions, however well-intentioned, but a few minutes ago Kit had shaken her shoulder until she sat up stiffly, pointing to the buildings coming into view.

She tried to gather her thoughts, to decide what to say and what to conceal, but her brain refused to give her a clear answer.

The cart rolled along a street now, lined with houses on either side. There seemed to be no one out, but the sounds and signs of normal life leaked from the windows: talking, hammering, laughter, the smell of cooking fish. To Nyssa it all seemed to belong to another world at the moment.

They stopped in front of a building set a little way back from the street, a vegetable patch in front of it.

The younger of their rescuers helped Nyssa down from the cart, Kit having adroitly avoided his proffered hand. "This is the village guesthouse," he said. "If there is any news, it will come here."

They followed him along the path. He pushed open the door and stood aside.

The room inside was brightly lit, and it took Nyssa's eyes a few seconds to adjust. When they did, directly in front of her she saw Aria, sitting in a cushioned chair by a fire and wearing a borrowed dress, a blanket around her shoulders. Her eyes opened wide as she saw Nyssa and Kit.

Off to the right Marius sat on a bed, an old woman bandaging one of his hands. As he saw Nyssa in the doorway he lurched to his feet, bandages and salve spilling from his lap, and crossed the distance between them in three strides to engulf her in an embrace that made her cry out in pain.

He released his grip. "You're hurt?"

"No . . . yes . . . just my ribs. I thought . . . I thought you were dead."

He folded her back into his arms, more gently this time. "And I thought I'd lost you. Both of you."

Marius and Nyssa were both in tears.

Aria rose carefully from her chair, seeing Kit look agitated at this display of emotion.

"I'm glad you're safe, Kit. Come to the fire and get warm. They'll bring you some clothes in a minute."

Marius released Nyssa, who went cautiously to hug Aria. The old woman who had been looking after Marius had tactfully disappeared to give them some measure of privacy. Aria made Nyssa take her chair and Kit sat down close to her feet.

They all looked at each other, surveying what damage the shipwreck had done to them. Kit seemed almost unscathed, Aria bedraggled and exhausted, but nothing worse. Marius's palms were raw from all the hours he had spent fighting the tiller of their poor lost boat, and below his left eye there was a long cut already crusted over, with the promise of a spectacular black eye to come. With nothing worse than Nyssa's battered ribs, the sea had treated them kindly.

For some moments it was enough to simply look, as they each took in the fact that they had all survived. It seemed that no one wanted to break the silence, and they all sat, as speechless as Kit, until there was a knock at the door and the old woman came back in with an armful of clothes.

"There'll be some food along in a minute," she said, handing garments to Nyssa and Kit, "and hot water so you can wash the sea out of your eyes properly." She looked at Marius. "I should finish doing your hands."

"There are other rooms where you can change," said Aria. "I'll show you."

The guesthouse had several rooms set around a central courtyard. Nyssa looked longingly at the bed in the one where she was changing. As her fears had receded, they had left behind a weariness so great that she knew if she lay down, even for a moment, she would be asleep. She resisted for the moment, though, anxious to hear Marius and Aria's story.

When she went back to the main room, there was a pot of soup on the table and loaves of barley bread. The old woman was gathering up her bandages.

"Sleep well tonight. No one will disturb you too early tomorrow. Come to the house opposite if you need anything—that's where I live."

As Aria ladled soup, Marius said, "So, what happened to you? Where did you come ashore? We looked for you."

Nyssa told him the little she could remember of her time in the sea and their rescue. For the moment she said nothing about the revelation that Kit was not mute. When she was finished, she turned the question back to Marius and Aria. "What happened to you?"

Marius glanced across at Aria. "She saved me. I would never have made it to shore without her."

"I did not," Aria retorted. "Don't be overdramatic. I just shouted at you."

He gave a chuckle and went on. "I got hold of a piece of planking as the boat broke up. I saw you and Kit for a few seconds, then you were gone. Aria suddenly appeared beside me, and then something hit me in the face" — he touched his swollen eye gingerly — "I think it was a piece of the mast. It nearly knocked me out, and I let go of the plank and went under.

"Next thing I knew, Aria had dragged me up by the collar, yelled at me to hold on, and kept on yelling until I came to my senses."

"I told you all I did was shout," Aria said to Nyssa with a smile. "The current took us more or less straight toward the shore, and it wasn't long before a couple of villagers found us. It seems boats founder regularly on those rocks."

"They call them the Dragon's Teeth," Marius added. "With good reason."

They lapsed into silence again, too tired to eat much, and shortly afterward gave up trying to stay awake and went to bed.

Nyssa had barely shut the door to her room when it opened again; it was Kit with a tangle of blankets in his arms, obviously intent on staying in the same room as her.

Without a word he spread them on the floor at the foot of the bed and curled up.

"Good night," she said, but there was only his quiet breathing in reply.

The next morning, Nyssa woke stiff as a board and sore all over, but feeling unreasonably optimistic. It was as though, having cheated death by drowning, she had cheated all the other possible fates as well.

She left the room quietly so as not to wake Kit, and found Aria in the courtyard, combing her wet hair as best she could with her fingers.

"There's plenty of hot water," she said, pointing to a doorway.

Nyssa bathed, and managed to wash the salt out of her hair.

"That's better," she said as she toweled it dry in the sun. She could see Kit watching curiously from the window. "Come on, Kit. Come and get clean. It feels good."

He looked at her doubtfully, then came out into the courtyard. He looked at the soap and basin as though he had never seen such things before.

Maybe he hasn't, Nyssa chided herself. She showed him how to wash his hair with soap and left him to experiment.

In the main room, Marius was still sleeping. *Not surprising*, thought Nyssa, remembering the hours during which he had fought the sea.

There was a knock at the door. When Nyssa opened it she found a young woman with a tray of food. She came in and set it on the table and gathered up the remnants of their supper.

"I'm Mariola," she said. "A couple of the men have gone

down to the shore to see if any more of your belongings have washed up. There wasn't much yesterday. Bethoc will be across to see you later."

"Bethoc?"

"The old woman who was here when the others arrived." She gestured to Marius, who had sat up, yawning, then flashed him a dazzling smile. "I'll leave you in peace to have your breakfast."

Nyssa went to fetch Kit and Aria while Marius dressed. As they ate, they began to take stock of their situation.

They were alive, more or less unhurt, and for the moment apparently safe from Alaric and the Shadowmen. That was the end of the good news, however. They didn't hold out much hope of retrieving any of their belongings from the wreck, which meant they were more or less destitute.

"So all we have are the clothes we came ashore in?" Nyssa asked, hoping she was somehow wrong. Marius nodded, cutting a slice of bread awkwardly because of his bandaged hands. "Here, let me," she said impatiently, taking the knife from him.

"There's a little money. I had a few gold pieces in the pouch on my belt, but that's all. My sword would go straight to the bottom, I've no knife. . . . What about yours?"

It was Nyssa's turn to shake her head.

"What are we going to do?"

"We can't stay here for long," said Marius. "Alaric will send Shadowmen here sooner or later. We need to get to the Mainland and disappear."

"Maybe they haven't even found the body yet," Aria said. "It's possible they might not connect it to us." She noticed that

Kit looked baffled. *Of course, he'd been drugged when it happened. He didn't know.* But why were Marius and Nyssa staring at her like that?

Marius and Nyssa glanced at each other anxiously. They'd almost forgotten over the past days that Aria didn't know everything. Not nearly everything.

"There are some things we need to tell you," said Nyssa slowly, wondering where to begin.

She didn't get the chance. They were interrupted by another knock at the door and the old woman they now knew to be Bethoc came in.

"Mariola told me you were awake." She came over and peered at Marius's swollen and rainbow-hued eye, touching it gently. As she did so, Nyssa noticed a green dolphin tattoo on her wrist. "I should look at your hands."

Nyssa gave her seat to Bethoc, glad for a pause before they had to explain to Aria just how much they had concealed from her. Then there was Kit to consider. How much did he already know? She had to get him to talk to her.

She touched him on the shoulder and gestured that he should follow her.

"I won't be long," she said to Aria with what she hoped was a reassuring smile.

She sat Kit down on a stone bench in the courtyard and turned him to face her.

"Kit, I need you to answer some questions. I need you to talk to me. It's safe to talk now. You have to get used to it again. You remember when we were a family, don't you?"

He nodded.

"And do you remember the raid, when the Shadowmen took you?"

His gaze slid away to the ground and he shrugged. She put a hand under his chin and tilted his head back until he had to look at her. "Do you, Kit? Do you remember?"

"Yes." It was a rusty whisper, nothing more.

She drew a breath. "Do you know *why* they came for you and me? Did you know it was us they wanted?"

Another nod.

"Why were we — are we — important to them?"

He touched the back of her head, then his own. "The words."

It was a relief to find that he knew. She had no idea how she would have gone about explaining that to him. It would be hard enough explaining to Aria.

When they went back inside, Bethoc had just finished with Marius's hands.

"What do you all say to a bit of a walk?" she said, to everyone's surprise. "Not far, mind you — I'm getting too old to drag my bones far nowadays — but you can see what we brought out of the sea." She sighed. "It's not a lot, I'm afraid, but there's a few bits and pieces you might be glad to see again."

They walked in a little group back along the street Nyssa and Kit had come through in the cart yesterday. Nyssa hadn't noticed much about it then. The houses were small and old, the wood scoured of paint by the salty wind. It didn't look as though anyone had much money to spare. The only sizeable building was a smoke shed, whose doors were open enough for her to make out racks of suspended fish. There were people out and about now, children playing and women coming and going between houses.

"The men are mostly out on the boats today," said Bethoc.

Mariola waved at them from a doorway as they passed. Others looked at them curiously, but no one approached. There was an odd atmosphere, Nyssa thought. Not threatening, but she couldn't quite identify it.

The village seemed to be on the highest point of the island but still close to the sea, with a little harbor. Nyssa watched the waves for a glimpse of the rocks where they had come to grief but they were under the water just now.

Looking the other way she saw no trees, just a hummocky expanse of rough ground and tough, thorny plants. It didn't look like a place where much would grow.

Near the point where the village petered out, Bethoc turned off to the left. She took them through an archway and into a stable yard. A cart stood there, a heap of flotsam in it.

"I'll wait here while you have a look through it." Bethoc sat herself down on a bale of hay.

They climbed into the cart and went through the salt-cured remains of their belongings. There were a few pieces of clothing that just needed washing and drying, one of Nyssa's knives tangled among them. Kit darted forward to pick something up. The flute. How could something so small and fragile have survived?

The rest was unsalvageable: torn clothing, single shoes and boots, fragments of their belongings. No sword. More important, in the short term at least, no money.

"I'm sorry it's not more," said Bethoc. "The men looked in all the likely places."

It was profoundly depressing to sit among this sea wrack — more so than if nothing had been salvaged. Only Kit looked happy, inspecting his flute to see whether it had been damaged.

"And now," Bethoc went on, "I think we should talk about why you are here, Keepers, and about what we do with you."

ALARIC

THE HUNT BEGINS

At first Alaric hardly registered that the boy had gone. He often disappeared for hours at a time, heedless of the punishments he knew would await him when he returned.

Alaric rather enjoyed the opportunities this afforded.

Never before, however, had he stayed away for a whole night. Had he perhaps killed himself? It seemed unlikely: He would surely have done so long ago if he intended to. Nothing had changed recently.

When word was brought to him that Captain Jaxom was missing, he wondered briefly if the two could be connected, but dismissed the idea almost at once. Jaxom had never shown any interest in the boy. His tastes lay elsewhere.

When Jaxom returned, of course, there would be a reckoning. In the meantime, there was the boy to find.

He called in his local informers as well as the Shadowmen.

"Search the town, and if he is not there, search the rest of the island. If anyone is hiding him, kill them. I will have him found."

13

THE TOMBS

Nyssa and Marius stared at Bethoc, trying not to show the alarm they felt. Kit pushed himself into a corner of the cart, cradling the flute. Aria was frowning, puzzled.

They waited for her to say something else.

"To be fair, I don't know if you're all Keepers," she went on, her shrewd eyes watching their reactions. "You two"—she gestured at Marius and Nyssa—"carry the sign of the Crane, I know. I couldn't help but see, the state your clothes were in when you were brought to the village. But you—Aria, is it? I don't know about you, or Kit here, who, it seems, can hear, but not speak."

Kit glanced around at the sound of his name, his expression apprehensive.

"So we have at least two Keepers, maybe four, shipwrecked on Drakona, coming from the direction of Thira, where no Keeper ever goes. You can't wonder that I'm curious."

Marius got down from the cart.

"Aria isn't a Keeper. The rest of us are, but she didn't know. Leave her out of whatever is going to happen."

Aria looked from Marius to Nyssa and back again in bafflement.

"What's going on? What are you talking about? Marius?"

Bethoc ignored her and went on. "But she's your friend, surely? You're traveling together." She cocked her head to one side, birdlike. "And this one," she pointed to Kit, "hasn't led the same sort of life as the rest of you. Look at him: skin and bones. Did you do that to him?" Her voice was suddenly crisp.

"Of course not." Marius's voice rose angrily. "He's my nephew, Nyssa's brother. I wouldn't treat a dog like that, never mind my own blood." He stopped abruptly, aware that he'd probably said too much.

"Boy! Kit! Look at me." To Nyssa's amazement, Kit uncurled himself and sat up. "Have these people treated you badly? Don't be afraid. We can deal with them if they have — after all, they should by rights be dead already — and keep you safe."

Kit looked terrified, but he shook his head and reached up to take Nyssa's hand. She gripped it tightly. Bethoc tapped her chin with a gnarled finger, thinking.

"By the way," she said absently, "I'm assuming you've realized it would be stupid to attack me. You've no way off the island without our help." No one answered her. "So, two questions: How do you come to be here, and how did Kit get into that state? Are you going to make me guess? It would probably save you time if you just told me. I've a feeling time might matter to you just now." She smiled expectantly.

Nyssa tried to think of a way out, a convincing lie, but her brain seemed to have frozen. Aria seemed too stunned to say anything.

Marius licked his lips. "Very well. As you say, we are at your mercy. Kit was taken from our family when he was very young. We found out recently that he was alive, and a slave. We went to rescue him."

"From Thira?"

There was a pause before he answered. "From Thira."

Bethoc nodded to herself. "Well, it makes sense of what I know—except for Aria's involvement."

"That was accidental," Marius said quickly.

The old woman got stiffly up from the hay bale, dusting down her skirt.

"I must take this to the rest of the Elders now, so that we can decide what to do. Good-bye." And she turned and walked away, under the archway and into the street.

The others stared after her in stunned silence.

"Was that what you needed to tell me?" asked Aria in a small voice.

Marius cleared his throat and went to sit on Bethoc's hay bale. Nyssa let go of Kit's hand and turned her full attention to Aria.

"It's part of it."

"Keepers? Like in the Legend?"

"Yes."

"But they don't exist. It's a legend; it's not true."

"Maybe not, but the Keepers are real." Nyssa pushed her sleeve up. "I always used to wonder what my tattoo meant. I had no family to tell me. I thought maybe it was a birth sign, like yours." She gestured to a spiral pattern of dots on Aria's ankle.

"No one ever recognized it or said anything about it, and I never met anyone else with the same design.

"And then the Shadowmen arrived on the island and everything changed. William and Marius had the same tattoo; Marius is my uncle. And the tattoos meant we were Keepers.

"I didn't believe it, either. I'd thought the Keepers and the Legend were just stories, too."

She paused, waiting for Aria to say something, but she sat staring, silent. So did Kit, hearing this for the first time, too.

"They told me that Alaric was hunting down Keepers, that Marius and I had to run away. Shadowmen came to the Drowned Boy." She felt a chill remembering how thoughtlessly she had edged closer in the cellar so that she could hear what was being said. If she'd known the danger . . .

"We fled the island. I knew there was something William and Marius hadn't told me. Something about *me*. I made Marius tell me." Nyssa flashed him an apologetic half smile and saw how keenly he was listening and watching for Aria's reaction. She took a deep breath and went on.

"I have another tattoo under my hair. It's supposed to be half of the spell, or whatever it was, that caused the Great Destruction. Alaric wasn't just looking for Keepers, he was looking for *me*. He already had the other half because he had Kit, and it's on Kit's head, too. We fled to the Mainland. And then we realized that Kit was alive and on Thira.

"You know the rest. I'm sorry. We didn't set out to deceive

you; we just never thought you would get tangled up in it all. It seemed safer for you not to know."

She glanced at Marius to see if he had anything to add, but he gestured no.

Aria shook her head slowly.

"Let me see your arm." She traced the lines of the Crane tattoo with a finger, then let Nyssa's sleeve fall back and climbed down from the cart.

"I'm going for a walk," she said. "I need to think."

"Do you want me . . . ," Nyssa began.

"No. No, I need to be on my own to think."

She moved past them like a sleepwalker.

Marius and Nyssa looked at each other bleakly.

"From one crisis to another," remarked Marius. "Surely we're due a few hours' peace?" From the cart came the sound of a wheezing note as Kit breathed into the flute. He looked up, smiling delightedly. "At least someone's happy."

-|-   -|-   -|-

There seemed nothing for them to do now except go back to the guesthouse and wait for Aria and Bethoc to return.

Kit went into the courtyard, but Nyssa lingered behind to speak to Marius.

"Since it seems to be the day for telling people things, I've some news for you, too: Kit can talk."

Marius did a double take. "What?"

"When we washed up on the shore . . . I woke up and he was saying my name. I managed to get him to say a couple of words this morning as well, but I don't think it's going to be easy to get him to talk normally. I think he's almost forgotten how to."

"I wonder how many years it is since he dared speak to someone? I don't suppose he's likely to speak to me yet?"

"I doubt it. I've only had half a dozen words out of him altogether. That's something else that's going to take time."

"If we have any, that is," said Marius gloomily. "For all we know, they're about to ship us back to Thira."

"And yet . . . it doesn't feel like that, does it? We aren't guarded."

"No, although maybe that's because they think there's no need. Let's just hope our instincts are right."

-|-   -|-   -|-

Aria returned in the middle of the afternoon. She sat down with a thud and reached to pour herself a glass of water. "It's hot out there," she said unnecessarily.

When it became apparent that Marius and Nyssa were waiting for her to say more, she put the glass down with a sigh. "It's not your fault, I know. I went through it all while I was walking. Nyssa thought she was just going to be hiding with me for a couple of days; why would she tell me all this? And then it all just grew from there without me thinking about it.

"Would I have got involved if I'd known the truth? Of course not, but the trouble I'm in now is not of your making." Nyssa came around behind her chair to give her a hug. "There isn't anything else you forgot to tell me, I hope?"

Nyssa straightened and went around the table to face her.

"Well, actually there is one thing . . ." She had to laugh at the expression on Aria's face. "Don't worry, it's nothing awful. Kit can speak, though for now he doesn't want to."

"Well, I suppose that's hardly surprising. Where is he now, by the way?"

"In the courtyard."

"And what about the village Elders? Have you heard what they've decided yet?"

Marius shook his head. "No. I don't know how it can be taking them so long to decide what to do about us."

Another two hours went by. Aria had questions now, of course, and they did their best to answer them.

"They'd be looking for us even if we hadn't killed Jaxom, wouldn't they?"

Marius nodded. "Afraid so."

There was a knock on the door.

"I suppose it's a good sign that they're actually knocking, instead of just bursting in," Marius muttered as he went to open it.

It wasn't only Bethoc this time, it was a deputation. A dozen people filed into the room. Nyssa recognized both of her rescuers and Mariola, but the rest of the faces were unfamiliar. Once again it was Bethoc who took the lead, seating herself by the hearth in the big chair with the carved arms.

"One of you fetch Kit, please. You should all hear what has been decided." Nyssa went quickly to bring Kit from the courtyard. "Sit down, please." Bethoc nodded to the chairs set around the table, smoothed her skirts over her knees, and began.

"Three of you are Keepers. The fourth is not, but travels with you as a friend in the enterprise that has put you in our hands.

"You admit that you have taken this boy from his masters in Thira?"

"Yes, but . . . ," Nyssa tried to interrupt.

Bethoc held up her hand. "Your turn to speak will come. Indulge an old woman's curiosity." She turned her gaze on Marius. "If you had not been wrecked, what was your plan?"

Marius took a deep breath. "To get far enough from Thira for Kit to be safe: probably on the Mainland. To live quietly there as a family and take care of him. You can see he needs that."

Bethoc nodded imperceptibly, shifting in her seat. "And you, Aria? Is that your plan, too?"

"I don't have a plan," said Aria flatly. "I don't know what I'm going to do."

Bethoc looked at her questioningly, but she stared back coolly and said no more.

"The Elders have talked among themselves. We have reached a decision about what we should do.

"We have long memories on this island. The tales of the old days have been passed down, mother to daughter, father to son.

"We still tell of how the Keepers caused the sea to rise up and cleanse the Shadow from the Archipelago: the Great Destruction, it is called on Drakona."

"That wretched Legend!" The words were out before Marius could stop them. "It's blighted my whole life, and Nyssa's and

Kit's as well—Aria's, too, now. None of us *wanted* to be born Keepers."

Bethoc stared him down into silence. "Perhaps you should hear what has been decided before you say any more." She ignored the mulish expression on his face and went on. "We call it the Great Destruction, but we never *blamed* the Keepers for it. They were asked to find a way to get rid of the Shadowmen, and they did. No one can foresee all the consequences of even the most trivial decision."

"That's certainly true," Aria muttered under her breath.

"Here, we still hold the Keepers in reverence. We will not send you back to Thira. We will do what we can to help you. But if a Shadow ship comes searching, I do not know if we can hide you for long. Tell us what you need, and we will try to provide it."

Nyssa sagged in her seat with relief. Marius took a moment to gather his thoughts before he spoke.

"We are putting you in danger by being here. If you could get us off the island, maybe to Idhra . . . We could take a ferry from there to the Mainland. And some food and clothes."

"And money, surely?"

"We wouldn't ask you for money."

Bethoc smiled. "And yet you can do little without it. Consider it a loan if it is easier for you. To be paid back next time the sea casts you up on these shores. Don't be too grateful—it won't be very much. As you see, we are not rich people." She got to her feet. "And now it's time that you met the rest of the villagers. We won't tell the children who you really are, though, or they'll be too overcome to do much more than stare at you and spill their food." Her mouth twitched.

"There is a meal prepared. You are an opportunity for us to have a celebration of sorts."

The deputation began to leave.

"We will expect you in an hour. Follow your ears."

She closed the door behind her, leaving them to digest what they had just been told.

Marius let out a long breath. "Well, I don't know what I was expecting, but it wasn't that. Perhaps we're about to get those few hours of peace I was longing for."

"What do you think, Kit?" Nyssa looked at him, hoping to pry a word loose, but all he did was smile. "All those people want to help us. We're safe here."

"Does that mean we can have an evening off from worrying?" asked Aria.

"I think it does," replied Marius with a smile.

·+·   ·+·   ·+·

When they came out onto the street an hour later they found it was true: All they needed to do was listen to know where to go.

Their ears led them to where they had been with Bethoc that morning, but now the stable yard was bright with lanterns and a sheep turned on a spit over a bed of charcoal. The stable doors on the far side of the yard were open, and through them could be seen not horses, but long tables set for a meal.

The whole village seemed to be here. People milled about the yard talking and drinking, or carrying plates and baskets of food. A fiddle struck up in one corner, voices joining in a song Nyssa didn't recognize.

She found someone pressing a cup of mulled cider into her hand. Kit was by her side, but Aria and Marius had drifted off to talk to some of the villagers. Marius was engaged in animated conversation with Mariola. She shook her long black hair back as she smiled up into Marius's face.

He was a handsome man. Stupid though it seemed, Nyssa had never really noticed before, but now she saw him as Mariola must: the untidy black hair that fell over his brown eyes, the lazy smile. Until the last few weeks he had just been Marius, sitting in his usual place in the Drowned Boy, then Marius her uncle, with whom she had fled from one danger to another. But she could see why he'd be a fascinating novelty to Mariola, stuck on this tiny island with the same faces, year after year.

After a while they were called to supper, but before they ate, a large communal cup was passed among them.

As Nyssa drank from it, she was aware of the goblet's great age. It was made from some dark wood, bound with dulled metal bands. The wood must once have been finely carved. Although most of the carvings had been smoothed away by generations of fingers pressing the bowl to generations of lips, traces of the designs were still visible. Nyssa looked at them, fascinated. She could see what looked like a dolphin—like the one on Bethoc's wrist, in fact. There were stars and crescent moons, lilies and patterns of dots, abstract designs that she recognized as clan tattoos. And there, near the rim of the cup, a Crane, almost identical to her own. It was as though all the clans of the Archipelago were joined in this one object.

"They say it was brought from Thira before the Great Destruction," said a voice on her left. She passed the cup to Kit on her right, and looked around. It was her rescuer.

"I've never thanked you properly," she said. "In fact, I don't even know your name — or the other man in the cart."

"Thomas," he said. "And my father, Eneas. There's no need for thanks. We are always glad to save someone from the Dragon's Teeth. We were relieved that you all got ashore: The sea is not always so kind. There have been times when we've seen a boat break up on the rocks and not so much as a splinter or a strand of hair comes up on the beach."

He excused himself and got up to help deal with the roast mutton. Nyssa looked around, searching for Aria's face, and found her near the head of a table, deep in conversation with Bethoc. She looked solemn, and Nyssa had the feeling that she was unburdening herself about something. Not too much, she hoped.

The evening passed in a haze of food and drink. Nyssa made her excuses and left early, trailed by Kit: Sitting in one place for so long was making her ribs hurt even more, and all the food and drink had made her sleepy.

She looked around to see where the others were before she went. Aria had been absorbed into a group of village women. Marius and Mariola were in a corner, still talking.

Aria arrived back at the guesthouse soon after Nyssa and Kit. Nyssa heard her pause outside the room they were sharing, but she didn't come in, and a few seconds later came the sound of Aria's own door closing.

It was much later when Marius returned, clumsily trying to be quiet and as a result making twice as much noise.

⊹   ⊹   ⊹

The next morning, Aria seemed in an uncommonly good mood; or at least she was singing, and generally making quite a large amount of noise.

Marius winced as Bethoc took the bandages off his hands.

"Did I hurt you?" she asked.

"No, it's not that," he replied, eyes narrowed.

"Well, they look fine, but you'll need to be careful with them for a few days. They'll be tender."

Marius touched his palms gingerly. "Thank you. Whatever it was you used on them, it certainly worked."

"*Mmnn* ... shame it doesn't help hangovers," Bethoc remarked drily as she gathered her things together.

There was a knock at the door. Bethoc put down her bandages and opened it to Thomas, who had a large wooden box in his arms. He put it down on the table, smiled, and left without a word.

"I thought you might like to see what's in here," Bethoc said, looking at the four fugitives.

Wordlessly, they gathered around the table.

"You don't seem to hold your own people in very high regard," she went on, looking directly at Marius. "Despite the fact that it's one of their ointments that's healing your hands so well. Perhaps if you knew something about them, you might be more proud to carry their heritage."

Marius held her gaze. "I doubt that," he said. "All they've brought to my life so far is grief and death."

"Well, for us the opposite is true," Bethoc said, lifting the lid of the box. "What they left us here has allowed us to put to sea for generations without fearing the Dragon's Teeth." She lifted a cloth-wrapped bundle from the box and set it down carefully. "For us, the Keepers have kept death at bay."

She unwrapped the object. It was a copper plaque, lovingly polished and incised over most of its surface with small symbols in groups of three or four, arranged in columns. A line of tiny Cranes stalked across the bottom, and, as with the ruined house on Thira, Nyssa felt the stirrings of a connection with these vanished people.

"The secret of how to read this has been passed down here on Drakona since the Keepers' time on Thira, before the first Shadowmen came."

"What does it do?" asked Aria.

"It tells us how to read the tides and currents all around this island, so our ships are never pulled onto the Teeth and wrecked. No one dies in sight of home here. I wonder how many lives we owe to this thing of the Keepers?"

Bethoc swaddled it in its wrappings again and picked up her bandages, preparing to leave.

"So, young man, you should not be too swift to dismiss your heritage as a curse. To us, it has always been a blessing."

Before Marius could answer, the door burst open. It was Thomas, breathless from running.

"A Shadow ship," he gasped. "It's making for the harbor."

For a few seconds there was an appalled silence. A bandage slipped from Bethoc's hand and unspooled on the floor, then she came to her senses.

"Fetch your father and Mariola," she snapped at Thomas. "Fast as you can."

He ran.

She turned to the others. "Get your things. They mustn't find anything of yours. We've got twenty minutes before they're here."

"Is there somewhere we can hide?" asked Marius.

"Yes, but you won't find it on your own. Get your things!"

They scattered. There wasn't much to gather up, and they were back in the main room with their belongings bundled up in a couple of minutes, just as Thomas returned with his father and Mariola.

"Eneas, you and Thomas take them to the tombs and hide them," said Bethoc. "Mariola, get all the children into the schoolroom and make sure they're busy. We don't want the Shadowmen talking to any of them in case they mention we've got visitors. I'll tidy up here. Now go!"

Eneas and Thomas led the fugitives out of the village and along half-hidden pathways among the scrub, careful to keep out of sight of the sea. Eneas was surprisingly spry for his age, and they found themselves trotting to keep up. No one spoke.

After about ten minutes they came to an area of hummocky ground and Eneas slowed down.

"Watch your step," said Thomas, catching Aria's wrist. She looked down and saw a narrow slot in the earth in front of her, an edge of white stone beyond it. By now Eneas had stopped and was peering around.

"What's he looking for?" Nyssa whispered to Marius.

"I don't know."

A moment later he evidently found what he was seeking and set off again, motioning them to follow. He stopped about thirty feet away.

"Give us a hand with this stone," he said to Marius as Thomas reached them. A flat white square of stone the length of a man's forearm lay in front of them.

They set about levering it up, and after a few seconds had it tilted up on one edge, leaning against a boulder.

Where it had lain was a hole in the earth, like a mouth to the Underworld, narrow white steps sloping downward.

"Come on," said Thomas, and started down them. Marius followed, then Aria, Nyssa last, Kit's hand clamped to her arm like a manacle. Eneas stayed where he was.

The stairs widened a little as they descended. Enough light leaked in to see dimly. Nyssa counted steps: twenty-six, then level ground and a doorway. She stepped through after the others and found herself in a circular chamber about ten feet across.

Thomas looked around at them. "We'll have to put the stone back. You're as well hidden here as anywhere on the island. I'll come back when it's safe."

He turned and went back up the stairs and a few seconds later came the thud of the stone dropping into place; darkness settled around them like a shroud.

-:|:-   -:|:-   -:|:-

The ship tied up in the little harbor. It was a fifteen-minute walk from there to the village. The Shadowmen took their time, watching automatically for any signs of attack. Not that there would be any here. The people of Drakona were smart enough to know that Alaric could have their little community wiped out anytime he felt like it, so they were careful to do nothing to offend him. There was no hint of insurrection here.

When they reached the village, everything seemed normal. They passed the schoolroom, children learning their letters. An old woman sat on a bench in the sun outside her house.

She got to her feet as they approached, and stepped into the roadway. "Bethoc, chief of the village Elders," she said by way of introduction. "What brings you here?"

The man in charge nodded in acknowledgment. "We're tracking escaped criminals. Murderers. A man and two girls. They've got a boy with them: yellow hair, mute. They stole him — he's one of Lord Alaric's slaves — and murdered a captain of the guard."

"Dangerous then, likely?"

"Definitely. We know they set off north from Thira in a small boat. Have they been here?"

Bethoc shook her head. "No, but there was a boat wrecked on the Dragon's Teeth day before yesterday. Could've been them, I suppose."

"Survivors? Bodies?"

She shook her head again. "Neither. You know what those currents are like. There was some wreckage, but no bodies. We gathered it up. Do you want a look? Maybe there would be something you'd recognize if it was them."

"I doubt that, but I'll take a look. Meanwhile, you won't mind if we have a look around." It wasn't a question.

Bethoc spread her arms. "Help yourself. There's nothing worth hiding."

-:-   -:-   -:-

The darkness wasn't total. There was a gray rectangle where the door was—some light must be getting in around the edge of the stone. There was also a small hole high in the roof, through which a narrow shaft of light fell like a spear to the floor.

Nyssa listened to the sound of breathing: Aria's ragged and quick, Kit's quiet and light, Marius's slow and regular. Her own was too fast, as was her heart. She could hear her blood beat in her ears.

They sat with their backs to the wall directly across from the door, close together. At first, they'd tried to talk in whispers, but the sound was dead and flat, and it discouraged them into silence. They were afraid to talk any more loudly in case someone on the surface might hear them.

"Rats in a bottle," Marius muttered to himself. This was a situation over which he had no control. That was the worst thing. And if they *were* betrayed, or discovered, there was nothing he could do. There wasn't so much as a loose stone down here to use as a weapon. All they could do was wait.

Aria knotted her hands together. She shut her eyes, then opened them again. Which was worse? Both were awful. There was just enough light to make it as unsettling to have her eyes open as it was to have them shut.

She felt the walls closing in.

Don't be stupid, she told herself. *Your friends are around you. They're not panicking. Soon Thomas and his father will come back and let you out.*

What if they didn't? What if the Shadowmen killed everyone? Would they be strong enough to push the stone away from the stairway? They could be trapped down here to die of thirst in the dark . . .

-:-   -:-   -:-

There was nothing among the wreckage that the Shadowmen recognized. Bethoc left them to nose around the village and resumed her place on the bench, apparently unconcerned, busying her fingers on a piece of lace.

There was no reason for them to suspect that the fugitives were here. They must be checking all the nearby islands. A couple of hours and they'd be gone.

-:-   -:-   -:-

Nyssa was thirsty, and because she had no water it was all she could think about. A drink. It would be the first thing she'd find when they got out of here.

To distract herself, she began to feel around. The floor was just bare earth, hard as iron, no stones protruding, no trace of damp. Bodies would last a long time down here. She wondered where they'd gone, who they'd been. The tombs seemed much too elaborate for the villagers of Drakona.

She shuffled around to feel the wall. Large blocks of smooth stone, carefully fitted together. Where they joined, there was hardly room to push a fingernail between them.

"What are you doing?" Marius hissed.

"Nothing."

She ran her fingertips across the stone and found a groove. It felt too smooth to be a natural feature. She traced it — a spiral? She felt farther over the surface of the wall and came across other shapes cut into the blocks. It was difficult to visualize what they must look like. If only there was some light.

-:-   -:-   -:-

Their orders had been clear. A thorough search. That meant the island, not just the village. A waste of time, of course: The people of Drakona would have looked a sight more nervous if they'd been hiding anything. Better not skimp on the search, though. Someone might report it if they did.

They took a couple of the men from the village, who helpfully pointed out a cave that might have offered a place to hide. Nothing, of course.

They moved inland throughout the afternoon, wandering now more or less at random.

"Watch where you step here," one of the villagers said. Flat stones were set into the scrubby turf in front of them.

"What are these for?"

"Tomb entrances — from the old days. Nothing left in them now, of course, all robbed centuries ago."

The Shadowman probed the stone in front of him with a toe. "How many men does it take to lift one of these?"

"Three, or four for some of the really big ones. We can get one up if you want a look."

-:-　　-:-　　-:-

They were aware of a mutter of voices from the surface. Kit clutched at Nyssa's arm again. They all stared at the dim outline of the door.

A sudden blast of light blinded them. They struggled stiffly to their feet. Marius pushed the others behind him and squinted into the light.

A figure appeared. Only one, so far. It came closer and resolved itself into a grinning Thomas.

"They're gone. You can come out now."

Before they left the hole, Nyssa showed Marius the carving in the stone. He peered at it. "It's just like the lettering on your head. Were these the Keepers' tombs?"

A voice from the surface distracted them.

"Come on out of there!" It was Aria. "They want to put the stone back."

Nyssa took one last look and followed the others up into the light. Marius and Thomas heaved the stone into place again.

"Whose tombs were these?" she asked.

"Keepers, of course. I thought Bethoc would have told you."

"She was interrupted — remember?"

He grinned. "Right enough. This was the Keepers' burial island, for hundreds of years. Our ancestors were their tomb keepers. They can't have been very good at it, though. There's not a thing left in any of them. Not just here, all over the island."

"This isn't the only site, then?" Aria asked.

"No. There must be nearly two hundred tombs scattered around."

Nyssa shivered, suddenly feeling as if she was surrounded by the dead. "Let's go back."

-|-   -|-   -|-

Two days later they left Drakona on a fishing vessel bound for Idhra. It looked reassuringly large after their poor little lost boat, but none of them was particularly looking forward to being at sea again. Except Kit, that was. It was obvious he couldn't wait for the boat to cast off so that he could begin scanning for fish and dolphins.

Thanks to the generosity of the villagers, they now had a couple of changes of clothes each and plenty of food. Their hosts had insisted Marius take a hunting knife, too, and a bag of money that would certainly get them as far as the Mainland.

Bethoc and a few of the other villagers, including Mariola, had come down to the harbor to see them off.

"Keep that brother of yours safe," Bethoc said to Nyssa. "And for goodness' sake, fatten him up a bit." She ruffled Kit's hair, and he gave her a quick smile.

"Remember what I told you," she went on, turning to Aria, who nodded but said nothing in reply.

"And you." She turned finally to Marius, opened her mouth, but then seemed to change her mind about what she meant to say. "You have a good heart. I wish you good fortune to go with it."

They carried their bags on board and found a spot where they wouldn't be in the way, and the ship eased out of the narrow harbor mouth as everyone waved good-bye.

-⁞-　-⁞-　-⁞-

The fishing boat wasn't designed with passengers in mind, so it was a rather cramped and uncomfortable three days as it took its normal fishing run to Idhra, hoping to fill its hold with tuna to sell at the market there.

They sat on the deck, upwind of the smell of tuna guts.

"What about these tattoos, then?" said Aria in a businesslike tone.

"Which ones?" asked Nyssa.

"The birds — the Cranes. How much of a danger are they?"

"No one recognized them for years on the island," said Nyssa, "but now . . ."

"Now that we're being hunted, they mark us out," said Marius. "We'll have to keep them hidden. If only there was a way to get rid of them."

"It would just draw attention to them if we tried to get someone to change them now," said Nyssa, pushing windblown hair out of her eyes.

"But we could disguise them as something else," said Aria. "You can buy pigment the same color and paint it on. It'll last for a week, maybe two."

"Really? I've never heard of that," said Nyssa.

"We used to use it in the House of White Lilies. Some of our performances called for symbols of particular clans, or birth signs, or . . . if no one had the right tattoo, we just added it." She looked straight at Marius as she spoke, as though daring him to say anything remotely disapproving, but he just stared at the deck. "So all you have to do is think of a way to turn the bird into something else. We can probably buy pigment on Idhra. We need to get dye for Kit's hair, anyway."

Kit looked up at the mention of his name. Nyssa thought she'd better explain.

"We're going to dye your hair the same color as mine. That way, if Shadowmen are looking for you, they'll be less likely to notice you."

He pulled a piece of yellow hair forward and stared at it as though trying to imagine the new color, then shrugged.

The fishermen caught some tuna, but it wasn't a particularly good trip for them. Still, if tuna was scarce just now, what they had caught would bring a higher price, so they headed into the harbor at Idhra in reasonably good spirits. Nyssa, Kit, Marius, and Aria stayed below while the crew checked for any obvious signs of Shadowmen, but there were none.

They unloaded their belongings, said another round of good-byes, and went off to find the cheapest lodgings in the town.

Once again, they were on their own.

ALARIC

THE MISSING SISTER

None of his men had found a trace of the boy. Alaric was furious, even though in a sense it didn't matter. He had copies of the tattoo; he didn't need the boy for that. But when he found the girl, he wanted them both in his palace so that he could show the people of the Archipelago he had won and what he could do if they continued to defy him.

He had the men search again: buildings, outhouses, caves, everything. The townspeople were questioned more closely.

And then, something.

One of them remembered seeing the boy early on the day he had disappeared, walking up from the slipway with a brown-haired girl who looked a little older than him. The boy had not looked frightened.

Alaric sat thinking about that for a long time. *Was it possible? Surely not. Could this girl be the elusive sister?*

He had no real reason to think so, and yet . . .

But why would she appear on Thira now? And from where? And how had she spirited the boy away?

He sent men to check the ferry records, and a number of interesting facts began to fall into place.

A girl answering the description of the one seen near the slipway had arrived on a ferry from Korce two weeks ago. She was with another young woman and a man.

Captain Jaxom and one of his men had visited their lodgings to find the reason for their visit. The other young woman was from a dance hall in Korce. The girl was her maid — supposedly — and the man her bodyguard.

Jaxom had set off to visit this young woman on the day he disappeared, which was also, of course, the day the boy had disappeared.

Their lodgings — which had previously been rented by two known rebels — were now shuttered and empty, the woman who owned them having supposedly gone to visit a sister.

Then Jaxom's body had been found, just off the road that led to Mili.

A man at Mili had sold a small boat to two young women and a man a week ago. None of them was from Thira.

There had been no sign of these three or the boat since the day of the disappearances.

It was tempting to see all these facts fitting together to form a pattern. If they did, then these three had killed Jaxom and taken the boy away in the boat.

So . . . how to track them down? A challenge indeed. But on the other hand, what a prize: Take one and you took them all.

KIT REMEMBERS

"Do you remember the raid?" she had said. "When the Shadowmen took you?"

There were so many things he worked hard not to remember. His mind was a frightening place. He kept it in check by locking memories away in imaginary boxes inside his head. Most of the time he could keep all the boxes shut, but sometimes one of them would open when he wasn't paying attention — when he was tired, or especially frightened — and then the memory would burst out. It was terribly hard to shut one of these escaped memories away again. It could use up all his strength for days. It helped if he cut himself. When he did that he could focus more easily on what he needed to do to shut the box.

He had managed to keep the box shut when she asked him the question, but his mind kept going back to it as he hung over the side of the boat on the way to Idhra, watching water and fish speed by below him.

What would happen if *he* opened the box — just a crack — and peeked inside? He had never tried to do that, had never even considered doing it. It took him a whole day to pluck up enough courage.

He opened the box in his mind . . .

He didn't feel well. He had a fever and a cough, so when Mamma took Nyssa out for a walk along the dunes, he was left with Grandmother. He heard the two of them go, Nyssa chattering away as usual. She hardly ever stopped talking. It was hard to find a gap in which to say something. Sometimes he didn't bother. He was content just to listen and watch.

That morning, Grandmother sang to him and made him some herb tea that soothed his throat and made him doze off.

He woke to the sound of shouting, alone in the house. Climbing from his bed, he looked out the window toward the center of the village.

There were strange men. Huge men, some of them on great horses. He saw a glitter of metal. They had swords. He couldn't make out what they were shouting at the villagers crowded into the space in front of them.

Where was Grandmother? She was so bent and small he couldn't see her, but there was Papa at the back of the crowd. Kit went to open the door and run to his father when there was a scream. He froze, one hand on the door latch. More screams.

He ran back to the window, stared wide-eyed for a few seconds, then crawled under his bed and curled up tight, with his hands over his ears.

They still found him, though.

By that time the screaming had stopped and the only noise was the crackling of flames. The door opened slowly and he watched a pair of boots move about the room. Cupboards and chests were opened and closed. The boots came over to his bed, and he heard the blankets being pulled back. The boots stepped back and a hand went to the floor as their owner knelt and balanced to look under the bed.

He saw Kit and smiled.

After he had looked at the back of his head, the man carried him from the house. He was too frightened to scream or struggle. He saw brief glimpses of scenes he would try for years to forget: houses in flames, bodies scattered over the ground.

"I've got one of them," shouted the man who held him.

Another of them turned to look. "Let's hope one's enough to stop him having us executed for failing."

Kit let the water come back into focus, concentrated on breathing. His heart was hammering and he was soaked in sweat and shivering violently. He had done it. He had opened one of the terrible boxes, then managed to shut it again without having to hurt himself. He could do it.

He wrapped his arms around his chest and tried to stop shaking.

‡   ‡   ‡

Drakona seemed a long time ago.

It was five weeks since the boat had put them ashore on Idhra. They'd only waited there long enough to catch the next ferry to the Mainland. Idhra was too small to be safe; it would be much easier to disappear on the Mainland than on any of the islands.

They'd worked their way slowly northeast, staying a few days here and there, Marius picking up bits and pieces of work to eke out their funds. At the first opportunity they bought pigment and dye for Kit's hair. When it was done, Aria and Marius stared at Nyssa and Kit.

"Now you look like brother and sister," said Marius, looking from one to the other.

Kit was fascinated by his new reflection and would stop to look at it in mirrors and puddles and ponds.

Marius had spent some time sketching possible ways to disguise the Crane tattoos, and they had agreed on an abstract, flowerlike design that wouldn't take too long to do, since there would be three for Aria to draw every week.

She worked quickly and carefully with a fine brush, tongue stuck out as she concentrated. It only took about ten minutes for each of them.

Nyssa squinted at her arm. "It can't be this simple, can it?"

"*Sshh!*" said Aria. "Nothing's ever too simple. There." She finished working on Marius's arm and sat back on her heels. "That's quite good. I can hardly see the bird, even though I know it's there. Let it dry before you pull your sleeve down."

Now feeling slightly less vulnerable, they pushed away from the busy coastal plains into the upland regions where towns were less frequent, looking for somewhere they could stay for a while at least.

Nyssa had thought that Aria might leave when they reached the Mainland.

"Do you want me to go?" she retorted when Nyssa broached the subject, looking her in the eye. "I understand. You're a family now. You don't need an outsider."

"Of course I don't want you to go, but don't you want to leave? You'd be safer well away from us. You could start to put your life back together."

"How will Marius feel about me staying?" Aria asked sharply.

"I'm sure he'd be pleased."

"Really? He still doesn't approve of me. He'll never think I'm respectable. Maybe he'd be happier if I wasn't around you or Kit."

"Don't be silly."

"I'm not."

But she stayed.

+ + +

There was one town they had stayed in for almost four weeks and had begun to think might be a place where they could at least sit out the winter. Marius had found work on a farm, and they had taken the cheapest lodgings they could. Aria had hired a loom and they had invested some of their small pot of cash in yarn and thread for her.

The weather was growing steadily colder. Soon they would have to buy warmer clothes. They worried about money all the time.

They still had to eat, though, and one evening they were sitting in a fleapit inn, concentrating on their bowls of stew, with half an ear on the conversations around them in the busy room and half an ear on their own.

A single word in one of the conversations caught their attention at once, the way the sound of your own name always shrieks at you through any level of noise.

"Shadowmen, you say?"

"Aye. I was down in Darfin last week, taking the wife down to see her mother while the road's still passable. Innkeeper there told me there were half a dozen around the town. Never saw them myself, mind you."

"Keep eating," said Marius under his breath, aware that they had all frozen mid-mouthful.

"What were they after, so far from Thira?"

"On the lookout for some criminals who escaped from Thira. Murderers. Apparently the trail led there. A man and two women and a mute boy with yellow hair. Didn't see them, either, mind." The man who was speaking took a thoughtful swallow of beer. "Shame, that. If they really are ruthless murderers, I could've sent them to see the wife's mother."

He and his companion roared with laughter, and the conversation turned to other things.

Nyssa, Marius, Aria, and Kit finished their meal mechanically. No one said a word until they were well away from the inn.

"Did we come through Darfin?" Nyssa asked.

"Yes," said Marius. "We stopped there for a night."

"What color was Kit's hair?"

"Brown by that time."

"So they might not pick up our trail there," Aria said, hoping against hope.

Marius grimaced. "We can't take the chance, can we? They could appear on our doorstep any day. We have to leave."

They were all as silent as Kit during the cold and gloomy trudge home. Except that it wasn't home anymore, was it?

Was this what it was always going to be like from now on? Nyssa wondered. She looked over at Aria's face, blankly neutral. They had to persuade her to leave: She'd have a better chance of some sort of normal life if she struck out on her own. Marius, Kit, and she were bound together, but Aria didn't have to be part of their fate, which at best seemed likely to be destitution, and at worst didn't bear thinking about.

They left the next morning with no clear idea of where they were heading, and too little money to make the journey comfortable.

The only good thing, Nyssa thought as they walked straight into the cold wind, was that they could talk without fear of being overheard.

Marius had done a lot of thinking during a largely sleepless night. He drew Nyssa back a little.

"We have to start to get Kit talking more normally," he said. "The Shadowmen are tracking a mute boy. It's far too noticeable anywhere we stop. It's only a matter of time before someone sets them on our trail again."

"I know," said Nyssa worriedly. "I'm afraid it won't be easy, though."

"I'm sure it won't. And I think it has to be your job. You're the one he trusts. You're the one he remembers."

She nodded.

"The other thing—and I don't have any ideas about it—is that we need some excuse to be traveling together like this. Not many people choose to move around at this time of year. If someone gets too interested, what do we say?" He pushed his hair out of his eyes and gave a rueful smile. "I'm not very good at being devious."

"Oh, I don't know. You managed to pretend not to be my uncle for years without me realizing."

"That was easy. It was wishful thinking," he deadpanned.

She jabbed an elbow hard into his ribs. "On the other hand, back on the island, when we ran away from the Drowned Boy, I knew perfectly well you didn't have a plan."

"Oh." He looked quite crestfallen.

"That's why I gave you such a hard time. I didn't want you thinking you could fool me."

"Well, I'm certainly cured of that."

✛ ✛ ✛

That night they made themselves as comfortable as they could in a hayloft. It was dry and reasonably warm, but very scratchy, and of course they couldn't risk a fire. The sweet, dusty smell rose around them as they passed out food and settled themselves in their blankets. It would be dark soon.

Marius was talking to Aria about reasons to be on the road at this time of year. It didn't sound as if they were coming up with anything. Nyssa heard Aria say, "We're a bit of an odd grouping as well. That doesn't help."

It was time to find Kit's voice.

He munched a piece of bread, gazing out of a break in the plank wall at the twilit landscape outside.

"Kit?" He turned to look at her. "I know you haven't really talked for a long time. I think I understand why you stopped." He gave her a look that said, clear as words, *You have no idea*, but she pressed on. "It's time to start again. It's safe to talk now. In fact, we *need* you to talk. You heard what those men said at the inn. The Shadowmen are hunting a mute, yellow-haired boy. We've sorted out the hair. Now we have to stop people thinking you're mute. You're not, anyway. You've just forgotten about talking. So we need to practice."

He nodded his head thoughtfully. After a minute he said, "Yes."

It still didn't sound like a normal voice, but it was a start.

⊹   ⊹   ⊹

The next day, they walked a little ahead of the others.

"You know I don't remember anything about living in the village with you when we were small?" He nodded. "I thought you could tell me about it."

And so it began. Haltingly, with great chasms of silence between the fragments of sound he'd almost forgotten how to make, he told her about her childhood.

"There was Papa, and Mamma, and Grandmother, and there was us. I don't remember Marius." The words didn't come out like that, of course. It took him almost five minutes to get that far.

"What did our mother look like?" Nyssa prompted him.

He closed his eyes for a few seconds as he walked along the road, getting the picture clear in his mind.

"She smelled nice. Like herbs. And apples. Her hair was curly, not like ours. Brown, like yours. I remember a blue dress. And the flute. Papa made it. Made it for her." He smiled at the memory. "She played every night when she put us to bed." He pulled it from his pocket and looked at it fondly, then fell silent.

Nyssa let him alone. How long must it have been since he said so much?

+   +   +

It was a half-ruined drover's hut that night. They tucked themselves into the end that still had a roof and lit a fire. Cold food again, though. Even with the fire it was difficult to feel warm.

"I've been thinking about what you said," Marius said to Aria, "about us being an odd group to be traveling together. You're right." He cleared his throat. "I thought that perhaps you and I could pose as . . ."

". . . as husband and wife?" Her voice would have frozen soup in a pot. Marius was suddenly very busy building up the fire.

"It was just an idea," he muttered. "Not a very good one, it seems."

"No," said Aria crisply.

"You think of something better, then."

"All right, I will."

There wasn't a lot more conversation that night.

-|-   -|-   -|-

"Grandmother used to sing a song about piglets. It always made you laugh. Me, too."

For a second, Nyssa felt she was about to remember the song, but it slipped away from her. She shook her head. "I don't remember. I wish I did. I wonder why you remember it all, but I forgot?"

Kit shrugged.

"Tell me something else. What did Father do?"

"He had some cows. And he fished. And he grew apples. Do you remember the orchard?"

Once again, none of this came out smoothly or easily. Every word was still a struggle, but his determination to do this was clear. She was full of admiration, seeing a glimpse of the inner strength that had sustained him through his terrible childhood.

When they stopped for a rest in the middle of the day, Marius said rather tentatively, "Well, did you think of anything?"

Aria tossed away her apple core.

"Actually, I did. The best lie is the one that's closest to the truth—you know that saying, don't you?" Marius nodded. "So we stick with the truth that Kit and Nyssa are brother and sister and that you're their uncle. The only thing we change is that I'm their aunt."

"But last night when I . . ."

She cut him off. "I'm not your wife. I'm your sister."

Marius took a moment to digest that. "And why are we running around the country with no money, and winter coming on?"

Aria allowed herself a very smug smile.

"Kit and Nyssa were orphaned recently. Their parents both died of a fever — completely unexpectedly. Their father — our brother — had overstretched his business, not expecting to die, of course. They left their children nothing but debt. Everything was sold but there still wasn't enough to pay off the creditors, so Kit and Nyssa were to be sold as indentured workers to clear the debt. We couldn't bear to see that happen, so we've gone on the run with them."

There was a short silence, while Nyssa, Kit, and Marius absorbed this.

"That's brilliant," said Marius at last, shaking his head slowly. "It accounts for . . . everything."

"And there are very few people who wouldn't be sympathetic to what we've done. Supposedly done," Aria pointed out.

"It even explains why we're so poor," said Nyssa. "That *is* brilliant." Aria was flushed with a mixture of pleasure and embarrassment. "How did you think of it?" she added.

Unexpectedly, Aria's face clouded. She shrugged. "Just an idea," she said, and it was obvious she wanted the matter left there.

+ + +

Four days later, they walked wearily through the outskirts of Armeni, the first town of any size they had come to since they had fled.

It nestled in a bowl-shaped valley at the foot of the mountains, protected from the worst of the winter weather that would soon come howling down from the north. There was an air of toughness and self-sufficiency about the town. It felt like a place where people were used to coping without too much contact with the outside world.

A week of walking in increasingly cold weather and sleeping in barns had done nothing to improve anyone's appearance. If there was a bright side, it was that traveling in this way had hardly eaten into their reserves of money at all.

They hoped to find work here for a few days or weeks to shore up their fragile finances. Surely they had come far enough to be relatively safe, for a while, at least? They took a dormitory room for the four of them in the cheapest inn they could find and set about making themselves look presentable enough to approach potential employers, changing gratefully into clean, dry clothes that weren't full of bits of hay and the smell of cattle.

Marius got the address of a work broker, who registered and matched up those seeking laborers with those looking for employment.

The girls and Kit got directions to some of the largest inns, hoping that they might be taken on in the kitchens. They had no luck at the first three, but when they knocked at the back door of the fourth and explained themselves, the innkeeper said, "I've been thinking I could do with a bit of help. There's not work for all of you, though. I want one person who can be a proper help with the cooking."

"I can do that," said Nyssa quickly, and told the woman about the Drowned Boy.

"All right," she said. "I'll give you a try for the next few days. I can't help the rest of you, though."

"Just a minute," said Aria. "Do you have any entertainers in the inn?"

"No."

"I can sing, talk to people, make them want to stay longer, buy more food and drink."

The woman looked at her narrowly.

"Nothing more than that," Aria said quickly. "Why not try me out for a couple of days? You'll know from your takings if it's worth your while. What have you got to lose?" She gave a beaming, innocent smile.

"All out in the open, mind," said the innkeeper. "Just the singing and talking. Nothing else."

Aria looked hurt. "Of course not. I'm an entertainer, not . . . anything else."

"And I hope you've got better clothes than that if you're hoping to charm my customers."

"Of course." She waved dismissively. "This was just for traveling."

"All right, then. Let's see what you can do on Thursday and Friday and Saturday. Then I'll decide. But I've got nothing for the boy."

"He could fetch and carry, couldn't he? You don't have to pay him — just a meal every day. He's strong, and he's quiet — aren't you, Kit?"

Kit nodded.

"Two for the price of one," said Aria brightly.

"I don't know . . ."

"Just try us all for a couple of days. We're good workers. You'll see."

The woman sighed. "All right. I'll give you a try. But, mind, I'm making no promises."

As they walked away down the street, Nyssa glanced sidelong at Aria.

"What?"

"Are you going to tell Marius what you're doing?"

"It's none of his business *what* I do," Aria replied tartly. "He's not my . . . father. Anyway, there's nothing wrong with what I'm going to be doing. Don't tell me you never flirted with men in the Drowned Boy to get them to leave you better tips or buy more drinks?"

"No!" She stopped to think. "Well, maybe a bit."

"There you are, then. Now I need to find somewhere to buy a decent dress and a few bits and pieces."

"Can we afford that?"

"We have to. Don't worry, I'll soon earn it back. I'll make sure she wants to keep me on."

When they got back to their lodgings, Marius was already there.

"Did you get anything?" asked Nyssa.

He nodded. "Fixing a roof. It'll keep me going for a couple of weeks—the whole thing's rotten. I'll be cutting shingles for days." He sighed. "I hate cutting shingles. Pay's not too bad, though. What about you three?"

"We all got jobs in the same inn. Place called the Woolpack. Not a proper job for Kit—no money, just meals. I'm in the kitchen with him, of course, and Aria . . ."

"I'm serving," she said with a smile.

"Good, good. Well, with any luck the Shadowmen won't track us here for a long time—if at all. We haven't left them much of a trail to follow."

-:-   -:-   -:-

"Four soups!" The kitchen door had opened just enough for the barman's red face to appear with the latest order. "And two mutton."

Kit moved to ladle out soup and Nyssa dished up the mutton, then cut bread to go with the meals. She loaded up the biggest wooden tray and Kit pulled the door wide so that she could get through. The inn was hot and bright with firelight, and seething with noise.

"Which table?" she called across the bar. The barman jerked a hand over his shoulder without turning around, busy with beer.

"Nearest the door," he yelled.

Aria caught sight of her and came over to help, reaching the bowls and plates across to the waiting customers. She wore the dress she'd bought the day after they arrived, kingfisher blue, with a neckline that was quite demure—unless she bent over a table to pick up glasses or put down plates, of course.

Aria had proved very popular with the customers, as had Nyssa's cooking. Mistress Marin, the innkeeper, had added up the takings at the end of their third trial night and raised her eyebrows.

"Well, you all seem to be earning your keep," she said drily. "Let's say you're hired, so long as things keep up this way."

That had been three weeks ago and so far things had kept up. Nyssa suspected that this was as close as she would ever come to her old life again. To be cooking in an inn kitchen soothed her more than she would ever have thought possible.

Kit was constantly at her side, helping her carry food back from the market, watching as she cooked—beginning to help, in fact. He picked things up quickly and could be left to make the bread every morning now, while Nyssa gave herself up to chopping and boiling and roasting and slicing.

Aria had dyed his hair again before the color could fade, and every week she repainted their tattoos.

They were making enough money between them to get by, and had taken a couple of rooms in a better lodging house. They didn't see a great deal of Marius most days: He was away early in the morning, first to cut or fit his wretched shingles and then to do an erratic succession of other jobs. Most nights he came into the Woolpack for a meal, though, and sometimes stayed for a little, to hear Aria sing. If he had any misgivings about her job, he had kept them to himself.

Kit was speaking a little more now, though Nyssa was beginning to doubt that he would ever feel comfortable talking.

No one mentioned Shadowmen.

Nyssa was right, he knew that. He had to talk, or his silence, which used to keep him safe, would put them all in danger. But they didn't understand just how difficult it was. They couldn't understand, of course. They had no idea what it had been like.

His early memories of life on Thira were patchy. At first, Alaric hadn't paid him any attention, once he'd had his head shaved and copied the writing he said was hidden there. Kit had often wondered why he hadn't just had him killed after that. Sometimes he wished he had.

Some of the other slaves looked out for him, as much as they dared. They would filch him bits and pieces of food from the kitchens so he didn't go too hungry, though he didn't need much when he was that young and too small to do much work.

When he was six or seven, though, Alaric seemed to remember that he was there and began to take a personal interest in him, and things got much worse. Alaric seemed to delight in setting him tasks that he wasn't quite old enough, or big enough, or strong enough to do properly. It took quite a time to realize that the White Wolf enjoyed having an excuse to punish him.

Sometimes, too, he would send for Kit just to beat him. One of the other slaves would scrub him clean in the bath and hand him a fresh tunic, never meeting his eyes. Then Kit would be taken to Alaric's rooms, where he'd be waiting, a cat-o'-nine-tails clenched in his fist.

Those were the worst times.

The hours he spent with the other slaves were even more important to him then. They were his only escape.

One of the kitchen girls — Ismene — who had always been fond of him, taught him his letters, so that when he was sent off through Alaric's palace on some errand, he would look at the torn books and scrolls that littered many of the rooms. They had been carelessly tossed from shelves and kicked aside or trodden underfoot by Alaric and his men, who had no regard for them at all. Kit would pick up pieces of parchment and smooth them out, carefully sounding out the words of those he could understand. Some of them were stories, others he didn't understand at all.

And then, one day, Alaric found out that the others had been helping him, Ismene in particular.

He came down to the kitchens himself, a thing unheard of, with two of his men, and had Ismene hanged from one of the beams while he and the other slaves were forced to watch.

After that no one helped him. No one spoke to him. Except Alaric. All that he could do was shut himself away in his own head.

He didn't speak again until he roused Nyssa on the beach at Drakona.

He came out of his reverie in the yard at the back of the Woolpack, shaking from head to foot, and was immediately sick. The hens he had been feeding pecked interestedly at the pool of vomit.

He tried for a long time to shut that box in his head, but he couldn't do it until he sneaked one of Nyssa's knives out of the kitchen.

-:-   -:-   -:-

When she saw his arms, and the clumsy bandages, Nyssa said, "Oh, Kit, what have you done?"

She washed the cuts and bound them up properly while he stared past her at the yellow-gray sky. She turned his arms over and touched the cross-hatching of silvery scars.

"Why do you do this, Kit? I don't understand. Why do you hurt yourself?"

He spoke, for once, without her having to urge him. "Don't ask. Never ask."

ALARIC

THE NET TIGHTENS

Alaric widened the search. He stared at his maps for some time, trying to decide what he would do if he were one of the fugitives.

Their boat was small and had been bought here on the north side of the island. To the south lay a seven-day passage for a boat that size, through open and unpredictable waters, before the next landfall. To the north, on the other hand, lay a scatter of islands that formed a chain of short hops from here to the Mainland.

So unless they were lunatics, they had gone north.

He sent a couple of boats off to do a sweep of the nearby islands. They had to come ashore somewhere to buy supplies. There would be someone who would talk for money. There always was.

After some thought he also sent off half a dozen men to Korce, just in case the other girl had been stupid enough to go back. She hadn't, of course, but another interesting fact emerged.

The girl, whose name was Aria, had only recently moved to the city from one of the islands where his sources had indicated the Keeper girl might be.

Aria had left for a few days in Thira with another girl: an old friend, Aria had told her mistress, who had appeared without warning and been allowed to stay in the House of White Lilies for a couple of nights.

And, of course, she hadn't returned.

Alaric was more convinced than ever that he had been right.

His men trawled the islands without any result, until they tried Idhra.

"Yes," said the man in the ferry office. "I remember them. Pretty girls, you see." He smiled at the memory. "Don't see so many of them as I used to. A man, too, and a yellow-haired boy. They were here about two weeks ago. Bought tickets for the Mainland. Singles."

The Shadowmen sent a coded message to Alaric, replenished their ship's supplies, and set off for the Mainland on the next tide.

15

ROON'S TRAVELING PLAYERS

Kit stood motionless, staring at the sky, a forgotten bucket of chicken feed hanging loosely from one hand. Around his feet the chickens pushed and squabbled, protesting their hunger.

Through the kitchen doorway behind him came the rhythmic sound of Nyssa chopping vegetables. He was oblivious to it, eyes fixed on the clouds heaped above him and what drifted from them. White flakes settled and melted on his upturned face. He wiped at them with a hand and looked in wonder at the film of water on it, then dropped the bucket and ran for the door. The chickens descended on the spilled food with squawks of delight.

Nyssa stopped what she was doing, trying to gauge the expression on his face. He tugged at her arm, trying to get her to come outside. She shook her head. "You have to say something to me. Tell me what you want."

He rolled his eyes, but he swallowed and thought and said, "Come and see. What is it?"

She smiled and went with him at once.

He almost pulled her out of the door. The chickens were still in an argumentative heap around the dropped bucket, but the ground around them had turned white.

"Snow! It's snowing, Kit!" She laughed and put out a hand to catch the fat white flakes that drifted down like feathers. "I always wondered what it looked like. I've heard about it, but I've never seen it before. It's frozen rain. William used to talk about it snowing sometimes when he was young."

Kit turned slowly on the spot, arms outspread, face upturned, hair starred with falling flakes. The snow was falling faster now, whirling around them. The hens went clucking and chuntering off to their house for shelter. Kit was fascinated by the sight of their tracks and his own footprints in the snow. Nyssa had never seen him this interested in anything but the sea, and he was shivering before she managed to persuade him to come inside.

Once it started, it seemed to snow more or less constantly for the next two weeks. Marius was unimpressed, having seen it before, but Aria was charmed. It was amazing, however, how fast the novelty wore off and it became simply an inconvenience.

It was the silence that Nyssa noticed most, lying in her bed in the morning with blankets and clothes heaped around her, a silence as though the landscape surrounding them was holding its breath. And then, when she opened the shutters and rubbed the frost from the glass, white flakes would still be drifting down.

Snow was nothing out of the ordinary in Armeni, and although there was almost a foot lying on the ground, people simply forced paths through it and got on with their normal business. The Woolpack certainly wasn't noticeably quieter.

There wasn't so much work available for Marius, though, and some days he spent hours in their lodgings, whittling at pieces of wood. Finally, when one was finished to his satisfaction, he handed it to Kit.

"Here. This is for you."

Kit looked from his face to what lay in his hand. After a few seconds he stretched out and took it cautiously.

"Go on. Try it."

It was a whistle. Kit raised it to his lips and blew, tried the different notes. After a while he lowered it and smiled a little at Marius.

"Thank you."

Nyssa's heart was in her mouth. It was the first time he'd said a word directly to Marius, the closest he'd come to touching him voluntarily. She caught Marius's eye and smiled.

+ + +

The year turned and the snow melted in town, though it still lay thick on the peaks around it. Between them, they were making enough money to get by. No rumors of Shadowmen disturbed Armeni's peace.

+ + +

"Do you remember when Grandmother made you a doll? You threw it in the fire because it had a green dress and you'd wanted a red one."

Nyssa shook her head. "No, I don't remember that, either. What a brat I must have been to do that. Are you sure you're not making it up?"

He shook his head. "You *were* a brat. Always wanted your own way, even then. Same as now."

It took her a few seconds to realize he was making a joke. She pushed him into a puddle of slush.

"You're the one who's a brat!" she said.

He shook his head. "I'm older. You should be polite to me."

She stopped and looked at him. It had never occurred to her. "Are you?"

He nodded. "Papa told me." He pointed at her. "Little sister! Hah!"

They arrived back at their lodgings to find two carts and several horses milling around in the yard as the stable boy tried to find space for all of them.

They went up to their room on the second floor and opened the door quietly so as not to disturb Aria, who was usually asleep at this time. Not today, though. She was wide-awake and looking miffed.

"What a noise there's been!" she said. "I haven't slept a wink. I don't know how many people have come in on those carts, but it sounds like an army. No," she corrected herself, "not an army. A circus. I don't know where they've gone now." She looked out the window at the continuing chaos in the yard. "That boy's going to get squashed."

"Why don't you go down and help him, Kit?" asked Nyssa.

He gave a sigh, but tramped off down the stairs again readily enough. The girls watched as the other boy gratefully accepted his gestured offer of help and they and the horses disappeared into the stables.

"Not a word," said Nyssa, sighing herself.

"He's getting better."

"I suppose so. But he'll never be an ordinary boy, will he?"

Aria rubbed Nyssa's shoulder in a gesture of comfort. "I doubt he will. How could he be?"

"I know."

Aria suddenly yawned hugely. "Well, if it's going to stay reasonably quiet, I'm going to have a sleep, otherwise I'll look a wreck tonight and customers will be leaving early to avoid seeing me instead of staying longer and drinking more."

Laughing, Nyssa pulled the shutters closed and, following Aria's example, kicked off her shoes and lay down on her own bed.

They were both dozing by the time Kit came back in. He was sharing the room with them — he couldn't be persuaded to share with Marius. "I can't, Nyssa," Kit had said, even more haltingly than usual. "I know he's not like . . . him . . . Alaric. I know he won't hurt me, but . . . I can't do it."

She could see that he wasn't going to change his mind, so she left it. In fact it made some sense, since Kit and the girls kept quite different hours from Marius. He, too, curled up on his bed and dozed off. It was quiet except for the droning buzz of a fly trapped behind the shutters.

They were all woken minutes later by a dreadful shriek from one of the other rooms, closely followed by the sound of a door crashing open, and footsteps thundering along the hallway and down the stairs.

Nyssa sat bolt upright, heart hammering; sleep fled, taking with it a vague memory of a woman's face smiling at her, curly brown hair, and the scent of apples. In the dimness of the shuttered room she could see that Aria and Kit looked as panic-stricken as she felt.

"What in the world was that?" she hissed. "It sounded like someone being murdered."

For a few seconds there was silence. They got up and went to the door to listen. Nothing. Aria was on the verge of opening it when there was another terrible scream, this time from the yard.

"She's dead! She's dead! I'll kill you, Lark!"

Nyssa, Kit, and Aria shot across the room and opened the shutters a little. After a few seconds they opened them wide and stared down, fascinated at the vision below them.

A little girl, eight or nine years old, stood in the yard. She had a tangle of black curls that came halfway down her back, and her sharp-featured face was clenched and scarlet with fury. Over her dress she wore a long purple cloak with a rip near one edge. It was much too big for her and trailed in the dirt.

They heard the sound of shutters opening a few rooms down from where they stood, and a boy's head popped out, black-haired and also rather red in the face.

"Shut up, Thorn! You'll wake everyone else."

"I don't care. She's dead."

"Don't be ridiculous. She's a doll, she can't be dead."

The girl held up a wooden doll's body in one hand, and its severed head in the other. "Of course she's dead. You pulled her head off!"

"Oh, for goodness' sake! You pulled it off yourself last week. It's only just been fixed. You know we can mend it easily enough. Anyway, never mind the stupid doll. Wait until Roon sees what you've done to the Queen of the Underworld's cloak. You'll be in big trouble."

Nyssa, Aria, and Kit were entranced. "Definitely a circus," muttered Aria.

Just then the girl seemed to notice for the first time that she had an audience. She stared hard at them for a few seconds, then stuck her tongue out and with an insolent toss of her head turned to come back into the building, cloak trailing behind her.

The boy at the window looked along at them with a sheepish smile. "Sorry," he said, shrugging as if to say, *What can I do*? He disappeared back inside, closing the shutters. Small bare feet stomped past in the corridor and a door banged shut.

"Well," said Aria. "I hope they won't be staying for long."

"The Queen of the Underworld's cloak," mused Nyssa. "What on earth did he mean?"

After that everything stayed quiet, and they went to sleep until it was time to go back to the Woolpack for the evening's work. It was only Wednesday, so it wasn't likely to be a particularly busy night, but word had got around the town about the good food and entertainment to be had at the inn, so it wasn't likely to be particularly quiet, either.

It had begun to drizzle as they walked along. The girls pulled up their shawls to protect their hair, but Kit opened his hands and stuck out his tongue, trying to catch raindrops, smiling good-naturedly as they laughed at him.

Back at the inn, using the skinny rabbits Marius had brought her, Nyssa had made a stew, adding barley and some winter vegetables. She missed the endless supply of fish she had been used to at the Drowned Boy, but she could produce something tasty, whatever ingredients she had.

When Marius came, she put a huge bowlful down in front of him on the table and sat down herself for a few minutes.

"What was it today?" she asked him as he spooned up the stew.

"Fencing," he said through a mouthful of rabbit. "Wood, not swords."

She grinned at him. "Did you see the new people at the lodging house?"

He shook his head and swallowed. "Heard them, though. Some man reciting poetry in a very loud voice, and a girl squealing." He broke off a piece of bread. "Did you squeal when you were younger?"

She shook her head. "I think Oonagh would soon have cured me of that if I'd tried it. We heard the girl this afternoon, though. What a fuss! All because her doll was broken. There's a boy, too—he doesn't seem to be so noisy—but I didn't hear any poetry."

"I wonder how many of them there are?" mused Marius. "It sounded like quite a few."

"Anyway, I'd better get back to the kitchen. Mistress Marin doesn't like to see me idle." Nyssa got up. "See you later."

He smiled good-bye at her and turned his attention fully to the stew.

The night wore on and the rain got heavier. New arrivals to the Woolpack steamed gently beside the fire as they ate and drank. Conversation rose and fell. Soon it would be time for Aria to sing.

The door banged open. Heads turned to see who had disturbed the peace. Silhouetted in the doorway was a tall, fat man, wearing a wide-brimmed hat with a feather in it. He stood quite still until he was sure that everyone's eyes were on him, then stepped all the way inside and, sweeping off his hat, bowed extravagantly to the room.

Nyssa, clearing plates, stopped what she was doing and looked up along with everyone else at the man who'd just come in.

He strode to the bar, unfastening his wet cloak with a flourish and dropping it and the hat with its soggy feather on an empty chair as he passed.

"A pint of your best, please," he said to the barman in a booming voice. Nyssa — and everyone else, for that matter — stared their fill at his broad back as he waited for his beer. There was a great deal of curly brown hair. It fell past his shoulders — much longer than was normal for a man to wear it in the Archipelago. He was dressed in a tunic and trousers of rather threadbare dark green velvet, with highly polished, down-at-the-heel boots of brown leather.

The barman set his beer before him, gawping openly. The man picked it up and turned to survey his audience.

"Good health, my friends." He lifted the mug in a toast, raised it to his lips, and drank it in a single draft. "Splendid," he said, wiping his mouth with the back of one hand.

He had gained everyone's rapt attention already, so they were ready to give him a hearing when he started to address them.

"Good evening, good people. My name is Mallery Roon." He gave another bow, as though receiving applause.

"I have the good fortune to be the actor-manager of the finest theater troupe in the Archipelago: Roon's Traveling Players. We entertain princes and paupers, honest men and villains, old and young. We have plays for poets, for lovers, for students of history, for the happy, and for the grieving."

The Queen of the Underworld's cloak, thought Nyssa. *Of course! That explained it. Aria hadn't been far wrong when she said a circus.*

"And now," Roon went on, "our tour of the Archipelago brings us to Armeni. Two days to refresh ourselves after the rigors of the road, to regild our scenery and make sure that our costumes and our voices are at their finest, and then we shall present to you, my friends, two new works: *The Queen of the Underworld's Daughter,* a tragedy" — he pressed his hands to his heart and closed his eyes with a sigh — "I can scarcely bear to think of it. Men will weep, my friends; men will weep.

"Our second offering will be *Love Lies Undone,* a furiously funny romance, sure to please the ladies of the town." He cast a suggestive glance at Aria, who was watching with a half smile from a corner of the room. "Both to be performed on Friday and Saturday at sunset. Until then, my friends, farewell!"

He bowed yet again, caught up his cloak and hat, and walked out of the inn like a king from his throne room. There was silence for a few seconds, then a great hubbub of voices and laughter. Roon had certainly had the effect he sought, for as Nyssa collected plates, he was the only topic of conversation.

Back in the kitchen she tried to explain to Kit, who had missed the performance, what was going on.

"I wonder if he's found the hole in the Queen of the Underworld's cloak," she said, half to herself.

When she went back out with food for a couple of late-comers, Marius had left, and Aria was about to sing. Her sweet voice followed Nyssa back into the kitchen.

"Shall we go and watch the Players, Kit? They used to come to the island sometimes. Not these ones, I mean. There are lots of different troupes. I suppose they all claim to be the best as well. Anyway, it'll be a change."

She stopped talking and looked at his confused expression. "I don't suppose traveling theaters came to Thira, did they?"

He shook his head, but he spoke, too. "No."

"Would you like to see them? All of us together?"

"Yes. But I'm not sure I understand what they do."

She smiled broadly. It had sounded almost like a normal sentence.

-:|:-   -:|:-   -:|:-

She'd half expected, as she went to bed late that night, to be woken by some sort of disturbance from along the corridor,

275

where Roon's Players seemed to occupy three or four rooms, but all was quiet throughout the night. The sound of sawing and hammering woke her the next morning, though Kit and Aria slept on through it. At first, she couldn't remember where she was.

She'd been in an orchard. She was very small, riding on someone's shoulders so she could reach up for apples and drop them into the basket he carried. Sometimes she pulled his hair, and he pretended to cry. He had black, wavy hair.

She woke up completely, trying to clutch at the remains of the dream, but it had slipped away.

There was another burst of hammering. Nyssa unlatched the shutters and looked out into the yard to see Marius hard at work on . . . something.

A few minutes later she was dressed and heading down the stairs to find out what he was doing.

He grinned at her sleepy face. He was sawing a broken corner off a big board painted with mountains.

"I've joined Roon's Traveling Players," he said, as the broken piece fell to the ground.

Nyssa looked at him quizzically.

"Mallery Roon went to the work broker yesterday. Scenery repairs needed. Costumes, too," he added as an afterthought. "I wondered if Aria might be interested in that."

"I'll ask her later." Curious, Nyssa wandered over to the heap of boards that was waiting for Marius's attention.

"It's a right mess," he said. "No one's been looking after it. Some of it's just about to fall to pieces." He spoke around a mouthful of nails as he fitted a new piece to the top of the mountains.

"Can we go to watch? I know we need to be careful with money, but . . ."

"I think we can afford to waste that much. I can't imagine it's going to cost a lot. Who knows, I might even be able to get us some free tickets. Anyway, we deserve to enjoy something once in a while."

-:-　　-:-　　-:-

Sunset. On an indeterminate patch of ground that was neither exactly in nor out of the town, Roon's Traveling Players (with Marius's help) had set up their stage. A line of blazing torches guided the citizens of Armeni, like large, earthbound moths, toward the frayed red curtain that, for the moment, hid the scenery.

Nyssa, Marius, Kit, and Aria sat on a blanket close to the stage. Despite what she had said to Kit, she was surprised that they had all managed to be here together, but Mistress Marin, with a sigh, had given all her staff the night off. So many people were going to see the performance that she had decided it wasn't even worth opening the inn that evening. Besides, she wanted to see the Players herself. With any luck, everyone would come to the Woolpack tomorrow to talk about it.

Certainly, as Nyssa looked around, at least half the town seemed to be jostling for space behind her. It was just as well that they'd come early, in spite of having free tickets, thanks to Marius.

Five minutes later, the torches were snuffed by a wiry man Nyssa had seen around the boarding house. The audience grew quiet, except for the monotonous crying of a small child somewhere. All attention was focused on the curtains now. After another few seconds, they moved apart, rather jerkily, to reveal Mallery Roon, his large frame clothed in a black robe embroidered with golden lightning brands, a crown of gold wire on his dark curls. Flickering lights at the front of the stage cast trembling shadows across his face.

He waited for absolute silence before he spoke.

"Good people! Be welcome here tonight. We seek to entertain you—that is our art. If we can move you to laughter and to tears, then we have succeeded.

"Now," he went on, sweeping his arms wide, "lay aside your toils, your cares of everyday. Free your hearts and minds and come with us. Come first to the Netherworld of the Gods." The lights on the stage somehow took on a red cast. "Come to the Underworld and hear the sorrowful—nay—the tragic tale of the Queen of the Underworld's Daughter."

A high, piping voice started up from somewhere behind the stage, a strange, mournful sound that had no words that Nyssa could make out. It made the hair stand up on the back of her neck.

Roon left the stage and another figure stepped forward into the light, robed in black, wearing a purple cloak that Nyssa recognized and what was obviously a wig of long, straight black hair. Under the makeup, Nyssa saw the wiry man who had doused the torches only moments before.

As the Queen of the Underworld began to speak, more lights revealed the scenery. She stood in her Throne Room, surveying her kingdom in a magic mirror.

Nyssa glanced once at the others. She could see that Marius was more interested in the carpentry than the drama, but Aria was clearly enjoying the shabby spectacle, and Kit's eyes were ablaze as he watched, openmouthed. Satisfied, Nyssa turned her full attention to the stage, and immersed herself in its imaginary worlds.

ALARIC

GONE AGAIN

Alaric frowned at the report in his hand, concealing the full extent of his anger through habit.

It seemed that the trail had gone cold. His men on the Mainland had tracked the fugitives with some certainty as far as Darfin, but after that they seemed to have disappeared.

What would he do if he was them?

Split up. That would be the logical thing, but he doubted they were basing their actions on logic. It was more likely to be sentiment, the so-called bonds of family and friendship.

Those bonds were useful to him in this case, since if they stayed together, they would certainly be easier to find again.

Well then . . . surely they would make for a large town, try to disappear into some anonymous backstreet life. They would have to do something to earn money. The boy was a useless slave, and he knew very little about the sister and the uncle. The girl from Korce, however, had a trade.

He sent the searchers their new instructions in cipher and another twenty men so they could widen their search.

It was time to encourage the local people to help with the search. He was sure they would soon realize the desirability of doing so.

16

LARK AND THORN

Mistress Marin's gamble had paid off. The Woolpack was as busy as Nyssa had ever seen it, and most of the conversation seemed to be about Roon's Traveling Players, one way or another.

Opinion seemed to be evenly divided regarding which play had been better. If there was a distinction, it was that more of the women had enjoyed a good cry at the tragic end of *The Queen of the Underworld's Daughter*, whereas the men tended to prefer the almost endless succession of jokes, many of them concerning sausages (since the hero was a pig farmer), that composed *Love Lies Undone*.

Nyssa and Aria had certainly enjoyed the tragedy more, and Kit had devoured both plays with openmouthed enthusiasm. Marius had admitted that the acting didn't really interest him, but he was fascinated by the technicalities, particularly how the lights on stage were made to change color.

They still weren't sure how many members of Roon's company there were. The little girl who'd made all the noise hadn't appeared onstage, though Nyssa suspected it might have been her singing

from behind the scenery at the beginning and end of the performance. She had recognized the boy from the window and Roon
himself and the wiry man from their lodgings, but the other faces
had been unfamiliar. None of them had been women, which had
seemed odd to Nyssa. The heroine of *Love Lies Undone*, for instance,
had been played by the boy. Admittedly, when she had watched
performances like this before, some of the female roles were taken
by men, but there was usually at least one woman onstage.

Nyssa tried to sort it out in her head, but each person seemed
to have played so many parts that it was impossible. In any case,
she was kept so busy doling out helpings of pie and soup and
bread that there wasn't much time to think.

It had been a good break, though. Despite how threadbare
the costumes and scenery looked in daylight, it was easy to lose
yourself in the event once the lights went down and the actors
began to speak.

Marius had been working with them again today, mending
something that had fallen to pieces during last night's performance — offstage, fortunately.

"They know it's all in a bit of a mess," he said to Nyssa.
"Apparently their last carpenter ran off with their only actress
three months ago, and nothing much has been done since." Marius
swallowed a spoonful of soup. "Not just an actress, either — she
was Roon's . . . common-law wife. Matthius told me."

Nyssa couldn't help smiling. "It's not like you to gossip."

Marius looked crestfallen. "I thought you'd be interested."

"Oh, I am!" said Nyssa quickly. "I'd wondered why there
were no women. That explains it. I don't suppose Roon's been

too keen to replace her, considering the circumstances."

Marius snorted. "No. Not after that — and the little girl's dead against it, anyway."

"The squealer?"

Marius nodded. "Yes. She's Roon's daughter. Matthius told me her name, too — something strange — but I forget what it was. The boy's his son."

"Matthius's son?"

"No — Roon's."

"Does he have a name?"

Marius made a wry face. "Forgot that, too. I'm new to this gossip game, remember."

She cuffed him around the head and went back into the kitchen.

⁒ ⁒ ⁒

By Sunday, there were few healthy people in Armeni who hadn't seen the Players, and they'd even agreed to do another show as word spread and people from outlying villages turned up to find out when they could watch the plays.

"It must be five years since we had anyone like this around here," explained Mistress Marin. "People are hungry for a bit of cheer in the middle of winter. It's a dreary time up here.

"You know that yourself," she added, nodding at Aria. "Look at how they've flocked in to hear you sing." She sniffed. "I must admit I was surprised by how popular that's been."

Aria smiled and thought it safest not to say anything in reply.

Roon himself came into the Woolpack that night, in an expansive mood, and bought drinks for everyone there. Aria watched from the kitchen doorway.

"Look at him — holding court as though he really was a king."

"Still acting?" asked Nyssa.

"Who knows? Maybe he actually thinks he is one."

"What age do you suppose he is?"

"Older than he wants everyone to think. I'm sure his hair's dyed. And I bet he uses belladonna to make his eyes look bigger."

The barman stuck his head around the door. "Mistress says five minutes, Aria."

"All right." She poured herself a glass of water. "See you later, Nyssa."

Roon stayed for both of Aria's performances, kissed her hand, and complimented her on her singing. Nyssa didn't hear their conversation, but whatever Aria said, it made Roon laugh.

‡   ‡   ‡

Marius was mending a throne, watched by Nyssa. He was fitting a new arm, which he would then have to work with a chisel until it matched the original.

"They've offered me a job, you know."

"I can see that." Nyssa pointed to the throne.

"No. I mean they've offered me a regular job as carpenter-handyman with Roon's Traveling Players."

Nyssa gaped at him.

"Don't worry, I'm not going to take it."

Nyssa didn't quite know what to say. She'd been assuming that Marius, Kit, and herself would stay together. It was what Marius always said, too, but surely he yearned for a proper life of his own? He deserved it, after what he'd done for the last few years.

"You could go with them, you know," she said slowly.

He stopped what he was doing, to look at her. "You mean it, don't you? You'd let me go." He put down the chisel and gave her a hug. "Don't worry. I'm not going anywhere without you and Kit. After what we've gone through to be together, we stay together. All right?"

"All right."

An hour later, Marius was still working on the throne, now with Kit watching closely and handing him tools.

"Hello," said a voice from above them. "Roon wants me to ask when it'll be ready."

Kit and Marius looked up. It was the boy—Roon's son.

"Another hour or so, I think."

"Thanks." He shut the window, and a few moments later appeared beside them in the courtyard. "Do you mind if I watch?"

Marius shook his head. "It's not very exciting, though."

"You're Marius, aren't you?" Marius nodded. "I'm Lark. Well, not really. My name's Zacharius, but no one ever calls me that." He turned to Kit. "What's your name?"

"This is Kit," said Marius quickly. "He prefers not to talk too much."

"I wish my sister was like that," said Lark reflectively. "She never shuts up."

"*Mmnn* . . . we've heard her," said Marius wryly.

Lark grimaced, but said nothing. He watched Marius

chiseling away at the wood for ten minutes before he got bored. Moving away to the edge of the courtyard he pulled a handful of small wooden balls from a pocket and began to juggle. Kit watched, entranced.

"Can you juggle?" Lark asked him. Kit shook his head. "I could teach you if you wanted."

Kit shot an inquiring glance at Marius.

"Go on," he said. "I can get the tools myself."

For the first fifteen minutes or so, there was a lot of laughter, and the sound of the wooden balls hitting the pavement, then all at once Kit began to get the hang of it.

"That's it, Kit! Well done. Keep going." Lark sounded genuinely excited. "Look at . . . oh . . . never mind. I'll get it."

Another five minutes passed. Marius glanced up to see Kit waiting for his attention.

"Look." He tossed three balls into the air one after another, caught them, tossed them up again, over and over until he dropped them.

"Very good," said Marius, grinning.

"He *is* good," said Lark. "I bet with a bit of time I could teach him some of the difficult stuff. Do you want to learn to juggle with four balls, Kit?"

"Yes," he replied, and they moved off to their practice ground, but just then Nyssa came to tell him it was time to go to the Woolpack and start the day's cooking. He insisted on showing her his new skill before he went, and nodded agreement to Lark's suggestion that they should meet up again later in the afternoon.

He was no help at all in the kitchen that day, spending every minute he could sneak trying to juggle onions. Nyssa half expected to find him tossing a clutch of knives in the air every time she turned around. She couldn't pretend that she minded, though; she was too pleased to see him unself-consciously enjoying himself.

✛   ✛   ✛

Roon was in the Woolpack again that night, with the man Nyssa now knew was called Matthius. To the disappointment of the locals, however, he wasn't buying drinks, but keeping himself to himself, though he did compliment Nyssa on her cooking. Both men applauded Aria's singing, and Roon called her over to have a drink with them — something that Mistress Marin wouldn't normally have encouraged. For Roon, though, she was happy to make an exception.

They left soon afterward, after announcing that their third and final performance would be the next night. Aria sang again, and the Woolpack gradually emptied.

Aria helped Nyssa and Kit tidy the kitchen, then they set off through the dark streets.

"He wants me to join them," Aria said suddenly.

"What?"

"Roon. He was trying to persuade me to join his Players while I was having that drink with them."

To Aria's surprise, Nyssa burst out laughing. "You as well!"

"What?"

"They want to take Marius on as a carpenter."

"Are you serious?"

"Yes, but he turned them down." She grew serious. "Tell me what Roon said."

"Just that they needed a singer and actress — had been looking for one for a couple of months — and would I like to join them for a trial."

"And would you?"

Aria was silent.

"Aria?"

"I don't know. I . . . I need some time to think."

"Wait until we tell Marius!"

"Don't," Aria said quickly. "I don't want to talk to anyone else about it until I've made my mind up. Please, Nyssa."

"All right. Did Roon say anything about Marius? Do you think he knows there's any connection between you?"

"I don't know — he didn't say anything. He might not know — we're not all together very much here."

"*Mmnn* . . . Wonder if they need a cook?" mused Nyssa, only half joking. "Seriously, though, Aria, you have to think about this. It would be a chance to start over, to leave all this business of Shadowmen and Keepers behind and have your own life again."

Aria didn't answer.

-:-   -:-   -:-

The third performance brought customers from out of town to the Woolpack, and they were all run off their feet keeping up with orders. A lot of folk seemed to be making it an excuse for a couple of days in town away from the bleak tedium of midwinter, so the following few days were busy, too, and there never seemed to be the right moment to bring the subject up with Aria again.

As it turned out, Marius brought it up first. He'd struck up a friendship with Matthius, and they often had a drink together.

Marius came back from one of these sessions looking thoughtful, and sought out Nyssa as soon as he could.

"What is it?" she asked.

"Matthius just told me that Roon's offered the singer from the Woolpack a three-month trial."

"Ah."

"You knew?"

Nyssa nodded. "She made me promise not to tell you. She wanted to think it over first."

"And is she going?"

"I don't know. I haven't managed to speak to her about it again."

"Matthius obviously has no idea that Aria and I know each other." He was silent for a few seconds. "Do you think she'll take it?"

"I don't know. You could both go."

"I told you before, I'm not taking the job. Anyway, I'm getting to like Armeni. I've had enough of traveling to last me a long time."

"Me, too. But it's a real chance for Aria to put us behind her and get a new life for herself. She'd be good. I'm sure they'd keep her on once they got to know her."

"You need to talk to her again."

⁜   ⁜   ⁜

Kit was having another juggling lesson — with four balls now — from Lark that afternoon, so Nyssa asked Aria to help her in the kitchen for a couple of hours. She did need help, but she was more interested in the chance of a private talk.

She passed Aria a pile of carrots to chop and started the discussion.

"Have you decided what to do about Roon's offer?"

Chop, chop, chop went the knife, then paused. Nyssa looked hard at the rabbit she was skinning.

"No." Aria sighed.

"You're not going, or you haven't decided?"

"I can't decide. Part of me thinks I should go. As you said, it's a chance to make a new life, maybe a better chance of safety. But another part of me doesn't want to start all over again with strangers. I'd miss you. All of you."

Nyssa pulled the rabbit skin off, inside out. "They offered Marius a job as carpenter, too, you know. He's staying here, though. He's fed up with traveling." She smiled. "Not really surprising when you think about it."

"No." She resumed her chopping. "Armeni's getting quite comfortable, isn't it?"

⁜   ⁜   ⁜

That evening, Aria told Roon that she wasn't taking up his offer.

He raised his eyebrows. "You would sooner stay *here*?"

She shrugged. "It suits me well enough for the moment."

"As you wish. If you want to waste your talent in this backwater, so be it."

Thwarted in his efforts to secure a leading lady or a carpenter, Roon decided that he would at least have the rest of the scenery overhauled while he had the chance, and arranged to keep the Company's rooms for several more days.

Kit was pleased. It gave him that much more time to learn whatever Lark could teach him about juggling. He practiced talking, too, when he was alone with him. Lark never seemed to find anything odd about how he spoke, unlike Thorn, who poked fun at his halting speech until her brother made her stop.

-|-   -|-   -|-

There was a new playbill tacked to the tree in the square that served as a notice board. Curious, Nyssa went to look as she headed home after a morning in the Woolpack's kitchen. Surely it couldn't be more Players?

She was close enough to see it clearly now. She read it once, then twice. She looked around to see if anyone was watching, pulled it down, stuffed it in her pocket, and walked quickly away.

She found Marius in the courtyard, his mouth full of nails. He looked at her and frowned. "What is it?" he said indistinctly.

"Not here. Come upstairs."

Alarmed, he followed her.

Aria had just finished dressing and was putting up her hair when they came in.

"Where's Kit?" Nyssa said without preamble.

"With Lark, I think. Why?"

She shut the door, pulled the crumpled paper from her pocket, and smoothed it out. She looked at it once more to make sure she hadn't imagined it, then handed it to Marius and Aria.

There was silence for a moment, then Marius merely said, "Well."

It wasn't a playbill.

REWARD
The Lord Alaric offers
a reward of
100 gold pieces
for information leading to
the capture of four
MURDERERS
escaped from Thira.
A man
Two young women
A yellow-haired mute boy

Nyssa's stomach felt as though it had been replaced by a small, very heavy stone.

All the color had drained from Aria's face. She sat down.

"When did that go up?" said Marius.

"It wasn't there this morning. Not that many people will have seen it."

"Maybe not, but there must be other notices. And someone putting them up."

"What do we do?" said Nyssa.

"Nothing." Marius sounded quite sure. "Kit's hair isn't yellow anymore, and Aria dyes it before it ever has a chance to fade. Our tattoos are disguised. Kit doesn't talk much, but he certainly isn't mute.

"There's no reason for anyone to link us to Thira — we've let our cover story leak out discreetly, so no doubt the entire town knows our supposed reasons for being here.

"We sit tight. If we suddenly disappear, it'll only get people wondering why. We can't go unless we have a good reason to leave."

Nyssa and Aria nodded. It made sense, although the first instinct of all of them was to run.

"Do we tell Kit?" Marius asked Nyssa.

"Tell me what?" said Kit from the open doorway.

There was no alternative now. Nyssa handed him the notice. He read it through and handed it back.

"I knew they'd come. We'll never be safe."

Nyssa wanted to say *Of course we'll be safe*, but what would that be but a hollow promise?

"We think the safest thing is to stay —"

Kit cut her off. "We should go with Roon. If Marius and Aria go, Lark thinks Roon might take you as cook."

They gaped at him. It was quite unexpected to hear him offer a forceful opinion. On the rare occasion a question was put to him, he usually just shrugged.

Moreover, he was right, and the rest of them hadn't thought of it. If they could go with Roon's Players, they immediately became part of a larger group, and one with every reason to be on the move.

"Just because I don't say much doesn't mean I don't know anything."

Marius took a deep breath. "I'm sorry. I shouldn't underestimate you."

The girls apologized, too, and they sat down to make plans.

　　　　‡　　　‡　　　‡

Roon looked dubious. He sat in the easy chair in his room, one booted ankle on the opposite knee, absently twirling a pen between his fingers.

Aria, Marius, and Nyssa stood before him, silently waiting while he considered the proposal Marius had just put to him. From outside came the noise of Thorn shouting unwanted advice to Lark as he practiced four-ball juggling with Kit.

"Why have you changed your minds?"

Marius replied. "Neither Aria nor I realized that you'd invited the other to join you. We want to stay together."

"It's your decision, naturally, Master Roon, but what are the chances that you'll find another two people who'll fit your needs as well as we do?" said Aria, pushing her luck.

Roon glared at her but, undaunted, she simply raised an eyebrow and smiled.

"And this way, all the domestic needs of the Company are taken care of without you having to give it any thought," she added. "You'll be free to concentrate on your true vocation: the writing and performing of plays."

"Don't try to beat me at my own game, young woman." Roon pointed the pen at Aria. "You have a persuasive tongue, though. I congratulate you on it." He paused. "But consider, if you will, this proposal: Leave the others behind and I'll double your wages."

Aria shook her head. "I'm afraid not. It's all of us or none. Shall we leave you to think it over?" She half turned toward the door and, following her lead, so did Marius and Nyssa.

"All right, all right, I'll take the four of you—but only for two months. After that, you and you"—he pointed at Aria and Marius—"will have to make up your minds about what you're doing. The boy and girl are on their own. I don't need a cook or a juggler."

It was the best they were going to do at the moment.

"Thank you, Master Roon. You'll see, you won't regret this," said Marius.

"Now go away, before I have second thoughts. I've got a play to finish here." And he uncrossed his legs and turned his chair to the paper-littered table.

"Just one more thing," Aria said irrepressibly. "Where is the Company going next?"

"Rushiadh," Roon said. "We have a three-week engagement for the Festival of the Spring Moon."

Marius pushed Nyssa out the door before Roon could see her jaw hit the floor.

ALARIC

THE VIEW FROM KIT'S WINDOW

Alaric stood in the tiny attic room at the top of his palace and looked around at the few things the boy had accumulated in however many years he had been there.

It had never occurred to him to wonder where the boy slept, but one of the other slaves had mentioned it the day before, hoping to win his favor. His curiosity had been piqued, and so he had climbed the filthy stair to the little rat's nest. There was no clue here of course about where he might have gone.

He looked out the window at the roofs of his city below. His city. That at least was still true, but unrest was spreading on the outer islands. His forces were stretched, no doubt about it. There were too many islands. It was that simple. Trying to keep them all under his yoke was like trying to herd cats.

As soon as his troops put down the rebels on one island, up would pop another group somewhere else. Why, even Thira wasn't immune. He'd had a dozen—or was it a couple of dozen—suspected rebels put very publicly to death over the last few months, but he still couldn't crush the unrest here. The town was awash with notices urging the people to rebel against him, and he had no idea where they were coming from or how they were produced so quickly. They'd begun to appear on some of the closest islands, too.

He needed the boy and his sister, hated to think of them together, out there, somehow still beyond his grasp, but there was no sign of them even though he had authorized a reward, and signs were going up all over the Archipelago and the Mainland.

He found it hard to understand how these four nobodies could elude his men for so long. Winter weather had made traveling difficult, they reported, as though that didn't apply equally to their quarry.

He turned to leave. He had kept the delegation from Rushiadh waiting for half an hour. That was probably enough. Some sort of invitation. He wouldn't go of course, but one must keep up diplomatic relations with one's neighbors. Perhaps he would send someone.

TRABZYN

Nyssa breathed in the familiar smell of tar and salt, listened to the creak and stretch of rope and the flap of unsecured canvas. She stood on board the sailing vessel *Shearwater*, three days out of Matala and bound for Trabzyn, the port and seaward defense of the powerful city-state of Rushiadh. The home of the Moon Priestesses and the Great Library. Here was her chance to find out more about the tattoos that she and Kit carried.

If Nyssa had wanted to believe in fate, this would have been unbeatable proof. *There's no such thing as fate*, she kept telling herself, *just coincidence.*

Back on a boat again. She counted them up: squid boat to the Mainland, ferry to Thira, their poor lost cockleshell to Drakona, fishing boat to Idhra, another ferry to the Mainland . . .

And now this. The *Shearwater* was an enormous vessel compared to anything she'd ever been on, plying one of the main routes across the Archipelago to Rushiadh. There must be almost one hundred and fifty passengers on board, crammed into tiny cabins like cells in a beehive, or traveling steerage on deck surrounded by bundles of belongings.

It would be another five days before they docked in Trabzyn. Even Kit might have wearied of the sea by then. She already had.

That wasn't exactly true. It was being squashed together with so many other people that was making her edgy. The four fugitives and Roon's Players were still getting to know one another, and with Thorn in particular, it wasn't a smooth process. She had made it clear from the moment she heard what her father had done that she resented the girls' presence, although she was completely indifferent to Marius and actually seemed to like Kit.

So it was a strain, always trying to be pleasant, to be unobtrusive, to be useful and so justify her presence somehow. Most of all it was a strain always to be on her guard, to be sure she hadn't let something incriminating slip for Thorn's sharp and unfriendly ears to pick up.

They'd worked out a week's notice at the Woolpack, under the accusing eyes of Mistress Marin, who was anticipating a sharp drop in her profits when they left. By that time the worst of the winter weather was over, and they had an uneventful, though wet and cold, ten-day journey to the port of Matala.

It had taken another week there to sell the carts and horses and crate up what they were taking with them to Rushiadh. Most of the scenery was staying behind, to be picked up at some unspecified date in the future. Roon had decided it wasn't grand enough for Rushiadh, so Marius's job at least was assured.

They'd kept a low profile in Matala as best as they could, after seeing two more reward notices pinned up there that they didn't dare risk removing. Nyssa even had to watch as though unconcerned when Thorn stopped especially to read one of them, eyes widening at the thought of a hundred gold pieces.

Don't panic, Nyssa chided herself, *she's only reading. If she'd made the connection, she would have been off to tell her father in seconds.*

Their passage on the *Shearwater* cost them nothing; it would be paid for by the authorities in Rushiadh who had invited them to perform. Nyssa suspected that this was the only reason why she and Kit weren't jostling for space on deck with the rest of the steerage passengers.

Nyssa and the others had been surprised when they were introduced properly to the Company to find just how small it was: only Roon and his children, big sandy-haired Matthius, the dark and wiry Pavlos, and Conor, a man so colorless and lacking in outward character that they hadn't even registered his presence before. Onstage, however, he was a man transformed, completely possessed by whatever part he was playing.

"A genius of the acting profession," said Roon, introducing him. "A blank sheet on which playwrights may write the lines that show their grasp of the human heart and mind."

They smiled and nodded and tried to stop their eyes from sliding to more interesting parts of the room: the door handle, for instance.

"My children you already know—Zacharius, who assures me

that Kit here is a natural juggler. Perhaps you two can entertain our clients as they queue up to see us? And Jessamy, my briar rose, my leopard cub."

Thorn glared at him through her black hair. "I still don't know why you need those silly girls, Papa. I'll be old enough to play the parts in another year, and Pavlos will do quite well until then."

Roon stroked her hair with an indulgent smile, as though she was a horse that needed calming, but she tossed her head and moved away from him.

On the journey to Matala, Thorn had made a point of staying aloof from the newcomers, except Kit, who she occasionally graced with a dazzling smile. She seemed surprised when this didn't immediately have the desired effect of making him her slave. Instead he treated her (wisely, Nyssa thought) like a beautiful but unpredictable wild animal, and kept his distance.

Nyssa sighed and roused herself. She'd put this off for too long already. She picked her way among the steerage passengers to the prow of the ship where Kit hung over the side, watching for dolphins, and tugged at his sleeve to get his attention.

"Kit, come down to the cabin." He waved her away. "I need to cut your hair." Now she had his attention. "I want to copy the writing."

"Why?"

"In Rushiadh I might be able to find out what it means. There's a famous library there — a place with hundreds of books. Maybe we'll find out something that will stop him from hunting us."

He shook his head.

"Don't you want to know what it says?"

He shrugged, but he peeled himself away from the rail with a resigned expression.

⁜   ⁜   ⁜

Half an hour later, it was done. Because his hair was dyed brown, it wasn't too obvious, especially since she'd given him a badly needed proper haircut at the same time. She looked at the lines of script she had copied.

Kit traced the shapes with a finger.

"Marius made a copy of my tattoo, but of course we lost that when the boat sank. I'll get him or Aria to do the same for me later."

There was a knock at the door and Lark came in. Nyssa hastily tidied the paper away.

"Hello, Nyssa. I've come to steal Kit. Time to try five balls." He stopped talking and took a good look at Kit. "It makes you look different now that it's shorter. Older. It suits you. Come on." He lobbed a ball at Kit, who caught it, grinning, and turned to go.

⁜   ⁜   ⁜

"There," said Aria. "It's done. That's the strangest thing I've ever seen." She looked critically at Nyssa's hair. "Shake your head. There, that's all right."

She passed the paper with the words over to Nyssa.

Once again Nyssa tried to imagine what they could mean, what they might sound like, but she had nowhere to start, nothing on which to base even the wildest guess.

"I'll make a copy and get Marius to keep it," she said. "I don't want to have to do that again. Especially with Thorn so keen to poke around in everything we do."

Aria sighed. "I'd better go. Roon wants me to rehearse a new scene he's written."

Roon was proving to be a demanding taskmaster, and Aria had been hard at work on the role of Queen of the Underworld since the day they finished at the Woolpack. As yet she had nothing to wear: Roon had decided that the old costumes were too shabby and that Rushiadh could be inveigled into meeting those costs along with all the new scenery he had already decided on.

When she'd finished making the copy of the tattoo, Nyssa went in search of Marius and found him on the afterdeck with Matthius, deep in discussion about the new set designs. Roon was determined that these performances in Rushiadh were going to make the Company's name.

She wanted a more private moment to hand over what she carried, so went instead to the clear area of deck that Lark and Kit had managed to find to practice in.

The two boys were passing the balls to each other now, Kit with a look of fierce concentration, tongue poking out, Lark laughing at him. Thorn sat nearby, dressed in improbable pink silk, the bag of juggling gear at her side.

Nyssa sat down on the other side of the bag and tried to count the balls as they flew back and forth. Five? Six? She couldn't track them quickly enough.

"He's good," Thorn said unexpectedly.

"Yes," Nyssa responded cautiously, for Thorn generally addressed about as many words to her as Kit did. "Your brother is a good teacher. Do you juggle?"

Thorn shook her head. "My hands are too small to do it well." She held one up for Nyssa to see: a chubby hand, with dirt ingrained under the bitten nails.

The boys had stopped in a welter of dropped balls; they came over.

"We're going to start with clubs," said Lark. "I'd stand farther back if I were you."

The warning proved to be justified as clubs flew everywhere except into Kit's and Lark's hands.

"This is dull," Thorn announced after a few minutes and wandered off, her too long dress gathered up in her fists.

As a club missed her narrowly, Nyssa decided that *dull* wasn't the right word, but that it would definitely be a good idea to leave. She got to her feet and went off to try again to speak to Marius.

⁜   ⁜   ⁜

The Company stood clustered together by the rail watching Trabzyn draw closer. All morning the scale of the landscape they were approaching had been growing clearer. Cliffs that were almost vertical reared out of the sea, the rock mortared at the top by buildings of silvery wood and pale stone, as inconceivably secure as limpets.

A single path zigzagged its way up from the harbor to the city gate. It was easy to see why Trabzyn was known as the

Shield. Its position made it nearly impregnable to attack by sea, and behind it the fertile plain and rich city of Rushiadh were well protected.

The *Shearwater* was like a disturbed anthill as it began to negotiate the tricky channel that led to the harbor. On deck, the steerage passengers milled about, re-roping bundles and searching for children, while those who had traveled below were busy bringing their gear up above.

Mooring lines were flung ashore, and the *Shearwater*'s rope fenders thudded against the harbor wall as she berthed. A few more minutes and the Company was making its way off the ship. After so long at sea, the quay seemed to shift under Nyssa's feet as she watched the steerage passengers begin to lug their belongings up the pathway.

Roon looked around to make sure all his subjects were present. "Come along then. The walk will do us good. Stretch the muscles after being cooped up for a week."

It took about twenty minutes to climb the sharply angled path. Every time they doubled back on themselves at a corner, another tier appeared above them, like so many giant steps. At each corner was a squat watchtower, massively built of stone, with narrow windows to allow archers to fire out in relative safety if Trabzyn was attacked.

The cliff face was covered in small, ground-hugging plants, mostly grayish green, some of them already coming into flower. The air was faintly scented by them, a pleasant antidote to the dung that littered the path. Every so often they came on an old man or woman scooping up the droppings into a container to sell to the town authorities as fertilizer.

Reaching the final stretch of road hot and breathless, the Company joined a queue of people outside the gates trying to get into the town. Entry was not automatic: A permit was needed, or a skill, or goods to sell. Arguments broke out frequently, but were short-lived as unsuccessful travelers were beaten away down the hill again by guards. There were guards up on the walls, too, with bows and spears. Vigilance at the gates never faltered.

Roon had a permit for the whole Company, so they weren't worried as they shuffled forward with the queue toward the massive gates.

They finally reached the front. An officer scrutinized the permit carefully, then handed it back.

"You need to see the placement officer to get somewhere to stay." He pointed to a nearby building. "I'd go now if I were you. There are a lot of people coming in today."

Nyssa, Kit, Marius, and Aria had no idea what the man meant, but Roon seemed to understand, so they followed along, trying to look as though they were used to this sort of thing, and joined another queue.

Roon explained as they waited.

"The state controls all the inns. The placement officer has records of where there are rooms free. He decides where we stay."

And so, some twenty minutes later, they emerged to look for the Inn of the Pearl Divers.

The directions they had been given took them into the heart of the town, away from the cliff edge. Trabzyn was roughly the shape of a bow, its curved edge the cliff, the straight side a heavily fortified wall, the whole town sloping down from the cliff toward the inland plain.

They looked at the web of streets spread out before them. Below them were terraces of houses and workshops, inns and storefronts. There was a strong smell of fish coming from a row of open-fronted booths nearby, displaying what was left of the morning's catch from the fishing boats moored far below in the harbor.

In the center of the town the ground rose again into a low hill, crowned with a collection of buildings that formed a hexagon around a large garden. Their walls were washed white, the roofs, red tiled. Bright geometric patterns outlined the doorways.

"What's that?" asked Aria.

"The Precincts of the Priestesses. They have small communities in towns of any size at all, throughout Rushiadh's entire empire. This is one of the largest outside Rushiadh City itself," Roon said. "Girls who are taken to be priestesses have their early training somewhere like this before they go to Rushiadh."

"*Taken* to be priestesses? You make it sound as though they don't have a choice."

"They don't. Free will plays no more part in the selection of priestesses than in the taking of slaves. The Searchers from Rushiadh go out every year looking for girls, three or four or five years old, and take them off to be trained."

"What happens to the parents of the girls who are chosen?" asked Nyssa.

Roon gave her an indulgent smile. "Nothing happens to them. To be a priestess is a position of great honor here, so they seldom object, but the family receives a payment, and the girls are never left to train in the same town, just in case.

"Are you listening, Thorn? Once a girl is taken, officially she has no parents anymore. She belongs to the Sacred Precincts and becomes a Daughter of the Goddess. The most gifted of them are sent to serve in the Temple in Rushiadh in due course. Perhaps I should offer you to them, though I suppose you're too old and too fierce for them."

Thorn smiled and stuck her tongue out at him.

-‡-   -‡-   -‡-

The inn was clean, comfortable, well run, and completely lacking in character. Roon gave them a couple of hours to unpack and rest, and then called a rehearsal, leaving Nyssa, Kit, and Marius free for the moment. Nyssa wanted to look for somewhere to buy fabric. It was time she and Aria got to work on the new costumes. Neither of them were seamstresses by trade, and it would take them some time.

When she told the other two what she was going to do, they decided to come along. They began walking in silence, getting the measure of the city.

"It's a relief to be away from everyone for a while, isn't it?" said Marius.

Kit nodded. "Too much talk," he said succinctly.

"I thought it was just me," said Nyssa.

"Oh no," said Marius. "It's a strain, having to think about everything before you say it. They're good people, though, even if Roon is a bit . . ."

Nyssa grinned. "Over the top?"

"That's one way of putting it. He's no fool, though." He frowned. "We mustn't underestimate him just because he has a fondness for velvet and feathers. Or that wildcat daughter of his," he added as an afterthought.

Everyone they passed looked busy, occupied with some task or other: taking a message to the harbor, choosing a fowl for the table, seeking the cheapest loan from the moneylenders. There were a great many of these, preying on the unprepared poor who traveled to Trabzyn hoping to find riches. Many of them reached the city of Rushiadh every year, not in triumph, but as slaves, their bodies claimed by the lenders in lieu of debts they couldn't clear any other way.

"This looks promising," said Nyssa, staring at bolts of cloth piled in a window. "Are you two . . ."

"We'll wait outside," said Marius firmly.

-‡-   -‡-   -‡-

They spent five days in Trabzyn, sewing, rehearsing, juggling, and putting the finishing touches to the designs for the new scenery. Roon had written a small part for Thorn as the Queen of the Underworld's handmaiden, in an attempt to placate her over the girls' presence, but she spent all her time onstage trying to upstage Aria and all her time off it making preposterous demands about her costume, so it hadn't had quite the effect he'd intended.

The five days wasn't their choice. Travel between Trabzyn and Rushiadh was controlled like so much else here by the priestesses, and the Company had been told to join a caravan of travelers on that day. Roon and Pavlos had to spend yet more time queuing up to obtain yet more vital permits for this, but with the rest of the queue providing a captive audience for him to talk at, Roon didn't seem to mind too much.

Kit was now proficient with five balls or three clubs, and he and Lark could pass to each other well enough for Roon to be thinking seriously about having them entertain the audience before the show. Nyssa had thought that Kit would reject the idea, but he was full of excitement at the prospect.

"I want to do that," he said. "I'm good enough now."

Kit was much more relaxed around Marius now, and was happy in Lark's company, though he kept his distance from Matthius, Pavlos, and Conor. Roon and Thorn he seemed to regard more as exotic animals than people, and he dealt with them with fascinated caution.

Their last evening in Trabzyn passed in a flurry of packing and sewing, and they waited at the landward gate early the next morning to load their bags once again.

The caravan was composed of carts with drivers, riding horses, and pack animals. These last were a mixture of mules and extraordinarily tall, lumpy animals.

"And what kind of beasts might those be?" said Marius, boggling.

"They call them *chamiel*," said Roon. "They are creatures of evil disposition but great endurance. Keep well away from them: The front spits and the rear kicks."

Nyssa watched as an improbably large portion of their copious luggage was strapped to a wooden framework on the chamiel's crooked back. It seemed to her unlikely that the poor beast would be able to stand up, much less walk.

When the luggage was stowed, they were ushered to their places on one of the carts. There was a canvas canopy to protect the passengers from the weather, and side panels that could be lowered to provide more shelter if it was needed.

They waited there for another half hour until the rest of the caravan was ready. Mounted guards moved around, checking that everything was in order, and finally issued the command to leave. The drivers flicked their reins onto the haunches of the horses, the chamiels lurched to their feet, their loads swaying alarmingly, and they were on their way.

18

RUSHIADH

They left Trabzyn behind them as the road carried them across the fertile plain that supplied Rushiadh with most of its food. Even this early in the spring, there were workers everywhere in the fields and orchards, planting, weeding, and irrigating. Roadside stalls sold the local produce: honey, eggs, a wide variety of vegetables, some of which Nyssa had never seen before. The road was busy with caravans like their own and farm wagons going to and from the city to deliver produce. There were riders and people on foot, and every so often a closed carriage would speed past, throwing a cloud of dust over them. Everyone else got out of the way when one was spotted.

"Rich people." Matthius spat on the road. "They're the same everywhere."

There were watchtowers about every hour's ride along the road, strongly garrisoned, and beacons ready to be lit to summon assistance if it was needed. It would be a foolish bandit who tried to make a living here.

Three times they passed gibbets at the side of the road from which the bodies of men and women swung rotting, their eyes taken by birds. The last one held four, of whom one was a boy who couldn't have been more than twelve years old. Nyssa wondered what his crime could have been.

Worse even than the gibbets, though, was the marble quarry they passed, where chained slaves worked at great slabs of stone, their faces so caked with dust that they seemed like ghosts, or statues with human eyes.

Roon decided that the Company should use the time to practice their lines. Nyssa, Kit, and Marius listened. Roon had done a lot of rewriting since they had watched the play in Armeni, to make full use of Aria's talents as well as to satisfy Thorn.

It was fascinating being this close to the actors without scenery, makeup, or costumes. Aria had to work much harder than the others to remember her lines, partly because she had one of the biggest parts, but mainly because it was all still so new to her. In the swaying wagon, only a couple of feet away, it was hard to believe in Lark as the queen's daughter, but even in such unpromising conditions, Conor was utterly convincing as Prince Amnatos, her mortal lover.

The road had been rising all morning, as they rolled into the foothills of the Lefkori Mountains. There was snow on the summits, but they wouldn't have to climb that far. A notch between the towering slopes was the entrance to the pass that the road followed.

It was noticeably colder, and the cultivation petered out before they reached the pass. The caravan guards were on high alert, as bandits often tried to prey on travelers here. Personally, Nyssa thought they'd have to be pretty optimistic—or desperate—to attack this group, since no one appeared to be much richer than Roon's Company, and *they* certainly didn't have much that would make it worth the risk of being killed by a guard.

They stopped briefly again at midday, but those in charge were clearly keen to press on and get out of the pass.

When they emerged in mid afternoon, it was to a totally new landscape. As far as they could see, in every direction the land stretched away from them, arid and seemingly lifeless, a wilderness of rock and sand. Nyssa could see now why the plain they had so recently left behind was so important to Rushiadh. The slope in front of them was littered with huge boulders, some the size of houses. The road curved around these and diminished into the hazy distance. Even the air was dusty and dry.

Roon produced a scarf of fine cotton from a pocket, and wound it around his face and throat so that it covered his nose and mouth.

The others stared at him.

"For the dust," he said. "Bad for the voice. Didn't I mention the dust?"

There was a general shaking of heads. *Typical,* thought Nyssa. *The one time it would be useful for him to tell us about something, and he doesn't.* The wagon creaked off down the hill.

By the time they reached the plain the temperature had risen dramatically. Dust clogged Nyssa's throat and sweat trickled down her face. Everyone else looked just as hot.

"I hope Roon buys good hair dye," Aria whispered mischievously to her, "or it'll be running down his face soon."

"What about Kit's?" Nyssa whispered back, alarmed.

"Don't worry. I never buy cheap cosmetics."

That day and the next passed in hot, dust-laden tedium. By now everyone had something around their faces, but the dust still found its way in. Lowering the canvas sides of the wagon didn't help, either: It was no less dusty, just more oppressive.

Several times they passed great standing stones, uprights and a lintel forming empty doorways.

"Shrines," said Roon. "The Horse Lords think they're doors to the Underworld." Nyssa was about to ask what he meant, when a plume of dust rose up on the horizon.

Advancing toward them, the dust cloud resolved itself into a group of riders approaching.

There were about twenty of them, identically dressed in robes of red and gold.

They swept through the middle of the train of wagons and carts and riders as though they didn't even exist, carelessly shifting their body weight to control the horses. Each man had an oiled braid of black hair that hung halfway down his back and carried a juniper branch. Nyssa just had time as they sped past to see that patterns of green and ocher lines were painted on the horses' necks.

They swerved to a halt in front of one of the stone shrines and jumped down from their horses. The branches were heaped on the ground under the lintel and set alight, then the men leaped back on the horses and galloped away into the distance, all without a word.

"Well," said Matthius. "Those'll be the Horse Lords, I take it." Roon nodded. "Who are they?"

"No one knows much about them. They are nomads. They live in the desert where no other folk can survive. Their special skills have been passed down through the generations—but I don't know how anyone could live out here. Their lives revolve around their horses. That's all anyone knows."

The rest of the day dragged past. It seemed as though they had been on this dusty road for weeks. Nyssa felt thirsty all the time. She was sure that if she tipped a water bottle over her head, it would be absorbed straightaway by her parched skin. They ate in near silence and fell into their beds, exhausted.

Nyssa stood in a shadowed alcove at the edge of a huge, marble-floored room. She held her breath, afraid the sound of it would give her away to the figure feeling its way blindly around the walls.

When it reached her and touched her she would be trapped, but if she moved, it would hear her, and there was no door through which she could escape. She tried to turn herself to marble, so that it would take her for one of the statues, but her flesh refused to turn to stone.

The figure was drawing closer, its hands making soft slapping noises as it patted its way across the wall. She panicked and tried to run, but found to her mounting horror that she couldn't move; her feet had obeyed her and turned to marble, rooted to the floor. She couldn't escape.

The figure was three feet away, two and a half. . . . She got a clear look at the face for the first time—white skin, white hair, the blank eyes of a statue. She screamed as Alaric's soft white hands came toward her.

Nyssa screamed and woke. The other people in the dormitory room were stirring around her, Aria in the next bed already stumbling toward her to see what was wrong.

"I'm sorry," Nyssa said to the room in general. "It was a bad dream. Go back to sleep."

Aria sat down on the bed and put an arm around Nyssa's shoulders. "Are you all right?"

She shuddered. "Yes. I'm fine. It was nothing." She couldn't bring herself to talk about those soft hands, pattering across the marble wall toward her. "Go back to bed. I'm all right."

⊹   ⊹   ⊹

Rushiadh appeared before them halfway through the final morning as a line on the horizon, and grew hour after hour, swimming out of the haze of dust thrown up by the horses, oxen, and chamiels of the caravan.

Rushiadh, the fabled city-state of the Priestesses of the Moon, one of the acknowledged wonders of the world.

A single, rounded hill rose out of the arid plain, necklaced with ocher walls on the lower slopes, white ones higher up, punctuated with columns and towers and beaded with colored roofs. At the summit stood a collection of buildings roofed with copper that flashed back the light like a burning glass, their walls gleaming salt white in the sun. The whole effect was dazzling.

"Behold Rushiadh," said Roon portentously, "and at its heart the Sacred Precincts of the Priestesses of the Moon."

A great wall surrounded the whole city, built not of stone, Roon said, but of mud brick. Nyssa assumed he was talking nonsense at first. How could anything — especially something that size — be built of mud? But as they waited in the inevitable queue outside one of the gates, she could see that it certainly wasn't stone.

It was a massive thing, perhaps twenty feet high and ten feet thick at the base, tapering as it rose. It was pierced by a series of gates, whose names they learned later: the Desert Gate, the Gate of Fire, the River Gate (though there was no river anymore), the Gate of Earth.

As had happened in Trabzyn, they had been assigned accommodation, but not at an inn this time. Instead, they had been given the use of a villa some way up the hill, where they could prepare everything for their performances. They left their baggage to be brought by porters and set off on foot.

It took them some time to get through the crowded streets to the villa, since it lay on the far side of the hill. Now that they were within the city, its beauty was clear. The houses had windows and pillars and swooping roofs, all shaped to be in harmony with one another. Trees provided much-needed shade on the streets, and doves flew and settled and flew again among their branches. The sun reflected on water here and there, for the city was famed for its fountains, which brought clear water to its inhabitants even through the longest droughts.

As they climbed, the buildings became ever grander, stone and marble replacing the mud brick, the streets becoming quieter. These were the dwellings of the rich.

"Well," said Pavlos in anticipation, "it looks as if they treat actors properly here."

-․‡-   -‡-   -‡-

The villa was indeed exquisite. It was two stories high and faced in pale pink marble with creeper-shaded verandas that looked out over the lower part of the city. Beds with linen sheets, soft towels. They went from room to room wide-eyed. None of them had ever stayed anywhere half as grand before. Roon acted as though he wasn't impressed, but convinced no one. Even Thorn couldn't find anything to complain about.

They had two weeks before the festival began in which to perfect every aspect of the play. Nyssa had expected to have plenty of free time in which to find her way to the Library, but now that they weren't staying in inns she had to cook all the Company's meals, of course.

She'd soon found her way to the nearest market and had been amazed at the choice of food. There were meat and fish of all sorts, fruit and vegetables she'd never even heard of before, spices so brightly colored that she thought they must be dyed until she got near enough to smell them.

To Nyssa, used to earning her keep by cooking, it was like opening a box full of presents. So many ingredients to choose from! The spices fascinated her most of all. She'd never used any of them before, having depended on the herbs that grew on the island for flavoring. She tried different ones every day, experimenting, asking the stallholders for advice about what would work.

In addition, the costumes still weren't finished, and Roon kept roping her in to go over the actors' lines with them.

Marius, with help from Matthius when he was free, spent every daylight hour hammering, sawing, or painting. Kit would often appear to help with the painting, and they would work side by side in companionable silence. It lifted Nyssa's heart to see Kit accepting Marius at last, and she knew how much it would mean to him.

A few days after they arrived, they went to see the theater where they would be performing. There was really no need for Nyssa to tag along, but she'd hardly set foot outside the villa except to buy food.

There were four theaters of varying sizes in the city. Roon pretended to take offense when he found that they were in the smallest, but no one paid any attention to his huffings. It was by far the grandest venue the Company had ever played in.

Marius and Matthius were immediately absorbed in measuring the space for scenery and deciding where to position their lights. Roon got Aria to sing while he prowled around checking the acoustics.

"How long will you be?" Nyssa asked Pavlos.

"An hour or so, I should think. You don't have to stay, though."

She needed no further encouragement and slipped away, Kit at her side like a shadow.

"The Library?" he said as they came out into the street.

"I thought I might at least try to find it. It's bound to be up near the top of the hill. In fact, maybe it's inside the Temple Precincts. I don't know."

All the time she was speaking they were climbing up the curving road. A little farther and they found themselves in front of a wall of white polished marble, elaborately carved. There were panels showing mythic scenes, abstract designs, beasts, landscapes, all manner of things. Although Nyssa knew they must be years old, they were so perfect that it was hard not to believe they had only just been finished. The gleaming wall was pierced by a wooden gate painted in patterns of blue and gold. It stood open, but was guarded by two enormous men.

"This is the entrance to the Temple Precincts. You may enter if you wish, mistress, but no man may come within the wall without permission of the Chief Priestess."

"No. That's all right. I was just trying to find the Great Library. We're lost."

"No. You are not lost. The Library is inside the Precincts. Do you wish to enter?"

"Not just now. Will I be allowed in if I come back another time?"

"Of course."

They turned to go. Nyssa was deep in thought as they made their way back down to the theater. Now that the possibility of finding what the tattoos meant was at last within reach, she found she was becoming more apprehensive by the moment. What would they do if she did find out? For good or ill it would surely change everything again.

╬   ╬   ╬

It was another six days before Nyssa had enough free time to return to the Library. This time she was alone, with half a day at her disposal and two pieces of paper hidden but rustling in her bodice.

She approached the Temple gate with some trepidation, imagining Shadowmen hidden and waiting for her just beyond it, despite what the guards had said. The two huge men were at their posts, but as unthreatening as they had been before. She walked through the gate and into the Temple Precincts as one of them rang a bell to signal the arrival of a visitor.

Before her spread a patchwork of gardens, pathways, and buildings, the hill crowned with the Temple itself. She had no business there of course, but she didn't know where she ought to go. She needn't have worried: As was true everywhere else in Rushiadh, there was someone to check what she wanted and tell her where to go.

A girl not much older than Nyssa herself appeared from the nearest building to find out what she was looking for. Her hair was loose and she wore a simple dress of leaf green. Nyssa tried to remember what Roon had told them about the priestesses.

"All except the most senior priestesses wear their hair loose. The color of their robes is a guide to how they serve the Goddess: those in green are healers, in red musicians. . . . I can't remember all of it. The darker the color, the more senior they are."

"Ah, the Library. Come with me." And with a smile she led Nyssa along curving paths to a white, two-story building set on the other side of the hill, surprisingly small for somewhere so famous. At the door, she was passed to a woman in a sky blue dress, her dark hair falling to her waist.

"My name is Xanthe. What do you seek in the Great Library?"

Nyssa pulled one of the pieces of paper from her bodice and smoothed it out.

"I want to find out what something means. My mother falls into trances sometimes, makes prophecies, speaks in tongues. Sometimes what she says comes true. She wrote some words down about a year ago in a language I don't understand — it looks like this." She handed a piece of paper to Xanthe with a few of the words from the tattoo on it. "I've not been able to find out anything about it. I'm here with some actors for the festival, so I thought, may as well try here, too, before I give up."

Nyssa hoped it sounded more convincing to Xanthe than it did to her.

The woman nodded absently, studying the paper. "This is not a language I know. . . . Come, I'll show you where you might begin to look."

They stood in an airy hallway with stairs at the far end to which Xanthe now walked. To Nyssa's surprise, she started down, not up.

The stairs turned back on themselves once, and they lost the sunlight. It grew no dimmer, however: Glass-shaded lamps hung from the ceiling every couple of paces, burning with a clear light that was almost as bright as the daylight.

Xanthe stopped going down, though the stairs continued farther than Nyssa could see, and pushed open a heavy door. She led Nyssa along the corridor beyond, stopped at another door, and pushed it open.

"This would be a good place to start," she said, motioning Nyssa inside.

Nyssa stood in the doorway, amazed. She had never seen so many books and scrolls, never even imagined so many. Every wall was shelved from floor to ceiling, each shelf full of books of all shapes, sizes, and ages, or piled with scrolls, their seals dangling free for easy identification. A man and two women worked silently at desks in the center of the room.

At home, Nyssa had barely known Rushiadh as more than a name. Now she was beginning to get an inkling of the power and immense history of the place.

"In this room we have samples of many languages from Rushiadh and all the lands under its rule, from the Archipelago, from the Eastern Kingdoms. I suggest you look here for something similar to your prophecy."

And with that she turned and left, catching Nyssa off guard. She had thought she would get some help to search, but clearly that wasn't how things worked.

Just looking around the walls almost made her despair. How many books were in this room? And this was where she should *start*! How could she ever have imagined that she would walk in here and find an answer?

Well, she was here now. It would be even more ridiculous to leave without trying. She found the shelves labeled LANGUAGES OF THE ARCHIPELAGO, and started with the top left-hand book.

An hour and a half later she'd checked two shelves and had a thumping headache. With some of the books it was obvious as soon as she opened them that they were no use to her. Sometimes the letter forms were so different that it only took a glance. Other books had to be looked at much more closely, though, and a couple she had left on one of the tables as perhaps being relevant.

She longed for a drink of water. The scholars in the room seemed hardly to have moved, poring over their volumes, making notes on sheaves of paper. How could they do this all day? She sighed and turned to the third shelf.

Just then the door opened and a priestess in robes of ink-dark blue entered. A woman, definitely, not a girl. She had hair as black as a rook's wing, drawn smoothly back into an elaborate knot at the nape of her neck, and the profile of an empress on a coin. She came straight over to Nyssa.

"Xanthe thought I might be able to help you. Is that the text?" She held out her hand and Nyssa gave her the paper. She studied it carefully for a minute or so, then handed it back.

"Well, you won't find anything *here* to help you. We'll have to go downstairs."

Nyssa's heart skipped a beat. "You mean you understand it?"

"Oh no. But I can tell it's much too old a language to be up here. Come."

She turned gracefully, led Nyssa out of the room and back to the stairs. This time they descended several flights. The woman walked swiftly and Nyssa had to hurry to keep up.

"How far down does this go?" she asked.

"There are seven levels below the ground, two above. They go far into the hillside. Visitors usually comment on how small the

Library looks from outside. This way." She opened a door and ushered Nyssa not into a corridor this time but a broad chamber, also brightly lit, and as crammed with books and scrolls as the room she had just left.

The priestess strode to the far side of the room and scanned the shelves.

"My name is Dido," she said absently. "I am the Guardian of the Library. Who are you?"

"I'm called Nyssa." She launched into her story as Dido moved to another section of shelving and took down a book.

"Which theater company?" Dido said, ignoring the false part of the story altogether.

"Roon's Traveling Players."

"Ah, yes. I'm looking forward to them: *The Queen of the Underworld's Daughter*, isn't it?"

"Yes," said Nyssa, surprised that she would know so much and be thinking of coming to such a lowly event as a play.

"And what part do you play?"

"Oh — I don't play anything. I'm the Company's cook."

"Ah." Dido rejected the book she was looking at and moved to a completely different part of the room. "An important job. I suppose you have other duties as well?"

"I help with the costumes and listen to people's lines."

Dido brought half a dozen books across to a table. "And have you been with the Company for long?"

"About a year," Nyssa improvised. "Before that I cooked for an inn."

"Try these." She pointed to the books. "I'm not sure, though — let me see the paper again." She seemed to look at it for a long time before she handed it back. "You have the rest of the text written down somewhere, I assume? Is it a long piece?"

"Not very long," faltered Nyssa, suddenly afraid. How much did Dido know?

"I'll send someone back later to see how you're getting on," the priestess added.

"I've only got a couple of hours before I have to go back. Can I come again if I don't find anything this time?"

"Yes, of course. I'd be disappointed if you were so easily defeated," she said. "And bring the whole text next time." With that, she left Nyssa to the new books.

With shaking fingers, Nyssa pulled the other piece of paper from her bodice, this one with the whole tattoo on it. The writing in the books certainly looked more like the symbols in the tattoo, but not the same. She shut the last book and got up with a sigh. She wasn't sure if she was supposed to wait for someone to escort her back to the entrance, but she didn't want to spend any more time than she had to in here. She could almost feel the books pressing in on her. She put the books carefully back on the shelves and climbed the stairs back to daylight.

Xanthe was in the entrance hall, so Nyssa was able to say thank you before she stepped out into the sun and air again. She made her way without further challenge out of the Temple Precincts and started down the hill, unaware of the figure that darted out of the gateway a little behind her and followed her back to the villa.

THE TRUTH

Roon gave everyone a morning to themselves the day before their first performance. The scenery was all in place, the costumes ready. Everyone — even Aria — knew their lines.

"Time to rest our voices," said Roon. "No shouting or singing today. Today we relax, tomorrow we perform."

One part of Nyssa longed to go straight to the Library, but she also wanted to spend some time alone with Marius, Kit, and Aria. She decided to do that first, and the four of them went out together soon after breakfast, to walk around the town and take in the beginning of the festival.

It was a beautiful morning: hyacinth blue sky streaming with pure white clouds, and just enough breeze to keep it pleasantly cool. They chose a route that took them past the Lotus Fountain, the largest in the city, its bowl carved like an enormous flower. The spray of water reached high above them and was blown on the breeze so that droplets pattered onto their upturned faces as they stood to watch, a welcome contrast to the dust-laden air.

Here in the upper part of the city there wasn't yet much in the way of celebration, but as they came down into the less refined areas, the festival was everywhere.

Even at this hour there were street entertainers out: stilt walkers and fire-eaters, jugglers and magicians, tumblers and snake charmers. There were food stalls selling dried fruits, pigeons cooked in honey, skewered meats, sweets, sherbets, and spiced wine. Nyssa knew enough about the spices now to be able to identify some of the scents: clove, cinnamon, the heady scent of nutmeg.

If the smell of the Archipelago was salt and herbs and grilled fish, here it was spices and dust and sweat.

They looked anxiously at every notice they saw pinned to doorposts, but they were simply flyers for theater companies and taverns.

There were people in many styles of dress, speaking in many different languages and dialects, obviously come from far and wide for the festival. There were pale-skinned northerners, and faces in every possible shade of brown, and a bewildering variety of hair and tattoos and jewelry. Some visitors looked to be from the Archipelago, and she saw two men who could only be Horse Lords, but she had no idea about many of the others.

Kit, with his newfound semiprofessional interest, was studying the jugglers.

"What a place," said Marius, with some understatement. "Of course, it won't always be as busy as this, but I don't suppose it's ever quiet—not by our standards, anyway."

"No. There would always be business here if you had a trade," said Aria absently.

"I thought you'd given that up," said Marius sharply.

Aria flushed. "I have. It's *you* who seems to have a problem remembering that. It's none of your business, anyway. You're not my father."

"Your *father*? Is that how . . ."

"What?"

"Oh, never mind."

Kit looked from one to the other, trying to understand the angry silence. He poked Nyssa in the ribs to see if she would explain, but she shook her head.

They bought some sticky grape paste and a bag of dried apricots at a stall, and covered the silence by eating until the atmosphere relaxed a bit, then dawdled along, watching a fire-eater and a troop of tumblers.

"Well, it doesn't look as though you'll be short of an audience," said Nyssa.

"Don't. I'm nervous enough as it is," replied Aria.

"You don't need to be," Marius objected. "You're good."

Aria didn't answer, but it seemed that peace had been restored.

No longer feeling that she had to stay as a buffer between them, Nyssa took her leave and set off for the Library.

Xanthe met her in the entrance again, almost as if she had been expecting her. "We thought you might have been back before now. I'm to take you to Dido — I think she has some more ideas about where you should look," she said.

This time Xanthe took her upstairs, knocked on a door, then ushered her in and left.

Nyssa had expected to find Dido poised over a book, and was surprised to find her lounging on a sofa near the open window, a tray of sweetmeats and a delicate flask of ruby-colored liquid on an inlaid table at her side.

"Ah, Nyssa. Come in, sit down. I'm happy to see you again. It's not often I'm presented with such an interesting problem. I've enjoyed pitting myself against the Library's desire to guard its secrets." She held out the tray of sweetmeats and Nyssa accepted one, rather in awe of the priestess and her surroundings. "Pomegranate juice?" Dido went on, and poured some without waiting for an answer.

Nyssa was glad to rest for a while in the airy room before she plunged again into the claustrophobic depths of the Library. The sweat from the climb up the hill was already drying on her forehead as she settled herself.

"How are the preparations going?"

"Finished, more or less. At least, we've been given the morning off."

"I think I could have enjoyed a life on the stage if I had not been chosen to be a priestess," Dido mused, sipping her drink. "But you are content to work behind the scenes?"

"Oh yes. I couldn't stand up there in front of everyone."

"And your brother, the juggler? Does he enjoy the performance or the practice more?"

Nyssa didn't remember mentioning a brother. She glanced at Dido, but the question was innocuous enough.

"He's certainly enjoyed learning. We'll see how he enjoys doing it in front of an audience." She realized just too late that this didn't really match with what she'd told Dido about being with Roon for a year. She took another swallow of the fruit juice to cover her confusion.

"And he's your twin. You did tell me that, didn't you?"

"I don't remember telling you that." Nyssa put down her glass in a panic.

"How strange . . . He is, though, isn't he?"

Rattled now, Nyssa couldn't decide whether it would be worse to confirm it or deny it.

"Yes," she said, hoping she hadn't just made a terrible error.

"Anyway, enough chitchat. I'm sure you're keen to get back to the books since you only have a morning." Dido put down her glass and got up, and Nyssa followed suit.

This time they went to the very bottom of the stairs, Dido carrying a lamp with her. The Precincts reminded Nyssa more and more of an anthill, busy on the surface, but with much more concealed below. Roon had been telling them only yesterday about the labyrinth that was reputed to lie beneath the Temple, heaped with the accumulated treasure of centuries. Perhaps the story was actually true, and this was the source of the power of the priestesses and their great city-state.

The door had to be unlocked before they could enter, and the room beyond was in darkness. It exhaled a smell of old paper and long-dried ink.

"Wait there until I light the lamps," Dido said. She moved around the room, kindling other lamps from the one she carried.

As the light grew, Nyssa looked around the chamber. The walls were roughly finished, and she could imagine the room being hollowed out of the hill long ago. The walls seemed to soak up sound, so that she was suddenly aware of the beat of her own pulse and of how alone the two of them were down here.

Dido finished with the lamps, went back to the door, and turned the key in the lock. She dropped the key into her pocket.

"Sit down," she said, motioning to a number of high-backed chairs set around a table. "I think I have the answer to your puzzle, but first we need to talk."

Nyssa's anxiety level rose sharply, from wary to frightened, but she could see no alternative to doing what Dido said. Wordlessly, she sat. Dido took a seat opposite her.

"You have lied from the moment you came in here. I do not know if you have a living mother, but these words did not come to her in a trance. I think it is time you showed me the rest of the text."

Nyssa was terrified, but locked inside this ancient chamber with Dido, she felt powerless to refuse what was effectively a demand. She took the copy of the tattoo from her bodice and slid it across the table.

Dido picked it up and studied it for several minutes.

"You may not know what these words mean, but you know what they are," she said finally.

Nyssa's throat contracted. She could hardly breathe, much less speak.

"The question is *how* do you know? How do you come to have them? I recognized them as soon as I saw them, of course; we in the Library have guarded them for centuries. But why would *you* recognize them?

"I set a watch on you and your companions after your first visit. Of course you didn't mention your brother to me then. You'd have to be careful about that, after all. You don't look like twins: That was a lucky guess. But put all the pieces together and out comes one question I must ask you: Are you the Bearer of these words? Don't pretend ignorance of what I mean."

Nyssa was so frightened that she could barely speak.

"No," was all she could manage.

Dido rose and came around the table. "You will not mind if I reassure myself that you're telling the truth? Untie your hair."

"No!" Nyssa surged to her feet and backed away, looking in vain for something she could use as a weapon. To her amazement and relief, Dido sat down again.

"And that, I think, is all the answer I need. I've often wondered what I would do if this moment came in my time. I must confess, I had thought you were probably all dead, or the White Wolf would have taken you by now.

"If you are truly the Bearer, you have nothing to fear from me. Will you let me look?"

"Why not?" said Nyssa shakily. "I'm in your power, after all." She unpinned her hair and shook it free.

Dido rose again and came around to stand behind her, lifting and parting Nyssa's hair with her fingers. Nyssa heard her take a sharp breath, then she let the hair fall and returned to her seat, two spots of color now in her cheeks. She looked at Nyssa as though seeing her for the first time.

"First, you should know you are safe here. No one in the Precincts will harm you. Indeed, no one else knows about you. Yours is one of the secrets passed on with the guardianship of the Library.

"The meaning of the words you carry is in this room, but you must be sure you want to know. Remember, the secret could be pried from you once you have it, so consider well before you take this knowledge, Keepers' Daughter."

"I *do* want to know. My family was killed for these words, my brother and I are hunted because of them. We want to know what they mean."

"Very well." Dido rose and went to a set of shelves near the door. The book she took down was small and thin, with a binding of battered brown leather. It looked like nothing. She put it on the table in front of Nyssa.

For a while all she could do was stare at the cover; then she roused herself and opened it. The words on the first page were so familiar, so unexpected that she thought it was a mistake, or a joke.

"This can't be right," she said, looking up at Dido.

Dido nodded. "Read," was all she said.

Nyssa read:

"*This is the Legend, as it has been passed down through the generations from the days before the earth and . . .*"

"But I already know this," she protested.

"Keep reading."

Nyssa read, every word echoing around in her head from a

hundred tellings in the Drowned Boy. The words that every child in the Archipelago knew.

"*. . . the Keepers were reviled and shunned and scattered. Thira was abandoned to become a haunt of spiders and snakes and scorpions.*

"*Thus were the Keepers punished for their presumption in awakening the Gods.*"

That was the end of the Legend, but it was not the end of the book. Nyssa read on.

"*After the disaster, some remnants of the Keepers made their way to the powerful state of Rushiadh and begged for succor. They were taken into the Temple and cared for, and for a few years they found peace there. But they could not settle away from the Archipelago, and at last they decided to return, whatever might befall them when they did so.*

"*Among them was one of those who had uttered the words believed to have brought down the cataclysm. She believed that the knowledge of those words must be safeguarded lest some evil reemerge.*

"*The Keepers had their own plans to keep the words safe among them, but they asked that the Great Library should hold the secret also.*

"*This the Priestesses agreed to, and they swore to keep them secret from any casual scholar and safe from those who might seek to use them, unless in time the meaning of the words was lost even to the Keepers and they should send one of their own seeking understanding.*

"*The Keepers returned to the Archipelago, and nothing more was heard from them again in Rushiadh.*"

There were two more pages.

On the first were written the characters now so familiar to Nyssa, and below them, written in the Common Tongue:

"There is no help
against the Shadow
that destroys the Light
but what courage
you find within
your own heart."

Nyssa stared and stared at the words as though the letters would at any moment rearrange themselves to say something quite different. She pulled the piece of paper from her bodice where she had returned it after Dido's scrutiny and compared the letters written there with the characters at the top of the page in front of her. There were two or three tiny differences, but surely nothing that could radically change the meaning. She looked up at Dido.

"But this can't be right. This can't be all it means. Have you seen what it says?"

The priestess nodded her head. "This book has been in the Great Library for generations. This is what the Guardian of the Library was told to write by the woman who spoke these words at the time of the cataclysm."

Nyssa shook her head. Whatever she had expected, it wasn't this.

"I joked once," she said, "that maybe we were being hunted for something that meant nothing, but I never thought . . ."

She turned to the final page. There were only a few lines to read this time.

"The words that preceded the destruction were spoken together by a man and a woman."

The words of the tattoos were written out again underneath, and below that, a translation, not of what they meant in the Common Tongue, but of how they should be pronounced in their original form.

Nyssa read them several times, her lips moving silently as she mouthed the strange words.

"And what happens if I speak these words aloud?"

Dido shrugged. "I know only what we all do: what it says in the Legend. But how can these words cause islands to be broken? I have no idea."

"Perhaps the Legend is just that, and there is nothing real in it at all." Nyssa sighed. "I can't think straight anymore."

"There is one more thing you should see," said Dido, rising again. Nyssa watched her reach behind a row of books to bring out a small metal cylinder and lay it on the table. Around its center marched a line of Cranes.

"What's this?" she asked.

Dido shook her head. "I do not know. It has never been opened. The first Guardian swore to put it only into the hands of a Bearer and never to open it. We have all kept faith."

Nyssa twisted the metal cap from the end of the tube and pulled out a small roll of parchment. The writing on it was faded, and she had to hold it near the lamp to make it out.

I write this in the Common Tongue, for I fear our Clan and its language may disappear and die.

Greetings, then, Bearer, Keepers' Daughter or Keepers' Son. I and your people must beg your forgiveness for the terrible burden you carry.

I was there at the Great Destruction, and I am the only one left now who knows the truth of it.

The words you carry were spoken by two of us together, as the Legend says, but not to the gods. We spoke to the people, trying to give them the heart to fight, for nothing we could do would save them. But as we did so, the earth broke and the sea boiled, and Thira was laid waste and so was the Shadow fleet.

The people believed that this was our doing, but it was not so.

Some of us escaped from the anger of the Archipelago and came to Rushiadh. There we thought long about how the Archipelago could be saved if the Shadow returned.

We let the world believe that we had caused the destruction by speaking these words, man and woman together. We let it be known, as though it was a secret poorly kept, that we tattooed the words of power onto the skulls of the firstborn twins of each generation, boy and girl, so that if the Shadow returned to threaten the Archipelago again, we could destroy them. Twins, we chose, because the Shadow Clan was always ruled by twins, believing them to be sacred and to carry magic within themselves.

And so we tattooed our children, though the words had no power except perhaps to inspire people to find courage *within themselves. And thus we made of our children a sacrifice to fear, and thus were we truly punished.*

Nyssa's hand shook as she read it again. She rolled it up to put back in its case. As she did so, the fragile paper cracked at its edges and small pieces crumbled away in her fingers. She stared at it numbly.

"Whatever you have read there is meant for you and your brother alone. You must take time to consider what it means for the two of you."

"Yes." Nyssa tried to gather her thoughts. "I should go back now. They'll wonder why I've been away so long."

Dido unlocked the door and snuffed the lamps and led Nyssa back up the stairs. By the time they reached the top, Nyssa had collected herself enough to be polite.

"Thank you for this. At least I have an answer now. Perhaps . . . perhaps we can use it to persuade the White Wolf to leave us alone."

"Perhaps. But he may find it hard to believe that that is all there is."

-⁚-   -⁚-   -⁚-

All the way down the hill to the villa, the words sounded like a drumbeat in Nyssa's head, over and over, over and over. She was still too shocked by the translation and the contents of the scroll to begin to think about what it might mean for her and Kit.

Back in the villa, there was no opportunity for private discussion. As soon as she shut the gate Thorn appeared, asking what there was to eat, followed by Lark and Kit, wearing tunics, baggy trousers, and turbans of bright silk that they had dug out of the costume chests.

"Roon says we're good enough to go on before the play begins," said Lark. "I've wanted a juggling partner for ages so I could do this."

Looking at Kit's happy face below the silk, Nyssa thought he was barely recognizable as the scrawny, terrified boy they had rescued from Thira.

She summoned the smile he deserved. "That's wonderful."

‡   ‡   ‡

It was evening before she managed to find privacy to speak to Marius, Kit, and Aria. She locked the door of the bedroom that she and Aria shared before she told them what had happened in the Great Library.

Kit fingered his head as though he might be able to feel the words. Aria said nothing, although Nyssa could tell she was desperate to ask questions.

Marius spoke. "And you believed this woman, this priestess? What was her name?"

"Dido. Yes, I did. Marius, I saw the book and the scroll myself. It was what's written on our heads."

"But why? All these deaths. My mother, my sister . . . All for *this*?" Without warning, Marius's temper snapped. He hurled his glass of wine at the wall and strode from the room, the door crashing shut behind him.

Nyssa started to go after him but Aria caught her arm. "Leave him be. He's too angry to listen to anyone just now. He'll get drunk, or get into a fight, and then he'll calm down, and tomorrow you'll be able to talk to him. You need time to think, too. And so do you, Kit."

She got up and went to tidy the broken glass and mop up the mess.

-+-   -+-   -+-

Aria was right. Next morning, Marius appeared, nursing a hangover, full of apologies.

"You've nothing to apologize for," said Nyssa. "Stop it."

"A rational man might stop searching if he found out what the tattoos mean," he said.

"Is Alaric a rational man? Even if he is, he wouldn't believe it on hearsay, and they won't let him see the books here. They're sworn not to. Now that I've found the answer, I'm not so sure it makes any difference to us at all."

"Nor am I. I think for the time being we just go on as we are and try to convince Roon to keep us all on — until we think of something better."

-+-   -+-   -+-

Opening night. The scenery was in place, the actors in costume. Aria was so nervous she'd been sick, and was touching up her makeup so she didn't look too pale. Nyssa was trying to ignore Thorn's complaints about the way her hair looked.

In the theater aisle, dressed in their silks, Kit and Lark tossed their clubs and balls back and forth. At the back of the stage, Marius prepared the last of the mixtures that would change the color of the lights, then rolled up his sleeves so that he wouldn't set fire to himself when he lit them.

Nyssa peeked around the curtain. The theater was almost full. People chatted to friends, or looked around to see who they recognized. In the most expensive seats, highborn residents of the city relaxed and gossiped, fanning themselves to keep cool.

"Right. Let's go," said Roon. "Marius, get the boys back here. Lark needs to change."

If Nyssa had been Lark, about to take the title part in a play in front of all these people, she would have been curled in a corner shaking with fear, not happily juggling in front of them until the last possible second.

Perhaps you had to be born to it, she thought.

Lark came rushing past her, grinning, to get into his dress and wig. Aria stood beside Nyssa, nervously twisting a strand of her hair around her fingers. Marius lit the lamps for the first scene, then, at a signal from Roon, wound the curtain back.

The noise of the audience stilled.

"Good people! Be welcome here tonight. Lay aside your toils and cares. Free your hearts and minds to come with us to the Netherworld of the Gods." Marius moved behind the scenery and kindled his red lamps. "Come now to the Underworld and hear the tragic tale of the Queen of the Underworld's Daughter."

Aria gave Nyssa's hand a quick squeeze, and made her entrance.

-‡-   -‡-   -‡-

The Queen of the Underworld howled in anguish over the body of her daughter. The curtain closed, Thorn sang her unearthly lament from behind it, and the audience broke into loud applause and shouts of approval.

Lark got to his feet, straightened his wig, and pulled Aria to her feet. Her eyes were brilliant, her face ecstatic.

"Listen to them," she said breathlessly. "Just listen to that."

"Places!" yelled Roon over the noise. The Players formed a line, and the curtain swept back again so they could take their bows. Once Marius had wound it shut for the final time, they relaxed, whooping in triumph, embracing, and congratulating each other.

Roon kissed Aria's hand. "Well done, my dear. An excellent start. You have the makings of a fine actress.

"Performance notes before you change," he called to everyone. "My dressing room, now."

The actors trooped off, leaving Nyssa, Kit, and Marius. Nyssa began to pick up discarded props and costumes from the wings while Marius snuffed the last of the stage lights, then the three of them reset the stage for the next performance. Kit and Nyssa left Marius checking that everything was where it should be and took the costumes back to the dressing rooms.

"So, how do you like being part of a traveling theater company?" she asked her brother.

"It's good."

"Should we try to convince them to keep us on?"

He gave her a lopsided smile and nodded vigorously.

Nyssa took her armful of clothes into Aria's dressing room and found her already there, taking off her makeup. She smiled at Nyssa in the mirror.

"Well done," said Nyssa, putting down the clothes and hugging her. "You were wonderful."

Aria beamed at her. "I loved it. I loved every second. Once I got on the stage, I wasn't nervous anymore. And at the end . . . I never imagined it would be like that."

"Perhaps you've found a new life."

"Perhaps. I mustn't get carried away, though. That's just one performance. It could all fall apart tomorrow."

"Pessimist."

"Realist. I can't afford not to be."

20

TAKEN

The first night proved to be a good indication of what was to follow. Aria got better and better with every performance, the juggling became more complex, the stage effects smoother. The theater was at least two-thirds full every night, and the audience loved the play. It seemed that all Roon's hopes for the visit to Rushiadh would be fulfilled.

The days took on a new pattern: late starts to the mornings, costume and scenery repairs. For Nyssa, cooking and shopping for food. The boys practiced their juggling every day, the actors their singing and lines. Roon shut himself away for a couple of hours each afternoon to work on a new play, inspired by his current success. He told Aria that he was writing the lead part specifically for her, then called her back and warned her not to let Thorn find out.

At some performances, there were parties of official visitors to the city in the audience, or groups of priestesses. At the end of the first week Nyssa saw Dido and Xanthe and realized she'd been too busy to give more than a passing thought to tattoos or any of the other things that seemed to have ruled her life for so long.

"Did you enjoy it?" she asked.

"Oh yes!" said Xanthe. "It was so sad."

"But only because the Queen of the Underworld's daughter didn't heed her mother's warnings," said Dido gravely. Then she smiled to take the sting from her words. "It was very good, Nyssa, especially the Queen and Prince Amnatos. I hear it's one of the most popular plays in the whole festival."

"Is it? I didn't know that."

"It's true among the priestesses, certainly."

"Nyssa! We need you back here," Marius called.

"We should go, anyway," said Dido. "But we might come back and see it again."

⊹   ⊹   ⊹

The second week came and went. The weather grew hotter by the day. No one ventured out without a water bottle, and no one ventured out near midday at all. It was hot in the Archipelago in the summer, of course, but Nyssa had never experienced anything like this. At home there had usually been a breeze from the sea to take the edge off the heat, but in Rushiadh, all that blew was a bad-tempered wind from the desert, which scoured everything and everyone with sand and made it even hotter.

They became aware of how few performances were left, and began to think about where they would go next. Nothing explicit was said, but Roon seemed to assume that all four of his new recruits would be involved. The new play, he said, was more than half-written. Perhaps they would stay on here to rehearse it.

On their fifth from final night, there was still a large block of empty seats in front of the stage when they began.

"Officials delayed at some banquet," said Roon dismissively. "They sent a lackey to tell me. I just hope they don't cause too much disturbance when they do get here. No manners, these people. Think they're more important than everyone else."

They began, despite the gap in the audience. From the stage, dazzled by lights, they couldn't really see the crowd, anyway. About half an hour into the performance they were aware of a shuffling and noise that must have been the empty seats filling up. It so happened that this took place in the middle of one of Roon's speeches. He paused theatrically, glaring into the lights until everything had settled, before he went on again.

Marius was waiting beside Nyssa and Kit in the wings, ready for the next lighting change, for which he had to go onstage between scenes.

"Why don't I get a costume?" he said jokingly to Kit. "You've got one and you don't set foot on the stage. I must be on there almost as much as Thorn, but I just have to go out in my own clothes."

Kit laughed.

Marius rolled up his sleeves and took and swig of water, then wiped the sweat from his brow. "I take it all back," he said. "I don't know how they stand wearing those costumes in this heat."

The scene ended to loud applause, and he darted onto the stage to light one set of lamps and snuff another.

"I take it that was the officials arriving?" Nyssa said to Pavlos as he came off.

"I suppose so. You can't really see anything from the stage, though, because of the lights. If the audience kept quiet, we'd think we were playing to an empty house. Strange to think they can see us so clearly—even Marius there."

"*Mmnn* . . . He was just claiming that he should have a costume because he goes onstage so much."

"Hah!" exclaimed Pavlos a bit too loudly, earning himself a poke in the ribs from Conor.

It was so hot that evening that all the performers had to redo their makeup during the intermission; it had almost sweated off. Nyssa and Kit were kept busy fetching bottles of water for the actors to drink whenever they came offstage.

The rest of the performance went well, though, and the curtain closed for the night to the enthusiastic approval they had come to expect.

The cleanup was now a well-rehearsed routine, and Kit and Nyssa helped Marius to move the scenery before taking costumes and props down to the dressing rooms.

"Look," said Nyssa, pointing to Marius's arm. "It must be hot. We'll have to watch that."

Marius looked at the smeared remains of his disguised tattoo, at the center of which the Crane could clearly be seen. "Oops," he said, pulling down his sleeve. "It's the heat from the lights. I'll get Aria to fix it tomorrow morning. What are yours like?"

The ink that disguised their tattoos was smeared as well, though not as badly as his. Aria would need a steady hand in the morning.

＋　　＋　　＋

"Another good night," Nyssa said to Aria, starting to hang up costumes.

"Yes — apart from all that noise when the latecomers arrived." She peered at her face in the mirror. "I thought Roon was going to get down off the stage and tell them to be quiet."

"I'd love to have seen that!" Nyssa chuckled.

The door opened. Nyssa turned, expecting to see one of the Company, but to her amazement it was Dido, alone. She looked agitated. Nyssa opened her mouth to speak, but Dido held up a hand to stop her.

"I'm sorry. There's not much time." She glanced at Aria. "I must speak to you on your own."

Nyssa looked at Dido's urgent face. "Aria knows everything — *everything*. You can speak in front of her."

"There are Shadowmen here. They have taken the man with the sign of the Crane. They'll be back here any minute looking for Keepers. You and your brother must come with me. Now."

Nyssa gaped. Aria sat frozen in the act of wiping off makeup.

"They've taken Marius?"

"I don't know his name. Hurry!"

The girls came to life. "I'll get Kit," said Aria. "Wait here." She rushed out.

"Are there cloaks in here, Nyssa? Hurry—we must get away from this place." Nyssa rummaged through a pile of clothes for cloaks. "Are there any more Keepers with you?"

Nyssa shook her head. "But they're hunting Aria as well. She must come with us."

"Very well, but no one else."

Aria and Kit appeared at that moment. Kit saw the strange woman, then looked at Nyssa's grim face.

"What?"

Nyssa tossed him a cloak. "Shadowmen. They've captured Marius." Her voice cracked as she said it. "The priestesses will help us, but we must go *now*."

They fastened the cloaks, pulled up their hoods, and followed Dido out of the building, then through a bewildering succession of twisting lanes until they emerged in front of the white marble wall that bounded the Precincts. A modest gate of dark wood stood before them; not the entrance that Nyssa had used before.

Dido glanced around and pulled a key on a chain from the neck of her robe. Silently she opened the gate, ushered them through, and locked it behind them again.

They were in a small, dark room. Dido moved across it and they heard the sound of tinder being struck. A lamp bloomed. Dido looked at the three white-faced fugitives and wondered if she'd done the right thing.

"You're safe here. Shadowmen would never be allowed to enter the Precincts. Sit down."

They were in some sort of storeroom. Numbly, they sat down on sacks of grain, pushing back their hoods.

"What happened?" It was Aria who had collected her wits enough to speak. "Are you sure they've taken Marius?"

Dido nodded gravely. "A delegation arrived from Thira a few days ago — ten men — but I didn't know until I found myself with them at a dinner tonight. I wouldn't have recognized them as Shadowmen — they were dressed in formal clothes.

"When I heard they were going on to see your play, I sent for Xanthe and arranged to be present myself, but I had no opportunity to send warning to you. I wasn't worried, though: I knew neither you nor your brother would be onstage.

"I sat beside one of them and Xanthe sat with another, so that we could try to distract them if it was necessary. But I was only thinking of you two. I didn't realize there was anyone else.

"When he — Marius, you say? — came on to change the lighting, you could see the tattoo. One of them must have noticed, and they started to whisper among themselves.

"As soon as the play finished, they rushed out. There was nothing we could do to stop them. Then six were sent back in. We tried to reach the man with the Crane tattoo, who was on the stage alone, but they were too fast. I don't think he had any idea what was happening. He had no chance to fight back or escape.

"I tried to protest. 'What did they think they were doing? They were guests of the city, how dare they attack another guest?' But the leader just laughed at me, and they dragged the man out. I sent Xanthe to follow them and find out where he'd been taken, and came to warn you myself."

Dido fell silent.

"Is he . . . did they hurt him?" said Nyssa fearfully.

"He was still on his feet when they took him out of the theater."

Kit had wound his arms as tight as he could around his rib cage, and was rocking back and forth. Aria's hands were over her mouth, stifling sobs. Nyssa felt as though the world had stopped, as though someone had reached into her chest and crushed her heart.

Dido spoke into the awful silence. "I can hide you in the Library for a short while. We'll wait here until there's no one around, then I'll take you. Xanthe will meet us there and tell us what has happened. I'm sorry."

Because she couldn't bear to look at their stricken faces anymore, Dido turned and pretended to look out the little window that faced into the Precincts. *It would have been much easier,* she thought, *just to pretend she hadn't known what was happening. There was nothing at stake for her if the Shadowmen chose to take all of this ragtag theater troupe.* Nothing except her integrity, of course.

-÷-   -÷-   -÷-

His mind had been elsewhere. He had thought he was safe here. He had let his guard down. He was an idiot.

He was a dead man.

The thoughts cycled ceaselessly through Marius's brain as he was forcibly marched down the hill to who knew where, hands bound behind him, knife tickling his ribs.

To a casual passerby he wouldn't look like a prisoner at all, just someone who'd had a bit too much to drink and was being helped home by his friends.

"Where are you taking me?" He couldn't stay silent any longer.

The knife jabbed him. "Be quiet, Keeper. We're taking you home with us for a bit of a party. The White Wolf's always interested in your kind. We might get a bonus for taking you back to Thira as a souvenir. Especially if you know anything interesting."

The tiniest spark of hope kindled in Marius's heart. Was it possible that they didn't actually know who he was, that they had taken him because of the Crane tattoo, nothing more?

He looked more carefully at the men around him, counting heads. As far as he could tell, no one had stayed behind at the theater, in which case they weren't yet looking for the others.

What about that priestess who had protested at his "arrest"? Would she have warned the others what had happened?

All he could do now to help them was pretend total ignorance of them, and hope that somehow he found a chance to escape.

-:-   -:-   -:-

Roon and the others were surprised to find that Aria, Marius, Kit, and Nyssa had left the theater without mentioning they were going, but since the Company often split into groups to eat or drink after a show, no one thought much of it that night.

⊹   ⊹   ⊹

"Put your hoods up again. I'll take you across to the Library. We shouldn't meet anyone at this time, but if we do, don't speak," said Dido.

They slipped from the storeroom into the night-scented gardens of the priestesses and walked toward the Library. Once they were inside, Dido took them straight down to the room where Nyssa had found the truth about the tattoos.

"No one comes in here without my permission. I have the only key. It's not comfortable, but it is safe." She looked around. "I'll bring down some food and water and try to find blankets. I'll be back soon."

They heard the key turn in the lock and sank despondently into chairs. Across the table from her, Nyssa watched Kit grimacing as though he was trying to speak, but couldn't. His face twisted in frustration and without warning he thrust his arm out and pressed the tender skin of his wrist against the hot lamp. He pulled it back with a yelp.

"What can we do? How do we help?" The painfully freed words tumbled out of him.

Kit's action shocked the girls out of their own defeated silence.

"Kit—your arm—let me see." Nyssa reached across, but he shook his head and cupped his burned wrist in his other palm.

"What do we do?" Aria echoed Kit's words. "We're the only people who can help Marius, but how?"

"Roon certainly won't lift a finger to help. It wouldn't be fair to expect him to. He shouldn't be involved. So it's just us."

"Dido said she'd sent someone to find out where he'd been taken, didn't she?" asked Aria.

"Yes. Perhaps once she comes back we can think what to do."

They sank back into silence until they heard footsteps coming down the stairs and the sound of the key in the lock. Dido and Xanthe appeared with an armful of blankets and a basket of food and water.

"Where is he? Is he all right?" Nyssa was on her feet before the door was even shut.

"He was all right when I left to come back here," said Xanthe. "They have taken him to the house they're staying in."

"Where is it?" asked Dido quickly.

"Kournas Street — the big residence."

"I'll get someone into the kitchens tomorrow to find out more."

"After they captured him they didn't look for anyone else in the theater," said Xanthe. "They just took him straight off."

"But why wouldn't they be searching for us if they found him? Do you think they don't know that we're all together?" mused Nyssa.

"If that's the case, it would make it easier to get you out of the city."

"But how will you get Marius away from the Shadowmen?" said Aria.

There was an awkward pause.

"I'm sorry: You don't understand. I can do nothing for your friend. Rushiadh and Thira are both power centers. They take care not to provoke each other. If it was known that the Temple had colluded in the escape of someone the Shadowmen will certainly claim is a wanted criminal, the consequences could be very unpleasant, especially now. Some of the islands are rebelling against the White Wolf. He would lash out especially hard at anything that seemed to challenge his authority, just to make the point that it's still he who is in control.

"The Library has a certain amount of . . . autonomy . . . from the rest of the Temple. Enough that I can hide you and help you to escape, but no more." She put down the blankets. "You should try to rest, and then think about where it would be safest for you to go."

She and Xanthe left, locking the door behind them.

A desperate silence fell again, unbroken for several minutes until Nyssa said, "I won't abandon him. I couldn't live with myself if I took the chance to run away and be safe. There is no safety, anyway." She shuddered, but felt she was beginning to think clearly. "Aria, will you take Kit with you and look after him? It's an impossible thing to ask, I know. . . . Maybe there's just a chance that you can both go back to the Company."

"No!"

The vehemence of the word shocked her. She looked up into Kit's eyes, saw them blazing with anger. He looked like a totally different person.

"I'm coming with you. Marius saved me from Alaric. I'm coming. I knew we would never be safe, anyway."

"No, Kit, please."

His face was utterly implacable, and it came to her again how strong he must be, under the fear, to have survived his life on Thira.

"I won't abandon him, either." Aria drew a shaky breath. "He . . . I . . . You are my family now. I won't leave you."

Nyssa looked into her friend's face and saw that she, too, had made up her mind.

"Very well, then." She poured the water with a shaky hand and started to pass out the food. "We must eat and drink and try to rest, while we wait for some news from Dido in the morning."

⁘ ⁘ ⁘

They took him into a big house some way down the hill, shoved him into a small, bare room, and locked the door. His hands were still tied, but it wouldn't have made any difference if they had been free: There was no window, and the locked door led only to a larger room full of his captors. The best he could do for now was to put his ear to the door and try to hear their plans for him.

"Are we really taking him back to Thira?"

"Why not? It might amuse the Wolf. You know what he's like about Keepers. There's plenty of room on the boat, after all."

So he was to meet the White Wolf face-to-face. There was only one way *that* was likely to end.

There was a general shuffling around. Chairs scraped and bottles chinked on glasses. "To unexpected bonuses," someone said, and everyone laughed.

To his surprise they left him alone after that. Presumably Alaric preferred his souvenirs undamaged. Eventually he lay down and thought of Nyssa and Kit and Aria, and tried to sleep.

-+- -+- -+-

Dido unlocked the door again.

"He's being taken to Thira," she said without preamble. "They leave for Trabzyn tomorrow. He's all right. At the moment they don't seem to realize his connection to you; just that he's a Keeper." She had brought more food, which she placed on the table. She sat down. "Have you had a chance to think?"

Nyssa looked at Aria and Kit. They nodded.

"Can you get us on a boat to Thira?"

"What?" Dido's eyes widened. "You're out of your minds. You should be heading as far from Thira as possible. You can't do this."

"It will be more difficult if we have to do it without your help, but it's what we're going to do. We have to try and find a way to rescue him. He's our uncle."

"You're insane. Have you any idea what it's *like* on Thira?"

"Yes," said Nyssa quietly. "My brother was the White Wolf's slave. Marius, Aria, and I stole him away."

"And you would go back there?" Dido was even more incredulous.

Nyssa gave a bleak smile. "At least they won't expect it."

Dido shook her head in bewilderment at their intentions. "Very well. I promised I would help you. But I didn't think you would want help to go to your deaths." She paused, thinking. "I'll send word to my family. They should be able to get you out of Rushiadh the day after tomorrow. You should be safe until then."

"Thank you. One more thing: We would like to send a message to the theater, explain why we disappeared without warning. The others deserve that."

Dido nodded. "It can't be sent until you've left, though. What if they were to betray you? And it can't mention that you've been hidden here."

"All right."

When Dido had gone, Nyssa got up purposefully and went to the bookcase beside the door. After a few minutes' search, she found what she was looking for—a small book and a scroll. She waited until Kit and Aria had both read them, watching as they sounded out the strange words, then took them back. They watched in silence as Nyssa slowly tore the papers to pieces and burned them to ashes in the lamp flame.

"One way or another," she said, "this ends with us."

✛   ✛   ✛

Xanthe came back with writing materials later that morning, and after much thought they wrote a short message to the Company:

We are sorry to disappear like this and leave you unable to stage the play. Please know this was never our intention. Marius has been arrested on false charges by men from the Archipelago. They will search for us, too. We would put you all in danger if we stayed with you.

Try not to think too badly of us. Good luck.

They all signed the letter. It wasn't the truth, of course, but the truth would have been no better. Nyssa was starting to think that truth was a highly overrated commodity, anyway.

A seemingly endless day of tension and boredom passed. It was almost impossible to keep track of time in the windowless room, and there was nothing they could do to make it pass more quickly. The books were impenetrable, even those in the Common Tongue.

At last they heard the key in the lock and Dido came in again.

"You leave tomorrow night," she said. "There will be someone at the door I brought you in by. My family has agreed to take you to Trabzyn and get you on a boat to Thira."

"We can't thank you enough," said Nyssa. "But I don't understand: I was told that when a girl is taken to be a priestess, she doesn't have contact with her family afterward."

Dido raised an eyebrow. "Not all families are happy to relinquish their daughters so completely. The poor ones can do nothing about it, of course, but if a family is rich or powerful enough, there are ways to stay in touch. Did you write your message?"

Aria handed it over and watched as Dido read it.

"Very discreet," she said approvingly. "I'll see that it's delivered once you're safely away. Do you want me to arrange to get your belongings before you go?"

"You can do that?"

"Oh yes. We can sneak someone in and out of any building in this city. Tell me where your things are and I'll have them fetched." Looking at their faces, she added, "There are a dozen reasons why tradesmen or gardeners or cleaners might visit your lodgings. After all, you never noticed the girl I sent to spy on you after we first met, Nyssa, did you?"

Nyssa opened her mouth, but couldn't think what to say.

⁜ ⁜ ⁜

They spent another uncomfortable night in the wretched room, lying sleepless on the floor with the books breathing in the dark around them. Nyssa's mind was filled with images that seemed to merge into one another: a white face with pale hair and cold eyes; William laughing in the kitchen of the Drowned Boy; Marius with an arrow in his shoulder; a doll in a green dress charring in a fire; an indistinct woman wearing a blue dress playing a bamboo flute.

As she had promised, Dido had most of their belongings brought to them in the middle of the morning.

"The Shadowmen left just after dawn," she said tersely. "You'll go an hour or so after midnight." She put a pile of books on the table in front of them. "I thought you should see these," she said. "They'll tell you more about what the Keepers were than anything you've seen before. They were put together by the first Guardians, when some of the Keepers fled here from Thira."

She opened one of the books.

"This page is from the Keepers' time, made by them on Thira. The facing page is a translation into the Common Tongue. They're all like that."

They clustered around, their minds diverted for a few minutes from Marius.

Neither Nyssa nor Aria had ever seen a book like it before. The lettering on the page from the Keepers' time was perfect, every letter evenly spaced, no sign of a pen nib blunting, no blots, no place where the ink had run dry. It was unnatural.

Somewhere in Nyssa's memory, something struggled to reach the surface. Perfect letters . . . something she'd seen . . .

"How did they do that?" she asked, too distracted by the writing itself to pay any mind yet to the content. "How did they get it so perfect?"

"We think it was done by a machine. It's called *printing*. These books were only rediscovered thirty years ago. We still haven't worked out how to do it ourselves, but give us a few years more . . ." Dido flashed an unexpected smile.

The memory that had been crawling to the surface of Nyssa's mind reached her consciousness.

"We've seen this before, Aria! Remember, on Thira? A sheet of paper you found in the street. I can't remember exactly what it said . . . But I knew there was something odd about it at the time—about how it was written. I couldn't think what it was, exactly, but I see it now. It was like this: too perfect. It must have been made the same way. Printed, not written."

Dido looked sharply at Nyssa. "Printing on Thira? Now? Surely not."

"I'm positive," said Nyssa. "I just didn't recognize what I was seeing. How could I? I'd never seen anything in my life that was written by a machine instead of a person. I didn't even know such a thing was possible."

"I remember now," Aria interrupted. "It said something like 'Citizens of Thira, be ready to fight back. Do not despair. The Tyrant will not prevail.'"

"This is incredible." Dido shook her head. "If you're right, then the resistance on Thira has rediscovered printing. No wonder rebellion is spreading."

"Why?" asked Nyssa.

"If you can print something, you can make as many copies as you want, all identical, all perfect — and very quickly. If the resistance can really do this, it can spread information much more easily.

"What a danger, though. If Alaric finds the machine . . ." She shivered, then seemed to remember why she had brought the books in the first place. "Anyway, I thought if you read these, it might help to pass the time. So few people now understand anything about the Keepers. If they're remembered at all, it's just as myths and magic, but the truth — if what's in these *is* the truth — is very different. I must go now. I'll be back after nightfall."

Nyssa moved the lamps to give the best light, and they

gathered around the table. Kit ran his fingers over a printed page.

"In Alaric's palace," he said, "there were pages of parchment like this, torn out of books. They used them to light fires."

They began to leaf through the books, wondering what they would find out, looking at the headings on the translated pages:

Of the Moon and the Tides
Of the Characters of Woods
Of the Treating of Wounds
Of Storms
Of the Dyeing of Leathers
Of the Finding of Fresh Water

There were stories, too:

The Tale of the Third Sister
The Tale of the Cobweb Necklace
How the Crane Saved the Emperor
The Ship That Sailed to the Moon

On and on the titles went, every few pages, through all the books.

They looked at each other.

"But these are . . . they're not . . . there's nothing . . . ," stammered Nyssa.

"I thought there would be something about magic," said Aria. "Spells or something."

Only Kit seemed unperturbed by what he read.

"Maybe there's something more if you read carefully enough," Nyssa suggested.

They each started to read one of the books more thoroughly. After half an hour, Nyssa and Aria looked at each other and shook their heads.

"Nothing."

"No magic at all."

Kit began to laugh. "Why would they *need* magic? The books tell them how to do everything they need."

They went back to their reading. After a while, Nyssa said, "Maybe it's the books themselves — the printing — that's the magic. You know what it says in the Legend about the Keepers sharing their knowledge? If every island had had all these books, they would be able to do just about anything. Maybe that's what the Keepers did that was so special. Imagine having books that contain the answer to anything you needed to know. . . ."

They looked at the books as though seeing them for the first time.

"I don't suppose you've found one called *How to Defeat the White Wolf* yet?" said Aria, with the ghost of a smile.

"Not yet," said Nyssa, and went back to reading.

Dido and Xanthe came for them after dark, to help move them and their things back to the storeroom. At least here they had a window and the night air blew in. They dozed and fretted the hours away until the priestess reappeared.

"Make yourselves ready," she said.

They wrapped their cloaks tight and waited, on edge, for whatever signal had been arranged. In the end it was nothing complicated: just a knock at the outer door. Dido opened it to two tall dark men who shared her profile.

"My cousins," she said, "Marcus and Adoni." She exchanged a few hurried words with them before embracing them and turning back to the fugitives.

"Go with them. There's a carriage waiting farther down the hill. If you should change your minds about your destination before you reach Trabzyn, tell them. They will give you what help they can. If not — good luck, you fools."

They stepped out of the Precincts and back into danger.

21

RETURN TO THIRA

For Marius it was almost a relief to reach Trabzyn. The journey back had been a hazy nightmare of heat and thirst. There was pain in his bound arms and shoulders from being tied to one of the ribs of the wagon and jarred every time it hit a rock or a pothole. He couldn't even wipe away the sweat dripping into his eyes. His captors hardly addressed a word to him, but they unbound him for a while each evening and gave him food and water. By then his arms were so painful that it was all he could do to raise the water bottle to his mouth.

Much of the time he spent adrift between sleep and waking. When he was alert, he talked to himself soundlessly in his head.

They're still safe. The Shadowmen didn't go after them. Every mile we go from Rushiadh makes them safer. I must stay strong. Stay ready for a chance.

When they came through the landward gate into Trabzyn, there was a brief wait while their papers were checked. For a moment Marius entertained a faint hope that he would appear as a discrepancy in the paperwork, but nothing came of it.

In the town the wagon was unloaded and the contents given to carriers to take down to the harbor. Marius was walked, at knifepoint again, down the zigzag path to where the familiar ominous shape of a Shadow ship waited on the dark water.

There were two or three Shadowmen on the ship, supervising the loading. They hailed their fellows as they approached. Marius was hustled up the gangway onto the deck.

"Look what we found!" His sleeve was hauled back roughly to show the tattoo.

"The Wolf will be pleased with that," one of them said.

Marius looked back up at the cliffs, saying a silent good-bye to Nyssa, Kit, and Aria.

"Take a long look, Keeper. You'll be in the hold for the journey."

They untied his hands then, and shoved him toward the ladder that led down to the hold. At that moment, the door of the deckhouse opened, and he found himself facing a blond-haired man. A man he recognized. The spark of hope he had nursed since his capture died. It was the man who'd been with Captain Jaxom the first time he came to their lodging: Merrick.

Merrick's jaw dropped. "Well, who have we here?" he said wryly. "Did you get the others, too?"

"What others?" said one of the men who'd been in Rushiadh, sounding less than pleased. "Do you not think one's enough?"

The blond man still hadn't taken his eyes from Marius's face. "You don't know who this is, do you?"

"He's a Keeper."

RETURN TO THIRA

"He's more than that. He's the one that the Wolf thinks was involved in Captain Jaxom's death and stole that dumb slave of his."

"Never!"

Merrick nodded. "We were told to look for four of them traveling together: him, two girls, and the mute boy."

"But there was just him."

"You're sure? You did check, didn't you?"

There was no answer.

"Didn't you?"

"We didn't *see* anyone else," said the man in charge of the expedition in Rushiadh, but he sounded doubtful now. "He was with a traveling theater company. We saw his tattoo when he was onstage, but none of the other actors had one, I'm sure of it." He sounded even less sure. "I could send some of our people back . . ."

Merrick shook his head impatiently. "There's no point. If they *were* with him, they'll be long gone. Best thing we can do now is get this one to the Wolf as quickly as possible and stick to your story that he was alone." He turned to Marius. "That's right, isn't it, Keeper?"

Marius swallowed. "Of course."

"Get him into the hold, then, and make sure it's secure. We don't want him going over the side."

-:-   -:-   -:-

Nyssa peeked around the curtain that shielded the window of the carriage from prying eyes, looking at one of the Horse Lords'

371

gates to the Underworld. It was less than five weeks since they had passed them, heading toward Rushiadh. She tried to remember what her feelings about the future had been the first time. Hope had been there, certainly. There was little of that now.

Dido's cousins had taken them swiftly by quiet lanes to a waiting carriage in the lower town. Marcus rode beside the driver and Adoni walked.

When they reached the city gates there was a long conversation between Adoni and the guards. Nyssa didn't dare look out to see what was happening, but she assumed a bribe was being negotiated, since the gates, now swinging open, were supposed to stay shut during the hours of darkness.

Adoni climbed in beside them, putting a finger to his lips to warn them to be silent, and they left the city behind.

They kept up a fast pace, stopping frequently to change horses, and staying each night in private houses. Everything had been arranged with care to speed them on their way. No one spoke to them much, not even the cousins. They were polite but distant, and clearly wanted to know as little as possible about the escapade in which Dido had involved them. Kit probably wouldn't have spoken, anyway, but Nyssa and Aria were relieved not to have to try to make conversation.

They reached Trabzyn late in the afternoon, the carriage clattering to a halt in a cobbled courtyard, and were ushered straight into another private house.

After they had eaten, Marcus said, "I'll go to the harbor and check that the Shadow ship has left for Thira." He paused. "Are you still sure that you want to go there?"

Nyssa nodded.

"Very well. Rest and refresh yourselves. I'll let you know what's happening as soon as I can."

He was back within an hour.

"They left on the morning tide. You go tomorrow morning. We've done well to only be twenty-four hours behind them. There's a room ready for you. You should try to get some sleep. I'll see that you're woken in plenty of time."

None of them was expecting any sleep, but fatigue had finally caught up with them and suddenly they were being shaken awake in the gray dawn.

They walked down the steep pathway, their bundles on a mule, to a small, sleek boat.

"This will take you anywhere in the Archipelago," said Adoni. "Dido was keen that we try to dissuade you from Thira, but she said we weren't to stop you if your minds were made up."

Nyssa looked at the others to see if they showed any signs of wavering.

"Thira," said Aria firmly. Kit nodded.

"You can't change your minds once you're on board. The captain will not accept orders from anyone outside the family," said Marcus.

"We won't be changing our minds," said Nyssa.

"Very well." Marcus shouted the captain over and spoke to him for some moments, then motioned the others on board and showed them to a comfortable cabin.

"This is smaller than a Shadow ship, but almost as fast, so

long as there's a wind. You should make Thira in five days. Good fortune go with you."

"Thank you," said Nyssa. "All. For everything."

Marcus and Adoni nodded and stepped back onto the dock-side; the boat cast off.

They watched the cliffs of Trabzyn shrink behind them in the morning light, Dido's words echoing in their minds.

"I didn't think you would want help to go to your deaths . . . Good luck, you fools."

-|-　　-|-　　-|-

He knew that they'd docked by the change in the motion of the ship and the increased noise. He'd let himself drift during the five-day voyage, allowing his mind to wander at will through his past and into futures that could only be imaginary, but now it was time to pull it back and tighten his focus to the present. He wouldn't give up hope yet; there were all sorts of things that could happen. Marius was finding a strength he never knew he had.

The hatch slid open and hot light flooded the hold. He shielded his eyes with his hand, squinting up as a ladder descended.

"Up you come, Keeper. Nearly there."

He climbed the ladder slowly to give his eyes time to adjust, so he wouldn't be like a mole caught in daylight when he reached the deck. He'd had enough of running. He'd face his fate with his head held high.

The dusty little harbor of Mili was before him; the sheds and motley collection of vessels as they had been before. And yet, not so. No ferries; but nothing odd about that, for they didn't dock every day. Half a dozen Shadow ships in, though, and a lot of Shadowmen on the dock—surely not because of him? There was an air of watchfulness that was even more intense than before.

He didn't have time to take in any more before his hands were bound in front of him and he was shoved down the gangway under the cold stares of the men who stood there.

"I'd keep very quiet if you want to get to Thira," Merrick said softly in his ear. "There are a lot of people here who would welcome the chance to deal with Jaxom's murderer themselves. Luckily for you, I'm not one of them, since his death brought me my promotion to captain."

Horses were brought up, and the party from the ship mounted. Marius's hands were tied with a long rope to someone's saddle horn. He wondered for a moment if he was going to be dragged to his death, but they set off at a steady walk for Thira.

The men from the ship talked to the others as they rode, catching up on the news.

"So, what's been going on?"

"Things aren't good. We've pulled out of another three of the outer islands altogether. Rebellion's spreading—just talk here so far. They'd never have the guts."

Someone else chimed in. "The Wolf's just looking for reasons to execute people. Keep them good and frightened, so they don't cause any trouble."

"Is he still in control?"

There was a harsh laugh. "You should ask him. That would be interesting. He must have a plan. He always does. He's letting all these stupid peasants on the other islands think they've got him worried, then he'll turn around and crush them to a pulp. You wait."

There was a trace of doubt in his voice, though.

Marius's mind kept flashing back to the last time he had been on this road. Wasn't that the path down to where the boat had been moored? And later, the turn they had taken to hide Jaxom's body. He'd hoped never to see these places again.

He peered into the trees, trying to decide if it was the right track, when suddenly the horse to which he was tied skittered sideways. He was jerked off his feet and fell heavily in the dust. As he did so, he heard a dull rumble, like far-off thunder, and the earth bucked beneath him for a few seconds. The horses whinnied and stamped in fear, and he curled up, arms over his head, trying to avoid being trodden on, then got to his feet as the riders brought their mounts under control again.

"Some things don't change, I see," one of the men from the ship said drily. "That was a big one."

The column moved off again.

"Yes, they've been stronger the last few weeks," someone said. Then the talk turned to hunting dogs and the tremor was forgotten.

In Thira itself, things were certainly different. Shadowmen patrolled everywhere, and the few citizens out on the streets walked swiftly and avoided eye contact. No one stopped to chat or pass the time of day or browse in shops. Fear hung in the air like a pall of fog.

They made their way along silent streets close to the shore. Marius glanced to his left at a crossroads and found he was looking down the street that led to the slipway where he'd first seen Kit. He saw, with a shock, the upper part of a building looming out of the sea beyond it. He was so surprised that he stopped, until a jerk on the rope almost pulled him off his feet.

"No time to admire the view, Keeper. It's always changing now; seems the town's hauling itself out of the sea again. This place is cursed." He spat on the ground.

They passed through the market square where Nyssa had first seen Shadowmen, but there were no stalls there now. Instead, a great iron cage squatted in the center. Some twenty men stood inside it, packed so tight that they could neither sit nor lie down. They were tattered and filthy, hollow-eyed, their faces without hope. It looked as if it was only the press of bodies around them that kept them upright.

Shadowmen guarded this horror, to make sure that no citizen would be tempted to pass a cup of water or crust of bread to any of the prisoners.

The contingent from the docks continued on up the hill until they reached the square with the broken fountain, Alaric's palace rising beyond it. A scaffold stood by the fountain. Four bodies hung by their bound wrists from a spar of wood across its center, their faces blackened and swollen. Around their throats, the cords that had been used to throttle them still bit into the dead flesh.

"They usually throttle the people they execute. They're famous for it. That's what those cords they carry are for." He remembered how matter-of-fact Aria had sounded when she said it. Thank God she would never have to see what it looked like.

In through the gates they went, past cold-eyed guards whose hands stayed on their sword hilts even as their supposed comrades entered. The men dismounted and tossed their reins to waiting slaves. Marius was untied from the saddle but his hands were kept bound. Four of the men from the ship pushed him up the stairs.

"Tell Lord Alaric that his delegation has returned from Rushiadh and has brought back someone who will be of great interest to him."

The men who guarded the doors ushered them through, and a slave was sent running to Alaric with the message.

Marius looked at the rotting beauty around him and, for the first time in his life, mourned the loss of what the Keepers had created. Rags of tapestry still clung to the walls in places. Torn parchment pages and scrolls littered the cracked marble tiles across which he walked.

They came into a huge, empty hall and stopped. And waited. After a while one of the men said in an undertone to another, "What's the longest you've stood here?"

"About an hour."

"I've waited nearly two. Let's hope he's keen to see what we've brought."

Twenty minutes passed and then came the approaching sound of several pairs of feet. Eight more Shadowmen entered the hall, and then Alaric.

He left his escort behind and came softly across the floor to the waiting party.

He glanced at Marius. "Why would this be of interest to me?"

Merrick ripped open Marius's sleeve. The telltale Crane tattoo stood out clearly.

"Ah," said Alaric. "You were right. I am always interested in Keepers."

"This isn't just any Keeper," said Merrick, trying not to let excitement show in his voice. "I recognize him. He's the one who was with the two girls. The one that might have killed Jaxom and taken your slave boy."

When he heard these words, Alaric became perfectly still, like a snake preparing to strike. Marius could only guess at what was going on behind those cold, pale eyes. *Eyes like those of a shark,* he thought.

"And the others?" Alaric said, very quietly.

"He was alone."

"I take it you did ask him if he knew where they are?"

"We did. He said not."

"As he would, of course. No matter, we'll find out soon enough if that is true."

For the first time, he addressed his prisoner directly. "I believe your name is Marius? I've wanted to meet you for a long time—long before this business of Captain Jaxom. Did you kill him, by the way?"

Marius said nothing.

"But what does it matter, anyway, in the larger scheme of things? You already expect to die here, don't you?" Alaric smiled. "But first we have so much to talk about, you and I."

To Marius's surprise and relief, the White Wolf turned away to give orders. "Lock him up and make sure there's no way for him to harm himself. Give him some food and water. I want him alive just now.

"And make sure that word gets out that we have him. There's always the chance he might act as bait for the others."

⊹   ⊹   ⊹

They had spent their time on board talking about all sorts of things, not just what lay ahead. They spoke of what they would have liked to do with the future. There wouldn't be much time once they reached Thira.

Somehow Nyssa had managed to persuade Aria not to come to the palace with her and Kit. "That way," she had said, "if we can't get out again, there's still a chance that you might be able to do something from outside." What she had really meant, though, was: *When we don't return, you'll be alive. You'll be a witness to our story, and at least we'll know that one of us survived.*

Nyssa had put hope aside, for her and, reluctantly, for Kit. He would not be dissuaded from coming with her, although he seemed as certain as she that it was a doomed undertaking. She didn't want to run anymore. She wanted an end to it. Either they would persuade Alaric that they weren't worth hunting, or they wouldn't.

On their last night at sea, Nyssa dreamed.

She wore a blue dress. There were flowers everywhere. Summer. She could hear her mother playing one of the tunes she had made up. Nyssa was hiding from her, playing, waiting to jump out at her, but when she did, Mamma didn't pretend to be surprised. "Hide again," she said. And then the men came.

The boat put them ashore on the south coast, outside a small village, and turned straight back out to sea. They shouldered their bundles and, avoiding the settlement, set off for Thira. Soon they found a track that joined a road after an hour or so. It was the middle of the day, but it would take them until nearly nightfall to reach the city.

They walked steadily, stopping a couple of times for a brief rest and a bite to eat. There were a few people out working in the fields, but they saw that some of the land had been abandoned: Olives were still on the trees, and last year's grapes hung withered on the vines.

To Nyssa and Aria, this was truly shocking. Whatever happened, food had to be grown, the land had to be worked. They couldn't begin to comprehend the sort of breakdown of normal life that could lead to this.

Once they noticed a group of men watching them from a shepherd's hut some way off. Uneasily, they quickened their pace.

The sun was sliding quickly toward the sea when Thira came into view. Their intention was to find a barn or stable near the edge of the city where they could pass the night, and in the morning Nyssa and Kit would go to Alaric's palace.

After another twenty minutes or so, Aria stopped, shushing the others.

"Did you hear that?"

They looked at her quizzically.

"I'm sure I heard someone behind us."

"Well, it is a road. Why shouldn't there be other people on it?"

"Then why can't we still hear them? They've stopped. I think someone's following us."

They peered back down the road, but the light was fading now and it was hard to make out what might lie in the distance.

"Let's go on," said Nyssa.

They walked in silence now, listening intently. After a few more minutes, they all picked up the sound of feet.

"What shall we do?" said Aria.

"Keep walking."

They each carried a knife. Nyssa tried to remember her lessons with Marius as she loosened hers in its sheath. If they could just get to the outskirts of the city, perhaps they'd be safe.

A figure stepped onto the road in front of them.

22

THE WOLF'S LAIR

They stopped. Nyssa drew her knife and, from the corner of her eye, saw Kit do the same.

"What do we do?" whispered Aria again.

"Walk on," said Nyssa. "There's no reason why we shouldn't be on the road."

They walked slowly on, trying not to look worried. The figure on the road became distinguishable as a man. They saw a knife at his waist, but for the moment it was in its sheath and his arms were folded.

They went to pass him.

"You're not heading for Thira, are you?"

It was obvious they were, so no point lying. "Yes," said Nyssa.

"You'll not get there before curfew. The light'll be gone in fifteen minutes. What are you thinking of?"

Curfew? This was something new.

"Best wait till morning. You don't want to be caught breaking curfew. There's a barn off the road this way where you can spend the night."

"No, it's all right, thank you. We've somewhere to go," lied Nyssa.

"I really think you'd be better with us," said another voice, from behind them. This time they had missed the approaching footsteps. "They'll be patrolling the road, too, later."

They turned to see another two men, also armed but for the moment unthreatening.

Nyssa couldn't see an alternative to going with them. Without the aid of surprise, there was no way they could make a clean break, and if the men were speaking the truth about curfew, they'd be running from one danger into another.

"All right," she said. "Thank you."

One of the men pointed to the knife she had forgotten was in her hand. "You don't need that. We mean you no harm. These are uncertain times, but we're just ordinary people like you."

Presumably to show their good faith, all three men went ahead of them, across an overgrown vineyard and over a thickly wooded ridge, and led them to the barn.

One of them knocked on the door. After a moment it opened a crack, then wider once whoever was inside had identified who it was. Inside, another three men and a woman sat around a small fire watching a pot, while from the shadows came the sound of someone singing tunelessly to himself.

"I hope you've got your own food," said one of the men who'd brought them in. "We've none to spare, I'm afraid."

"No, that's all right," Nyssa started to say, but the voice from the shadows interrupted her.

"What do you mean, none to spare? We've plenty of bread, at least. I should know." A figure, its arms full of loaves, emerged into the pool of firelight. With a shock, Nyssa and Aria recognized the gossiping baker from Thira, just as he recognized them.

"Well, well," he said slowly, a loaf slipping from his grasp. "I didn't expect to see you again."

"You know them?" The woman by the fire looked up sharply.

"I've met them. They were the ones staying at Niobe's when that Shadowman disappeared." The baker peered at Kit. "This one wasn't with them, though. It was an older man." He put the rest of the loaves down on a wooden crate. "Niobe found a bloodstain on the floor that someone had tried to hide. She reckoned you'd killed him. Seemed too much of a coincidence to swallow, you all just disappearing like that.

"Caused her a few problems, that did, coming so soon after those other two who'd been staying with her were caught. She thought they'd twig that she was a resistance organizer, but they still didn't. The fools." He spat into the fire to emphasize the point.

"Did you kill him?"

"It was self-defense," said Aria.

"I'm sure it was, my dear," he said, looking her up and down. "Well done, anyway. It's one less piece of filth for us to deal with when the signal comes." He picked up a loaf and handed it to Kit with a smile. "Sit down. Get comfortable. Not that that's easy."

Bemused and relieved, they sat.

"Me and Niobe thought you'd got off the island," he went on.

"We did," said Nyssa. "But we came back. Just today. We need to find someone in Thira."

"You'd best be careful, then," said one of the men who'd accosted them on the road. "It's a dangerous place now. Even more than it was. Alaric knows there's rebellion brewing, and he's determined to crush it. I've got to go in tomorrow, anyway. You can come with me. Do you know where this person is that you're looking for?"

Nyssa swallowed. "The Shadowmen have him. We think he's in Alaric's palace."

There was silence. Everyone knew what that meant.

Eventually, the woman beside the fire stirred. "We can probably stretch the food to do for all of us."

-:-   -:-   -:-

Nyssa, Kit, and Aria became aware later that the others had drawn aside and were discussing them. They pretended not to notice and concentrated on getting comfortable for the night as the man who had confronted them on the road came over to talk to them.

"How sure are you that Alaric has your friend?"

"Totally. I wish there was some doubt."

He nodded, thinking. "You stand the best chance of getting him out if Alaric is distracted. Don't try tomorrow. Wait for another twenty-four hours and he'll be distracted all right. That's when the uprising begins all over the island."

"Uprising?" echoed Kit.

"We've been planning it for months, trying to persuade people we can do this, getting messages to the other islands so they'll be ready, too. There are rebel cells all over the Archipelago, just waiting for the signal to strike. We're going to push Alaric and his men off the islands."

"Can you do it?" asked Nyssa.

"We'll know if we've done it on Thira in forty-eight hours."

"I don't know . . . ," Nyssa mused. "I don't want to wait another day. We could be too late."

"I'll take you to a safe house in the city tomorrow morning. We can talk further then."

-:-   -:-   -:-

They arrived in Thira in the middle of the morning. To their surprise, their guide led them back to Niobe's house. From the outside it looked deserted, the shutters closed and barred, but when he knocked, the door opened and they were ushered inside.

It took a moment for their eyes to adjust to the dim light. When they did so, they found they were facing half a dozen people. Niobe stood at the front of the group, hands on hips.

"You lot! I never thought I'd see you again." She looked to the man who had brought them. "What's the story?"

They let him explain.

"But we can't wait. We're afraid Alaric will kill him," Nyssa interjected once he had finished.

Niobe sighed.

"I'm afraid you don't have a choice, my dear. Now that you know about the uprising, we can't let you walk into Alaric's arms."

"But we won't tell him! We're on the same side."

"I don't doubt that, but the timing of the uprising is much too valuable a bargaining chip. It might save your friend's life. How could you not use it? You'll have to stay with us until tomorrow."

"He could be dead by then!" Aria argued.

"He could be dead already," said Niobe calmly. "This is your best chance. If you walk in there and the White Wolf is concentrating on you, none of you will come out again. You can go tomorrow, first thing. By then it won't make any difference even if you *do* tell him."

Nyssa opened her mouth to protest, but Kit put a hand on her arm.

"She's right," he said unexpectedly. "We don't have a plan for getting out. I know you think you can persuade Alaric to let us go." He shook his head. "It won't work. This way we might have a chance."

It was clear there was no alternative, anyway. They wouldn't be allowed to leave now, knowing what they did.

+ + +

They were aware that someone was always watching them discreetly as they sat around in the dusty rooms waiting, once again, for morning.

As she paced the room restlessly that night, unable to sleep, Nyssa accidentally knocked over a pile of papers. Kneeling to pick them up, her attention was caught by the too perfect lettering.

"Look," she said to the others. "These are printed."

Aria and Kit came to see.

"I think they're instructions for the rebels," Nyssa said, reading. "So that everyone knows exactly what to do."

They tidied them up quickly.

"I wonder where the machine is that makes them?" Aria mused.

Two or three times, flakes of plaster were dislodged from the walls by small earth tremors, a detail of life on Thira that Nyssa and Aria had quite forgotten.

At last, the morning sun pushed in around the shutters. "You can leave whenever you want now," Niobe told them. "Good luck."

Nyssa, Kit, and Aria looked at one another.

"You should eat something before you go," said Aria.

Kit shook his head.

"I don't think I could swallow anything," said Nyssa, trying to smile.

Aria licked dry lips.

"Well then," said Nyssa.

Aria hugged the two of them so tight it hurt, but somehow managed to keep the tremor from her voice. "Don't be long."

⁛   ⁛   ⁛

As Nyssa and Kit walked through the town they, too, were aware of the changes that Marius had noticed: the sense of watchfulness and fear.

They saw from the far side of the market square the great prison cage, packed to the gills. They backed away to skirt around the square, not wanting to look more closely than they had to.

"I want to go to the slipway," said Kit.

Nyssa nodded, thinking of their first meeting there. They worked their way around the square, and Kit led her down a narrow lane that seemed vaguely familiar from the dreams she used to have.

She gasped, and Kit came to an abrupt halt, as they reached the end of the lane.

The slipway lay before them, but far more of it was uncovered than had been the case before. Drowned buildings loomed farther out of the water, and at the submerged foot of the slipway the great temple building had emerged. What remained of the roof was crusted with weeds, crisped to black now by the sun. Columns and window frames were swagged with it, too, and they could see a line that marked how far the sea crawled up the walls when the tide came in. Nyssa reckoned that at least half its height was permanently uncovered now. She looked around for the statue she had seen gaze up at her from underwater in her dreams; it, too, should have emerged.

It was there, but it had been daubed with paint, then smashed.

"How has this happened?" she wondered aloud.

"The earth tremors," said Kit.

A gull circled and landed on the temple roof, then flew down into it through a hole.

As they turned away, Kit caught Nyssa's sleeve.

"Wait—what's that?"

She looked where he was pointing, to something under the water.

At first she thought it was weeds, coiling and dancing in the current, but her blood chilled as she realized it was long hair, drifting above the heads of three women. Through the clear water she could see that their wrists were bound and their ankles tied to large stones. They'd been drowned deliberately.

"They must have been alive as the tide came in," Kit whispered. "They must have known they were going to die."

With difficulty, they dragged their eyes away from the floating corpses and started slowly up toward Alaric's palace.

They changed routes several times to avoid Shadowmen: a lunatic lack of logic, considering they were about to give themselves up, anyway.

The ground trembled slightly under Nyssa's feet as they walked. It was such a small movement that she wondered if she'd imagined it, but when she looked at Kit, he nodded. He had felt it, too.

And then they were there. Alaric's palace loomed before them across the square, guards alert at the gate. After one quick glance at the scaffold and its dreadful burden, they both avoided looking at it, trying not to think about it.

"Please don't come inside," Nyssa tried again.

Kit smiled. "I never believed I'd really escaped, anyway."

Side by side they walked up to one of the guards.

"We have come to see Lord Alaric."

The guard looked at them as though they were insane. "Really? And why would he want to see you?"

"Because of this." Nyssa pushed up her sleeve. The guard looked hard at her tattoo, then back into her face.

"You must be out of your minds," he said, and waved to a comrade halfway up the steps to come down.

They were taken inside and searched thoroughly while a slave was dispatched with a message. Kit looked at him curiously, but it was no one he'd seen before. They stood silently, surrounded by guards.

The slave returned ten minutes later with a whispered message.

"Well, it seems he wants to see you," their guard said wryly. He gestured toward a corridor. "After you."

Nyssa's heart was hammering now and her legs felt unsteady. It had been one thing to be courageous when they were planning this, but now it was all she could do not to fall to the ground in terror. She wondered if Kit was as frightened as she was. So far no one seemed to have recognized him, though that was hardly surprising: Even if his hair hadn't been dyed, he would have looked very different from when he was last here. She glanced around at her brother, but he scarcely seemed to notice, lost somewhere in his own thoughts.

They were led into a hall with a floor of black-and-white marble tiles, like a huge chessboard, and a single thronelike chair at the far end, and there they stopped and waited for fate.

Alaric didn't keep them waiting long, his interest too piqued by the idea of two young Keepers walking into his palace of their own accord. He dispensed with his personal guards, judging that those already in the hall would be sufficient, and went in alone.

A girl and a boy, brown haired and, he noticed as he came closer, with the same bright brown eyes. There was something about the boy . . .

His normally impenetrable self-control slipped and he drew a sharp breath as he realized who was standing in front of him. He looked from the boy to the girl and back again.

The man from Nyssa's nightmares stood before her, corpse-pale against his dark clothes, a long, thin knife at his belt. Not as tall as she had thought, some tiny dispassionate bit of her brain told her; but even more frightening, the rest screamed at her.

She saw the instant when he recognized Kit, saw the realization of who they were flood through his brain, watched his eyes widen as it did so.

He walked slowly around them. Her flesh crawled as she heard his soft footsteps behind her. If he touched her, she knew she would scream. She forced herself to hold still, and he continued until he stood before her again.

He wanted to savor this moment, so he said nothing. He surveyed them as though they were horses he was considering. He smelled an herbal scent from the girl's hair. A pretty girl, though pale as a wraith. And the boy. Who would have thought he could change so much in a few months?

He walked slowly to his chair and sat, chin on hand, considering exactly how to deal with this. Finally he decided to hear what they — well, the girl, anyway — had to say. He'd almost forgotten that the boy couldn't speak.

"You asked to see me, I believe?" he said, his voice like an empty tomb.

"You know who we are?" said Nyssa shakily.

"I know that *that* is my property." He pointed at Kit. "And I assume you are its sister."

"His name is Kit," she said, anger making her voice a little stronger. "And yes, I am his sister. We know why you've been hunting us, and we've come to tell you it's pointless."

"Nothing I do is pointless," he said with a smile that made her quail.

Nyssa went on before her courage and voice could fail completely. "You have another Keeper here, a man called Marius. Let him go in exchange for us. You must know there's nothing he can give you."

"Ah yes, your uncle. I think a family reunion is in order, don't you?" He gestured to one of the guards, who immediately left the room.

Nyssa opened her mouth to speak again, but Alaric held up a hand. "It would be courteous to wait for your uncle, don't you think?"

Silence oozed around them. Nyssa thought she felt another tiny earth tremor as she waited, but decided it was more likely her own legs trembling.

After a few moments there was a noise of footsteps and two Shadowmen brought Marius into the hall. He was gaunt and unkempt, his hands bound in front of him but, as far as Nyssa and Kit could tell, unharmed.

And then he saw them.

A look of the utmost horror dawned on his face. His legs buckled under him, and he fell to his knees with a howl of anguish. Nyssa and Kit tried to run to him, but they were restrained by the guards. Struggle as they might, they couldn't get free.

"Marius! It's all right. We're all right," yelled Nyssa, but he didn't seem to hear.

He struggled to his feet and made to lunge at Alaric, but the guards were expecting it and kicked his legs from under him. He found a sword point at his throat.

"Control yourselves," said Alaric coldly. "None of you has been harmed. I am waiting to hear what you have to say."

Nyssa looked at Marius panting on the floor, struggling to deal with the ultimate disaster of finding her and Kit in Alaric's hands.

"You might want to hear it privately," she managed to say.

The White Wolf smiled. "I have no secrets from my brothers in arms, my Shadowmen."

"Very well." She cleared her throat. "You've been hunting me and Kit for the words we carry, even though you don't know what they mean. You think they'll bring you more power.

"You're wrong. I found what they mean, in the Great Library of Rushiadh. There's no power in them. They couldn't do what the Legend claims. It was all a bluff: The Keepers were just trying to make everyone believe they had the power to destroy the Shadowmen. But they didn't."

Alaric sighed. "Do you not think I sent people to the Great Library long ago? They checked it from top to bottom and found nothing. Remember—I've had half the words for years, ever since I took your brother. You're lying."

"I'm not! You know we were in Rushiadh—that was where your men captured Marius. The Guardians of the Library have kept the translation a secret since the time of the Keepers. They were sworn only to let a Bearer of the words see it."

"So, where is this translation?"

Nyssa swallowed. "I burned it."

"Not really a good idea if you wanted to be taken seriously," Alaric said in a silky voice.

"But I remember it: *'There is no help against the Shadow that destroys the Light but what courage you find within your own heart,'*" Nyssa said desperately.

"Dear gods," said Alaric. "Unbelievable *and* trite."

"It's true! That's all it means. I know how to say the words, how to pronounce them. I'll show you that they have no power."

Taking a deep breath, she spoke the words in the Keepers' tongue.

She felt the hands on her arms tighten. Alaric seemed to freeze, watching intently. Marius, too, was still, his eyes fixed on her.

A tiny part of her had still thought that something might happen, but nothing did. Nothing.

She heard Alaric release a breath, and then there was some sort of commotion at the entrance to the hall: the sound of running feet. A Shadowman appeared, breathing hard, and stopped just inside the door.

Alaric rose, all his attention now on the man who had just come in. He motioned him over and was given a lengthy whispered report, the urgency of which was obvious, even to the prisoners.

This is it, thought Nyssa. *The rebellion's starting. We must be ready in case there's a chance to escape.* She glanced at Kit, saw his almost imperceptible nod.

Alaric gave a few brief orders in an undertone, and the man left as hurriedly as he had arrived. Alaric stared after him for a few seconds, then returned to his seat.

"I'm afraid we'll have to postpone the rest of our talk," he said. "As you can no doubt see, I have more pressing issues to attend to.

"As for the words, it really doesn't matter to me anymore whether they hold any power. It is what *others* believe that matters. If the words have power, I can threaten to unleash it against them. If they have none, I can claim to have defeated it. Either way, I win.

"For now, you'll be —"

He was interrupted by the sound of another voice: Kit's. "Say it again, Nyssa. Both of us, together. Remember what the Legend says."

The Wolf's eyes opened wide. "It can speak! I had no idea." He rose. "Entertaining though this revelation is, I must still postpone attending to you properly until later."

"Wait and see. The people will defeat you," Kit said, in a voice filled with venom. And then he began chanting. Nyssa had no idea why he was doing this — what could it achieve?

But after a second's hesitation, she joined her voice with his.

In that moment everything was still. Alaric seemed to register Kit's words and stared at him, a shadow of doubt on his face. The strange words reverberated and then faded into silence. Nothing.

The Wolf laughed, and turned to leave.

There was a rumble: booted feet running along a corridor. Nyssa found her arms free and turned to see what was happening. She couldn't see anyone coming, but the noise went on. She saw that Kit was free as well, the guards looking as baffled as she was. The ones holding Marius had more presence of mind, however, and the sword remained poised above his throat.

The noise stopped suddenly. They all looked at each other uncertainly.

"As I was saying," said Alaric, forcing their attention back to him, "put them in the —"

There was an enormous crash, as though they were inside a thunderbolt. The marble tiles under their feet shook and splintered, and part of the roof came rumbling in.

The guards took to their heels at once, running for the corridor that led to the front doors of the palace. Alaric stood his ground on the bucking floor for a few seconds, then turned and ran in the opposite direction.

Marius came to his senses first. "Get out! Run!"

The noise went on, louder and louder. Paneling burst off the walls in a shower of splintered wood. Kit grabbed Nyssa's hand and pulled her to one side just as a roof beam crashed through the floor where she'd been standing.

"Don't wait!" Marius yelled. "Run!"

Ignoring what he'd said, Nyssa raced to pick up the dropped sword beside him and cut his hands loose. He got to his feet and they held each other for support as the room shuddered around them.

The noise stopped and for a moment everything was still.

"Quickly!" Marius started across the debris that now littered the broken floor to follow the guards who had fled.

"No!" Kit yelled.

He pulled Nyssa in the opposite direction. Marius skidded to a halt, the sword now in his hand. "No! This is the way out. Come on."

Kit shook his head frantically, struggling to say the words. "There's a safer way. The Keepers made it for this."

"All right," said Marius, and they ran.

The noise started to build again, a grinding roar like nothing they had ever imagined, let alone heard. Shards of the building cascaded down around them.

They followed Kit along corridors and around corners, down two flights of stairs that were somehow intact. At the bottom was a door of black wood. He turned the handle and hauled it open with difficulty, pushed them through, and dragged it shut behind them. In darkness now, the noise was even more terrifying, but the floor was steady beneath their feet.

"Wait," Kit's voice said, barely audible. Nyssa and Marius were aware of him moving, and then after a few seconds there was a faint spark, which grew until they could see his face in the flickering light of a lantern.

The noise died away again. They looked at each other. Nyssa threw her arms around Marius. He kissed the top of her head.

"Kit," he said, "what is this place? How did you know about it?"

"I read about it in one of the scrolls in the palace. Then I found it. The Keepers made it to survive earthquakes, as an escape route."

He gestured for them to follow him and, with the lantern held high, led the way.

They were in a tunnel that bored through what seemed to be solid rock. The walls were a reddish color, with dark patches here and there where it was damp. It was just high enough for Marius to walk upright. The floor was cut rock, too, finished to be more or less flat; shiny in places where feet had polished it over centuries. It sloped steeply down.

They followed it without speaking, Kit first with the light, then Nyssa, Marius at the rear with the sword gripped in his hand. The shape of the walls threw back the sound of their breath, so that their progress was far from silent. The corridor twisted and turned to avoid outcrops of rock too hard for the tunnelers.

"Do you know where this goes?" Nyssa whispered to the back of Kit's head. He nodded without turning around.

Five minutes later they reached another door. Kit handed Nyssa the lantern and pulled it open. It moved smooth and silent in his hands, and they were blinded as light flooded into the tunnel. They stood still for a moment, letting their eyes adjust. Nyssa blew out the lamp and set it down. They stepped out into a large circular room. Opposite them was a set of double doors, flanked by two enormous statues of the Earth Goddess, her snakes coiling up one arm, a vine up the other, her feet half transformed into olive tree roots. One of the statues was tilted at an angle where a corner of its plinth had broken; it leaned against the wall as though the Goddess was resting.

Other smaller statues of the lesser gods were spaced in niches at intervals around the walls, the windows above them, long devoid of glass, letting in light and the sound of shouting — in fact, of fighting.

They started across the room toward the outer doors, all their attention on what they could hear happening outside. They didn't look around them, intent on their escape. They didn't see Alaric rise from his place of concealment behind one of the statues. They never heard him come silently up behind them, missed the flash of light on metal as he drew the long, thin knife from its sheath. It glittered as it rose, and then Alaric brought it down with savage strength and plunged it into Marius's back.

The sword fell from Marius's hand and landed with a clatter on the tiles. Nyssa and Kit turned in time to see the look of shock and pain on his face as he fell.

Alaric calmly sheathed the bloody knife and bent to pick up the sword.

Nyssa clutched at Kit. "Marius!" she screamed. "Oh my God, no, Marius!" But he lay unmoving in a slowly spreading pool of blood.

23

AFTERMATH

Alaric stepped over Marius's body and walked unhurriedly toward them.

"Your turn," he said. "I have a rebellion to deal with. You'll still be useful dead, and much less trouble."

Kit was pulling Nyssa backward toward the doors as Alaric advanced implacably, his pale eyes glittering like sea ice in his white face. They were between the statues now. Kit let go of her and began to fumble with the doors.

"I have the key," said Alaric, smiling, as he closed in on them.

"Listen to what's happening outside!" Nyssa yelled at him desperately. "The people are rebelling. You're defeated. You should be running. You're a dead man!"

She heard the doors rattling as Kit desperately tried to force them open, and then, without warning, the earth gave another convulsive shudder that threw the two of them to the floor in a tangle of limbs.

A shadow passed over their faces.

Time seemed to stretch. Nyssa turned her head to see the statue of the Earth Goddess lean away from the wall and topple, with infinite slowness. She saw Alaric's expression change as he realized what was happening and threw himself sideways, but it wasn't enough. The statue crashed down on top of him, shattering into fragments and throwing up a cloud of marble dust.

Silence fell.

Dust settled.

Nyssa and Kit pulled themselves up, clinging to each other for support. Alaric lay beneath the toppled statue of the Earth Goddess in a ghastly welter of broken marble and shattered bone and torn flesh.

Kit stared at him, transfixed.

Trying to avoid looking at Alaric's crushed body, Nyssa edged around the remains of the statue and stumbled to where Marius lay, falling on her knees beside him, heedless of the blood.

"Marius?" she shouted, stroking his face. "Marius, wake up. We're safe now. Wake up, Marius." But he was as still and pale as the broken Goddess.

Her shouts roused Kit, who wrenched his eyes away from the jumble of marble and flesh that used to be his tormentor. Seeing Marius, he stumbled to his uncle's side, putting a hand to Marius's wrist and then to his throat, searching. Nothing. He frowned and moved his fingers slightly.

"He's alive!" He pulled Nyssa's fingers to where his had been. At first she could feel nothing, but then . . . a thin thread of pulse.

"He's still alive!" Nyssa's brain switched back on. "Kit—find Aria and get help. I'll stay here."

Kit shot to his feet and skidded across the floor to the doors.

"The key!" he yelled, suddenly remembering.

Nyssa looked up. "Alaric said he had it."

For a few seconds, Kit didn't think he'd be able to do it. Everything about Alaric that he'd tried so hard to avoid remembering came back in a rush.

He's dead, he can't hurt me anymore, he thought suddenly, then realized he'd spoken aloud. So he said it again with more conviction. "He's dead, he can't hurt me anymore."

Overcoming his fear and revulsion, he knelt beside Alaric's body, searching for the key. What would he do if he couldn't find it? Could he climb to one of the windows and get out that way?

His hands closed around the cold metal of a key in one of Alaric's pockets. He tugged it free, and as he did so, to his unutterable horror, Alaric's eyes opened.

Kit scrambled back, his feet slipping on the bloody floor. He looked into Alaric's eyes, looked at the ruin of the man who had almost destroyed him, and realized that it was him, and not Alaric, who would survive this.

"My sister told you," he said very quietly. "You're a dead man."

Alaric struggled to speak, but only a froth of blood came from his lips. He shuddered and was still, eyes staring sightlessly at the ceiling.

"Kit!" Nyssa yelled. "For God's sake, hurry!"

He came to himself then, jumped to his feet, turned the key in the locked doors, and ran.

Nyssa ripped the sleeves from her dress and tried to staunch the bleeding, talking to Marius all the while.

"We're safe, Marius. Alaric is dead. Wake up. Please wake up." She heard the sound of the doors opening and looked up to see Kit had gone. He had disappeared into the mayhem outside.

There was nothing more she could do. The cloths she had bound around the wound were already red. She pressed on them as hard as she could.

"Stay with us, Marius. Please try."

-:-   -:-   -:-

Kit ran. The noise of fighting came and went, and he changed routes several times to avoid getting caught up in it. All the boxes in his head were threatening to burst open. Too much had happened. There was no time to deal with them now. Nyssa and Marius were depending on him.

He skidded around a corner, found himself on the edge of a pitched battle, backtracked, and ran again.

He could see Niobe's house. Breath sobbing in his lungs, he reached it and banged on the door.

-:-   -:-   -:-

Nyssa, Kit, and Aria sat silent in their old room in Niobe's house. Aria had helped Nyssa to change out of her bloodstained clothes, dressing her as though she was a child, but she couldn't get the smell of blood out of her nostrils. She couldn't help looking at her hands every so often, half expecting them to be clotted with red, even though she remembered Aria washing them.

When Kit had hurtled into the house, he had found not only Aria, but Niobe and half a dozen of the resistance fighters. Once he'd managed to get enough words out to explain what had happened, they had rushed into the dangerous streets to get Marius and Nyssa back to Niobe's.

Outside, the noise of fighting from the town ebbed and flowed. Every so often someone would come in and reassure them they were safe, but it didn't matter now.

They waited.

Niobe came into the room with the doctor. Nyssa saw Aria's knuckles whiten.

"The bleeding has stopped," the doctor said. They waited for more.

"That's good, isn't it?" said Aria.

"Yes . . . but he's lost so much blood. . . . I'm sorry. There's nothing I can do. It's unlikely that he'll survive."

Aria put her face in her hands.

"He can't die," said Nyssa in disbelief. "Not after everything."

"I'm sorry," the doctor repeated.

They were dimly aware of Niobe and the doctor leaving, and then of raised voices at the top of the stairs and a door slamming.

"I'm going to sit with him," said Nyssa, rising.

Just then the door flew open. Niobe stood there, flushed and agitated. "Don't let him die. Keep him alive. I'll be half an hour. I'd never forgive myself if I didn't try. Half an hour."

She turned and rushed down the stairs. They looked at one another, baffled.

"Come on," said Nyssa.

In the little room across the landing Marius lay, pale as wax, barely breathing. Partially hidden under the bed was a basin of bloodied cloths. They stood at the door, frightened to go closer. It was Kit who moved first, stroking Marius's hand briefly before he sat on the floor at the head of the bed. Nyssa and Aria perched carefully on the edge of the mattress, and Nyssa picked up Marius's hand. It was icy cold and she rubbed it in a vain effort to warm it.

Aria found words. "Come on, Marius. Alaric is dead. We're in the middle of a rebellion. You don't want to miss this, do you? Nyssa and Kit and I are waiting for you. We will wait for you."

The minutes crawled by, and then they heard the outer door slam and two sets of footsteps coming up the stairs. Nyssa clutched Marius's cold hand tighter.

They could hear Niobe's voice. "Never mind that. Just do it! If ever there was a time to try . . ."

The door opened and Niobe half pushed a small, plump, gray-haired man into the room, then shut the door behind the pair of them as though she feared he might escape her.

"I've brought another doctor," she said breathlessly.

The man clutched a small wooden case to his chest. He looked at Marius and the others and licked his lips nervously.

Niobe gave him a poke in the back. "Get on with it!"

He put the case down on the table and gathered his shredded dignity. "I need to examine him," he said in a surprisingly deep voice.

They moved away from the bed. The new doctor felt Marius's pulse, looked at his eyes and tongue, checked the wound.

"He'll likely die," he said.

"We know that," Niobe said in an exasperated voice. "That's why I came for you. These people have helped free us from the White Wolf. It's because of them he's dead, and it's because of the Wolf this man is dying."

The doctor looked at the bleak faces in front of him. "I've made it my business to study what remains of Keeper lore about healing," he said. "Not everything is lost. They sometimes saved people by letting blood flow from the healthy to the sick." He saw hope in their eyes and held up a hand. "My knowledge is incomplete."

He pulled the tattered remnants of a book from his case. "I found this several years ago, but the pages are badly damaged. I have had to guess at the missing parts."

Nyssa could just read the faded title. *Of the Lore of Blood.*

"I do this only rarely," he went on. "Sometimes it works, but at other times it makes the person receiving the blood even more ill. Weak as this man already is, if that happens it will surely kill him.

"There is a small chance that he will survive if we do nothing. If we give him blood, I cannot predict the outcome." He paused. "There is a better chance if the blood comes from a blood relative."

"I'm his niece," said Nyssa at once.

"And I'm his nephew," Kit added.

The doctor nodded. "Then you must decide if you want me to do this."

Nyssa looked at Aria. "What do we do?"

Aria shook her head. "This isn't my decision."

"Kit?" said Nyssa, badly not wanting the decision to be hers.

"Do it," he said immediately, to her surprise. She looked into his eyes, found no trace of doubt there, and turned to the doctor. "Do it."

He nodded. "Boiling water to clean the equipment," he said to Niobe.

Nyssa came forward. "What do I do?"

He shook his head. "Nothing. I'll use the boy."

Before she could protest, Kit caught her arm. "Let me," he said. "I want to. I owe him this."

She nodded slowly and stepped back.

"Leave us now," the doctor said. "I'll come for you if . . . if I need to."

For the best part of an hour, Nyssa and Aria sat in silence in the other room, listening for any tiny sound that might give them a clue to what was happening. It grew dark, but neither of them rose to light a lamp. The sound of fighting had died away completely now.

They heard the other door open and shut, and then their own door opened and the doctor stood there, behind him Kit, his arm bandaged.

"He's still alive," the doctor said without preamble. "If the treatment is going to kill him, it will do so in the next couple of hours. If he's still alive in the morning, he has some chance. The boy should rest now."

They spent the endless night in Marius's room, listening to every change in his breathing, Kit dozing under a blanket on the floor. Once or twice Marius muttered something, but they couldn't make it out.

Nyssa woke with a start. She'd fallen asleep sitting on the floor, her head resting against the bed. The room was quiet: Kit on the floor, Aria fast asleep in the chair in the dawn light. With terrible foreboding, Nyssa looked directly at Marius and took his hand.

It was still cold, but was—surely—a little less icy? She looked at his chest and watched, with a relief that left her weak, as it gently rose and fell.

Aria stirred and moved in the chair. "Is he . . ."

"He's alive," said Nyssa. "He's still alive."

After that, though the doctor urged caution, nothing would convince them that Marius wouldn't recover, as if by sheer force of will they could make it happen.

⊹   ⊹   ⊹

Nyssa was sitting with him the first time he fully woke. He saw her and frowned, trying to work out what was going on.

"Welcome back," she said, making an effort to keep her voice level. "You've got a lot to catch up on."

After that, he grew a little better each day, though it would clearly be some time before he would be well enough to travel. They told him things piece by piece: how Alaric had died; how the rebellion had kindled and spread so that now the Shadowmen, who without their leader seemed to have lost the will to fight, were being driven out of every island of the Archipelago; what Kit had done for him when he lay close to death.

It was several more days before he was alone with Kit. The boy was looking out the window, watching a gang of men repair earthquake damage to one of the opposite buildings.

"You saved me, you know," Marius said.

Kit turned from the window, looked at him for a moment, and smiled. "No," he said. "*You* saved *me*." He pushed his sleeve back and looked at the web of old scars on his arm and the single new one. "I used blood and pain to help me forget," he said. "I don't need to do that anymore. I never thought my blood could help anyone but me." He smiled. "Nyssa kept telling me we were safe, but now I think we really are."

-‡-   -‡-   -‡-

Nyssa, Kit, and Aria had plenty of time on their hands as they waited for Marius to recover. Aria wrote a long letter to Roon, explaining what had happened — with a fair few omissions — and sent it to Dido in Rushiadh in the hope that she would know where the Players had gone.

They discovered that they'd been living on top of the printing machine when they found a trapdoor open in one of Niobe's rooms on the ground floor, and went down into the cellar.

Niobe was there with two men, arranging tiny metal squares in a frame. As she looked at them, Nyssa suddenly remembered picking up the metal letter in the doorway two days before they stole Kit away from Thira.

"Just wait until Marius sees this," said Aria in tones of awe, walking around the huge machine. "He'll never want to leave."

Kit picked up a sheet of paper, the ink still damp.

VICTORY!

The bravery of the people of Thira
has led to the destruction of the Tyrant Alaric.
His forces are fleeing all over the Archipelago.
Soon all the islands will be free of the Shadowmen.
Many lives have been lost, but those who have
died have sacrificed their lives for the
FREEDOM of their people.

WE ARE FREE!

"Was this here when we stayed in the house before?" Nyssa asked Niobe.

She nodded. "We managed to put it together and get it working about a year ago." She looked at the machine with affection. "The rebellion could never have happened without it. We smuggled information from this house all over the Archipelago. We had to make the people believe they could win — that was the hardest thing. They'd forgotten what freedom felt like."

"The Keepers had machines like this, didn't they?" Aria said. "Is this one of theirs that somehow survived?"

Niobe shook her head. "We built it from scratch. It took us five years to piece together the plans from the fragments we found, and another two to build it." She patted the machine as though it was a favorite dog. "It's been our secret weapon."

Nyssa thought about the books Dido had shown them.

"This is what made the Keepers great," she said, and began to explain about what she'd learned.

-:-   -:-   -:-

They explored the changed landscape of the town, staring in amazement at buildings newly emerged from the sea. They even went back to the place where Alaric had died and Marius had come so close: the Temple of the Earth Goddess, as Nyssa might have realized at the time from the statues, had she not been in terror of her life. There was no trace now of the horrors that had happened there.

It seemed that there was a network of tunnels linking the Temple with the palace where Alaric had made his spider's nest and a number of other major buildings. There was even rumored to be one beneath the seabed that led to the now fully emerged Temple of the Sea God, but so far no one had been able to find it.

-:-   -:-   -:-

One afternoon, as Nyssa and Kit sat in Marius's room, Marius said to his niece, "What do you think really happened that day?"

She frowned. "What do you mean?"

"The earthquake."

"It was an earthquake, Thira has them all the time," she said flatly.

"But coming so soon after you both said the words . . ."

"No! It was a coincidence, that's all. There had been tremors already that day. I told you what I found out in the Library. Kit and Aria saw it, too."

Marius looked at Kit, who looked back at him calmly but didn't say anything.

"But," Marius continued, "we don't know that was actually a true translation. You don't wonder whether—"

"No!" She clutched the arms of the chair. "No," she said more calmly. "Everyone says the tremors had been stronger over the last few weeks. It was just . . ."

". . . an extraordinary coincidence?"

"Yes."

Marius took another look at Kit, but he just smiled and shrugged.

They didn't speak of it again.

✢   ✢   ✢

Another week passed, and Marius was out of bed and sitting in a chair for part of each day. He gazed out the window, bored rigid by inactivity, and was pleased to hear the door open.

It was Aria with a tray of food and a smile on her face.

"Well, what did the doctor say today?"

"Good news. He says I'll be fit to travel in another week."

She put the tray down and fixed him with a knowing eye. "Liar! I asked him myself and he said a fortnight at least."

Marius held up his hands in a gesture of surrender. "All right—but he's a pessimist, you have to agree. At least he admits I can start going outside. If it wasn't for you, I'd have lost my mind, stuck in this room all day. Does Nyssa know how long he said it'll be?"

"I haven't seen her yet."

"Don't tell her, please."

She passed him a plate of food. "It doesn't matter if I do or not, she always knows when you lie to her, anyway."

He sagged visibly. "I know. I wish I knew how she does it."

Aria chuckled. "She's gone to the carrier's office to see if there's a letter back from William."

For a moment neither of them spoke, then Marius said, "Nyssa's impatient to get back — to get Kit to somewhere he can start to think of as home. I'll be glad to get back to some sort of normal life as well. This has all been . . ." He shook his head. "I still can't believe it's all over."

Aria looked at him hard, then lifted a jug of water.

"Where will you go when the three of us go back there?"

She paused for a few seconds in the act of pouring the water, then went on. Only when she had finished did she say, "I don't know yet. I haven't decided." She handed the glass to him. "I'll see you later, then."

"I thought you were going to have something to eat," he said, confused.

"No. No, I've got to . . . I promised Niobe," she said vaguely, and went out.

"Wait! There's something I need to ask . . ."

But she was already gone.

✢   ✢   ✢

He didn't see her again that day or, oddly, the next, but he was quite unprepared when Nyssa crashed into his room the day after that and woke him from a doze, her face like a fury.

"What have you done, you stupid man?" she yelled at him.

"Me? What?" He struggled to gather his thoughts.

"Aria. What did you say to her? I knew she was upset about something but she wouldn't say what. And now I find this" — she waved a piece of paper at him — "and it's too late, she's gone."

"Gone? What do you mean, *gone*?"

"What do you think I mean, you idiot?" she ranted at him. "Packed up and left. Left us." She advanced on him and thrust the paper at him. "Read it yourself."

Dear Nyssa,

i couldn't bear to say good-bye, so i'm taking the coward's way out. i know you'll all be leaving to go home to William soon, and i don't really want to be left here alone, so i decided to go before that.

Please forgive me for not telling you first. Kiss Kit for me and say good-bye to Marius. i'll write to you sometime and tell you where i end up, and i'll be able to think of you all, safe at the Drowned Boy.

Your friend always,

Aria

Marius stared at it, his mind suddenly blank. Nyssa sat down miserably on the bed.

"She's gone," he said slowly. "She's really gone?"

"Yes," she said patiently. "What did you say that made her do it?"

"*Me*? I didn't say anything." He tried to recall their last conversation. "I just asked her what she would do once you and I and Kit went home. I thought she'd say she was coming, too, but she didn't. I was going to talk to her again, but now she's . . ."

". . . gone. You know why she didn't say she was coming, don't you? She wanted to be asked, and now she thinks you didn't ask her because you're ashamed of what she used to be."

His face registered such shock that she regretted putting it so baldly.

"How could she . . . No, how could I be ashamed of Aria?" He put his head in his hands. "I thought . . . I was afraid to ask her to come with me. What could I offer her? I've no money, no house. . . ." He looked up. "What have I done?"

"You stupid man," said Nyssa gently, and put her arms around him.

-|-   -|-   -|-

They stepped from the boat — the last boat, Nyssa fervently hoped — onto the quayside and for a moment did nothing but look around them. For Nyssa and Marius it was like stepping from a dream back into reality. They knew every building, every fishing boat. Familiar faces stared at them curiously.

"Let's get out of here before we have to start answering questions," said Marius.

They picked up their bags. "We're home, Kit," said Nyssa. "From now on, this is home."

He stared around him curiously. *Home.* It was a strange idea. He wondered how long it would take him to get used to it.

Ten minutes later, they were outside the Drowned Boy. The

faded sign creaked in the breeze, just as it always had. Marius set his hand to the door, but Nyssa shook her head. "It'll still be bolted. Kitchen door."

She walked, half in a dream, around to the back of the building, and opened the kitchen door.

William stood with his back to her on the far side of the room, stirring a large pot. When he heard the door he stopped what he was doing and stood very still, and then he turned slowly, as though he was half-afraid of what he might see.

He took a deep breath at the sight of Nyssa, and then he was across the room in two strides to wrap her in his arms.

Eventually he let her go and turned to embrace Marius. "Are you really all right?"

"I'm fine now."

"This is Kit," said Nyssa unnecessarily.

William restrained himself, remembering Nyssa's letters. He offered his hand to shake, and Kit took it with hardly any hesitation. "Welcome, Kit. I'm so pleased you're here with us at last."

"And it's truly over?"

"It's over," said Marius firmly.

"Sit down, sit down," said William, suddenly starting to fuss. "Let me get you something to eat." He set to filling plates, and for the next half hour they ate and talked.

When they had finished, William said, "The food wasn't very good, was it?"

"Not very," said Nyssa, smiling. "Who's been doing the cooking for the customers?"

"Me."

"Oh dear." She stood up and began to clear the table. "I think I'll make a fish stew tomorrow, shall I?"

William grinned. "That would be perfect, lass. You'd best make plenty; once word spreads that you're back, they'll be queuing up to get in."

"And what a story we'll have to tell them," said Nyssa, looking at Marius and Kit. "Though not the real one, obviously."

-¦-   -¦-   -¦-

The curtain closed, and Aria let the smile drop from her face as she left the stage.

"You're quite good sometimes," said Thorn grudgingly. "But you don't wave your arms enough." She demonstrated how she thought Aria's performance could be improved.

"Thank you," said Aria gravely. "I'll try to remember."

"Oh, I'll remind you," Thorn said eagerly.

"I'm sure you will."

Back in her dressing room, she looked at her face in the mirror for a moment before she unpinned her elaborate wig and set it on the stand.

It was a good life she had now: work she enjoyed, an income, friends, a future. She avoided her own eyes in the mirror and opened a pot of cream to take off her makeup.

There was a knock at the door.

She paused, her fingers in the cream. *If this was one of Roon's plays,* she thought, *the door would open and . . .*

The door opened.

"Roon wants to know if you're coming to eat," said Lark.

"No," she said after a couple of seconds. "I'm tired. I'll just go back to the inn."

The door closed.

Idiot, she chided herself, and went back to her makeup.

It was raining when she left the theater. She pulled her hood up and hugged her cloak tight around her, hurrying along.

Footsteps behind her. She stopped and turned, peering through the rain. A man's figure, cloaked and indistinct. For an instant she was frightened; then he spoke.

"Aria?"

Was her imagination playing tricks on her?

"Marius?" She took a few steps toward him to make sure he was real. "It's really you! What are you doing here? Has something happened to Nyssa? Kit?" Her heart was hammering.

"They're fine."

"Then why are you here? How did you find me?"

He smiled at that. "It took a while. I came to apologize."

"What for?"

"For not asking you to come with us—with me. I'm not *ashamed* of you. I just don't have anything to offer you. You've got a good life now—I watched you tonight—and I have nothing to compare with it. I couldn't ask you to give it up to be a farmer's wife. I had no right. But I couldn't bear the idea that you thought I was ashamed of you. So I came to apologize."

Aria somehow found it difficult to breathe. "You stupid man."

Marius looked hurt. "That's what Nyssa said, too."

She burst out laughing.

ANOTHER LEGEND

Nyssa sat on the wooden bench outside the house, shelling beans. Beside her Aria was hemming a skirt. William and Marius had gone off for a day's hunting and wouldn't be back until close to sunset.

"It's so peaceful out here," said Nyssa. "It's always good to get away from the Drowned Boy for a couple of days."

"Oh, I don't know. I quite enjoy the bustle when I visit, not to mention the fact that I'm allowed through the front door now."

"You wouldn't want the bustle every day, though, would you?"

"No."

"We had a ballad singer in last week. He gave us 'The Death of the White Wolf.' Apparently the Earth Goddess rose up and killed him herself."

"I suppose that's true, in a way. I know what you said about the words not meaning anything, but don't you ever wonder if that's what . . ."

"No. I've told you that a hundred times."

"And Kit?"

"What about him?"

"What does he believe?"

"I think it doesn't matter to him. He's safe. He's talking. He's home."

Aria left a few seconds' silence.

"So, a new legend begins. Makes you wonder about the first one, doesn't it?"

"*Mmnn...*" Nyssa got to her feet. "I forgot—I've got a present for you."

She disappeared into the house and came back a minute later with two slim books, which she handed to Aria.

"Aha! Niobe's latest. You've no idea how much I enjoyed *Of the Cures for Diseases of Sheep*," Aria said, grinning.

"There was a long letter from her, too," said Nyssa. "There are five printing machines on Thira now, and more being built. They've also sent a copy of the plans to Rushiadh, so they can start making printed books."

Aria had opened one of the volumes.

"*The Ship That Sailed to the Moon*. A proper story—how wonderful! Not that *Diseases of Sheep* didn't fascinate the children."

She looked at the other one and sobered. "*Of the Lore of the Keepers Regarding Blood*," she read. "Is this...?"

Nyssa nodded. "The doctor who saved Marius put this one together from the bits of the old Keeper book he had and what he had learned himself over the years."

Aria turned the pages carefully. She shook her head. "How many is that now?"

"Close to thirty. Did you ever think you'd own thirty books?"

Aria laughed at the thought, shaking her head.

"And this is just the start. If you think about it, *really* think about it, imagine what the Archipelago can do. If someone on one island has something worth saying, all they have to do is take it to Thira and it can be all over the place in a few months. Everyone can know everything.

"Look how far we've already come. It's only six years since Alaric was overthrown, but it's like a new world."

"Or perhaps a very old one?"

"Perhaps."

They sat in companionable silence until the peace was shattered by a shriek, and a small girl came hurtling around the corner, clutching a bamboo flute that her father had made for her. For a second Nyssa had the strangest sensation that she was staring back through time, looking at herself. Her memories of the time before the Shadowmen invaded were still fragmentary, but sometimes she thought she could remember her mother's face.

"Thea!" remonstrated Aria. "Not so loud."

"Cousin Kit's chasing me."

"Ah. Why not hide in the kennel?"

Thea crawled quickly into hiding. A few seconds later Kit appeared, strolling nonchalantly, trailed by a boy a year or so older than Thea.

As he walked, Kit juggled a trio of apples, taking a bite from one every so often without losing the rhythm.

"*Please* teach me to do it," the boy said, obviously not for the first time.

"No! Then you'll be as good as me and I'll have nothing left to impress you with."

Kit turned suddenly and threw an apple at him. Surprised, the boy fumbled it but managed to catch it before it hit the ground.

"See! I can do it."

"Your hands are too small, Will," said Nyssa. "You'll have to be patient, wait till you're older."

"It's not fair," said Will mutinously. Kit dropped the remaining apples and swept the boy off his feet. In seconds they were rolling across the dusty ground, laughing.

"Kit," called Aria. "Leave that horrible boy of mine alone and get ready or you'll be late. You're supposed to meet Marius and William in an hour, and you know how grumpy William gets if he's missing the chance to shoot something. He might start aiming at you."

He ignored her completely and kept on tickling Will.

"Who'd have thought he'd ever be the way he is now?" Aria mused. "When you think what he was like when we brought him off Thira . . .

"Are all those girls still mooning over him?" she added.

Nyssa laughed. "Can't get enough of him. Good looks and a tragic past are an irresistible combination. I don't think he even notices them fluttering around him, though."

"And is Laszlo still fluttering around you?"

Nyssa flushed. "Don't start."

"It's about time you took mercy on the poor soul and gave him some hope, you know."

"I'm not sure I want to be tied to someone else. Apart from all of you, of course. The world's a much bigger place than I ever imagined. I don't want to spend my whole life behind the bar of the Drowned Boy. I want to be free to see some more of it if I decide to."

Thea emerged from the kennel to see what she was missing and joined in the wrestling match.

"I'm sure I remember you saying it was peaceful here a minute ago," remarked Aria, watching her children batter their cousin enthusiastically.

"*Mmnn* . . . You know, there's a bucket of water just here that we could throw over them."

They got to their feet.

THE END

AUTHOR'S NOTE

You might have wondered about the dedication...

I'm often asked, "Where do you get your ideas from?" The answer is that you never know where they're going to come from. Which means you have to be ready for them all the time.

Some of the most important ideas for *The Keepers' Tattoo* came from eavesdropping on conversations on buses (sorry!). So: Thanks to the teenager who, when her friend asked her what she was doing on Saturday night, said (or I'm sure she *didn't* say, but this is what I seemed to hear...), "The Shadowmen are coming for me"; and to the two men who were fantasizing about having a map of their favorite ski resort tattooed on their heads...

And, most important, thanks to the real Aria, who let me steal her name after we got talking—also on the bus—one day. I'm sure she is as brilliant, brave, and beautiful as *my* Aria, but of course she bears no other resemblance to her.

Many people helped *The Keepers' Tattoo* on its way: Thanks to my agent, Kathryn Ross, for having faith in it, and to everyone at Chicken House for their enthusiasm and attention to detail; to Charles Brookman, for advice on how quickly Kit could learn to juggle, and of course to my family, for everything else.